Paul Mann is forty-three, married with three children and lives in South Australia. Born in England he began his career as a newspaper journalist and later moved to magazines.

He has worked in London, New York, Toronto, Montreal, Vancouver, and Sydney. Since turning free-lance in 1983 he has written for leading newspapers and magazines throughout Australia. *The Beirut Contract* is his second novel. He is currently at work on his third novel, *The Traitor's Contract*.

GW00806301

Also by Paul Mann
in Pan Books

THE LIBYAN CONTRACT

THE
BEIRUT
CONTRACT

Paul Mann

PAN BOOKS
London, Sydney and Auckland

First published 1989 by Pan Books (Australia) Pty Ltd
First published in Great Britain 1991 by Pan Books Ltd,
Cavaye Place, London SW10 9PG
1 3 5 7 9 8 6 4 2
© Paul Mann 1989
ISBN 0 330 31349 5

Printed in England by Clays Ltd, St Ives plc

This book is sold subject to the condition that it shall not,
by way of trade or otherwise, be lent, re-sold, hired out,
or otherwise circulated without the publisher's prior consent
in any form of binding or cover other than that in which
it is published and without a similar condition including this
condition being imposed on the subsequent purchaser

For Nancy,
without whom I would be living in a bar
in Thailand with three wives.

CONTENTS

EXECUTIVE ORDER 12333, December 4, 1981 from the office of the President of the United States.

SUBJECT: Special activities, defined as:

... activities conducted in support of national foreign policy objectives abroad which are planned and executed so that the role of the United States Government is not apparent or acknowledged publicly ...

1

TERROR INCORPORATED

Beirut, 1987

The pain was back. Familiar pain, nagging its way into his reluctant consciousness like a shrew. The human body was supposed to carry no memory of pain but Wallace knew that was another of life's cruel jokes. He knew this pain well and feared it. It had started in the same place, on the right side of the upper jaw. A persistent arthritic burn, at first focused on the temporal joint, it had radiated sharply outwards in a series of agonising bursts, lighting up every jangled neuron in his skull. It had since evolved into a relentless pulse behind the right eyeball which somehow found an excruciating resonance in the clenched cords and muscles of his neck, as though a nerve had been pulled unbearably tightly around that hemisphere of his skull. Wallace knew there was no such nerve but that didn't erase the pain that seared every conduit in his face. Even his sinus membranes and his right ear had begun to ache and the nerves in his jaw had become so inflamed that the slightest accidental grating of his teeth caused a surge of pain that made him gasp.

The middle-aged American scholar stopped tapping at the word processor. He took off his glasses and closed his eyes to shut out the luminous green figures on the screen in front of him. He rubbed the bridge of his nose between his thumb and forefinger and heaved the sigh of a man exhausted beyond all acceptable limits of human tolerance. A greasy film of sweat covered his worn face, and there were damp crescents in the armpits of his rumpled, short-sleeved khaki shirt.

Stress. The Syrian army doctor had diagnosed it with a condescending smirk. Stress which expressed itself in the constant tensing and flexing of his jaw while he was asleep, grating the teeth and grinding tired bundles of nerve fibre against bone. The result was pain which would not be denied. Wallace had never had a high pain threshold; he would never be able to withstand any form of physical torture and he knew damn well that he wasn't cut out for this kind of work. He was already run down to the point where his health was almost broken. His psychological will was stronger but even that couldn't last much longer. Yet somehow he had to find the reserves to go on. He was just an ordinary man thrust into an extraordinary place and time. Wallace smiled grimly to himself, opened his eyes and began rummaging in the top drawer of the desk for the foil-packed codeine capsules he kept there. Who wouldn't be stressed being an American in Beirut in 1987? He found the codeine, snapped two capsules from their plastic bubbles and swallowed them with the cold dregs of a half-finished cup of coffee. Wallace glanced up at the digital clock on the wall of his borrowed office. It said 6:47 pm. Lieutenant Nazul from the Syrian Army's Sixth Armoured Division would be arriving soon with car and escort to take him home. If the house at Jubail, half an hour's drive north of Beirut, could still be called home since his wife had taken their two girls back to Maryland. That had been eleven months ago and Wallace was looking forward to joining them as soon as his work in Beirut was complete.

Bill Wallace had never thought of himself as the heroic type. Neither had his wife. Following the bombing of the US Marine barracks in Beirut in 1983, the withdrawal of US forces, and the subsequent advice from the State Department to all American civilians remaining in Lebanon that their safety could no longer be guaranteed, most of his colleagues at the American University had faced reality and left. Bill Wallace had only stayed on at the personal request of

10

the American Under-Secretary at the Embassy, a man who almost certainly worked for one of his country's multifarious intelligence-gathering services. Wallace had been asked to compile a report about the economic and political structures necessary to establish a new, western-friendly Lebanon in the aftermath of the civil war. Wallace knew the report was destined for the CIA and his former employers at the National Security Agency before it ever reached the Secretary Of State's desk. Wallace also knew that the entire project was an exercise in futility. In the unlikely event of an imminent end to the carnage and chaos, the picture would have changed a dozen times before the report reached Washington.

Even as he typed, the exhausted scholar knew his report would be obsolete the moment he finished it. Still, he had been asked to serve his country. It didn't matter that the Under-Secretary was a dimwit and an asshole who had no idea what he was asking Bill Wallace to do — and probably didn't care. Wallace could not find it in himself to refuse. In his mind that would have been an act close to treason. And there was always a chance — a slim chance — that his report might prove useful in helping the US build a framework for diplomatic policy once the Lebanese maelstrom had settled. If it ever did. Wallace was an authority on Lebanese political history; this wasn't difficult work for him — only dangerous. Indeed, it was a logical extension of the job Wallace had come to Lebanon to do in 1972, when Beirut was a different place and Lebanon a different world. Back then, he recalled, Beirut was the most beautiful city he had ever seen, a shining white city on the edge of the ocean with the snow-capped peaks of the Jabal Lubnan mountains running parallel to the coast in the middle distance. Without doubt it was the most beautiful, the most worldly and the most exciting city in the Middle East, a city of character and sophistication, distinguished by exotic Ottoman architecture from three centuries of Turkish occupation, and wide boulevards from a century of French colonialism. After

11

France ceded Lebanon its independence amid the ashes of World War II, Beirut quickly established itself as the banking capital of the Middle East and one of the leading sin capitals of the world. It became a place where armaments, heroin and hashish, beautiful women and blonde, blue-eyed children could be bought by anyone with the right money. Beirut was the most Western of Arab cities and the most Arab of Western cities, a free market and a crossroads where the Arab world could meet the West to do business. And when business was done, Beirut was known throughout the world for the opulence of its casinos and the decadence of its nightclubs. Even now, Wallace knew, the casinos still flourished in Beirut and violent, well-barbered men and their elegant mistresses gathered there to gamble and plot amid the rubble and the madness. If nothing else, Beirut was a monument to the tenacity of human greed.

When Bill Wallace first arrived in Beirut he was thirty-eight years old and the youngest professor of Middle Eastern studies in the United States. He had loved Lebanon from the moment he set foot on the sizzling airport tarmac. So had his wife, Mary, a languages specialist whom he had met at NSA headquarters outside Baltimore, where they were both employed as cryptographic analysts specialising in the Middle East. When he was offered the position of senior lecturer in Political Science at the American University in Beirut, he and his wife had been thrilled. They saw it as an irresistible opportunity to live in the region they had spent their lives studying from afar and to which they had made only occasional precious forays. They also saw it as a chance to break free from the claustrophobic bonds of the NSA. It had since transpired that this was a naive belief. Once you had been to bed with Uncle Sam he liked to make sure you never strayed too far. Several times Wallace had been asked to compile special reports for his former employers at the NSA. But back then, married four years with their daughter, Cassie, less than two years old, and with another on the way, all things seemed possible. They had not hesitated.

They decided to live in Jubail, an historic backwater on the Mediterranean coast, thirty-five kilometres north of Beirut. Jubail appealed to them because it was small and liveable but mostly because it had been built on the ruins of Byblos, the ancient city-state of the Phoenicians, forerunners of the trade-worshipping Lebanese. It amused them both that Byblos, had also been the home of a cult which celebrated its worship of the Greek goddess Aphrodite and her lover, Adonis, with marathon orgies. Within a year they had bought land at Jubail and built a home they believed would always be theirs. Even if Bill had been posted back to the US, they decided they would keep their home in Lebanon and retire there one day. Professor Wallace enjoyed his work at the university, teaching Lebanese students the science of politics and the role of the Middle East in international affairs. He and his wife made friends easily. They counted Lebanese of many faiths among their friends, Christians and Muslims alike. Their second daughter, to whom they gave the pretty Arab name Rabiha, was born at the American Hospital in Beirut. But the Wallaces never forgot how much easier it was for them to cross ethnic lines because of the neutrality their American citizenship gave them. They knew that beneath the veneer of nationhood, Lebanon was a melting pot which could boil over at any time. Despite his occasional report to the NSA, Wallace never thought of himself as a spy. The very thought of anything so melodramatic would prompt a wry smile. He had always considered himself a mere scholar, an academic who occasionally contributed to the general flow of information to his government, much of which went straight into a computer index after the briefest inspection by some bored junior intelligence officer at the NSA. Much of his work was so broad and interpretive, anyway, that he could not see any specific political or military application — his business was the promotion and dissemination of knowledge, not espionage.

13

On weekends and holidays Bill and Mary Wallace piled the girls into their Volkswagen campervan and drove the length and breadth of Lebanon. They crossed the borders of Syria, Iraq and Jordan with impunity, visiting Damascus, Baghdad, Amman, dropping in on old university friends at archaeological digs or picking over ancient cities like Petra. It was a halcyon time and they thought it would last forever. For a while, it seemed, there might be lasting peace in the Middle East. Then it was 1975 and their world erupted around them. Lebanon's fragile harmony exploded into a symphony of hate. Like every other American in Lebanon at the time, Bill Wallace was shocked by the suddenness and ferocity of the change. He too had heard the rumblings and seen the signs but simply had never dreamed that the Lebanese, the charming, urbane, educated Lebanese, were capable of turning on each other like rabid dogs and transforming their beautiful country into the world's first anarchist state. This was part of the reason he felt obliged to stay on now to finish this damned report. It was not only loyalty to his own country. He felt a sense of duty to Lebanon too, an obligation to restore some dignity to the mayhem, if only on paper.

At first, foreigners like the Wallaces were in no danger. As long as they kept their noses out of the fighting between Christian and Muslim they were left in peace. By 1976, it looked very much as though the war would run its course and that both sides, exhausted by the fighting, would make a truce. But it was only the lull before the storm. Instead of graduating towards a workable peace, darker forces triumphed: the nation tottered briefly on the edge of peace, then toppled into the abyss. Spurred by the fanaticism and the grand designs of puppet masters in Syria, Iraq and Iran, territorial and religious grievances which had been suppressed in Lebanon for generations flared. The restless Druze asserted their sovereignty in the mountains, Christian Phalangists took over southern Lebanon, the Palestinian Liberation Organisation took advantage of the mayhem to assert total control

14

of Chatila, Sabra, Mar Elias and Bourj al Barajneh camps in Beirut. Then Khomeini returned to Iran, Iraq's Hussein seized the opportunity to invade, and one of the most bloody and inconclusive conflicts of the twentieth century followed. In 1982 Israel invaded Lebanon and expelled the PLO from Beirut. Brief intervention by the US to provide support for the government of President Gemayel and the beleaguered Lebanese army in the wake of the Israeli withdrawal, proved disastrous. Yet again, the US found itself musclebound and at the mercy of a lone fanatic at the wheel of a truck packed with explosives. Following the massacre of US Marines in 1983, the Americans cut their losses and pulled out, contenting themselves with a few parting shots from the battleship Missouri. Once more Khomeini railed against 'The Great Satan' and threatened to export his lunatic brand of Islamic fundamentalism to the world. For the Shi'ite minorities in Lebanon this was like a call to arms. Suddenly, as though from nowhere, Amal and Hezbollah Muslim militia appeared on the battlefield, re-drawing the military and political picture in Lebanon once more.

Then they started taking hostages.

It didn't matter whom. Anyone foreign was a potential target. American, British, French, it made little difference, as long as they could be used to extort cash, arms or other favours from their government. Only France made shameful deals with terrorists to free its citizens. The US and Britain refused to negotiate and more than a dozen hostages of both nationalities settled down to a long wait at the hands of murderous and irrational captors.

That was when Bill and Mary Wallace decided it was time that they too left Lebanon. A decade of watching a country they loved tear itself apart had taken its toll. Beirut was no longer recognisable. It had been transformed from one of the most elegant cities in the eastern Mediterranean into a vision of hell. Many of their Lebanese friends had fled, disappeared or been killed in the street-fighting and indis-

15

criminate bombing. Mary and the girls had been relatively safe in their home at Jubail, but in late 1986 Bill had loaded them into the Volkswagen and waved them an emotional farewell on the journey to Damascus. A message from the US Ambassador in Beirut a few days later informed Bill that they had arrived safely and boarded a flight to London where they had caught a connecting flight to Washington. That was almost a year ago. Mary had rented a house in Baltimore and the girls were finishing high school. It was impossible to get mail in and out of Lebanon anymore, except by diplomatic pouch and that was no longer practical either, because it meant Wallace would have to run an unacceptable risk by driving into the city to collect letters from the heavily-guarded US Embassy. Still, Mary made her weekly phone call to the house at Jubail, like clockwork, every Sunday night and, when Bill could be there to take the call, they would talk for an hour or more, trying vainly not to inflame the fears that clouded their lives. It wasn't easy.

Wallace estimated that he only had another month, perhaps two at the most, to go on his report. With President Assad of Syria making conciliatory noises towards the US and demonstrating a willingness to militarily impose peace in Beirut there was a dim ray of renewed hope for the future. It was the importance of Bill Wallace to the US Embassy which had afforded him the privilege of a Syrian escort. At the request of Wallace's Under-Secretary, the US Ambassador had made diplomatic representations directly to the Syrian High Command and Assad about Wallace. It was an example of Assad's desire that Syria be seen as crucial to the peace-keeping process in Beirut that the Syrian High Command had ordered General Mazaq, commander of the Sixth Armoured Division occupying northeastern Beirut and eastern Lebanon, to ensure Wallace's safety. The wily Mazaq had assigned Lieutenant Nazul and two men to act as permanent escort to the ridiculous American professor. Nazul spoke a little English and, besides, he was a little too clever for his own good. It would keep him out of the way for a while. And if something went wrong, Mazaq reflected, so much the better.

This was the reason Wallace was no longer working at the American University campus in Beirut. The Syrians knew they could not guarantee his safety there. Instead they had moved him and his work to this windowless dungeon in Broummana on the northeastern outskirts of the city. Formerly a textiles mill, it had been taken over by the Syrian army as a maintenance depot for its light armoured vehicles. Wallace could have worked at home in Jubail but if he was a kidnapping target it was wise not to settle into too much of a rut. This was why some nights he did not return home at all but had to billet down with his Syrian escorts at whatever hotel, camp or military depot they chose to take him.

Tonight he was going home. It was Friday. He had told Lieutenant Nazul in emphatic terms that he needed to spend at least one night in his own bed this week. The amiable Syrian officer had promised him the weekend but told Wallace they would have to keep their hour of departure vague as a precaution. To Wallace this meant anytime between five and eight. He hoped Nazul would get here soon. There was nothing else to do in this squalid factory office with its peeling grey paint and someone else's furniture except work. And the pain in the right side of his head had made that impossible. Wallace was now fifty-three but he looked older. A shrivelled twig of a man with lank brown hair, he was actually of average height but seemed smaller to most people because of his shrunken academic posture. His face wore a permanently anguished look and his sad, bloodshot eyes were deeply puddled in wrinkles. He was not a man to pose a physical threat to anyone, but beneath the unimpressive exterior lurked a wry and perceptive wit — the traditional survival tool of the weakling.

He was working in what had been the book-keeper's office, which was why there were no windows and only one door.

17

It had also been the mill strongroom and he could see the scarred cement slab where the safe had once been bolted to the floor. He had nosed around on his arrival two weeks before and all the files and ledgers were still here waiting for someone to return when Lebanon was whole once more and there were reliable markets for suit cloth. Wallace put his glasses back on, squinted at the VDU screen and a spasm of pain lanced across the right side of his skull in protest. He reluctantly switched off the PC and waited for the codeine to take effect. The pain was getting worse. He reached into the bottom drawer of the desk where he had a half-pint bottle of Black and White whiskey, all he had been able to buy on the black market out here in Broummana. There was a rust-streaked sink in one corner and he threw in the remains of his coffee, then splashed three fingers of scotch into the cup and took a deep swallow. The whiskey instantly scoured the staleness from his mouth and he swirled it around his tender gums for a moment before swallowing it and savouring the warm, strong glow that reached deep into his gut. Wallace plucked another small bottle out of the drawer, shook out a couple of Vitamin C tablets and washed them back with another drink of whiskey. Codeine, Vitamin C and scotch. Something had to work — at this point he didn't mind which. Wallace sat back down at the desk and picked up the only photograph of Mary and the girls he carried with him in a small brass frame that fitted snugly into a shirt pocket. It was a colour snapshot taken on the beach near their house at Jubail two summers ago and showed the three of them sitting on a blanket, happy and relaxed in swimsuits Not the most recent picture — Mary had sent a shot of the three of them in front of the rented townhouse in Baltimore a few months earlier — but this one was Wallace's favourite. Mostly because Mary looked so young and pretty, more like the vibrant, clever redhead he had married than the fretful wife and mother with grey-flecked hair she had become. The girls were thirteen and fifteen at the time and hadn't wanted

18

their picture taken but Wallace had coaxed them into smiling and fluked a shot of almost professional quality. He held the cool brass frame in one hand and ran the fingertips of the other gently across the glass plate almost as if he were caressing the pretty faces. The ache in his face began to subside.

The door opened without warning and Lieutenant Nazul stood in the doorway, wearing the tiger-striped battle dress of his unit, a half smile on his dark face. Wallace glanced up at the clock: 7.04 pm.

'I thought you might hear the resounding clang of the whiskey being opened,' Wallace chided him in barely accented Arabic.

Like most Syrians, Nazul was Sunni Muslim and not supposed to touch alcohol but Wallace had long since learned that Islam relaxed its grip exponentially the further an Arab travelled from home.

'A happy coincidence, Professor Wallace.' The lieutenant smiled disarmingly. He took off the pale blue beret of his unit, threw it on the desk and slumped heavily into a chair opposite Wallace. The American handed Nazul a paper cup containing a couple of fingers of scotch. The Syrian officer raised the cup in silent salute to the American professor and took an appreciative sip.

'Allah does move in mysterious ways,' Wallace murmured. He raised his own drink in return and added mischievously, 'Allahu Akhbar.' God Is Great. It wasn't the most diplomatic toast ever made to an Arab soldier. Nazul shifted uneasily in his chair but Wallace knew he was on safe ground. Here was an Arab who enjoyed Westernisation and was no longer comfortable with all the strictures of Islam.

Nazul shrugged. 'One of the small comforts of the professional soldier in a hostile land,' he said. Then he smiled, savouring the soothing blaze of the scotch in his belly. This was the West's most potent weapon, he thought. Nazul had often wondered why the West didn't save itself a fortune on the arms race and just flood the Middle East and the

19

Eastern Bloc countries with cheap scotch. Arabs liked scotch. Much more than vodka. It was by far the natural antidote to the subversive tide of heroin and hashish he saw flowing daily from the Shi'ite drug factories of the Beqa'a to the streets of Europe and North America.

Lieutenant Adnan Nazul was thirty-four and had been a professional soldier since his conscription into the Syrian army at eighteen. Born in the old desert city of Palmyra, Nazul had faced a dull future working his family's meagre orange groves — until he joined the army and discovered an aptitude for soldiering. He had served first as a gunner aboard one of the 2,500 Soviet built T-62 main battle tanks with which the Syrian army was equipped in the late '60s and '70s and had later trained as a tank commander aboard the newer T-72s at the Soviet Union's massive training camp and Red Army base near Buchara, in Uzbekskaja province, 150 kilometres from the border with Afghanistan. It was country almost identical to the scrubby mountain and desert terrain of the Middle East and ideal for the Soviets to train the tank crews of client Arab states like Syria for the next round of live ammunition war games with Israel.

Nazul made a good tank commander. Natural intelligence and affability had singled him out for officer training and three years ago he had made first lieutenant. He was due for a captaincy soon, he knew. He'd be a colonel by the time he was forty. Beyond the rank of colonel, promotion could come with deadly swiftness in the Syrian army. Generals had a habit of disappearing if they were unfortunate enough to incur Assad's displeasure and that meant everyone moved up a step. It was a promotion process which carried terrible risks — but there were rewards too. Nazul had faith in his ability to stay out of trouble. President Assad could be as generous as he was dangerous. A few years in the Syrian top brass could set up a man for life. A bank account in Zurich, a little careful planning and Nazul calculated he could escape to a cosy retirement in the West. Southern France appealed to him the most. The lieutenant didn't mind his latest assignment. It made a change from the boredom of endless drills and inspections, punctuated by the sudden explosions of violence, brief exchanges of fire with whichever militia sought to assert itself on a particular day. It was only gratifying when Nazul could order a couple of rounds of 125mm antipersonnel high explosive into some sniper's nest in an apartment block but he had been reprimanded recently for wasting money and even that small pleasure had been taken away. The infantry had been given the task of engaging and subduing local militias and life for the tank regiments had settled into the monotony of occupation in the northeastern sector. The Syrians may have brought peace to this quadrant of the shattered city but it was a thankless task. The Lebanese had viewed them as liberators at first but now, wary of Assad's long term plans, they regarded them as an army of occupation only marginally more tolerable than the Israelis.

Nazul liked this frail, flustered American professor. He felt pity for him. He was just another little man out of his depth. At least he had had the manners to learn the language of his host country, unlike any other American Nazul had ever met. From his perspective, Wallace saw a charming opportunist who had chosen soldiering as his ticket to the good life. Nazul must have some courage, Wallace conceded, because, in the Syrian army at least, that was a high-risk strategy. Nazul might make it, Wallace thought. He had a lot going for him. He was a handsome man with the thick black moustache favoured by Arab men and the olive-dark soulful eyes Western women found so beguiling.

The two exchanged small talk while they sipped their whiskey. It had been a quiet day, Nazul told him. Quiet for Beirut, that was. No car bombs. Sporadic fighting had continued between Hezbollah and Amal militia on the southern side of the Green Line, he said. The city south of the Green Line was still no-man's-land to the Syrians, although there were rumours that Assad planned to join the Lebanese army in a 'pacification' action there too. At this stage Assad appeared content to play a waiting game. It was the best strategy. If he waited long enough, all of northern Lebanon, including Beirut, would simply topple into his grasp. The Maronite Christians and Phalangists could have the southern half of the country and annihilate the remaining Palestinians between them. The Israelis would still have their buffer zone and Syria would have all the north, which would give Assad virtually all of the historic lands of ancient Assyria. That was assuming those fanatical Shi'ites backed by Iran and Iraq continued to blast each other into oblivion. They didn't seem to need too much encouragement.

Even then there were the Druze to contend with and the PLO was already infiltrating back into the Lebanon, north of Sidon, to the increasing annoyance of Amal. Meanwhile the Americans still propped up Gemayel. Lebanon! It was wiser to wait and see.

'Time to go home, professor,' Nazul said, draining his cup. Wallace wearily stood up, pocketed the photograph of his family and collected his few belongings, filled with relief at the thought that tonight he would be in his own house surrounded by the comforts of the home he and Mary had built.

Nazul replaced his beret, hawked and spat noisily into the nearby sink to get some of the whiskey off his breath, then led Wallace from the bleak little office, along a short corridor lined with other equally squalid offices and out through the main building now cleared of its weaving looms, and crowded instead with Soviet-built armoured personnel carriers, trucks and jeeps. A steel-helmeted guard with an AK-47 was standing at the sliding door to the floodlit delivery bay and parked right outside was another drab green Soviet jeep bearing the insignia of the Sixth Syrian Armoured Division. A soldier armed with one of the new compact Soviet-made AKRs, for easier portability in the confines of the jeep, stood to attention when Nazul appeared. The driver stayed at the wheel, eyes trained stolidly on the windshield.

It was cool outside — despite the taint of war, the air tasted fresh and sweet, especially after a day in that stifling, miserable, windowless office. Far to the south he could hear the crackle of small arms fire, punctuated by the occasional heavier thud of a rocket or artillery shell rearranging the rubble in the smouldering southern suburbs. Nazul motioned the guard into the front passenger seat and he and Wallace climbed into the back, as usual. Nazul adjusted the holster of the automatic pistol on his hip and left the flap open. The moment they were settled the driver started the jeep, reversed out of the bay and began driving northwest out of Broummana to connect with the main coastal highway north which would lead them first through Jounie, the teeming ferry terminal for boats travelling to and from Cyprus — and a main conduit for Shi'ite and Palestinian terrorists entering and leaving Lebanon. From there it was a short, easy drive to Jubail. Wallace luxuriated in the cool rush of wind that swept over him as the jeep hummed along the almost deserted highway towards the coast, the air freshening noticeably the closer they got to the sea. The whiskey and the codeine had worked their anaesthetic alchemy and the pain had eased to an unpleasant memory.

They encountered their first checkpoint five kilometres north of Bouranna. The sinister hulk of a T-72 was pulled halfway across the road, its massive 125mm gun trained toward the city. A red and white striped barrier-rail had been pulled across the rest of the road while two armed soldiers checked vehicles through a narrow gap. Several other troops lolled beside an APC at the side of the road, making tea over an open fire. There was no sign of the tank commander on the T-72 but Nazul saw the machine gunner half out of the turret, his 12.7mm anti-aircraft machine gun trained on the highway leading north. At least, Nazul noted, the commander had both highway approaches to the checkpoint covered. Heading out of Beirut, there were only two vehicles in front of them. The first was an ancient Citroen truck laden with the furniture and household possessions of the family of four squeezed into the cabin — more refugees leaving for the relative peace of the northern countryside. The real madness was that it had taken them this long, Wallace thought. The second vehicle was a dust-streaked white taxi containing only the driver and one male passenger. The guards made them get out and checked their wallets before letting them through. Nazul couldn't see if the soldiers had taken any money — the road toll troops often exacted when they found civilians carrying American dollars. Nobody liked America but everyone liked American dollars. The checkpoint guards tensed visibly as the jeep pulled up at the barrier and they recognised the rank of the officer in the back seat. Nazul, his driver and the guard presented their ID and Nazul vouched for his passenger. The soldiers glanced at the tired little civilian, then saluted and pulled the barrier back to allow the jeep through. The driver accelerated away and Wallace breathed deeply.

Another twenty minutes, perhaps thirty at the most, and he would be home. He fiddled absently with the straps of the cheap plastic Pan-Am bag on his lap that contained his overnight things which had lasted him six days. His khaki shirt and pants were dirty and uncomfortable. He was aching for a cool shower and another scotch, this time with ice. He would probably have to spend a polite half-hour with Lieutenant Nazul before retreating to the bedroom where he could enjoy some blessed privacy, secure in the knowledge that the driver would remain outside with the jeep and the guard would be at the front door all night, with Nazul asleep on the folding bed in the living room.

They cleared another checkpoint just south of Jounie. Nazul spent a little too long chatting with the officer in charge for Wallace's liking but he said nothing and they were on their way again in a few minutes. Wallace glanced at his watch. It was almost eight o'clock. The Mediterranean had been clearly in view for the past ten kilometres and Wallace could see the last dying embers of the sun on the western horizon. It was a cloudless night with a quarter moon and he could see the great silver slash of the Milky Way with its countless stars. It made him feel good just to look at it, even though he didn't know why. He and his wife had spent many summer nights such as this on the terrace of their home, enjoying a martini before dinner.

They were suddenly on the final, familiar descent into Jubail. One last checkpoint and he was home. There was no T-72 this time, just two trucks, a jeep-mounted machine gun and another candy-striped barrier. There were two guards again. Nazul saw they were wearing the shoulder flashes of his regiment. He didn't recognise either of them but that was not unusual. There were 600 men in his regiment. The checkpoint seemed quieter than usual. No sign of the other soldiers from the trucks making tea to sweeten their army rations like troops at the other checkpoints. The driver pulled to a smooth stop a few metres before the barrier and Nazul reached into his breast pocket to produce his ID for the third and final time. The two checkpoint guards ambled casually out towards them from behind the barrier, AK-47s cradled in their arms. A little too casually Nazul thought. He opened his mouth to say something and the first guard fired a burst of 7.62mm shells into Nazul's face at point-blank range. Wallace screamed in horror as a fountain of blood and fragments of bone and scalp from the officer's shattered skull spattered over him. At the same moment the other guard fired a long, concentrated burst into the driver and guard in the front seat. They weren't even given a second to plead for their lives. The escort trooper toppled slowly out of the jeep and onto the road, his torso ripped by bullets. His useless steel helmet fell to the ground with a hollow clang, rolled briefly, then stopped. The driver slumped forward over the wheel and the jeep's horn began to blare. The checkpoint guard pushed him roughly back onto the seat,

25

his bloodied head lolling on his shoulder, and everything fell silent again. Except for the screaming. Wallace could hear himself screaming, a shrill almost feminine sound, yet he couldn't stop himself. He was on the verge of hysteria. For a moment he sensed that he had drifted free from his body and was looking down on the murderous scene from above. He could see himself amidst the carnage, still screaming. Other men spilled out of the trucks. They weren't wearing Syrian army uniforms. There were at least a dozen of them and they were wearing a ragbag assortment of military clothing.

The pain brought him back. A sudden surge of pain jarred every nerve in the right side of his head. Wallace fought it, forced himself back to reason. His sanity depended on it. Their accents. There was something different about their accents. These soldiers weren't Syrians at all. They were speaking Arabic with a Lebanese accent. He struggled to place the accent. It was the harsher, more guttural inflections of the southern suburbs. But there was something else too. His mind strained to make sense of it all.

The soldier who had shot Nazul was still standing beside the jeep looking down at Wallace with a contemptuous smile. Wallace looked up at the man, his eyes glazed with dread, as the other armed men swarmed around the jeep. The man turned to his comrades and laughed. 'American... strong American, huh,' he said. And it all slid into place. Shi'ite Muslim. That was the accent. He hadn't heard it since he had last visited the southern suburbs of Beirut nearly four years before but he recognised it now.

These men were Shi'ite militia. They had to be. Only Shi'ites killed like this. They were men from Amal or Hezbollah. Or worse. They could be from one of The Shi'ite lunatic fringe terrorist groups: Guardians of the Islamic Revolution, Islamic Jihad or Red Jihad. All of them with links to the notorious psychopath Abu Nidal and his freelance group of Palestinian terrorists. Whoever they were, they had attacked

26

the checkpoint earlier, killed or disabled the Syrian guards and dressed two of their men in Syrian uniforms to ambush Nazul and take Wallace hostage.

Hostage!

The word seared into his brain and Wallace almost gagged. It was the last coherent thought he would have for a long time. The man dressed in a dead Syrian's uniform turned back to Wallace and the smile turned to a sneer as he looked down on the terrified American professor. Then he raised the AK-47 and smashed the hard wooden stock into the right side of Bill Wallace's face and the pain evaporated into a welcoming cloud of blackness.

Andros Island, Bahamas, June 10, Present Day

There was blood in the water. The blacktip reef shark sensed it as he nosed gracefully between the pillars of coral in five fathoms of pristine ocean. Seven gill slits on either side of his sleek grey body rippled like palm fronds as he sifted oxygen from the salt water, the sensors in his skin alert to any tremor of distress in the passing current. A school of tiny, glittering silversides scattered out of his path like exploding shrapnel as he prowled hungrily beneath a rock arch, then glided downward to skim the white, coarse-grained sand, searching, sensors straining like antenna. There it was again. And again: a flurry, a disturbance. The shark's primitive brain processed the message from the web of electrodes genetically impregnated in his tissue and recognised the signal. Everything else was reflex. The most lethal and efficient eating machine on earth twisted toward the signal and with a hard flick of its long tail accelerated towards the source of his next meal.

The man saw it first and he decided not to alarm the woman. She had her back to him and had just summoned all her courage to handfeed pieces of conch to a receptive moray in the coral wall. Both divers were unprotected in the warm Caribbean water except for the lightweight blue

27

lycra suits they wore to guard against coral grazes. It wasn't a big shark, a metre and a half in length maybe, but big enough to do serious damage if it wanted to.

Apparently it wanted to. The blacktip glided towards them like a sleek grey lance, a beautiful, evil sight. Homing in relentlessly on the source of those excited vibrations, the minor turbulence of a moray eel tearing at fragments of tattered conch meat. The man finned around to face the shark, his right hand gripping a coral spur to give himself leverage in the water. With his left hand he drew a wicked looking dive knife from the rubber sheath strapped to his left shin and positioned himself carefully. It only took a couple of seconds but the shark was almost upon them. The man seemed to know that the shark would ignore him and his partner. It was only interested in the source of those feeding signals. But, in the swift, single-minded lunge for food, the deadly, serrated teeth in that snapping jaw could easily slice off his dive partner's hand. And that wasn't likely to be a positive experience for a woman undergoing her first dive in open ocean.

There was less than a metre to go. The man glimpsed his reflection for a second in the shark's dead black eyes then lunged upward with the knife. The point of the blade bit deep into the shark's body just behind the jaw and the shark slit itself open from head to tail on the momentum of its own attack. The clear, clean water suddenly clouded with blood. The shark cannoned off the coral wall and twisted erratically away, spinning and flailing towards the sandy bottom in its death throes, leaving a long billowing trail of blood and entrails. The man grabbed the woman by the shoulder and yanked her away from the moray's lair in case the eel lunged out wildly in search of more unscheduled food. He saw her eyes widen in shock as she saw the blood in the water and the knife in his other hand and quickly gave her the okay signal followed by an upward jab of his thumb toward the surface.

'Jesus Christ!' she sputtered, a moment after breaking surface and ripping the regulator out of her mouth. 'What the hell was that all about?'

There was an unmistakeable note of anxiety in her voice but he was pleased to see she had it under control.

'A small blacktip wanted to get in on lunch,' the man said, keeping his voice deliberately calm. 'I'm afraid I had to discourage him.' His voice was English with a faint trace of Scots. Hers was an unmistakeable cultured Boston drawl.

Her eyes grew even wider now and her voice went up another octave.

'A blacktip what... a shark... a fucking shark?'

'Just a little one... a baby...'

'Jesus Christ... get me out of the water.'

'That's a good idea,' he grinned. There was no way of knowing what the dying shark would attract in the next half-hour or so. 'But take it easy,' he cautioned. 'Nice, easy kicks back to the ship. You'll get there much faster and in much better shape.'

The woman jammed the snorkel in her mouth and began finning rapidly towards their host vessel, anchored fifty metres away. The man wasn't sure if she would heed his warning and he swam with her until the moment of panic had passed and she had settled into a steady, sensible rhythm. If he had to tow her back he wasn't sure who would have been more humiliated.

He quickly scanned the horizon with an easy 360 degree turn. The ship was alone on the wide blue ocean. They still had this corner of the Caribbean to themselves. When his eyes fixed on the ship again, towering in front of them like a floating white castle, he paused for a moment just to admire her. Even though he had spent many hours on board he had never lost that sense of awe he felt just looking at her, enjoying her lines, her power, the extraordinary beauty of her engineering. The 2,200 tonne *American Endeavour* was one of the most beautiful private cruising yachts in the world.

Her raked superstructure gave just a hint of the thrust from the massive BMW marine diesel turbines that could propel her through the water at 26 knots for 4,500 nautical miles without refuelling. Her bridge was equipped with state-of-the-art electronics and her 72 metre length and 16½ metre beam accommodated six staterooms, a dozen double cabins and twenty-two singles. Her permanent crew of twenty-five was composed exclusively of Americans, all ex-Navy or Marine Corps. Nor was the *American Endeavour* quite as innocent as she looked. Concealed behind that racy white superstructure were 60mm cannons fore and aft, the launch tubes for six Sea Wasp surface-to-surface missiles and another half-dozen Sea Hawk surface-to-air missiles.

The man gave a strong kick and finned powerfully through the light swells to catch up with his partner. She had almost reached the dive platform, a few steps below an open side hatch, where a crewman wearing white shorts and T-shirt waited patiently, smoking a Lucky Strike. The crewman was in his early fifties with sinewy limbs the colour of aged teak. His grey hair was slicked straight back and tiny droplets of sweat trembled in his woolly sideburns. On his right forearm was the faint blue outline of a globe and anchor tattoo, the emblem of the Marine Corps. The woman reached the platform breathing heavily into her snorkel. The crewman flicked his cigarette into the water where it sizzled briefly then he bent down to take her weightbelt and tank.

She pulled the snorkel out of her mouth but was still too breathless to say or do anything for a couple of minutes. By that time the man had swum up alongside her and had begun to help her out of her gear.

She finally got her breath back. 'A shark!' she said, her voice a blend of disbelief and exasperation. 'A million square miles of ocean and he finds a goddamn shark and... he kills it — can you believe it?'

The crewman helped the woman out of the water and looked at her with genuine interest. She was in her late-twenties with strong, sensual features, dark eyes and rich, blue-black hair that hung to her shoulders. The wet lycra suit clung to a body that was almost perfect, a body of curves, of rounded hips and full breasts rather than the linear muscularity of so many modern women. She wore only bikini pants beneath the skintight lycra suit and both men noticed her nipples were hard and swollen under the wet fabric, whether from excitement or the coolness of the water, neither could tell. Even bedraggled by the ocean, she was lovely.

'A shark?' The crewman's voice was thick and phlegmy from forty years as a two-packs-a-day man.

'Yeah, a goddamn shark.' She plucked a fluffy yellow towel from a fresh stack just inside the hatch and dabbed at her streaming face.

'How big?'

'How *big*?' she echoed 'Who cares how big? It was a shark. There was blood and guts everywhere... it was disgusting. I nearly threw up in my goddamn regulator.'

'Gee...' The crewman looked bemused. 'You're lucky. I musta done a hundred dives or more before I saw my first shark. They sure are beautiful aren't they?'

The woman stopped towelling her hair and looked first at the crewman then down at the man who was still floating lazily in the water, watching her with a half smile on his face.

'*Lucky*?' She stared in disbelief. 'First he talks me into getting into the ocean, much against my better judgement, then he gets me to feed something that looks like a dick with teeth, then he lays on a shark because I might be getting a little bored and just in case that isn't enough he sticks a goddamn knife in the thing, right next to me there in the water so I can have a good look at its insides too. Jesus Christ! What next... Moby Dick?'

The crewman shook his head slowly. 'Gee,' he said. He bent down and picked up the mouthpiece to her SCUBA gear. 'Y'know,' he added, 'if you ever think you're going to throw up when you're under the water, make sure you take the regulator out of your mouth first because the lumpy bits —'

'Jesus Christ.' She stopped him going any further. She could see the ex-Marine was having trouble keeping a smile from his crafty, weatherbeaten face. She looked hard at him then at the man in the water. 'Gee,' she said, her voice leaden with sarcasm then she threw the towel down and disappeared through the hatch into the ship.

The crewman looked at the man in the water and they both grinned in that ageless male conspiracy. The man passed up his weightbelt and tank then heaved himself up onto the dive platform.

'I thought girls just wanted to have fun,' he deadpanned, picking up the discarded towel and wiping his face.

The crewman decided that he liked this tough limey. The guy looked smooth and talked smooth but he was okay where it mattered. And he had a few sharp edges. Edges that could cut deep.

He looked to be in his late 30s. His eyes were bright hazel, like hard, shiny pebbles from a Scottish brook, and his wet, chestnut hair was matted thickly to his skull. When he peeled off the thin wetsuit and stood only in his white swimming shorts, he revealed a muscular, lightly-tanned body marred by a constellation of strange, pink scars across his back which reached around to his ribcage. They were scars which had to have been caused by something violent, painful and fairly recent. Despite the scars, he looked strong and fit though there was a hint of fleshiness in the male danger area just above the hips which suggested he hadn't done any hard, sustained exercise for a while. Been convalescing, the crewman guessed.

The door to the bathroom was closed when the man reached their cabin a few minutes later and he could hear the shower running. He wanted to join her and harden up those nipples a little more. The sight of her in that clinging lycra suit had

32

created an urgent need in him but the closed door was an unmistakeable sign. Lynch looked at his dive watch. Nearly midday. Colin Lynch, formerly Lieutenant Lynch of Her Majesty's Royal Navy, formerly of Britain's elite Special Boat Squadron, most recently resigned from Britain's Counter Terrorism Command, took off his wet swimsuit, wrapped a towel around his waist and lay on the huge bed that dominated the bedroom of the VIP suite. It was the second grandest stateroom aboard the ship, the master stateroom was permanently reserved for the *American Endeavour*'s owner, Jack Halloran.

James Fitzgerald Halloran was president of the US conglomerate, Standard Transport Charter, and a dozen of its subsidiaries with interests in oil, mining, rail, shipping, trucking, cattle and real estate. Many of them were companies that Lynch had not even heard of yet. The rich American had made good his promise to let Lynch and his beautiful companion enjoy the restorative pleasures of the luxurious ship in exchange for services rendered — services which had put Lynch in a private hospital in Syracuse for three months recovering from burns, shrapnel wounds and other injuries which included three broken ribs, blast trauma and perforated ear drums. The only good thing about it had been that the beautiful woman in the bathroom had never left his side the whole time. Janice Street had suddenly become the most important person in Lynch's life. Little more than a year ago he hadn't known she existed. And the likelihood of them ever meeting conventionally had been slim. But, Lynch reflected, ever since his move from regular service into the shadow world of freelance counter terrorism, everything about his life had been distinctly unconventional. He liked that. Lynch glanced around the luxurious surrounds of the cabin again, the expensive Italian furniture, the silk-padded cabin walls, the plush, pale rose leather sofas. How many gay Brahmas had gone into those, he wondered. His eyes were drawn naturally to the tinted, blastproof glass of the big, rectangular window which framed the serene Bahamian waters outside. Lynch was no hayseed. He prided himself on his ability to move easily and comfortably from one social strata to another. It was a knack he had acquired. He was well aware that survival depended on the speed with which one adapted to environmental change, whether it was the jungles of Timor or the corridors of Whitehall. Lately it had been corporate America and the mercenary arena — Wall Street and the Third World. He had a feeling that all those years of specialist training might not be enough — but there was no going home for him now, even if he wanted to. Lynch was comfortable with most aspects of his new life in the United States. He had worked with US Special Forces on clandestine operations in the Philippines and Cuba. He had once mined a boat in New York harbour, a small, Panamanian-registered freighter packed with Armalites and half a million rounds of 5.56mm ammunition destined for the IRA — arms that were never delivered because two days out into international waters, a delayed-action fuse triggered the mine which, in turn, ignited the ammo and exploded the boat into splinters, scattering the crew and cargo over a wide area of the Atlantic. The Americans suspected British intelligence on that operation but they had never had it confirmed, officially or unofficially. Still, the Americans appreciated talent and now Lynch was in their pay, though he had often been given cause to wonder who his real masters were. Once a man had served with the intelligence community or any of the West's elite fighting units like the SAS, SBS, CTC, or US Special Operations Forces such as Delta, Seals or the 2nd Air Division, there was no such thing as just letting him go. No such thing as an easy retirement. They always made sure you knew that they knew where you were. Despite the deposit of one million dollars US in a Zurich account under a fake name following the successful completion of the Libyan contract, Lynch knew he had no real independence. He probably never would. The new name came with a new identity and a brand new green card, all provided by Halloran, a man whose power, it seemed, was limitless. This made Lynch wonder if Halloran too was really as independent of the US Government as he pretended to be — especially when Halloran could cough up a bona fide resident alien's card even the US Immigration Department couldn't query.

He heard the shower stop and a few minutes later Janice emerged from the bathroom wearing a fluffy yellow bathrobe. She said nothing but stood in the doorway and looked at him for a long time. Her face was solemn but he discerned an unmistakeable glow in her smoky brown eyes. She held a hairbrush in her right hand and walked over to a mirrored dresser, sat down and began brushing the tangles out of her hair. She hadn't said a word but the way she walked, the minutely exaggerated sway of her hips, the subtle movement of her body beneath the bathrobe said that he was more than forgiven. Janice examined her face in the mirror and she too saw that her anger — anger bred of a little girl's fear of the deep, yawning ocean and all the terrors it contained — had passed. She had only agreed to let him teach her to dive because she loved him and he loved the water so much. She wanted to learn everything she could about him. She would even conquer lifelong fears for him. The last few days aboard the *Endeavour* had been among the happiest of her life. Certainly the happiest since that summer evening in London the year before when she had met Lynch in a Thames-side pub and known instantly that he was the man she had been waiting for. But then they had only been allowed a few brief, artificial months together before he had disappeared on that Libyan job. She had initially been assigned by Halloran to keep an eye on Lynch. Falling in love hadn't been part of the plan for either of them. She smiled at the memory. They had both thought themselves immune to the complications of something as unnecessary as love.

Then there had been the waiting in New York. Month

35

after month when she tried to get on with what had once been her life — and couldn't. She couldn't rest until she knew what had happened to him and she couldn't bear to learn that he had been killed or maimed when she did find out. Finally she had learned he was alive. Halloran had told her Lynch was virtually unharmed. She still hadn't forgiven Halloran for that. She was entirely unprepared for the man she saw in the hospital bed in Syracuse. It had taken months for the broken ribs to knit, the myriad cuts and burns to heal. There were so many that it took an age for the fine grafts of the surgeons to take effect. Even then some had become infected and had to be done over again. Despite the pain he had never complained. That traditional, damned limey understatement. 'A few cuts and scrapes after a little spot of bother with the Libyans,' was how he had described it. A little spot of bother! Now he was whole again — and she could feel him slipping away from her.

She finished brushing her hair and swung around on the dresser chair to face him, her bathrobe falling open to reveal shapely brown legs. She left it open.

'Such a damn boy,' she said finally.

Lynch looked back at her and smiled. He swung his legs off the bed and walked towards the bathroom but she caught his hand and swung him back around to face her. 'Don't shower yet,' she said. She pulled him closer and pressed her face against his body. They stayed like that for a long time, savouring the moment, knowing that everything was okay again. For a while. He lovingly touched her head and cheek and she kissed him. Then she began tracing the hard ridges of his belly with her tongue. After a moment she reached up and began to unloosen his towel. 'I like my boys with a little salt,' she said.

It was just after three in the afternoon and they had eaten a late lunch on the fantail. The sun had turned the ocean to crushed emeralds and now that the steward had cleared away the dishes a pleasant drowsiness had settled over the whole ship. Janice was lying face down on a flag-sized towel spread across the scrubbed teak deck, the straps of her one-piece swimsuit tucked inside. Lynch had put on a pair of white trousers and a long sleeved Sea Island cotton shirt to protect his lighter skin against burning. He sat alongside Janice on a cushioned steamer chair, alternately browsing through the *Sports Illustrated* on his lap and casting long admiring looks over the woman he had just made love to for hours. Her skin was the colour of biscuit, almost identical to the coffee coloured one-piece swimsuit she wore. If you glanced at her quickly you could be mistaken for thinking she was still nude. As he looked at her Lynch realised he still had a lot more to learn about this beautiful Radcliffe-educated daughter of a small-town Maine doctor, a woman who had once chosen to sleep with Jack Halloran's rich and powerful friends, to cull favours and win confidences in exchange for the comforts and privilege of wealth. And she *was* moderately wealthy. Lynch had stayed at her Manhattan apartment for a month after getting out of hospital, a ninth-floor corner apartment on Park Avenue which had cost $1.4 million when she had bought it two years earlier with the help of an interest-free loan from Halloran. He had seen her portfolio and knew she had at least three million in savings funds and investments. And that was just what he knew about. With his recent paycheque it was enough for them to live comfortably together. Then why wasn't he entirely comfortable, Lynch wondered. Suddenly he had everything he had ever wanted from life: a beautiful woman who loved him, money, and a peaceful retirement just waiting for him. If he wanted it.

If he wanted it? He'd had plenty of time to pick over that one in hospital and he still hadn't been able to answer it honestly. Not even to himself. Lynch had learned to avoid too much self-analysis. He was like the man on the tightrope, he thought. He was only in trouble the moment he looked down and thought about what he was doing. Now it was harder than ever because Janice was forcing him to make a decision. Gently, subliminally perhaps, but nevertheless a decision about how he intended to live the rest of his life. So far he had avoided it by lying to her and to himself. The truth was, he knew, that he liked the military life. And, God help him, he liked being a mercenary. Mercenary imperatives cut right through that world of suffocating red tape he had once inhabited. He knew it was brutal. But you could get a lot done at the point of a gun as long as you were sure you were right. Right? That was another question. All he could manage on that one was that there were people in the world who were causing a helluva lot of unnecessary suffering. And that was wrong. It was a simple answer to a complicated question. But it would have to do for now. He would leave the diplomacy to others. After all, diplomacy was just war for people who were afraid of guns.

Lynch knew he loved Janice as much as he could love anyone. That in itself was a trial. There were times when the demands of commitment made him feel claustrophobic. Nor was he used to Janice's world. He was nagged by a constant sense of dislocation as he shared her life of sheltered opulence with all its attendant insularity, its safeness, its... softness. He liked luxury but he loathed the decadence that seemed to be its constant companion.

It had started soon after Lynch had felt sufficiently recovered to start laying the foundations of his new identity and his new life. The two of them had taken Janice's silver-grey BMW and scoured the New England states looking for an appropriate retreat for Lynch. She refused to let him consider Maine. A little too close to home, she said. He ruled it out, anyway, because most of Maine was too accessible from the coast and therefore vulnerable to any seaborne hit team that might want to take him out. The further inland the better. He would have preferred somewhere like Wyoming or Montana and had to lie to her that he was only kidding when he saw the look on her face. He finally settled on a small lodge just outside Stowe in Vermont. Stowe was a popular ski resort for the northeastern United States and Janice thought it might be a little busy. Lynch pointed out that it was small enough to be manageable and big enough for a newcomer with a funny accent to blend in without attracting too much attention. And, he pointed out, it was only 150 kilometres from Montreal so he could slip across the border in an hour and have all of Quebec to hide in — an area the size of western Europe. In the past, Lynch had helped train RCMP Emergency Response Teams in special exercises around the eastern provinces. He knew the country, he was an all-weather expert at living off the land and if he wanted to he could get lost and stay lost indefinitely.

He and Janice had spent two months furnishing the lodge outside Stowe. Two happy, innocent months. The lodge was high on a rock shelf in a keyhole gully with the nearest neighbours, a wizened hippie couple, half a mile away on the other side of a fir-crested ridge. It had been a kind of idyll for them both. Her apartment in New York, his lodge in Vermont. Yet there were always unacknowledged tensions between them both. For Janice, sharing her life with Lynch was like trying to relax in a lull between storms — even when there was no sign of a storm on the horizon. For Lynch, even at its best, there was an artificiality about it that bothered him. It couldn't last, he told himself. Not because he didn't want it to. But because he believed it would be impossible to change the momentum of his life, a momentum built up through twenty years of active soldiering and cemented by all the survival habits a man accumulates along the way. Travel fast, travel light, travel alone. In his world there was no such thing as excess baggage.

They had told no-one about the Vermont hideaway so they had both been surprised when the phone rang one night and it was Halloran on the other end, inviting them to spend a couple of weeks as his guests aboard *American Endeavour*.

The number was supposedly silent though Lynch would have given it to Halloran eventually. He was impressed that Halloran had found it so quickly, especially as he had had the phone connected in a different false name from the one Halloran had given him on his green card.

'It's my business to know where you are,' Halloran had reminded him before ringing off.

The idea of two weeks cruising the Caribbean appealed to them. They had flown to Miami, caught a connecting flight to the Bahamas and boarded the ship at Nassau a week before. For Lynch, as well as Janice, boarding the *American Endeavour* had been like reuniting with an old friend, even though the last time Lynch had seen the ship it had been in the dead of night in the Gulf of Sidra twenty sea miles off the Libyan coast. This time he had enjoyed her as she was meant to be enjoyed: in the company of a beautiful woman, the two of them the only guests on board, a congenial crew to wait on them, and a captain instructed to take them wherever they wanted to go in the northern Caribbean.

Lazing in the sun on the fantail they both wondered how long the honeymoon could last. They did not have to wait long for their answer. Lynch heard it first. He stood up and shaded his eyes to scan the horizon and caught a rapidly growing dot about 10 klicks off. Captain Penny hadn't said anything about other visitors. A moment later Janice heard the chopper too. She made a face and stood up. It could have been a private charter, sightseers, Bahamian coastguard or customs patrol. God knew these waters were busy enough with drug runners between the islands and the mainland US. But the way the chopper was making a beeline for the *American Endeavour* suggested it was someone for them. Their suspicion was confirmed a moment later when some crewmen bustled out to clear the helipad. Janice made a skirt of her towel and Lynch picked his glass up from the table. The helipad was only twelve metres away on the raised afterdeck and they were going to catch some wash from the props. The chopper swooped in low behind the stern, banked and settled into a hovering position above the afterdeck. The bright afternoon sun glinted off the cockpit canopy, preventing them from seeing who was inside. Lynch riffled his memory. It was a Puma — the sleek, fast business chopper built by Aerospatiale of France. With its range of 705 kilometres and maximum speed of 278 kmh it could have made the flight from the Florida coast, 250 kilometres away, in less than an hour. Lynch had noted the absence of a chopper on board the vessel when they had boarded at Nassau but thought little of it. They wouldn't need one. Now they had their answer.

The pilot eased the chopper neatly onto the helipad. It bounced briefly then settled. Lynch and Janice turned their backs to the wash. Lynch could see Janice's lips moving but couldn't hear what she was saying above the noise of the rotors. He caught something about her hair and smiled. Whoever it was wouldn't be getting a warm reception from Janice. The pilot shut down the engines and they both turned back as the turbines sighed to a full stop. A cockpit door swung open and a moment later the beefy face of Jack Halloran appeared.

'Oh no,' Janice groaned, turning away again. 'There's been no time. I didn't think it would be this soon. This is what the bastard had in mind all along.'

She flicked a sharp, anxious glance at Lynch. The intensity of her reaction surprised him but it wasn't entirely unexpected. Since she and Lynch had begun living together she had no longer been available for Halloran to participate in any of his activities in the same accommodating manner she had in the past. To Halloran's credit he had accepted her decision with equanimity. Superficially, at least, Lynch was a realist. He knew that Halloran, more than any other person, had been responsible for Janice achieving the financial independence which now enabled her to say no to him. But Lynch suspected that Janice had become a trifle paranoid where

41

Halloran was concerned. What was it about the sanctimoniousness of the reformed hooker? Not that Janice's past had ever bothered Lynch. He had often enjoyed the company of classy hookers and knew many of the world's best whorehouses. It was the ideal solution for a man in his line of business and he liked the honesty of the hooker–client relationship. A straightforward cash exchange for an hour or two of erotic stimulation and a pleasurable hydraulic adjustment, and, if you got the right girl, good conversation and a few laughs along the way.

Once, on a three-month assignment in Singapore advising the Police Tactical Team at Changi airport, he had a Chinese girl move in with him. They had grown to like each other, too. Afterwards he sent her money occasionally until she sent him a sweet letter saying she had married a rich shipping broker. If anything, Lynch had found that there were times when Janice's recycled virtue irked him a little. Then again, he had to concede, she had plenty of reasons to be wary of Halloran. She had known him for almost ten years, ever since he had plucked her out of Radcliffe College for a rather specialised executive role in his corporate empire. Janice knew from long experience how persuasive, how cunning and how utterly ruthless Halloran could be in the pursuit of his goals. And, quite sensibly, she was afraid of Halloran. Lynch already knew how dangerous Halloran could be. Behind the avuncular charm was a man who would not hesitate to do murder to get his way. Or rather, to have someone do murder on his behalf. Halloran had already warned Lynch, in that deceptively amiable way of his, that if Lynch ever jeopardised his security he would have Lynch terminated without hesitation. As confident as Lynch was of his own survival skills, he believed Halloran was one of the few men on earth with the resources and the will to do it.

Halloran trotted down the steps from the helipad, leaving the pilot to boss around two crewmen while they secured the chopper. He was beaming like the proverbial rich uncle.

'Enjoying my little yacht?'

He didn't wait for an answer. Halloran never waited for answers. *He* controlled all the questions and answers in his world. Instead, he gave Janice a proprietorial kiss on the cheek and lingered just a fraction too long for her liking. The bastard did it on purpose, she thought. Then he turned to Lynch and gave him the kind of rasping, bone-crushing handshake that only farmers or cowboys still give.

'You're looking good, Lynch,' he said. 'Glad to see you one hundred per cent again.'

'Try seventy-five,' Janice added coolly.

The last time Lynch had seen Halloran had been in the hospital room he had called his home for three months following his transfer from the US Navy hospital at Norfolk, Virginia where he had first been treated following his medivac after the Libyan job. That had been nearly five months ago. Lynch suspected Janice was right. Halloran probably wanted something. He wasn't the type for idle socialising. The ship's Executive Officer, an olive-toned, serious-looking young man in crisp whites, arrived and gave Halloran a smart salute.

'Sir, welcome aboard, sir.'

Not long out of the service at all, Lynch thought.

'The captain sends his compliments and asks if there's anything you need.'

Halloran nodded. 'See my pilot to one of the double suites. We'll stay at anchor here. I see no reason to disrupt my guests' vacation ... for now.' He let the words hang for a moment. 'I'll be flying out again in the morning. Tell Captain Penny I'll be dining in my stateroom with Mr Lynch and Miss Street at eight o'clock and I want the conference room prepared for a meeting to follow. Right now, why don't you get the steward to organise a couple of cold beers for me.'

Halloran didn't have to say which beer. He could have the ship stocked with all the premium beers in the world but he always drank Budweiser, the beer he'd been weaned on as a 17-year-old in the Marine Corps during the Korean

43

War. He turned to Janice and Lynch but they shook their heads. The XO saluted smartly again and left. Halloran was wearing tan pants, a khaki windbreaker and a blue checked shirt with a couple of buttons undone to reveal a forest of silvery chest hair. He took off the jacket, threw it into a nearby steamer chair and sat down at the circular metal table bolted to the deck. Lynch and Janice sat opposite Halloran and waited.

Halloran would soon turn sixty but had a full head of bristly grey hair that gave his face a tough, pugnacious look. It was a face with the burnished glow of a man who spends a lot of time outdoors or one who spends a lot of time indoors drinking whiskey. But the eyes were piercing blue and you only had to look into them once to know you were dealing with a man used to getting his own way. Despite a gut that overlapped a polished silver rodeo buckle, Halloran's heavy build suggested a lot of latent physical power. There was something about Halloran that commanded attention. It wasn't easy to relax around him, Lynch had noticed. Even when he was making small talk he always gave the impression that he had more important things on his mind.

Halloran had started the day in Washington, he said, where he had spent the previous two days in frustrating discussions with senior officials at the State Department. He didn't say if he'd been to the White House this time. It wouldn't have surprised Lynch or Janice if he had. As Halloran often boasted, in the three decades that followed his accumulation of great wealth and influence he had eaten more dinners at the White House than any single President. From Washington he had flown to Miami by private jet to pick up the chopper, he said. They had taken off from Miami only ninety minutes ago.

When Halloran had invited Lynch and Janice to use his yacht he gave the impression that it was awaiting their pleasure. He had told them they could go anywhere in the northern Caribbean they chose. Lynch now realised that he had wanted

44

them somewhere private and protected, but easily accessible to him. On his own yacht moored within ninety minutes fast chopper ride of the east coast was the perfect place. And, Lynch reflected, Captain Penny would have kept his boss informed of their exact location at all times. As Janice often said, when you worked for Halloran you had all the freedom in the world... within limits.

The conversation stopped for a moment as the steward delivered Halloran's beer. Two frosted cans in a silver ice bucket. No glass. Halloran plucked a can from the ice, popped it open, and took a long, satisfying pull.

'I want you to do another job for me,' Halloran said, looking at Lynch and coming abruptly to the point.

The sudden silence weighed a ton.

Janice was the first to speak. 'He always gets a power surge close to Independence Day,' she said caustically.

Halloran let it pass. Lynch said nothing. He squinted over the ship's rail at the glittering ocean. This was how it happened, he was thinking. Out of the blue on a clear, innocent day. He might have guessed. No warning for either of them. Especially not for Janice. No time to keep secrets from her now, he realised.

Lynch felt Janice's eyes on him. Was that her fear he could feel... or his own guilt?

Halloran spoke again. 'You know about our hostages in Beirut — '

'No.' Janice interrupted, leaning forward in her chair, hands knuckled in her lap, showing white through the tan. 'This isn't goddamn fair...' Her words trailed away. They had been directed at Halloran but her eyes never left Lynch.

'I think Janice is opposed to the idea,' Lynch said dryly.

Halloran hesitated only for a moment, long enough to frame the words precisely the way he wanted and to give them all equal emphasis. 'If we don't go and get them,' he said, 'those guys are never coming home.'

Janice's next words surprised Lynch. She played her biggest

card right there and then. It was all the more surprising because they had never directly discussed this moment between them, even though they knew it had to come. Sooner or later.

'If you discuss this with him now,' she said, 'I'm flying back to New York. Tonight.'

Halloran's eyes narrowed a fraction. This was a woman who had once been under his total control. Both men knew now that something had changed. Forever. Janice had seized her independence and she was fighting for the only thing that made that independence worth having. All the warmth had gone out of the day. The air between them sizzled with static electricity.

Lynch looked at Janice, his eyes deliberately expressionless. He opened his mouth to speak, searching for that calm, neutral tone intended to impose a certain civility on situations such as this. But Janice saw it coming and got up before he could speak. The look in his eyes was exactly what she didn't want to see — because there was nothing there for her. Already, he realised, she knew him a little too well. Janice left the table without another word. Both men watched her go.

'Shit,' Lynch said. But he couldn't bring himself to go after her. If he did, he knew it meant surrendering control of the only life he had ever known for the tenderest of traps: life with Janice in a world where he wasn't even sure he belonged. It wasn't a decision he was ready to make. If he stayed, at least it would be the world he knew.

Janice disappeared from view and Lynch turned his attention to Halloran. He scanned the fleshy red face for any sign of triumph but found nothing. Halloran could deadpan with the best of them.

'Hostages?' Lynch prompted.

Halloran was in no mood to waste more time. 'I've spent the past two days talking to those pukes at the State Department,' he said. 'They're still involved in negotiations with Tehran through our Embassy people in Jordan. They're willing to unfreeze Iranian assets in the US in exchange for

46

the nine remaining American hostages in Beirut. Iran is a lot more willing to behave since its war with Iraq ended and the mullahs found out that they're going to be back in the Stone Age without Western aid. And Western aid means American goodwill. For its part, the administration has been trying to undermine Khomeini's hard line successors, and build a few bridges to the emerging power structure in Tehran. Khomeini's death has changed nothing behind the scenes. The problem is that Tehran doesn't control the fate of our hostages anymore. Our hostages are held by the lunatic fringe in Lebanon, primarily the Shi'ite militia — Hezbollah or Party Of God. We've known for some time that most of the Shi'ite militias get their money from Tehran. As long as the mullahs can see some possibility of getting back $5 billion of their frozen US funds to rebuild their armed forces, it is in their interests to pretend that they still control the militias and, hence, the fate of our hostages. Unfortunately for the hostages, the State Department seems to think it's more important to play along with their contacts in the Iranian government than to look at more realistic ways of getting our people out. We know that Tehran's grip on Hezbollah has been slipping ever since the USS *Vincennes* blew that Iranian Airbus out of the sky in '88 and the Iranians didn't react. None of the old ranting and raving, none of the old threats of dire revenge on the Great Satan or any of that shit. Hezbollah wanted to execute a couple of the hostages in revenge but Tehran wouldn't permit it. The mullahs knew our hostages would one day be worth more to them alive than dead. So they contented themselves with a propaganda war and kept stringing the State Department along. Hezbollah couldn't stomach that. What happened was that Tehran pushed them further into the arms of Abu Nidal and all those other murdering fanatics who hate all things American. The crazy thing about this whole situation is that as long as Tehran controlled those bastards' purse strings they acted as a moderating influence.'

47

Halloran sipped his beer. 'How do you like those apples — Tehran as a moderating influence? But it's true — if the Shi'ite militias in Lebanon didn't do what Tehran wanted they got no more arms with which to wage war against the enemies of Islam. Hezbollah believe they have a sacred duty to take their holy war, their *jihad* to the rest of the world, preferably to the mainland of the United States. Now Iran has exhausted itself and decided to be reasonable for a while Hezbollah have decided they're a bunch of wimps in Tehran. Consequently Hezbollah have been trying to reduce their dependence on Iran, to break Tehran's control and make their own policy. We think they may have found a way to do it.'

Lynch was transfixed. Halloran leaned forward, his body tense. 'The loonies inside Hezbollah are on the verge of a deal which could bring them millions of dollars and give them the power to operate as an independent force wherever and whenever they like,' he said, 'If that happens, the most murderous and dedicated group of anti-American fanatics in the Middle East will be free to wage a campaign of terror against the US and its citizens, anywhere in the world — a campaign that will make the terrorism of the past twenty years look like a practice match.'

Halloran took another pull on his beer to give Lynch a moment to absorb the implications of what he had just said.

'You know what really irks me about these bastards?' Halloran said. 'They cause trouble and pain that is out of all proportion to their goddamn importance in the world.'

Lynch smiled faintly. He had entertained the same thought.

Halloran shuffled in his seat then added: 'We won't be able to count on any regional assistance for this operation. Not from our intelligence people, Special Forces, not from the Israelis, the Christian Phalange, the Lebanese Army or the Syrians. The Syrians have been co-operating with the State Department in certain areas but they have their own objectives in Lebanon, and for the purposes of this operation

48

we must consider them a hostile force. Syria's Assad has been behaving himself in public lately but it still suits him to have the Druze, Sunni and Shi'ite militias wreaking havoc in Beirut and southern Lebanon, until he can consolidate his grip on the whole northern half of the country, which your schoolbook history will tell you was all part of the old Assyrian Empire. That bastard is as cunning as a shithouse rat. He wants the whole goddamn country if he can get it and as long as the State Department buys his line that he's doing his best to enforce peace and stability in the region, he can keep pursuing that strategy. Superficially, Assad has been posing as regional peacekeeper to keep the major powers out of his hair. That keeps us out of the picture and gives Assad the room to pursue his own objectives. And the State Department thanks him and plays along!' Halloran grunted. 'Small wonder nobody knows what the US is doing in the Middle East. *We* don't fucking know!'

'Now we have the State Department trying to make a deal with Tehran over the lives of our hostages when the current leadership in Iran no longer controls the fate of these hostages. If the mullahs pull this one off, if they get everything they want from the US then throw up their hands in frustration and say they're terribly sorry but they don't control the fate of the hostages after all, they'll make even bigger fools of us than they did over Irangate.'

Lynch had to admit he was impressed. But the Scot in him was naturally sceptical. 'How do you know all this?' he asked.

'Because,' Halloran sat back in his chair with the air of a man about to play his trump card, 'while the State Department has been considering demands from Tehran over the hostages, some of our other government agencies have been getting parallel demands from other groups for the same fucking hostages!' He paused. 'Until now, our policy has been to treat these other demands as bogus. Largely because they were laughably unrealistic. Stupid stuff ... twenty million per

49

hostage, the release of all Shi'ite prisoners in Kuwaiti, Omani, Saudi and Egyptian prisons, that kind of thing. But ten days ago a junior attache at our Embassy in Amman was invited to a meeting with a man who claimed to be an intermediary acting on behalf of Hezbollah. At that meeting the attache was given a set of demands we believe were genuine.'

'What kind of demands?'

'Hezbollah delivers all nine American hostages still held captive in Beirut. That suggests they can get the co-operation of other Shi'ite factions for the time needed to make this deal. They're asking five million dollars per hostage. It's close to what the French paid for their hostages. That's one reason why we think it may be genuine. The problem is... nine hostages. At five million per that represents forty-five million dollars.'

Lynch shrugged. 'Considering the money the US has lost in the Gulf already, it could be a bargain.'

'Yes,' Halloran agreed. 'And think of what the world's most fanatical anti-American terrorist organisation could do with forty-five million dollars.'

'What other reason do you have to believe the offer was genuine?'

'It came in the form of an ultimatum. Either we signalled our acceptance of the deal within thirty days or Hezbollah would sell our hostages elsewhere.'

'Sounds like a standard threat.'

'It isn't.'

'How do you know?'

'We aren't the only people in the market to buy American hostages.'

'Who else is there?'

'The PLO.'

'The PLO... Arafat's men?' Lynch was incredulous. 'But he's almost respectable, for Christ's sake. What is it... seventy-odd countries which recognise a Palestinian state now? And apart from all of that Hezbollah helped drive the PLO out of Lebanon.'

'Yes,' Halloran nodded. 'But you know what those bastards are like over there. They mutate like a goddamn virus. And they change allegiance as fast as they change form. Arafat's recognition of Israel's right to exist has put him in deep shit with Fatah's hard liners. People forget that Al Fatah is the PLO's military wing and it was Fatah which set up Black September. On top of that there are still half a dozen Palestinian splinter groups dedicated to the overthrow of Yasser Arafat and the destruction of Israel by force. That's not counting all those other crazy fucking towel-heads in Lebanon. Even his old terrorist pal, Abu Nidal, has sworn to knock him off. And that bastard has tried twice already.' Halloran shook his head. 'No,' he added. 'What Arafat is trying to do is buy himself a little insurance.'

'Insurance?'

Halloran smiled and Lynch realised it was in grudging respect for the PLO Chairman's cunning.

'If there is one thing the PLO has it is plenty of money,' Halloran said. 'Yasser Arafat is going to use some of that money to buy friends and influence people. The PLO is going to buy our hostages from Hezbollah and all the other factions in Beirut.'

Lynch thought for a moment. 'Maybe it's better for the hostages. At least we can deal with the PLO.'

'Maybe. Maybe not.'

'What do you mean?'

'Arafat's position has never been more precarious. He'll have to show some pretty fancy footwork if he doesn't want to get bumped off by any of the cutthroats he used to run with. He needs new allies. Allies where he never had any before.'

'Such as?'

Halloran pursed his lips. 'Oh… American Jews,' he said with just a trace of irony.

Lynch's eyebrows arched.

'Don't look so surprised,' Halloran said. 'Arafat has already met with Jewish Americans in Stockholm. It's part of his

51

strategy to drive the wedge even deeper between America and Israel. That's what he has to do now, get America more on his side and isolate Israel as much as he can. And since the US started talking to the PLO, I think he has a good chance of pulling it off.'

Halloran paused. 'It's a confident man who thinks he can outsmart Yasser Arafat. I don't think there's anyone in the State Department who's up to it. That's what worries me. And a neat little propaganda coup about now would strengthen Arafat's hand even further... say securing the release of US hostages in the Lebanon. Something the US or no other power has been able to do. Can you imagine the impact it would have if Arafat were to call a press conference, then release the American hostages one at a time? He could run for Mayor of New York after that. The US would probably hand him the West Bank on a plate. And at the very least...' there was a hard glitter in Halloran's eyes, 'Arafat could ask the US for a nice little aid package to help him set up the new state of Palestine. Something to establish an equitable balance of power between Israel and Palestine. Under the circumstances it would be hard to see how the US could ignore such a request. Imagine that... from our number one terrorist enemy to friendly head of state in twenty years. Pretty fancy dancing if he can pull it off.'

Lynch whistled softly. 'You've got to admire the bastard's nerve.'

'Arafat has never gambled small,' Halloran said. 'He's playing for Palestinian statehood here... not to mention his own immortality. And it's my bet that he's going to get it — in five to ten years at the outside, maybe sooner. These things have a habit of moving fast when they gain momentum.'

Lynch thought for a moment. 'Would any of that be so bad?' he mused.

'Depends on which side of the fence you're watching it from,' Halloran answered. 'You don't have to look too hard to see problems for the US in all of this. To be backed into

52

a diplomatic corner by Yasser Arafat and at the same time for Arafat to give money to splinter terrorist groups. The administration comes out looking like a bunch of goddamn farm boys compared to Arafat, and at the same time Arafat keeps his credentials high with the fanatics in the Middle East by giving them money to continue their campaign of terror against the US. It's a no-lose situation for him and plenty of shit on the face for Uncle Sam. They'd be pissing themselves laughing all over the Middle East at the US.... again. Meanwhile we'd have our hands full fighting off a new wave of terrorism. Not a pretty picture for us, huh? Those hostages are pawns in a mighty big and dangerous game, Lynch. It's changing all the time and the longer it goes on, the worse it gets for us. We have to get them out and put an end to Arafat's little scheme. If he wants to set up a Palestinian State he can do it on a different agenda, not one that puts us in the shithouse. The US can't be seen to have a hand in it so it has to be an unofficial operation. Arafat, Assad, Tehran, the militias, they'll all get the message that we weren't dumb enough to fall for their little trick and that we're not prepared to be fucked around any more. They have to know that. A certain amount of executive force will be required to impress that fact upon them. That's why we... I want you.'

Lynch didn't respond immediately. Then: 'What price is the PLO paying for the hostages?'

'Around one and a quarter million US per head.'

Lynch shrugged. 'Presumably Hezbollah don't care where the money comes from. Why don't you send word to Hezbollah that you'll up the ante. Offer one and a half million... two million a head if it'll get the hostages back. It's a much more discreet way of doing it.'

'Well...' Halloran drawled it out, a half smile on his big beefy face. 'Apart from the morality involved...'

Lynch snorted. He well knew that his own government and the US government used third parties all the time to negotiate directly with terrorists when it suited their purpose.

Halloran ignored him and continued. 'Apart from the dubious morality of going behind the government's back to do business with terrorists, there is also the problem that the price goes right back up through the roof when they know they're dealing with Americans or American agents. We can't afford it and we can't justify putting that kind of money in their hands to enable them to wage war against us. That's quite apart from the fact that we don't want to risk giving them another hostage.'

'Ahh,' Lynch nodded. 'So you've tried it already and lost one agent.'

'Yes,' Halloran said shortly. He tended to forget Lynch wasn't just a dumb soldier.

'What sort of timescale are we looking at?'

'We've got twenty days to give them an affirmative.'

'And then?'

'Well, it starts to work in our favour for a while. Briefly, and I mean very briefly, they bring the hostages together in one place where they can be collected when the money has been paid. We have to string Hezbollah's negotiators along just long enough to let us put in a team to pull the hostages out.'

'Just like that.'

'Yeah,' Halloran's face split into a grin. 'Just like that.'

Both men stayed silent for a while. 'Besides,' Halloran added, growing serious again. 'I have a personal score to settle with some of those fuckin' sand apes. You remember when those bastards blew up the Marine barracks in Beirut — killed 241 men?'

Lynch nodded.

Halloran's eyes hardened visibly. 'The Syrians were behind that,' he said. 'Just another little example of Middle Eastern tactical thinking to get the US out and leave the way clear for Assad to play regional peacekeeper. When that happened I wanted to land every goddamn bulldozer in the Fifth Fleet and push the whole goddamn country right across the border into Assad's lap. He wants it — he can fuckin' have it.'

'This has nothing to do with Syria,' Lynch said.

'Don't you believe it,' Halloran replied. 'The Shi'ite militias are holed up in the Beqa'a Valley under Syrian protection. That's where intelligence tells us the hostages will be gathered for the handover. It would suit me nicely if Assad got his fingers burnt while you boys were there.'

Lynch shook his head. 'I'll go in and get your hostages for you,' he said. 'But there are to be no punitive strikes against the Syrian military.'

Halloran looked pained for a moment. 'What's so special about the Syrians to you?' he asked.

'Nothing.'

'So?'

'KISS,' Lynch said.

'What?'

'KISS,' Lynch repeated. 'US Special Forces expression, I believe. Keep It Simple Stupid. Going in and getting the hostages back in one piece will be hard enough. We don't want to complicate matters further by going out of our way to take action against Syrian military personnel to satisfy one of your old grudges. Simply not very efficient, old boy. Get in, get the hostages, get out. That's how I see the job. If you want me to take it, that's how I'll do it.'

'And if anybody gets in your way they get dead?' Halloran pushed.

Lynch nodded. 'Count on it.'

'Good enough,' Halloran said. 'You have to go through Syrians to get to the militia... they're that close.'

Lynch shrugged lightly. 'Whatever it takes to do the job,' he said.

Halloran finished his beer but held the empty can in his beefy fist and looked at Lynch. 'Money?' was all he said.

Lynch looked directly back at him. It would have been impossible for either one to know what the other was thinking.

But Lynch had learned something about the fee structure which applied to freelance military operations of this nature. He didn't hesitate.

'Two million US to plan and lead the operation,' Lynch said. 'Half a million for each of the men. No insurance. I choose the team.'

'No problem with that,' Halloran said. 'But we choose the men together.'

'Okay,' Lynch said. 'You provide all the equipment.'

Halloran smiled again. 'Toys for the boys? You wouldn't fucking believe what I can put in your hands, pal.'

Lynch glanced at his surroundings and thought of the battery of Sea Wolf missiles hidden aft. 'Oh, yes I would,' he replied quietly.

The main business was done. Lynch looked out over the ocean. The same gorgeous day, the sparkling Caribbean, the dusty green slopes of Andros Island. All beautiful. All despoiled by casual talk of murder.

It didn't show but Lynch had discovered something unpleasant in himself. He had been lying to Janice for months, he realised, casual, frighteningly easy deceptions about the way he intended to lead his new life. Most disturbing of all he had been lying to himself. It wasn't until the offer had been put baldly in front of him and the sudden involuntary thrill of electricity had coursed through his body that he had realised how much he needed the military world. He had found his niche early in life. There was always the next operation to look forward to, the next mission, the next assignment. Without that, he had found, he could never really relax. He could rest between jobs, but he could not make a lifetime out of recreation. It would be too empty, too purposeless. To have meaning his life had to have direction. And the only direction he knew was the next job. Lynch felt uneasy. He didn't much care for what he was learning about himself. He gained a sudden insight into why former comrades in arms had chosen the mercenary life after leaving their regular units. At the time he had assumed the professional soldier's casual contempt for the mercenary, the soldier of fortune and his 'need' for action. But now he was beginning to understand. He simply didn't have a lot of choice, no matter how alluring Janice and her world might be.

Even Halloran looked curious. He studied the phlegmatic Scot carefully.

'I never usually ask,' he said after a long pause. 'But I thought I was going to have to work harder than this. You're more complicated than the others I deal with in this line of work, Lynch. Are you sure you're ready to do this job?'

Lynch hesitated. He felt awkward and resented Halloran for pressing him. He had no easy answer. Halloran had to know that. The American was pushing for something more, the authority in their relationship perhaps. Lynch wasn't prepared to give him more. It was enough that he did the work. He didn't have to like himself as well. And that was nobody's business but his own.

'It's what I do best,' he said finally.

Halloran finished his beer. He toyed with the can for a moment and flicked it carelessly over the guard rail into the pristine blue sea. Lynch watched it glitter prettily for a moment as it caught the sun before hitting the water and bobbing away in the slight current, another piece of indestructible jetsam. 'Goddamn,' Halloran grumbled, opening the second can. 'I hope you're not going to give me any of that crisis of conscience bullshit.'

Lynch watched a few drops of ice water form dark splashes on Halloran's blue shirt then scanned his face for a sign of the sarcasm he knew must be there, but couldn't find any. If it was a bluff, Lynch had to concede, it was a good one.

'Perhaps I might just be getting to like it,' he said.

Halloran shook his head. 'You're no psychopath, Lynch,' he said. 'I think I know what's eating you. You're a professional fighting man. You've served with some of the finest fighting units in the world. Now you no longer have a country, a home... or a reason to continue doing what you do. And that bothers a man like you because of all that goddamn British properness you've been indoctrinated with all your life.' Halloran paused and an ironic gleam crept into his eye. 'The most civilised people in the world, the British,' he said. 'It's all fine and dandy to butcher the natives as long as it's done with propriety and there's gin and tonic to follow.'

Halloran waited but Lynch didn't bite.

'Well...' Halloran added, 'I've got news for you, Lynch. What we do is right. You can bet your goddamn soul on that. So I don't want any problems with the rightness of the cause here. There's no room for tormented souls in any of my operations. You're no good to me unless I know you can give me one hundred per cent performance. And I'm not talking about your physical toughness. I know the shape you're in. I'm concerned about mental toughness. And I don't want any fucking around here. I don't want you leading this operation unless you can guarantee me that hundred per cent. When you're on the ball, Lynch, you're the best there is. That's why I came to you first. Still got the booze licked?'

Lynch felt a sudden flush of anger but controlled it. Halloran was only testing him. Pushing, prodding, niggling. It was all part of the process to pull him into line, exactly where Halloran wanted.

'I haven't had a drink in eighteen months,' Lynch replied quietly. 'But you already know that.'

Halloran smiled then added, 'Janice isn't working for me anymore... but you already know that.'

The two men eyed each other for a moment then Halloran spoke, his voice hard and businesslike again. 'You know the rules. Once you're in you're in 'till the fat lady sings or you go out feet first. You take the job now, Lynch, you see it through. There's no dropping out halfway if you decide things might be getting a little too dirty. And, given the time pressures we'll be operating under, this one is going to be a bitch.

So, if there's anything you want to tell me, you'd better tell me now.'

Lynch deliberately kept his voice at a dead monotone. 'I'll give you a professional job,' he said.

Halloran smiled again at the faint hint of menace. He liked that. He was satisfied. The big American stretched and took another deep pull on his Budweiser.

'You know something, Lynch,' Halloran said, visibly more relaxed. 'People love drama. Most people get it vicariously from TV and movies. You get it from real life because you like it, Lynch. You enjoy it. You've lived with it for so long you can't live without it. There's nothing to be ashamed of in that. But don't make the mistake of confusing drama with bloodlust, Lynch. They aren't the same thing at all. Look at all the guys who can't stop talking about their experiences in World War II. The greatest adventure of their lives. The war only lasted three or four years for most of them, but it dominates the rest of their days. When a guy parachutes into Nazi-occupied France at night with a rifle strapped to his chest, forty-eight hours before D-Day what the hell can ever compare with that again in his lifetime? It's not the bloodshed that's thrilling... it's the drama, the theatre of war and the certainty in the rightness of your cause. It has been very unfashionable to say so, Lynch, but for many people war is the most exciting time they will ever have. Dreadful, terrible, bloody, yes, all of that. But dramatic too. And without that drama men like us may as well be dead.'

He waited for a second. 'You know what one of those Red Brigade bastards said in Italy, after planting the bomb at Bologna railway station that killed a couple of hundred people? At his interrogation, he was asked why they had killed men, women and children. You know what he said? He said, "There are no innocents... no innocents". Well,' Halloran grunted, 'I think that's clear enough, don't you? I'm willing to take them at their word.

'There's something else, too,' he added. 'If I believed in

God, Lynch, I would wake up every morning and thank him for giving me a new war to fight... and real bastards to fight against. There's no law that says we don't have to enjoy what we do, Lynch. I like exterminating these bastards. It gives me a sense of pride. That's why I do it.'

Lynch eyed Halloran warily. He considered himself the most self-contained of men and preferred it that way. He didn't enjoy being read like a book. First Janice, now Halloran. It was turning into an enlightening afternoon.

'Let me tell you something funny,' Halloran went on. 'A couple of years ago one of the hostages from the Iranian Embassy siege was killed in an automobile accident. It rated a couple of paragraphs in the newspaper. So what did that life really count for when the hostage was released, anyway? Nothing. Nobody even knows their names. All the world remembers is that America was humiliated by a rabble. And when Carter finally did something, all we did was bump into each other in the dark and make even bigger fools of ourselves.'

Lynch well remembered the debacle at Desert One, the landing site in the desert outside Tehran where US Special Forces bungled their first hostage rescue attempt, leaving eight charred bodies, millions of dollars worth of wrecked aircraft, equipment and secret papers. It had become a textbook example to special forces units around the world of how not to run an operation.

'You see,' Halloran continued, 'the lives of the hostages aren't what this is all about. What really matters is that we have to deprive those fanatics in Beirut of the power they command when they take Americans prisoner. And we have to do it cleanly, swiftly and with lethal resolve. Not because the life of any individual hostage is that important. It is what they represent that is important. Because every day those bastards hang on to our people, America dies a little. Democracy dies a little. That's the big picture. That's what really matters. Every day they hold Americans hostage they exercise power over us — and we have to take that power away from them. That's why I do it, Lynch. Because I can make a difference to the big picture. And that's why you do it too. You couldn't go back to civilian life now. You'd die of inertia.'

Halloran paused then abruptly changed tack and Lynch found himself bristling as the conversation cut a little too closely to the bone.

'You and Janice are supposed to be in love,' Halloran said.

'Supposed.' Halloran's use of the word annoyed Lynch but, again, he let it go.

'Love,' Halloran was saying. 'That's a drama. Domestic drama. The tiny, insignificant kind of bullshit drama that's available to everybody. But it's not enough, is it? It soon settles down to boredom and routine. Oh yeah, it can stay sweet and cosy for a while but the drama doesn't last, does it? Sooner or later the pettiness overwhelms the pleasure. That's what you're really afraid of, isn't it, Lynch? Face it. You like to play with the big boys. It's what you've been trained for all your life. War. The ultimate theatre of man. Janice knows it, I know it. It's time you accepted it. My world is a dirty, dangerous place, Lynch, but it's where you belong. Where you've always belonged. That's why I'm here today. That's why you're here today.'

Lynch said nothing. There were times when he could dislike Halloran intensely and this was one of them. Lynch didn't mind being bought... but he didn't like being owned. He stood up to go.

'One last thing,' Halloran said. 'Don't worry about Janice. She'll come around. It's only love.'

Halloran finished his second beer, pulled back his fist and flung the can high over the stern rail.

Lynch's left hand moved like a striking cobra, his arm a silent blur. The can seemed to vanish before it had begun its high sparkling trajectory towards the ocean. Plucked from thin air only to materialise a moment later in Lynch's hand where he flipped it a couple of times with studied nonchalance.

'Reflexes still pretty good,' Halloran huffed.

'Bit rusty... haven't worked out much this year.'

Lynch played with the can for a moment then looked down at Halloran. 'Something important you don't know about me.'

'Oh?'

Lynch flicked the can back into Halloran's lap. 'I can't stand people who litter,' he said. Then he padded silently away.

Halloran watched him go for a moment then looked down to see a huge dark stain spreading across his crotch as the beer dregs spilled from the can.

'You bastard.'

Janice hadn't come around. But there was surprisingly little anger in her voice — only resignation, as though a long held fear had merely been confirmed. She was already packed, her two blue canvas bags in the middle of the floor. She had put on the lightweight cream-coloured skirt suit she wore for travelling and was sitting on the edge of the bed near the telephone, face tense, legs crossed and her raised foot bobbing rapidly.

He waited in the doorway, unsure of where to begin.

'You said yourself he could be persuasive...' he began. But it sounded lame, even to Lynch.

'How much persuading did you take?'

He walked over to the bed and sat down beside her. She didn't pull away but Lynch felt a sheet of ice come down between them. Her reaction wasn't entirely unexpected but if Lynch could have controlled the timing...

He tried again, struggling to start on a lighter note. 'What we have here,' he said, 'is a failure to communicate.'

Janice wasn't buying. 'No,' she said. 'I think you communicated your priorities quite well.'

He waited. 'I don't know if this makes it any easier,' he

said. 'But I didn't know myself until an hour ago.'

'Yes,' she said. 'It makes it easier.'

He watched her profile but she wouldn't turn her head to look at him.

'But it doesn't change anything,' he said for her.

'Not a goddamn thing,' she said.

He sighed. Her strength was one of the things he liked about her.

'What are you going to do now?'

'Go back to New York.' Her voice had a brittleness to it he didn't like. She took a deep breath and looked at the floor. She seemed about to say something then changed her mind. 'Come and get your things when you're ready,' was all she said.

'Jesus Christ,' he said softly. Less than four hours ago they had made love on this bed. Now they were like two different people. 'You can't be serious,' he said. 'You can't want it to end like this?'

'You made your mind up first,' she said. 'This is my response. You didn't come to your goddamn decision an hour ago. You decided months ago, probably the day you got out of hospital if the truth were known. You've been kidding me and kidding yourself ever since. Well...' she hesitated for a moment, 'I didn't make up my mind in five minutes either. I decided a while ago that if you went back to work for him I would have to end it. I told you before, I'm not the grieving widow type. And I'll be damned if I'll be stuck with a supporting role in your life. I have my own life to lead. With or without you.'

Lynch smiled. 'For what it's worth,' he said quietly, 'I happen to believe in what Halloran is doing this time.'

She laughed. 'He uses people. He used me. He's using you.'

'I know,' Lynch said. 'Maybe I'm prepared to be used for a while if it suits me. It suited you for ten years.'

She jerked around to look at him. 'You fucking bastard.'

This time there was real anger in the words.

'It just so happens that I think those hostages should have been pulled out of Lebanon years ago,' Lynch said. 'It seems to me that Jack Halloran is one of the few men I've met who has the ability to get things done. I want to do this.'

'And the next one and the next one,' she said. 'That is assuming you get back from this job in one piece.'

An awkward silence fell between them. It only lasted a moment then the cabin phone chimed. Janice picked it up.

'Yes,' she said. 'Can you put me through to him now?'

There was a brief wait then Halloran came on the line. Lynch could hear the voice from where he was sitting.

'Jack... can your pilot take me back to the mainland tonight?' she asked. Lynch got up and walked across the stateroom to look at the ocean. A few long strands of wispy stratus had appeared on the western horizon, chopping and dicing the dying sun into slivers of crimson and violet. There was going to be a spectacular sunset. He could still hear Halloran's voice through the earpiece of the phone across the cabin but he couldn't make out what was being said. He guessed Halloran was trying to talk her out of it. He failed. 'Good,' she said at last. 'Ask Captain Penny to send somebody down for my bags, would you? I'll wait on deck.'

She got up to go. Lynch turned to try and reason with her again but the right words just weren't there. He watched her collect her purse and a few of her things then go to the cabin door.

'Tell me,' she said, before closing the door. 'How much *is* Jack paying you?'

But she had gone before he could answer. Touché, Lynch thought. This was one hell of a tough woman he was losing. Suddenly he wanted her very badly. He went over to the liquor cabinet and poured himself half a glass of scotch.

Dinner was a subdued affair. The two men ate in Halloran's vast stateroom amid decor that looked to Lynch as though it had been pillaged from the Palace Of Versailles. Lynch had no appetite and the fresh fish, although beautifully cooked, was wasted on him. The scotch hadn't helped. After eighteen months dry, it had hit him like a truck after just two mouthfuls and he had poured the rest down the sink. They were almost finished their meal when they heard the chopper return. No doubt the pilot was hoping those spoiled rich bastards below would leave him alone long enough to get some rest.

'Give her a few days...' Halloran left the rest unsaid. He had a great reservoir of affection for Janice but he wasn't about to let her jeopardise the upcoming operation by putting added pressure on Lynch either. Lynch settled those fears a moment later when he pushed his barely touched dinner away and reached for the fresh, strong coffee the steward had just brought.

'Got a plan?' he asked.

'The beginnings of one,' Halloran answered. He dabbed at his mouth with a napkin and got up. Lynch had noted earlier that Halloran was wearing clean khaki pants. Halloran motioned Lynch to follow him and they crossed the huge stateroom to the adjoining conference room. Unlike the master stateroom this room had no windows or portholes. It was situated amidships and fitted with concealed lighting which kept it in continuous twilight. It was oval in shape with a matching oval table of highly polished rosewood. The table and a dozen chairs were empty. The walls were panelled with what looked like a synthetic, pale wood laminate. Lynch discovered why when Halloran pushed one of the metal studs in the green leather inlay at the head of the table. An entire section of wall panelling at the end of the room slid back to reveal a huge TV monitor. At the same time a computer keyboard hissed into view through a slot beneath the screen.

Halloran punched a few keys and a kaleidoscope of figures, codes and patterns danced across the screen in dazzling technicolour. A computer map of the Middle East flashed up. Halloran tapped more keys and the computer obediently enlarged Lebanon with a series of fast focuses until the entire screen was filled with a detailed map of northern Lebanon. Halloran plucked a tiny flashlight from a socket in the computer console and beamed a spot of red light at a small town about forty kilometres east of Beirut, close to the Lebanese border with Syria. The town was called Ba'albek. 'That's where all the remaining hostages will be taken, starting twenty days from now,' he said. 'According to my information that's where the handover will take place. We project the handover will take place within a week to ten days after the hostages have been brought to Ba'albek.'

'That soon?'

'Once they've got the deal set they have no reason to fuck around anymore,' Halloran said. 'In fact, the faster they can get their hands on the money and unload the hostages, the happier they'll be.'

Lynch whistled softly. 'Doesn't give us a lot of time, does it?'

'There's something else,' Halloran said.

Lynch waited.

'It would be nice if you could have our people out by the Fourth of July.'

'The fourth...' then the penny dropped for Lynch. The Fourth of July was American Independence Day. That was what Janice had meant earlier in the day.

'What's the matter?' Halloran grinned. 'Starting to look a little hard already?' He didn't wait for a response. 'Hezbollah have not and will not receive a response to the demands they made in Amman and the State Department is dragging things out with the Iranians till they see what we can do. That way Syrian intelligence will think we're just continuing to be strung along as usual and they won't have anything important to pass on to their proxies in Hezbollah. The only place for Hezbollah to go now is the PLO. As far as we can tell, negotiations are at an advanced stage in that area and the handover should proceed unless something totally unexpected happens, which is always a possibility with these

66

assholes. Hezbollah still have to get the hostages from the southern suburbs of Beirut and elsewhere to Ba'albek. Hezbollah have five hostages, Amal have two, Islamic Jihad and Red Jihad have one each. Naturally, they all get a cut of the ransom. We'll monitor the situation as the next few weeks progress and as the deal gets closer we'll move into position in a neighbouring country, preparatory to launching our strike. This time the launch zone will be Turkey, not Israel, for reasons which will become clear in a moment. There will be an optimum two or three day period at most when we can be sure of striking with any certainty of success. Timing will have to be exquisite because there will never be another chance like this.'

He glanced over at Lynch but Lynch said nothing. Halloran flicked the spot back to the map. 'Ba'albek is at the northeastern end of the Beqa'a Valley and that's all solid Shi'ite country,' he said. 'Hezbollah will arrange a forty-eight hour ceasefire with the other Shi'ite militias for the duration of the handover. We will get only a few hours notice and that's when we will have to move. What that means is that when the ceasefire commences it should be relatively safe to get to Ba'albek. But,' he grinned again, 'Ba'albek itself will be like an armed camp for the period of the handover and they'll be ready for trouble. In addition to Hezbollah militiamen we can expect Syrian army units to be in the area with some heavy weapons, including tanks. Officially, the Syrians don't know anything about it. Unofficially it's going to happen under their protection. The Syrians have their own proxy Palestinian militia in the Beqa'a too. They're called Saiqa — it means "Thunderbolt" — and they're the military arm of the Vanguards of the Popular War for the Liberation of Palestine. They're members of the Palestinian branch of the ruling Syrian Ba'ath party and they form part of the Syrian Army's Palestinian battalion. They're pro-Fatah too, which means they can be expected to help protect the handover to the PLO as well.'

Halloran watched a slight smile form on Lynch's face.

'Strength?' Lynch asked.

'Thought you'd never ask,' Halloran said. 'Hezbollah have between 1,500 and 2,500 fighters in Lebanon. At least 500 of those are quartered at the Sheikh Abdullah Barracks in Ba'albek. We must expect at least another 500, maybe a thousand in Ba'albek itself to guarantee the security of the handover. The other Shi'ite militias will provide bodyguard escorts for their hostages only. Once they've delivered their cargo they won't stick around. During the actual handover the PLO can be expected to have an armed presence too, if only to make the point that they're still a force in Lebanon. No more than a couple of hundred fighters probably to provide security and escort for the hostages to their new destination, wherever that is. Saiqa aren't much of a force to be reckoned with at all, say 150-200 fighters from the Palestinian battalion. They'll be around but they aren't expected to play much of a part.'

'That's a relief,' Lynch said. 'For a while there I thought we might be outnumbered.'

Halloran sniffed. 'You can count on anything up to 2,000 armed militiamen — and that's in addition to whatever the Syrians will have in the area at the time. Could be a whole battalion, though most of them will be outside Ba'albek itself. Get in and out fast enough, an operation of swift, surgical precision. Hey, they won't even know you're there.'

Lynch looked at him.

'Yeah,' the American said. 'Gonna be a gun collector's delight. Janice's bed starting to look pretty nice about now?'

'Fuck you, Halloran.'

Halloran flicked back to the screen. 'The PLO will collect the hostages for delivery to another country. We don't know where. Arafat has bases all through the Middle East. It could be Iraq, Tunisia, Algeria, Northern Yemen, even Madagascar, for Christ's sake. Arafat's money and men just about installed Madagascar's President for life. That's one of the safest fall-back bases the PLO has.' Halloran turned to Lynch. 'One of the biggest mistakes successive US administrations have made is to underestimate the wealth and influence of the PLO in the Middle East, Lynch. If the PLO was listed on the New York Stock Exchange it would be in the top 100 companies. It has gold, real estate and hard currency reserves amounting to five billion dollars US ... that we know of.'

'Almost as big as STC,' Lynch said.

Halloran bit. 'On known equity the PLO would be ranked in the high 60s. STC is presently ranked at 37.'

Halloran punched the keyboard until a new diagram flashed up on the enlarged screen. It looked like a diagram of a family tree, except the name at the top read: Palestine Liberation Organisation. Underneath was a whole network of branches which delineated the many offshoots of the PLO: the executive committee, the political, planning and information departments, the central committee, the Palestine National Council. From each of these were even more departments, titled propaganda, social affairs, various Palestinian unions, and the Palestine National Fund with a breakdown of investments in farms, property and factories throughout the Middle East. Finally there were its many known terrorist offshoots: Al Fatah, Black September, the Palestine Liberation Front, the Popular Front for the Liberation of Palestine, the PFLP-General Command, As-Saiqa.

Lynch blinked.

'Terror Incorporated,' Halloran said dryly. 'The PLO is the world's biggest and most sophisticated terrorist organisation. And whatever else Yasser Arafat says in public — he's still sitting in the chairman's seat.

'The PLO has its own fleet of aircraft and Arafat virtually runs the PLO from the air. Palestinians are scattered in key positions throughout the Middle East. They keep the oil industry running and they have big cash deposits, usually in US currency, in the banks of half a dozen Arab countries we consider friendly. Arafat gets most of his money from a five per cent income tax on all Palestinians working through-

69

out the Middle East and through donations from countries like Saudi Arabia who aren't averse to playing on both sides of the fence either. It'd be a big mistake to underestimate the power of the PLO. The Israelis sure as hell don't. That's why they'd be going apeshit if they thought Arafat could pull off a propaganda coup like this. We'd better hope that they don't. The last thing I want is you and Mossad fighting each other to get at the hostages.'

'I'd be inclined to let 'em.'

'Yeah,' Halloran nodded. 'The problem is that it would suit the Israelis just to liquidate the hostages. They don't have to pull a snatch. It would be a straight assassination job for them. This is American hostages we're talking about here, not Israelis. Ever since we recognised the PLO the Israelis have been a little cool on the finer points of our activities in the Middle East. With the hostages dead Mossad will still have deprived Arafat of his propaganda victory. We'd rather have them alive.'

Halloran punched another button and enlarged the map to include the eastern Mediterranean, showing the coastline of Turkey and the divided Greek-Turkish island of Cyprus. 'My plan is that we launch an airborn penetration of the northern Lebanese coast using the new generation of glider parachutes developed for Delta — your friends in the SAS have been using something like them for years and there's a good chance we may have to call on their expertise.'

'I know them,' Lynch said. 'HAHO. High Altitude, High Opening. Exit from an aircraft 40 to 50 klicks out at sea, well beyond territorial limits, then glide inland, invisible to radar.'

'They're the ones,' Halloran said. 'Except you won't have seen anything like the parachutes we have now. The 'chutes we've developed are better, stronger, more manoeuvrable. You can drop a man carrying a lot of ordnance in the middle of the night with just about pinpoint accuracy and nobody's going to know he's there till he's sitting on their face.'

70

Lynch nodded. 'Then what?'

'Our best intelligence says the handover of cash and hostages will take place inside Sheikh Abdullah Barracks. The barracks used to be occupied by Hezbollah and a couple of hundred Iranian Revolutionary Guards. Since Hezbollah's disaffection with Tehran the Iranians have been kicked out and now it's exclusively Hezbollah.

'You will land in citrus groves adjacent to the highway that connects Ba'albek to Homs in Syria, around about here...' He flashed the red pinprick to a small town called El Laboue, about ten kilometres north of Ba'albek. 'You will land undetected, conceal your 'chutes, commandeer transport and proceed south. You'll come to Sheikh Abdullah Barracks first. They're on a hill overlooking the town of Ba'albek. They're hard to miss. Even if the handover is not there you will have to neutralise the forces within the barracks. Otherwise you will not be able to proceed to the Hezbollah command post. You will, therefore, neutralise the barracks and the command post, secure the location where the hostages are held and take them under your protection.'

'Well,' Lynch said dryly. 'I see no problems with any of that.'

'Glad to hear it,' Halloran answered with equal cool.

'And when we've got them, what do we do with them?' Lynch asked.

Halloran flashed the red light in a direct line from the town of Ba'albek to Lebanon's southern border with Israel. 'It's about one hundred kilometres, give or take a few, from Ba'albek to the Israeli buffer zone,' Halloran said. 'The moment you have the hostages safe you commandeer a fast vehicle and go like hell for the Israeli border. We can arrange for a safe reception. That much the Israelis will guarantee.'

'I thought they weren't supposed to know anything about the operation?'

'They won't,' Halloran said. 'Till it's over.'

'They won't like that.'

71

'It'll be too late for them to do anything. Besides, it will still be in their interests to have the hostages out of Lebanon. It's just that we'd prefer it if they were still breathing.'

'The plan needs a little refining, I think,' Lynch added.

'That's what you're here for,' Halloran answered. 'You've got three weeks to put a team together and rehearse the job. Then you go in. It may be a little earlier than that or later if they get nervous. At this point our greatest ally is the fact that Hezbollah's lunatic fringe needs the money and now they've got a deal they want to get it closed fast and easy. We'll know when they're moving and we'll just have to roll with the changes. We're monitoring it all the time.'

'Where are you getting this intelligence?'

Halloran eyed Lynch, wondering how much he could afford to reveal. 'You ever hear of the Lebanese Forces Second Bureau?'

Lynch shook his head.

'That's the Lebanese Army's secret service. The Lebanese Forces were built on Lebanon's Christian militias and they put forward a pretty interesting peace formula back in June '88. They told the State Department they'd kick the Syrians, Iranians and Israelis out of the country, then disarm the militias internally. The idea was then to bring in a United Nations peacekeeping force consisting of US troops and troops from neutral Arab countries like Egypt and Saudi Arabia. You can imagine how well the idea of sending US troops back to Lebanon would have gone down at home in an election year. But we've had good communication with the Second Bureau ever since and they'll do anything to help us break down the power of the Muslim militias.' Halloran paused. 'There's no need for you to know everything. It's probably better that you don't.'

'I have a certain interest in knowing how good it is.'

'It's good.' Halloran answered bluntly. 'The best.'

Lynch was annoyed but was careful not to show how much. He projected his mind forward. 'Where's the rest of the team?' he asked.

72

Halloran tapped more keys. The map dematerialised. A moment later the first file spooled up: *Tuckey, Emmet, ex-USN, ex-SEAL. Rank: Ensign. Address: 18 Tulane Drive, West Bay, Panama City, Florida. Phone: 221 4989.* Lynch quickly scanned the information on the screen and learned that Tuckey was now married. The name of his wife, Luisa, formerly Aguerra, suggested Mexican American. He also operated an ocean salvage business out of Panama City and was the owner of a modest ten metre salvage vessel called *Reef Runner.*

'Think he's okay?' Halloran asked.

Lynch recalled the lanky blonde ex-US Navy Seal who had seemed so unsuited to special operations work and yet who had out-gritted the best of them when things got rough. Still, Lynch had reservations. 'I'm not sure,' he said. 'I don't think his heart's in the work.'

Halloran snorted. 'I don't give a goddamn where his heart is as long as his balls are in my pocket.' Lynch wondered if Halloran talked about him the same way when he wasn't around. He concluded that there was no reason to believe Halloran considered him any different to all his other human assets.

Halloran summoned up two more names: *Reece, Henry, ex-USMC. Rank: Sergeant.* Then *Bono, Samuel Jefferson, ex-USMC. Rank: Private first class.*

'Jefferson,' Lynch grinned. 'Bono's middle name is Jefferson?' Then he realised that his details would be in Halloran's computer too. Both Reece and Bono showed the same address, which didn't surprise Lynch. The two ex-marines had been pals for a long time. It wasn't as precise as Tuckey's. The mailing address was given as: *c/- PO Box 110, Hibbing, Minnesota.* No phone number. Though there was a location note which put the ranch 22 kilometres east of US 169 on State Highway 37.

'They've got some kind of property up near the Canadian border,' Halloran explained. 'A farm with a couple of hundred acres. Fucking slum, I understand.'

Obviously, Lynch realised, they'd had the same thought as him. He guessed that Halloran hadn't seen either of them since the bloody conclusion to their last job. He wondered if Reece's arm had healed from the bullet he took and how they'd both react to a surprise visit. Part of him was looking forward to finding out.

'Availability?'

'They're all available,' Halloran said. 'You'll have to move fast.'

'Fast?' he echoed Halloran with an extra touch of sarcasm. 'You're looking at twenty days to put together a team and rehearse an operation to accomplish something no Western power has been able to do in eight years. No-one has ever rescued a hostage from Lebanon.'

'The SAS, West Germany's GSG9 and Delta do it in less than twenty days during aircraft hijack and siege situations. Do I have to remind you what your own SAS did at the Iranian Embassy in London in under six days, including the building of a full-scale replica of the Embassy?'

'Can you build me a full-scale replica of Lebanon?' Lynch asked. 'Besides, in London they were operating in their own backyard. They had all the equipment and support they needed and they knew exactly where the hostages were, right down to which room they were in. There's a difference.'

Halloran smiled. 'If it was easy I would have got somebody else.'

Lynch looked at him. 'What would you have done if I'd said no?'

'I knew you wouldn't,' Halloran said.

Lynch thought the American sounded awfully sure of himself. Too damn sure.

'How?'

'Janice told me.'

The words hit Lynch like a hammer blow. This time he could not keep the shock from his face. He saw Halloran watching him carefully, perhaps just a faint gleam of pleasure in those hard blue eyes.

'But she...'

'No,' Halloran interrupted. 'She isn't working for me anymore. But I called her a few weeks back and sounded her out in general kind of terms. Asked her how she thought you'd react, what she really thought.'

'And she told you...'

'She said she didn't like it, she would fight it. But she said it was your decision. And,' he paused, 'she said you'd probably do it.'

'Shit.'

Halloran shut down the computer, pressed the button on the table and the wall swallowed the big screen and keyboard with a faint electronic sigh. 'She's a smart girl,' Halloran said. 'I trusted her judgement.'

'Even though...'

'That's right... even though it might make her unhappy. This business isn't about making people happy, Lynch. None of it. When can you leave?'

Lynch was looking at Halloran but thinking of Janice. She had known all along, even when they had accepted the invitation to visit Halloran's ship. She must have known Halloran was up to something. She had sensed the inevitable. No wonder she had seemed so resigned in their cabin that afternoon. She was expecting it, all along. She knew both men too well, he realised. Intimately. Anger flushed him.

'Damn,' he said. 'How does tomorrow grab you?'

2

THE DEATH OF BAMBI

Florida, USA, June 11

Lynch flew to the mainland with Halloran early the next
morning. They parted company on the tarmac at Miami,
Lynch to catch a flight to Pensacola to track down Tuckey,
Halloran to fly his personal jet to New York where they
would meet in forty-eight hours to discuss progress. Lynch
booked himself onto the next available Floridair flight to
Pensacola. He had been given $10,000 cash to cover immediate
expenses. Lynch could feel himself being drawn inexorably
into Halloran's mink-lined, steel-clawed embrace.

The two-hour Floridair flight would get him into Pensacola
around lunchtime. Salvage work was unpredictable business,
he knew; if Tuckey had a job, he could be anywhere in the
Gulf of Mexico for a week or more and Lynch would have
to charter a boat or float chopper to reach him. If there
was no work Tuckey could be killing time at home or at
the dock. Or, he might simply have gone fishing for a few
days and told no-one. With the million dollar pay-out from
their last job he would have enough money left over from
the purchase of a new house and boat to not have to hustle
for work. Lynch decided against an early warning phone
call. He didn't want to give Tuckey time to think about it.
The former SEAL was a good, solid operator with what
Lynch considered to be the most valuable of qualifications:
he was combat tried and proven. This was not going to be
an operation for beginners. There would be no time to train
men how to act under live fire and he didn't want to worry

about it. Lynch wanted Tuckey back on the team because it would be one less thing to worry about when the bullets started flying.

Lynch bought a tourist map of Florida and estimated the driving time from Pensacola to Panama City at a couple of hours, maximum. He might grab some lunch on the way and kill an hour or two so as to time his arrival at Tuckey's home for the late afternoon. If Tuckey was around that was when he would most likely be at home, especially with a new wife to worry about.

Lynch read the *Miami Herald* on the flight to Pensacola, his eye drawn automatically to a story about the renewed fighting in Lebanon. There was a photograph of a wounded Palestinian woman being carried into a camp infirmary. It looked like a squalid place. The doctors were gaunt and hollow-eyed from lack of sleep. There was a haunted look about their faces. Lynch recalled the same faces from photographs he'd seen of Nazi concentration camp survivors. A couple of Syrian and Lebanese soldiers were just visible in the background, weapons cradled impotently in their arms. The text described the sudden flare-up between rival Shi'ite militias. The picture caption said the Palestinian woman had been shot in the back by an Amal sniper while bringing water into the camp. She was expected to live, but she would be paralysed from the waist down.

The Floridair Boeing 737 wheeled over the Gulf of Mexico to make its approach into Hagler Field and Lynch got a glimpse of the giant Eglin Air Force Base which, along with the three naval installations, make Pensacola the biggest service town on the Florida coast. Panama City was really only an extension of Pensacola. No wonder Tuckey felt at home here, Lynch thought. In the terminal he rented a spanking new Mercury from Hertz. It was canary yellow and the dashboard was maroon plastic. He drove south out of the airport towards Fort Walton Beach then east onto Highway 98 for the two-hour drive along the coast to Panama City.

The drive along the gulf would have been pretty under other circumstances but Lynch kept wondering about what kind of reception he'd get from Tuckey. A long, inviting ribbon of white sand unravelled past the passenger window and finally he succumbed at a place called Sunnyside Beach. He was making too fast a time, anyway, he decided. Driving the Mercury was like riding a magic carpet. It was all too easy to slip past the state limit of 55mph and he kept having to take his foot off the gas pedal. He picked a fast food joint specialising in seafood. It was called 'Cap'n Cook'. Lynch ordered something called Mermaid's Treasure Chest and a girl with steel bands on her teeth handed him a styrofoam bucket filled with heavily battered and deep fried bicycle tubes and told him to have a nice day. Outside he decided he wasn't that hungry and left the bucket on a nearby picnic bench. It was swamped by ravening gulls the moment he took his hand away. Lynch decided to walk along the beach a while. He thought about Janice, about Halloran and the job ahead but all that did was raise more questions, none of which could be answered right now. He pushed the jostling doubts from his mind and determined to enjoy his brief interlude. Because it was a weekday the beach wasn't crowded. He thought about stripping off his jeans and sports shirt and going for a swim but decided against it. There was probably some law against swimming in your underwear in Florida. He passed a noisy group of young people, fit young men with service haircuts enjoying a day off with their girlfriends. Not one of them was older than twenty — well-fed, tanned and healthy. A gleaming new Bronco with a pile of clothes thrown promiscuously in the back was parked nearby and a ghetto-blaster was playing down the Top 40. They had a cooler filled with food and drink, and a couple of windsurfers had been left to wallow at the waterline because there was no wind. He watched one of the girls for a moment, a freckled brunette with an impossibly perfect figure, and felt a pang of jealousy for something he had never had. These were the luckiest kids in the world, Lynch thought. There had never been a time in his life when he had been this carefree. What wouldn't he have given to have grown up amidst affluence such as this instead of the bleak British Isles and the cold, hard streets of Dumfries? During his youth, courtship had been a freezing, hand-holding walk around town, a half-pint made to last an hour so they could take refuge in the warmth of the pub and a late-night grope at the bus stop with a girlfriend in a lumpy coat who smelled of body odour and Woolworth's perfume. The sixties were supposed to have been a time of affluence, but Lynch had never seen it. He had turned twenty the day the sixties ended. That was the year he left home to go to naval college at Dartmouth and he had not looked back since. He had been twenty-six before he could afford his first car. Lynch looked at these confident, boisterous American kids with their magazine cover teeth and tans and wondered if they knew how lucky they were. And how hard they were willing to fight to keep what they had. Lynch smiled at himself. He was getting old, he decided, old and unforgiving. He checked his watch. A little after four. Time to head back to the car.

He drove slowly. Forty-five minutes later he was turning into Tulane Drive looking for Tuckey's house. It was a newer housing development, from the look of the trees, about ten years old. Ranch-style homes, timber and brick, neatly mown lawns, sprinklers, kids' bicycles in the drive, pools, barbecues, two car garages. Suburban. Middle class. Anonymous. A good place to hide, Lynch thought. He found number 18 and parked at the kerb.

An attractive Hispanic woman in her early twenties with a glossy curtain of blue-black hair reaching down to her waist opened the door. She was wearing a little blue cotton smock and from the size of her belly, Lynch guessed, she was about six months pregnant. Tuckey hadn't wasted any time when he got back from their last job. Lynch introduced himself as an old Navy friend of her husband. She smiled and disappeared and a moment later Tuckey appeared. He was sweating and wearing dirty white shorts and T-shirt. His blonde hair had grown longer and he had put on some weight but he still looked five years younger than the last time Lynch had seen him. From the dirt smeared on his arms and legs he'd been building something in the back yard. And from the look on his face he wasn't pleased to see Lynch at his front door. He recovered quickly and they shook hands. More for Luisa's benefit, Lynch felt, Tuckey invited him in and led him through the darkened house to a patio out the back that had a newly finished look about it. At the bottom of the yard were the foundations for something else.

'Putting in a shade house for Luisa and the baby,' Tuckey explained. 'Thought it would be nice, y'know? Want a beer?'

Lynch didn't but he nodded anyway.

'Honey?'

Luisa was watching from the doorway. She smiled, nodded and vanished inside to get a couple of beers for her husband and his friend. She had smiled with her lips but not her eyes, Lynch realised. He saw something else too. She was afraid of him. Afraid of what he might mean to her husband.

'Don't take this personally,' Tuckey whispered as soon as his wife had gone. 'But I was kinda hoping I'd never see you again as long as I lived.'

'What makes you think I'm bringing bad news?' Lynch sought to reassure him.

'Anything you and Halloran have to say to me is bad news,' Tuckey said. 'The cheque didn't bounce and I'm grateful for that — but that's it. There aren't a helluva lot of good times for you and me to chew over.'

There was nothing hostile in it but Tuckey was right.

'Half a million dollars?' Lynch tried.

The former SEAL gave a short laugh and looked away. 'Half a million? Try ten. It's the same thing. No more deals for that bastard. I'm not interested. People have a habit of dying around him.' He stopped and looked back at Lynch.

'I'm surprised you want anything to do with him after what you went through. How's the skin on your back?'

Lynch shrugged. 'Thicker than ever.'

'It'd want to be.' Tuckey couldn't conceal the glimmer of disgust in his eyes. 'And goin' back for more huh? Shit.'

Luisa arrived with two cans of Blue Ribbon. She smiled again as she handed him the beer but there was no mistaking her true feeling. She was certain he was bad news. She hovered for a moment longer, uncertain whether to stay or go. Tuckey answered the question for her.

'Honey, me and Mr Lynch here have a little business to discuss. Could you give us a few minutes? We won't be long.' Luisa nodded and went back inside.

'Doesn't she know anything about you?' Lynch asked.

'She knows I was in the navy. She knows I was in the SEALS. She knows I went through a lot of hairy shit but she doesn't know anything about... any other business.'

Lynch sipped at the cold beer and waited.

'We've known each other a coupla years,' Tuckey added. 'It wasn't real serious at first. But when I came back from Libya all I wanted to do was crawl into bed next to her and stay there. I told her some of the things I did were special ops... secret stuff that I can't talk about. I think she buys most of that. But she's not stupid. She knows there's been some bad shit. She doesn't know somebody could arrive on my doorstep any day and blow me away for what we did.'

He hesitated. 'I can live with that, you know. But I saw the best man I knew in all the world die on that job. A better man than me... and you, Lynch.' He took a pull on his beer. 'I don't know how else to put it except... all the heart went out of me after that. I haven't got the guts for any more of that shit. Call it cowardice, call it anything you like. I want to quit while I'm ahead. I still have my health, I have a nice little business — I suppose you know all about that. I have Luisa and we're going to have a family.

81

Maybe in time some of that bad shit . . . some of the memories will stop coming back. Maybe I'll get close to finding that peace of mind shit everybody's always talking about. Half a million? Man, there's no amount of money in the world would make me go through something like that again. No amount of money in the world . . .'

The words trailed away and Lynch realised it was pointless arguing. He wasn't like Halloran. If Tuckey didn't have the heart for another operation there was no sense in trying to manipulate him into it. Lynch hadn't touched his beer. He set it down on a nearby table and got up.

'This is no line of work for a family man,' he said. 'I think you just caught a bad case of common sense.'

Tuckey looked back at him for the first time with genuine sympathy.

They watched the yellow Mercury glide up the street and they kept watching until it disappeared from view. Then Luisa went to her husband and held him for a long time. She looked up into his open farm boy's face and she saw that she wasn't losing him after all. Then she took his hand and held it against her swollen belly. He felt the vague flutter of a foot or a tiny clenched fist. Tuckey smiled.

'It's a boy,' Luisa said softly. 'I know it's a boy.'

Hibbing, Minnesota, June 12

It was too late to catch a flight anywhere important when Lynch got back to Pensacola so he booked into the Howard Johnson's under his assumed American name of Robert Prentiss and earned a funny look from the desk clerk when he paid cash. He ate in his room and stayed up late watching television but when he tried to go to sleep discovered that bed was a big empty place without Janice. How soon he missed her, he thought. He got up early the next day, drove back to Hagler Field, caught a commuter flight to New Orleans then flew Delta to Minneapolis St. Paul. He had to wait a couple of hours to catch another commuter flight to Duluth, in the southwest corner of Lake Superior and by the time he picked up his bags it was getting dark again. When he got to the Hertz counter he wondered about the kind of vehicle he should rent this time. He thought about Reece and Bono, considered the type of country and decided on a Dodge pick-up. Within minutes he was driving north again. According to the map he got from the Hertz girl he would find Reece and Bono's place on State Highway 37, little more than halfway between 53 and 169 towards Hibbing. Lynch didn't know anything about Hibbing except that Bob Dylan had grown up there. Once upon a time that might have mattered to him.

It was pushing eight o'clock before he found the farm through process of elimination. It wasn't signposted from the highway. He passed their turn-off twice, eliminating the other farms with names painted on their front gate mailboxes. There was only one unmarked gravel road and it led off at an angle behind a strand of trees. It paralleled the highway for a hundred yards then turned abruptly south and deteriorated rapidly into a bumpy dirt track. He knew he'd found the right place when he came to a sturdy metal gate fastened with a heavy padlock. There was an unexpectedly smart sign in the shape of a shield fastened to the middle bar of the gate. He had to bend down to read the words in the beam of the pick-up's headlights. The white painted words said: 'Private Property — Intruders Met By Armed Response'. A fancy piece of scrollwork stretched across the top of the shield and said 'Beverly Hills Security Service'. Lynch smiled. He couldn't take the Dodge any further and he didn't know how far it was to the house. He switched off the lights and the engine then vaulted easily over the gate, flanked on both sides by a new barbed wire fence, and set off up the track. There was almost a half moon, and no cloud to obscure the starlight so he had little trouble finding his way. It was still half an hour before he reached the farm house and there were no lights. He approached the house carefully in case Reece and Bono had seen him coming and mistaken him for a hostile visitor. They had money now, contacts and access to all kinds of dangerous exploding toys. And he knew how much they liked toys. He wouldn't have put it past them to have a few security sensors planted along the track and around the gate to alert them to intruders. So he played it straight, walked carefully, deliberately up the steps to the front porch, in full view of anyone watching from inside the darkened house, hands by his sides, and knocked on the door. No answer. He knocked again but after a few minutes was satisfied there really was no-one at home. He decided to have a look around. This meant taking his life in his hands, he knew. A chance visitor was one thing but a nosy visitor was something else. He was almost positive that Reece and Bono would have decided that nosy visitors would have to be discouraged. He trod warily along the porch, eyes straining in the gloom for clues to how long they'd been away, how long they might stay away. Hours, days, weeks? They could have gone into town for dinner and a few beers. Or they could have gone away for a month to God knows where. It was too much to expect them to give up freelance work altogether. Even if they had each earned a million dollars in the past year. Still, Halloran's latest intelligence had them in Hibbing. Lynch came to a window and peered inside. Nothing. A screen had been pulled down. The same at the other two windows on the front. He prowled cautiously around the rest of the house. At least there were no guard dogs loose. That could be an ominous sign in itself. No dogs meant no-one needed to feed them, which meant the two ex-Marines expected to be away for a while. It was a ramshackle, two-storey farmhouse. All timber and, by the look of it, the boys hadn't spent much time or money on restoration. That gave him an idea. He decided to try an old trick. Doors and windows were obvious targets for intruders and so they were always turned into strongpoints. If there were any alarms or booby traps that was where they would be. So he decided to ignore all the doors and windows. He would go through a wall.

It took a few minutes of picking around the farm yard but he finally found what he wanted attached to the door of a dilapidated barn filled with rusting, antiquated farming machinery. A bolt. Just a steel bolt with the tip filed to a blunt point by years of use. He pocketed the bolt, returned to the house and felt along the timber panels of the kitchen wall with his fingertips. The wood nearest the outlet pipe was usually the best, softened and rotted by years of hot dishwater splashing back from the drain. He scratched with his fingertips and grunted with quiet satisfaction. Then he produced the bolt and began gouging into the soft timber. It took him ten minutes to make a hole big enough to get his fist through. He reached inside and heaved at the soft timber. There was no need for silence and he ripped at the wood with all his might, rending the old planks away from the wall till they snapped like pistol shots where the soft wood reached the dry wood. There were a few sheets of insulation to be punched through but they were no obstacle. Lynch worried for a moment that they might be fibreglass. They weren't. They were asbestos. Lynch decided he'd have to warn Reece and Bono they were living in a death trap. Another ten minutes and there was a hole big enough for him to crawl through. He squirmed around the hot water pipes and entered the house through the cupboard beneath the kitchen sink. Once inside he picked his way carefully between the furniture. He had to make sure. He left the lights off and waited till his eyes were used to the deeper gloom. The air inside had a sour smell. Accumulated dirt and zero ventilation, Lynch realised. The boys weren't very proud housekeepers. He painstakingly examined the kitchen first, cheap metal and plastic laminate table and chairs, dirty dishes in the sink. An entire car engine sat on a couple of sheets of newspaper on the kitchen floor, silently leaking oil. Something scuttled softly across the draining board beside the sink.

Lynch stared. He sensed rather than saw something odd, then he felt delicately across the sill of the window over the sink and found it. A wire attached to both the blind and the window catch and leading to a canister attached to the window frame. He left it all alone. It was the same story at the back door and every other window in the house. A length of wire tied to the handle of each window blind and to each window and door frame and leading to a canister about the size of a can of beans attached to a wall hook close by. The *pièce de résistance* was at the front door. Anybody stupid enough to force the front door was in for a most unpleasant surprise. Like all northern farmhouses the front door led into a small square cubicle not much larger than a washroom stall, a cloakroom where they could leave their boots and hang their thick coats in winter. There was another door, with a frosted glass window, leading into the living room. It took Lynch a while to figure it out, but he realised the front door wasn't wired at all, only this inner door. The wire and canister was inside the cloakroom, in the confined space between the two doors. He spent a tense twenty minutes feeling around one of the canisters nearest a front window till he was satisfied. It was one of the oldest tricks in the world to stick a grenade in a can with the pin out and the lever held in place by the sides of the can. A wire attached to the grenade led to a door or window. Someone opened the door, unwittingly pulled the wire which tugged the grenade out of the can ... and bang. The Japanese used them a lot to booby-trap jungle trails on Pacific islands during World War II. These weren't real grenades though, Lynch was relieved to discover. Blowing up an intruder with a grenade would attract a degree of official curiosity, even in northern Minnesota. These were flash-bangs, also known as stun grenades, the kind used by the SAS and other Special Forces in assaults on planes and buildings where it was necessary to disable everyone for a few precious seconds without causing permanent injury. Stun grenades contained thousands of magnesium particles and fulminate of mercury. When detonated the grenade would create a deafening explosion and a flash of light with an intensity of 50,000 watts, leaving anyone in the area deafened, blinded and disoriented for a minimum of seven seconds. But it caused no serious damage. Unless you put one in your mouth. Or were trapped in a small, enclosed space with one, such as a farmhouse cloakroom about two metres square. It wouldn't kill an intruder but it would frighten the living Christ out of him. Once he'd recovered, even the most hardened burglar would be convinced that he'd just escaped death by a whisker and he'd want to leave in a hurry and never come back. Lynch carefully removed one of the grenades and examined it. Not just a conventional stun grenade either, he realised, but the latest kind. These would flash and explode like firecrackers, six or seven times in four seconds and create much more fear and havoc. Lynch had a thought. It took him a few more minutes to relocate the stun grenade in the toilet bowl but when he left the farmhouse Lynch was wearing his first real smile for days.

It was a few minutes after ten pm when Lynch drove the Dodge through downtown Hibbing. Less than twelve hours to go before his next scheduled contact with Halloran in New York and all he had to report was one rejection and the fact that he hadn't the faintest idea where the other two were. Not a promising start to a mission with a tight schedule. Hibbing was like a thousand other small towns in the Midwest. Tired, quiet and broke. It wasn't that late, the night was pleasant and warm and yet the streets were almost deserted.

Lynch knew what he was looking for but he hadn't found it yet. Every town, however small, has its sleazy side and its sleazy bars. He found it a few minutes later, a roadhouse on the other side of a car wrecker's yard, shoved just outside the city limits like a poor relation. Lynch heard it before

87

he saw it. The country music boom was still going strong on this juke box. Bono's kind of music. A hot pink neon scrawl proclaimed 'Sockeye's Bar 'n' Grill'. A greying piece of cardboard in a grimy window announced '*Happy Hour — 4 to 7 every nite*'. It had to be a good bet.

He parked the Dodge in the first vacant space amidst a battery of mud spattered pick-ups and went inside. Obviously the news that smoking was hazardous to your health hadn't got this far inland yet. Lynch nearly gagged when he stepped through the door and his newly-healed eardrums ached under the noise level. The bar was a museum of living Americana, he thought, as he walked past two pool tables to the bar. There was a small dance floor, an empty stage, tables and a few booths and a line of swivel chairs along the bar. A kitchen hatch at the far end of the room had a blackboard menu alongside and served a variety of deep fried offal. The roadhouse was half-full, he estimated, a young, rough crowd mostly, tattoos and plaid shirts, and a few unhealthy looking men and women who were old enough to know better but never would. Half a dozen couples grappled on the dance floor. The place stank of cigarette smoke, beer, cooking fat and sweat. Lynch picked an empty stool and ordered a beer. Nobody seemed too interested in him. A couple was working the bar, a husband and wife team, he guessed, after a few minutes of listening to them bicker. She was a short, tough-looking brunette in her thirties, with eyes like slits, and she was dressed all in black. He was older, with receding brown hair and chin stubble. He wore jeans and a red plaid shirt with the sleeves rolled up to reveal hefty, tattooed forearms but he still didn't look anywhere near as tough as his wife. Lynch decided to try the man first. He knew it was a bad line but he was in a hurry.

'I'm looking for a couple of friends,' he said, trying to disguise his English accent. 'New to town. I think they might come here sometimes.'

'Yeah?' the man answered. 'So fuckin' what?' Then he erupted in a loud braying laugh at his own joke. The bartender's wife gave him a look of infinite boredom.

Somehow Lynch knew that politesse was not going to be the right approach at Sockeye's. He dropped his voice a little and leaned over the bar with a slightly conspiratorial look on his face. The bartender didn't look impressed but he was automatically drawn closer to his side of the bar. Lynch's hand flicked across the wet bar top, seized the man's wrist, gave it a brutal twist and crushed it so hard that they both heard the small wrist bones begin to crackle. The bartender winced and Lynch fixed him with a look that said he wasn't the type to make an empty threat. 'So,' Lynch gave him his most threatening smile, 'tell me what you know or I'm going to punch you right out of your fuckin' tattoos.'

The bartender stared at Lynch, eyes glazed with sudden fear and anger. Lynch knew what he was thinking but no-one else in the bar seemed to have noticed anything yet.

'I'm going to let go of your arm now,' Lynch said. 'And if you yell or reach for the Louisville Slugger I just know you have underneath, I'm going to come right over this bar and put you in hospital for six months.' Lynch knew it was essential to keep the momentum of intimidation going, to hold the initiative before the bartender could start thinking too hard. He gave the man's wrist an extra grind and sent a savage spasm of pain up to the elbow joint to show that he knew what he was doing, then let it drop.

The man began rubbing his wrist with the other hand but he never took his eyes off Lynch. Lynch wasn't a big man, being average height and of a wiry, medium build but there was an unmistakeable hardness about him and just enough hint of menace in the confident way he carried himself. The message had reached the bartender.

'Where'd you learn that shit?' he asked.

Lynch gave him that dangerous smile again. It wasn't the moment to be modest. 'Special Forces,' he said.

The bartender looked at him. 'Oh, man,' he said. 'Okay, whaddya want?'

'Couple of ex-Marines. One's a nuggety little dark haired

guy, the other guy's big, overweight, ugly, red hair...' He corrected himself. '*Some* red hair.'

The bartender sniffed and wiped his nose with the back of his good hand.

Lynch continued. 'Big guy's kind of mean. You never know which way he's going to go. Got a real bad temper. The little guy's always easing him down. Kind of like a double act, like Mutt and Jeff. Know what I mean?'

Lynch saw the glint of recognition in the bartender's eyes. 'I know the guys you mean,' he said. 'Came in here six, seven months back. One of our local boys thought the big guy looked kinda funny. Couldn't keep it to himself. Good fight, though. Your boy took a while to warm up but he handed out a real good lickin' when he got started. Trouble is they did eighteen hunnerd dollars worth of damage to this place.'

Lynch looked around. 'You'd never know,' he said.

The bartender shrugged. 'Your pal threw in nine hunnerd the next day. Said that was his share. The other guy still hasn't paid his half. That's why your pals can still come back. The other guy don't.'

Lynch nodded.

'Somethin' else. Few days after that some of the boys went out to your friends' place to get even. Don't know for sure what happened but whatever it was scared the shit out of 'em and they've been real polite to your friends ever since.'

Lynch thought about the reception Reece and Bono would have arranged in their own backyard. The local toughs must have thought they'd been teleported to a bad night in Vietnam. He smiled — so much for Reece and Bono keeping a low profile.

'They been around lately?'

The bartender shook his head. 'Not for a couple of weeks. They mostly come in the afternoons when it's quiet, play pool, have a coupla beers. Then they don't come aroun' for a few weeks. Go huntin' up north, I think. That's all they say when you ask 'em. Been huntin' they say.'

Lynch nodded and looked at the bartender's wife who had wandered over to see what was keeping her husband so interested.

'Know where they usually go?'

'Up north of Ely, I think,' the bartender said. 'Lake country. Easy to get lost if you don't know your way around.'

Lynch nodded and got up to go.

'Hey,' the bartender called him. Lynch turned on his way to the door. The bartender was leaning back on the bar with his good hand raised in the arm wrestling position. 'Wanna make it the best outta three?'

Lynch checked the map in the cabin light of the Dodge. Ely was a town with a population of around 7,000 about sixty miles northeast of Hibbing. The roads got smaller, narrower and twistier. Lynch looked at his watch. Gone 10.30. About an hour to reach Ely. He had no choice.

Ely was deserted when he drove down the main street close to midnight. He hunted around for a few minutes then decided there was nothing for it but to wake the local forest ranger up. If Reece and Bono were in the area the ranger ought to know. The ranger was a young man with black hair, part Indian, Lynch guessed, and he was up anyway. Lynch could hear soft rock playing inside the ranger's house and smelled a sweet pungent smell that could only be one thing. The young man stepped out into the porch light and closed the door behind him, his pupils the size of hub caps.

'Yeah, I seen 'em,' he said after a few minutes wary conversation.

Lynch followed the ranger's directions. It had been a long day. He was starting to feel it but he could last a long time yet. He'd grown used to going without sleep and putting in hard time during his years with the Special Boat Squadron. It was part of the job. It started with those damn exercises where they worked you to the point of exhaustion in the Scottish highlands for seventy-two hours at a stretch then put you in a warm room with a training film of stultifying boredom and asked you detailed questions about it afterwards. Nevertheless, he'd taken a battering on the last job and he was pleased his stamina was holding. He had come this far. He would find the two ex-Marines tonight... and he would have a little fun along the way. He turned off at the Chevron Station, as the young ranger had directed and followed the dirt road for twelve kilometres till he came to a firebreak. A couple of miles up the firebreak he ought to find their Chevy wagon parked in some bushes and they were a couple of kilometres in from there camped on the bank of an inlet to Birch Lake.

The night was warm and quiet. The noise of an approaching vehicle would carry a long way. When he found the firebreak he drove in about a hundred metres then parked and shut down the engine and lights. While his eyes adjusted to the dark again he fished around in his travel bag till he found a dark blue T-shirt. With the blue shirt, jeans and some dirt rubbed on his sneakers and arms he was almost invisible. He began a slow, steady jog along the dirt track that paralleled the tree line of the firebreak until he found the Chevy. It was locked but he found what he needed in the back — a filthy gunny sack. Then he began picking a way through the forest as quietly as he knew how. Even someone listening a few yards away would not have heard him coming. All those special exercises in the woods of eastern Canada paid off now. He knew this kind of country well. Mostly birch, maple, ash and plenty of conifers: spruce, larch, fir, yew and sequoias. His biggest worry was running into a bear. There were no grizzlies this far south he knew, but he was only 32 kilometres from the Canadian border and the vast wooded wilderness that lay beyond. There would be plenty of black or brown bears up there. They didn't need a passport to cross the border and an angry brown bear protecting her cub could do a lot of damage to an unarmed man. Lynch breathed deeply. The night air had been scented by resins oozing from the buds of the big pines all around him and he stopped for a moment to savour the smell. The forest floor was carpeted in pine needles and it was tempting to lie down and go to sleep but Lynch knew if he did he wouldn't wake up until morning. He forced himself to focus on the task at hand. It took him almost two hours of patient searching before a scratching, snuffling sound in the undergrowth told him he'd found what he wanted. It was only a small raccoon but ideal for his purpose. The startled creature thrashed and scratched viciously when Lynch grabbed it but quietened abruptly the moment it was bundled into the sack. Lynch had scouted the woods well enough by now to have a fair idea where Reece and Bono were camped and he made directly for the lakeshore, his furry cargo fuming silently in the sack.

After a while he spotted firelight through the trees, and slowed to a near crawl. He needn't have worried. As he approached the clearing he heard the big man's contented snoring. Bono was on the far side of the camp fire, closest to the lakeshore, flat on his back in a sleeping bag. A half empty bottle of Jack Daniel's was stuck in the dirt near his head. There were a couple of backpacks propped against a tree and each man had a hunting rifle by his side, each zipped into its carrying case. Reece was closest to the tree line, sleeping on his side so Lynch could see his face. First he had to neutralise Reece. Lynch hung the gunny sack from a nearby branch and stealthily approached his target. Lynch knew that if the two men weren't quite so relaxed and drunk, it wouldn't have been this easy. But Reece was young, fit and strong so he still had to be careful. Lynch quietly picked up the rifle, lay it across the man's chest then clamped it down heavily with one hand and a knee while putting his free hand over Reece's mouth. In his sleep the ex-Marine suddenly had a horrific dream that he had been nailed to the ground. There was a terrible pressure on his face and chest and he couldn't breathe. He arched his back and tried to throw the weight off but it wouldn't budge. Then he woke up and heard a voice in one ear, a whisper, urgent and familiar.

'It's me... Lynch,' the voice said. 'Malta... Libya... remember? It's Lynch... Jack Halloran sent me.'

The eyes blinked awake. At first they couldn't make sense of the face. It was streaked with dirt and the firelight cast sinister, deceptive shadows. Then he remembered. Lynch saw the sudden gleam of recognition in Reece's eyes.

'I'm taking my hands away,' Lynch said, still whispering. He put a finger to his lips to signal silence and got up, laying the rifle back down on the ground. Reece sat up and rubbed his face. His chest felt as if he'd been kicked by a horse.

'Was that really necess —' he began.

Lynch motioned him to be quiet and looked across at Bono. The big man stirred but didn't wake up. Lynch crouched down beside Reece. 'I wanted to give Bono a surprise,' he said. 'I've brought a little bed warmer for him.' Reece was confused but wide-awake now. He climbed out of his sleeping bag, scratched at the crotch of his marine issue shorts and watched.

Lynch plucked the gunny sack from the tree branch. The tormented creature inside coughed and struggled. Lynch padded soundlessly across the clearing and swiftly emptied the sack into Bono's sleeping bag. Suddenly freed from its tormentor, the raccoon made a dash for safety, only to find itself in a bigger prison. Except this time it was trapped with something bigger and more threatening. Believing it was fighting for its life, the terrified raccoon began clawing, biting and scratching at the larger animal next to it. It took a moment for Bono to react. As he watched, Lynch realised the big man must have been in a very deep alcoholic stupor. First there was an angry grunt, then a deafening bellow of real pain. Then Bono's body convulsed and his legs thrashed as he tried to escape from whatever it was that was trying to savage him. He couldn't get free from the sleeping bag either, and all he managed was to wrench and throw himself across the ground in a bizarre kind of St. Vitus's dance, getting himself more and more entangled with the sleeping bag and the raccoon. A stream of foul language poured from his mouth, half fury, half fear, because he still had no idea what was mauling him. Lynch had forgotten how difficult it was for a panic-stricken man to get out of a sleeping bag in an emergency. Bono heard a whoop of laughter from the other side of the fire and caught sight of Reece and another man watching. Watching and not helping. Bono didn't recognise the other man's dirt-streaked face but suddenly realised he was the victim of a cruel practical joke.

'You cocksucker!' he roared like a wounded animal. 'I'll eat your fucking face...'

The raccoon dug its claws deep into a fleshy thigh and held on. Bono screamed and kicked harder. Suddenly he was free. He scambled away from the still thrashing sleeping bag and leaped to his feet. Both Lynch and Reece saw blood flowing from a series of deep claw marks on the big man's bare legs and laughed even harder. Like Reece, Bono was wearing Marine issue boxer shorts and T-shirt, except they were now ripped and spattered with blood. The big man stared at the sleeping bag for a moment and watched the bulge of the animal inside still thrashing and snarling and spitting. Bono reached down, seized the sleeping bag with both hands and swung it wildly around his shoulders. When he had enough momentum the big man gave one final almighty swing and hurled the sleeping bag as far away from him as he could make it go. The weight of the raccoon carried the sleeping bag high into the trees, flapping behind it like the tail of a quilted comet. They heard the snap of small branches as the airborne raccoon crashed through the pines then a moment later the thud as it hit the ground. There was a sudden silence and that was followed by the scratching sounds of the dazed raccoon scuttling away across the pine needles.

Bono turned to face his own tormentors. The stranger was grinning quietly through smudges of dirt on his face but Reece was bent double again with a peculiarly high, breathless kind of laugh.

'Oh yeah,' Bono growled, his voice deep and slushy as though he hadn't cleared his throat properly. 'Pretty fuckin' funny, pal.' Then he advanced across the clearing towards them both. 'Now we'll see if you can laugh when I rip your fuckin' plums off.'

Reece couldn't stop laughing, but Lynch braced himself just in case. Bono was a powerful man and if he was genuinely enraged Lynch knew he was capable of inflicting a lot of harm. The big man stood almost two metres high and weighed 125 kilos. There was flab on him but Lynch knew he could be frighteningly fast on his feet for such an ungainly looking man. His puggish nose looked like it had been broken more than once, his face was disfigured with old acne scars and his mouth was an ugly gash. A few wispy red curls clung patchily to a scalp that had the look of sandstone. His massive shoulders and forearms were covered by brassy coils of red body hair and as he drew closer Lynch caught the rank stench of stale booze and sweat.

Lynch backed away and Bono circled after him, the big man's arms flexed like a wrestler, hands poised like grappling hooks. 'Don't you ever take a bath, you big ugly bastard?' Lynch joked, trying to humour Bono back into self-control. It was the first time Bono had heard Lynch speak. The big man hesitated, cocked his head slightly and squinted at the face of the man only a few feet away. Lynch remembered the dirt on his face and wiped it away with the back of one hand. While he had Bono momentarily stalled Lynch decided to play on military conditioning. Maybe Bono's fifteen years in the Marine Corps had left a reflex that was still obedient to military authority. Lynch injected his voice with the note of command.

'If this was a real operation you wouldn't just have a few scratches on your arse,' he said. 'You'd be dead ... Jefferson.'

Bono stopped and straightened. Lynch saw the tension

go out of the massive shoulders and arms and the fury replaced by uncertainty.

'Jefferson... how'd you know my middle name is Jefferson?'

Reece had stopped laughing and caught his breath. He stepped between the two of them and looked at Bono. 'It's Lynch, you stupid bastard. The limey from the job in Libya... one of the good guys, remember?'

Bono still wasn't convinced, but at least he had stopped threatening and started listening. There was a moment's silence until the realisation penetrated his anger.

'Lynch?' he repeated 'The guy from...?' Reece was right. Lynch was one of the good guys and there weren't too many of them in their books. But Bono was still angry and the claw marks on his legs hurt like hell.

'What the fuck are you — ?' he started, then seemed to think better of it. 'Oh, never mind,' he said and turned away. He walked back into the middle of the campsite, planted both feet hard in the dirt, closed his eyes and tilted back his head. Lynch and Reece watched him but there was only silence. Then they heard it. It started as a grumble and built into a deep, gravel-throated growl. It seemed to boil up from somewhere deep inside him, to gather volume and momentum until it erupted from his throat like a geyser, a great thunderous roar of unbridled rage and frustration. It was like the bellow of a stricken beast and it shuddered and reverberated around the clearing until it threatened to wake the entire forest. It was a sound that seemed as though it would go on forever until Lynch realised Bono had stopped, and what they could hear now was the echo rolling back and forth across the still waters of the inlet.

Bono opened his eyes, shook his great whiskery jowls and smacked his lips. Then he looked back at Lynch and Reece who stood by in astonished silence.

'That's better,' Bono said. He picked up the half-drunk bottle of bourbon and took a series of long, greedy swallows.

'Kind of like a great big mind-shit,' he added. 'Really blows away all them internal cobwebs.' He looked down at his legs and carelessly splashed some bourbon on the scratches.

'Shit,' he winced, 'that smarts.' He glanced back at Lynch and jabbed a grimy finger in his direction. 'If I have to get any of them goddamn rabies shots after this I'll find one of them critters and come round to your house and cram it up your ass.'

Lynch and Reece relaxed. Bono was back in good humour.

'Quit complainin',' Reece said. 'That's the closest thing to a pussy you've had in your sleeping bag in a long time.'

Bono lay down heavily on his side by the fire and took another swig of bourbon. Lynch and Reece squatted down beside him.

'Got anything to drink besides that?' Lynch asked, nodding at the whiskey.

'Coffee,' Reece answered. 'Mostly all we bring on these trips is the three B's: bacon, beans and bourbon.'

'And Bambi,' Bono mumbled.

'Bambi?'

'Yeah,' Bono added, staring absently into the fire. 'We shot Bambi. Day before yesterday. Cute little four pointer. Ate the little fucker all up. Tasted real nice. Might send the horns to Disney.'

Reece threw another log on the campfire, sending a flurry of sparks scurrying up into the night sky then looked around for the coffee pot. When he found it he shook in some instant coffee, filled it from the lake and then ground it into the hot coals beside the freshly burning log. The black curly hair was a little longer, Lynch thought, but the tough olive face was still deceptively boyish considering the life Reece had led.

Lynch glanced around. 'This isn't hunting season,' he thought aloud.

'It is for us.' Bono said. 'The ranger's cool. We told him we'd only be here a week and he could spend the whole time chasin' after us or take the two grand we offered and go buy some more of that laughin' weed. He's on our side. Any rubbernecks come up he steers 'em someplace else. It's only for a week. And we don't make a lot of noise with these.' Bono nodded at the rifle bag nearby. Lynch unzipped the bag and pulled out a Heckler and Koch G11, the state-of-the-art West German assault rifle they had used on their last operation.

Suddenly it wasn't all so funny. 'Where'd you get this?' he asked.

'Relax,' Bono said. 'It ain't one of yours. We bought it in L.A. You got the bucks you can buy anything you want in the US of A.'

Lynch shook his head.

'Ammo doesn't have any casings so there's nothin' to find in case some asshole comes sniffin' around later,' Bono added. 'Nice, light, quiet and plenty of whack... nearly got Bambi airborne.'

Lynch was thinking. Bar brawls, $2,000 bribes to dope-smoking rangers, shooting out of season with prohibited weapons even NATO didn't have yet. 'God almighty,' he sighed, 'don't you guys know anything about keeping a low profile?'

Bono shrugged. 'We get bored, man. And there's just somethin' about me that likes comin' into the woods, shootin' things and eatin' 'em.'

'I think it's time we got you guys out of here for a while,' he said, getting up and walking down to the lake. He stripped off quickly and plunged into the water to wash off the dirt that still caked his arms, face and neck. The water in the shallows was tepid and felt refreshing after the long day he'd put in. He looked around the moonlit lake, at the tall pines against the starry northern sky, and thought what an ideal setting it would make for a spot of skinnydipping with Janice. He waded, dripping, onto dry land and dried himself as best as he could with his T-shirt then put it back on with his jeans. The coffee was boiling and he squatted down beside the fire again to warm himself inside and out.

'I think it's time you two dangerous bastards went back to work,' he said.

The two men looked at him expectantly.

'Got anything specific in mind by any chance?' Bono asked.

'As a matter of fact . . .' Lynch answered with equal sarcasm. It took him twenty minutes to outline the operation. When he had finished the two former marines looked at each other. 'Only half a million?' Bono queried.

'Short, simple job,' Lynch lied. 'In and out in less than thirty days. This time next month you'll be half a million dollars richer . . . and it's still more money than you ever made in the Marine Corps.'

'Who's bullshittin' who?' Reece said. 'I'm in.' He looked over at his partner lying by the fire like an ugly red elephant seal. 'What else are we doin' that's so important? Let's go get some real action, huh? Travel to distant lands, blow the fuck out of the natives.'

Bono tilted the bottle in salute. His fleshy lips formed an unpleasant smile. 'Yeah,' he growled. 'Let's go kill us some shites.'

'It's pronounced — ' Reece started.

'I know what they call themselves,' Bono interrupted. 'What I call 'em is something else.'

Lynch lay down with his head on a borrowed backpack, basking in the glow of the fire, hoping the coffee wouldn't keep him awake. He might get two or three hours sleep if he was lucky. Then he'd have to get to New York to keep an appointment with Halloran. Two days down. Eighteen to go before they had to be ready. And he still only had half a team.

He had other business to take care of in New York too. There was someone else he wanted to see. Badly.

3
EXECUTIVE IMPERATIVE

New York, June 13

Lynch was awake and on his way back to the Dodge by dawn. He passed up the offer of beans and re-fried Bambi for breakfast. He also told Reece and Bono to pack up, go home and stay there until he or somebody from STC contacted them. They were to be ready to leave at a moment's notice any time in the following forty-eight hours, he said. Lynch drove as fast as he dared but it was still almost eleven when he got back to Duluth airport. The woman at the Hertz counter eyed him with distaste when he dropped off the keys.

'Car all right?' she asked.

He forced himself to smile. 'Handled like a dream.' It was only when he saw himself in the washroom mirror he realised she hadn't been asking if he liked the car. She wanted to know if the car had survived him. His eyes were bloodshot and underlined with exhaustion. His clothes were creased and filthy, he smelled bad, his hair stuck up in different directions and there were pine needles clinging to him. He shaved, washed, changed his clothes and made the midday flight to Chicago. As usual they were stacking flights at O'Hare but he caught the next available eastern flight to New York. Three hours later he was in the back seat of a yellow cab, speeding from La Guardia airport across the Triborough Bridge, the glass and steel ramparts of Manhattan gleaming in the late afternoon sunshine across the East River to his left. Another ten minutes and he would be at the east coast headquarters of Standard Transport Charter in Manhattan.

Even losing an hour by flying from Central Standard to Eastern Standard Time he thought he would make STC before they closed for the day. The offices of STC were in a forty-eight storey skyscraper overlooking Columbus Circle. Halloran owned the building and STC occupied the top twelve floors. Lynch only just made it. It was a few minutes after six and an armed security guard at the big, double glass doors was checking people out but not letting anybody in. Lynch hefted his two light travel bags up to the door and gave his name as Prentiss. The guard at the security desk inside had cleared him within seconds and nobody asked to look inside his bags.

He took the express elevator to the forty-sixth level and walked out onto the Chief Executive's floor. Another security guard was waiting behind a solid marble security desk; the wall behind him was one entire slab of the same creamy Italian marble. The only embellishment was the gleaming steel plate logo of Standard Transport Charter, the *S* and the *C* arranged to create the subliminal suggestion of dollar and cent symbols around the larger, central *T* for Transport. The guard was expecting him.

'Mr Halloran's office is at the end of that corridor,' the guard said, nodding to his left. Lynch walked down a long, wide marble corridor punctuated by closed doors. There was so much marble he felt like a messenger bringing bad news to Imperial Rome. Except an American Caesar was waiting to see him. He passed through a deserted waiting room lined with leather sofas, plants and a brass-framed coffee table neatly stacked with copies of respectable magazines like *Forbes* and *Fortune*. Then there was the Executive Secretary's office where a middle-aged woman with expensive grey hair waited at her own marble desk. She was wearing the kind of smart black skirt suit and white blouse favoured by executive secretaries throughout the corporate world and pretending to go over some papers. Lynch dropped his bags. They barely made a sound when they hit the thickly carpeted floor. The woman looked up, nodded politely to Lynch then clicked on her intercom. 'Mr Prentiss has just arrived,' she said. She studied Lynch for a moment. Her face registered neither approval nor disapproval. If she knew Lynch's phoney name how much else did she know about him, he wondered.

'I'm Mrs Wilson.' She introduced herself without getting up. Her voice was as clear and as flawless as crystal and uncontaminated by any identifying accent. Lynch noted the formal prefix, 'Mrs'. Clearly she was not a woman with whom one embarked on first name terms immediately. Very un-American. 'You may leave your bags here, Mr Prentiss,' she said. 'They'll be safe.' Lynch did as he was told. From the look of her office Halloran's secretary had a couple of secretaries of her own. There was an unmarked door set flush in the leather-lined wall next to Mrs Wilson's desk. It looked like aged mahogany, and was the only piece of furniture in the room that wasn't some shade of cream or beige. The door swung inward without making a sound. A man Lynch had never seen before was standing on the other side, blocking Lynch's path. A tall man, almost a full head taller than Lynch, he had flowing blonde hair, clear grey eyes and a superior patrician look about him that Lynch disliked immediately. He wore an expensive charcoal grey suit with a white shirt and a beautifully patterned tie that looked as though it had cost more than everything Lynch carried in his luggage.

'Please come in, Mr Lynch,' he said, and stepped aside. Was that a sneer in the voice or had Lynch imagined it?

The office was the size of a tennis court. It occupied one corner of the building and it had disconcerting floor to ceiling windows on two sides which offered a view of a fiery Manhattan sunset that must have been worth millions.

Halloran was talking on the phone, leaning back in a huge swivel chair behind a desk that looked as if it had been carved from a single piece of American oak. The desk was remarkably uncluttered except for the telephone and one of the new Apple terminals. Lynch was surprised though he knew he shouldn't have been. He had simply never seen Halloran in a proper, pinstripe business suit before. He looked about as comfortable as a prizefighter dressed up for his sister's wedding. Halloran beckoned Lynch to a seat. The patrician young man guided him to one of two leather straight-backed chairs facing Halloran, then glided away, making as little noise as the electronic security locks in the office door. Lynch watched him go and speculated that the slight bulge beneath the jacket, around the small of the back where a man's clothing hangs most loosely, was a holstered automatic. The office was decorated as though the interior designer had been halfway through when he'd been fired and Halloran had done the rest of the job himself. The two interior walls were covered with silk; beige again. The carpet was the colour of milky coffee and there were a couple of modern Italian side tables that looked like they would break if you sneezed on them. The rest of the room's furnishings went to the other extreme. They were all robustly masculine and eminently predictable for a man of Halloran's entrenched conservatism; a couple of tan leather couches, solid oak coffee table, matching book-case containing a few token, leather-bound volumes of American classics. Faulkner and Hemingway were popular, Lynch noted. There was a startlingly ugly bronze bust of John F. Kennedy, one of Halloran's heroes, and nearby was a black and white photographic portrait of former President Eisenhower with a dedication scrawled across the bottom that said: 'To Jack, a great American and a lousy golf partner — Ike'. What really drew Lynch's eye were a couple of paintings on the walls, scenes of the old west. One showed a Sioux brave on horseback riding down a buffalo, the other a trio of cowhands tending branding irons in a fire with cattle milling in the background, somewhere in the desert country of the southwest. Lynch realised that they were Remington originals. Then he recalled that Halloran was from New Mexico. To him, New York was a branch office. Halloran tossed the phone back into its cradle, swung back his swivel chair and put his feet up on the desk. Despite the pinstripes he was wearing beautifully-tooled black cowboy boots.

He looked Lynch up and down. 'You look like you spent the night under a tree with a bottle.' he said.

'Close,' Lynch answered. He wondered if Halloran was psychic too.

Halloran waited.

'Tuckey's a definite negative.' Lynch said. 'Reece and Bono would do the job for nothing.'

The American grimaced. 'You sure Tuckey can't be talked around?'

Lynch nodded slowly. 'Not now. Not ever.'

'Okay,' Halloran said, leaning forward, fingers interlocking on his desk. 'We'll go without him. Like Al Capone said — nobody's indispensable.'

'Another hero of yours?'

'Capone?' Halloran shrugged. 'A master of the corporate takeover. Just a little ahead of his time.'

Lynch couldn't tell if he was serious.

'Coffee?'

'Tea.'

'Any special kind?'

'Twinings English Breakfast.'

'Sure, I don't drink anything else.' Halloran called to the blonde man who had taken a seat on one of the couches and who appeared deeply absorbed in the *Wall Street Journal*. 'Howard, bring me a beer,' he said, 'and see if the kitchen can rustle up a decent pot of tea for Mr Lynch here. Twinings English Breakfast, I believe.'

'If we haven't got it, we can get it,' Howard said. The young man conjured a revolving cocktail bar out of one wall and brought Halloran his Bud. Then he left the room to get Lynch his tea, moving across the carpet on polished leather shoes as noiselessly as if he were on castors.

'Howard's a Harvard man,' Halloran said.

'How interesting. How come he knows my real name?'

'He's my personal assistant. He can be trusted.'

Lynch said nothing. Halloran took a sip of beer. 'Harvard via Langley,' he added. 'Howard believes he can be more effective working for me than the CIA. He's smart, too. Already made a million running his own investment portfolio. He's twenty-eight.'

Lynch disliked Howard even more. He changed the subject. 'We need another three men,' he said. 'A four-man team might do it but six is better. It splits into three teams of two; far more effective that way. And we're going to need firepower and flexibility where we're going.' Lynch wanted to get things rolling. He was starting to feel the strain. He wanted to finish his business with Halloran then grab a hotel room and twelve hours sleep. The clock seemed to be gaining on him. If they could put probes out for replacements tonight things would still be moving while he slept.

Halloran wasn't used to being prompted. 'Okay,' he said, swinging his feet off the desk. 'Let's do it.' He shoved his beer aside, leaned forward in his chair and booted the PC. The terminal was linked into a mainframe at his primary computer centre in Albuquerque. From his desk Halloran could summon the records on just about every man and woman who had served in any branch of the American armed forces in the past twenty years.

They spent the next five hours hunched over Halloran's PC sifting through scores of files on men who either were available for freelance operations or whom Halloran believed could be available if he decided it were necessary. Lynch's tea arrived. Twinings English Breakfast Tea. Just the way he liked it, in a china teapot with a real cup and saucer. Then Howard glided back to the couch, took out a pocket calculator and resumed his diligent study of the *Wall Street Journal*.

Not surprisingly many of the faces summoned up on the PC screen were familiar to Lynch even though they were predominantly American. Most were serving with existing units. Others were known mercenaries. Lynch had been in here once, he knew. Now he was on another file — one marked 'Bought', he suspected. But he was a lot fussier than Halloran. Most of the candidates were quickly discounted. In Lynch's opinion they were unreliable, untrustworthy or unstable. Some were retired, deceased or had just plain disappeared from the face of the earth. Others, Lynch knew, were outright fruitcakes who advertised in *Soldier Of Fortune* magazine and were to be avoided like the plague.

'Time for a spring clean,' Halloran mused as they passed over one face after another. He had taken off his jacket and loosened his tie. Even Howard had removed his jacket, though his hair still looked pretty. Halloran sent him for sandwiches. It was a demeaning errand but Howard's face showed nothing. For what Halloran would be paying, Lynch realised, Howard was happy to get sandwiches.

Lynch was tired but the selection process he was involved in now was vital. The calibre of the men he and Halloran chose would decide the success or failure of the operation. Lynch couldn't afford to drop concentration for a moment. If Reece and Bono had come up for consideration under Lynch's merciless eye for the first time tonight they too would have been rejected. It was only because Halloran was a grunt in Korea that he had such a soft spot for the Corps and liked to hire marines. But Reece and Bono were valuable assets. They had proven their operational worth, and shown their mettle in close combat. For that alone they were superior to all the unknowns scrolling up on the computer screen.

The two men finally composed a short list of six candidates. All but two came under the US Army's Special Forces Command, SOCOM. The other two were with the Navy's SEALs and were discounted first because Lynch needed men whose primary expertise was airborne warfare. That left two men from the 7th Ranger Regiment's 1st Battalion at Fort Hunter in Georgia, and two men from Delta Force at Fort Bragg, North Carolina.

In the end they came down on the side of the men from

Delta because both had actual covert operations experience, whereas the two Rangers had only conventional combat experience in Grenada.

Lynch spooled up the first of the Delta Force candidates. The computer-enhanced picture didn't tell much about Master Sergeant Charles Vance, instructor-specialist on permanent attachment to Delta Force HQ, The Stockade, at Fort Bragg. It was just the usual military mugshot of a hard-looking bastard with close-cropped hair. Anybody could look tough. The report which accompanied the mugshot told Lynch more. Vance was thirty-five, originally from Oregon, unmarried, and unusual in the fact that he'd been with Delta for eight years, almost from the beginning. This meant he'd survived the worst of its growing pains. Furthermore, he had been part of the Delta team which secretly stormed a hijacked passenger aircraft at Bangkok, killing four hijackers with no loss of life to the passengers. Like many of his colleagues in Britain's Counter Terrorism Command at the time, Lynch had studied the operation closely and concluded that no-one, not even the SAS, could have done it better. Vance was also a seasoned jumper with wide experience in HAHO, HALO and the new glider 'chutes.

The second candidate was a Sergeant Leon Cooper. Again the mugshot told Lynch little except that Cooper was a thin, fairish man from Mobile, Alabama. Single, and aged twenty-six, he had been with Delta four years. His most recent work had been on special operations inside Nicaragua, including sabotage and assassination of key military commanders. He too was an experienced jumper. But one word in particular among the list of his qualifications convinced Lynch that Cooper should be on the team. Marksman. Lynch knew there would be situations during the upcoming operation when an expert sniper might mean the difference between success or failure. The Lebanese militia's style of combat was to use relays of fighters to pour automatic fire into a position in the general hope that they would hit something. The firepower

108

of modern weapons meant they usually did. However, a good sniper who could take out a man with every bullet in his magazine would blunt the impetus of any militia attack. Lynch was curious to see how the Shi'ite militias would stand up to a real casualty toll. Cooper would help him find out. Lynch and Halloran finished reading the two files at the same time. Both Vance and Cooper had sound psychological profiles. Both were considered to be amongst Delta's best men.

'Halloran looked at Lynch expectantly.

'They'll do,' Lynch said.

'They fucking better,' Halloran grumbled. He ordered Howard to fetch him another Budweiser.

'Assuming they'll join the operation, how soon can we have them?'

'I'll call my people at the State Department tonight,' Halloran said. He looked at his watch. It was close to midnight. 'They'll pull the necessary strings. If I have to I'll go through the White House and invoke Executive Order 12333.'

'What's that?'

Halloran grunted. 'It is the power to do anything,' he said.

'We need power like that,' Lynch said without a hint of irony. 'We're going to need another limey on the team too.'

'What's the matter, getting lonely?'

'Yep.' Lynch was deadpan. 'And we need somebody with extensive experience working in the Middle East. Somebody who can speak Arabic. And that is our department.' By 'our' Lynch meant Britain. There was little doubt that Britain's special forces had the edge in operational experience throughout the Middle East.

'That means SAS,' Lynch continued. 'Those guys drop in and out of Middle Eastern hot spots all the time. The Yemen, Oman, Iran, Kurdistan...'

'Kurdistan?'

'Sure... you don't think the problems the Iranians and Soviets have been having with the Kurds in their border regions are coincidental?'

Halloran listened.

'That's what the SAS has traditionally done best... make life hard for people who make life hard for us. They're used to working deep cover for months in hostile country, winning the natives' confidence, going native themselves, adopting the local customs, speaking the native dialect perfectly. Teaching them the mechanics of insurrection and sabotage, and occasionally shooting somebody in the head as a good example. The extraordinary thing is that sometimes they come out again.'

'Lawrence of fuckin' Arabia,' Halloran mumbled.

Lynch patted him on the shoulder. 'Now you're getting the idea.'

'I'll give Malcolm Porter a call in London,' Halloran said. 'See who he can come up with.' Sir Malcolm Porter was Lynch's former boss at CTC and he also happened to be a former Commanding Officer of the Special Air Service. If he couldn't find the right man for them, no-one could.

Lynch felt relieved. Three long, busy days were coming to a close. He turned away from the monitor and rubbed his eyes. Green snowflakes danced behind his eyelids.

'Stay at the company's place on Riverside,' Halloran offered. 'We keep a couple of townhouses there. They're secure. Howard will organise a key and a car for you.'

Lynch got up to go. Halloran walked him to the door and Howard followed.

'Feeling a little beat?' Halloran asked.

Lynch shrugged. 'This is the easy part.'

'Bet your ass.'

Lynch looked at him. 'I'm waiting till we get to the fun part.'

Mrs Wilson was still at her desk, still immaculate and composed, still rearranging papers and making calls. STC was a twenty-four hour empire and there were troops in different time zones all over the world who had to be kept on their mettle. Halloran chose his people well, Lynch decided.

110

No wonder he could take long absences. Howard murmured instructions to Mrs Wilson and a car, a driver and a key to one of STC's executive townhouses were all swiftly arranged. While his two aides were occupied Halloran took Lynch by the elbow and steered him out of earshot.

'Do you think Tuckey could be a problem?'

'Not a chance.'

Halloran shoved his hands deep into his trouser pockets and rocked back and forth on his cowboy heels. 'If there's a danger, even the suspicion of a threat that he might jeopardise the success of this operation...' Halloran left the rest unsaid but the meaning was implicit.

Lynch shook his head. 'No. Absolutely not. Tuckey wants to forget everything about us. You, me, everything. He's no threat to anybody.'

Halloran looked doubtful. 'All the same...'

'I told you, *no*.' Lynch unintentionally raised his voice. Howard and Mrs Wilson looked up but Halloran dissuaded them with a look and they went back to business.

'Tuckey won't be a problem,' Lynch emphasised softly. 'I guarantee it.'

Halloran nodded thoughtfully, then walked back towards his office. 'Get some sleep,' he said. 'I'll talk to you tomorrow.' He disappeared back into his bulletproof coccoon.

Howard handed Lynch a set of keys. 'These are for the townhouse. A driver and a car will be waiting out the front by the time you get down.' Lynch pocketed the keys and turned to go.

'Mr Prentiss?' This time it was the crystal chimes of Mrs Wilson. 'You may need these.' Lynch had forgotten his bags. He slung one over his shoulder, grabbed the other and headed for the elevators without another word. As he rode down his mind was filled with what Halloran had just said. Jesus Christ. What if he decided to snuff Tuckey as a precaution? There was nothing Lynch could do to stop it. Perhaps Janice was right about Halloran. The cost of getting involved with him was already higher than expected. Janice! He wanted to call her now but he was too tired.

The same armed security guard who had let him in unlocked the door for him. The sultry, fume-laden air of a June night in Manhattan smacked him in the face and ran damp, sweaty hands over him the moment he stepped out of the air conditioning. A shiny black Lincoln Continental was parked at the kerb with a uniformed driver waiting by the rear passenger door. He reached for the luggage but Lynch shrugged him away, threw his bags untidily in the back seat and climbed in after them. The driver got behind the wheel and pulled out into the blaring bedlam that passed for traffic in New York, even at midnight. Lynch settled back into the smoky blue upholstery with its prickly nap of odourless, everlasting synthetic velvet and let the limousine's air conditioning wash over him. There was a compact liquor cabinet in the seat in front of him. Lynch felt trapped inside a huge lethal machine that ran on power and money. A machine that could turn on him... just like that.

'Yes sir?'

'What?'

'You snapped your fingers, sir.'

'Did I? Sorry... just thinking out loud.'

'Anything you want sir... just ask.'

The power, Lynch thought. The power to do anything you want.

New York, June 14

The recuperative power of the human body was a mysterious but wonderful process, Lynch thought for the millionth time in his life. He thanked God for it in his line of work. Lynch was looking over his shoulder at his naked back in the bathroom mirror. He brushed the fingers of his right hand lightly over the insensate tadpoles of pink scar tissue that flecked his torso. Fifty-eight in all, the doctors had told him

— fifty-eight shrapnel fragments which had peppered him when the Stinger missile had slammed into the armoured car on the end of the jetty in Tripoli and blown him into the water like a rag doll. Fifty-eight permanent little scars and two patches of second degree burns across the neck and shoulders where the blast had spilled around the hulk of the armoured vehicle that had saved his life. Plastic surgery had erased most of the scarring with tissue taken from his left buttock and grown artificially in the laboratory. Nice new strips of pink skin had come out of the lab and knitted beautifully into the raw abrasions on his shoulders. He had declined the suggestion of plastic surgery for the constellation of smaller scars. It was enough that they had healed. He had spent enough time in hospital. The broken ribs had healed. Most of the pain had gone. He had wanted out.

Lynch finished towelling himself dry. There was an extraordinary range of expensive aftershaves, colognes and masculine beautifying gels in the bathroom cabinet. He chose one that wasn't too pungent and grimaced as it cauterised the microscopic shaving cuts on his neck and face. When he finally emerged from the bathroom he felt ready to face Halloran again. A good night's sleep was half the battle. Lynch had fallen into bed around 12.30 am. There had been no calls; now it was nearly one o'clock in the afternoon and he was starving. He picked through the clothes in his travel bags. They looked like dish rags. Even modern clothing wasn't meant to withstand being squashed into a couple of small canvas bags for four days. He found the least rumpled clean shirt and put it on with his last clean socks and underwear. The jeans still smelled rank but they were wearable. His sneakers were a write-off, but he had a pair of casual brown leather loafers in reserve. He would pick up a few things at Bloomingdales later. He had clean clothes at Janice's apartment but that was a bridge he still had to cross.

Lynch heard the maid busying herself in the kitchen, and the cleaning lady was there vacuuming non-existent footprints

113

out of the carpets. Both were employed by STC to keep the company townhouses immaculate and its corporate gladiators fed, watered and ready for combat. If they only knew, he thought. Lynch introduced himself and the maid offered to fix him something to eat. He said he wanted the kind of meal an NFL linebacker would have for breakfast. She made him blueberry pancakes with bacon and eggs. He almost ate it all. The next step was the hardest. He went to the drawing room, picked up the phone and dialled Janice's number. Her answering machine said she was out but would be back in a while. At least it wasn't the tape that said she was away for a few days. He hung up without leaving a message. He thought about phoning Halloran but decided it was pointless. When Halloran wanted you, he called you. Or his secretary did. And you made yourself available. When you wanted him it was another story. It depended on whether he wanted to talk to you or not whether you got through. The Big Man Syndrome. Lynch decided to go shopping.

He returned a couple of hours later with new jeans, a pair of grey pants, a couple of shirts and a pair of Nikes. At least it was June and he didn't need anything heavier. New York was hot, humid and overcast. People were snarling at each other earlier this year. In another couple of weeks it would be high summer and the city would be uninhabitable. All the people who could afford it got out for July and August, leaving the muggers a clear run at the tourists. He dialled Janice's number again and this time she was home.

'Did you call earlier?'

'Yes.'

'I thought you were the one who didn't leave a message.'

He couldn't tell anything about her real mood from the tone of her voice. It was absolutely neutral.

'Can I come around and see you?'

'Now?'

'Yes.'

There was a pause. 'Okay.'

'Just okay?'

'You were expecting a brass band and the Rockettes?'

That was more like it. She wasn't happy but at least her sense of humour hadn't deserted her entirely.

'I'll be there in half an hour.'

It wasn't far from Riverside Drive to Janice's apartment which overlooked Central Park, so Lynch walked. He needed to compose himself. He was worried by the way events were unfolding. Things were beyond his reach, out of his control. He didn't like that. Perhaps it was this business with Janice which had thrown him out more than he expected. That wasn't good. Halloran was right — a man with personal problems was a liability on a job like this. And he was supposed to be team leader. Something else was gnawing at him too. The little discussion with Halloran about Tuckey last night. That bothered him. Things just didn't feel right: too many wild cards, too little time, one distraction too many. He turned left at the Dakota. One thing at a time, he decided. Keep It Simple, Stupid. Put things in perspective. Get this business with Janice sorted out first, attend to Halloran later.

When she let him in, the apartment felt familiar and foreign all at the same time. The mood was different. Lynch knew he had to be imagining it but it actually felt cool compared to the warmth he had previously known there. This had been the only place he could call home after he had got out of hospital. He had spent several weeks here. They had made love, told jokes, and traded secrets and intimacies here. It had become their place. That had all changed in a matter of days. When they had left here, ten days before, they had been lovers looking forward to a couple of weeks vacation in the Caribbean aboard the yacht of a rich friend. That had all been shattered. Lynch was a stranger to this apartment now.

Her eyes seemed a little puffy. Otherwise, he thought, she looked perfect. She wasn't much of a crier, anyway, Lynch knew. Like him she kept it all inside, dealt with it alone, lived with it privately until it became manageable. If anything it made him feel relieved that she wouldn't have shed too many tears over him. It was one of the qualities he admired in her. She was in bare feet, as usual, and wearing jeans and a dark blue shirt which suited her dark colouring. Her hair was pinned into a chignon, though a few shiny black tendrils had escaped and curled prettily around her neck. She walked over to a sofa against the window and sat down, legs curled underneath her, arms folded across her chest. He stood in the middle of the room, hands stuck awkwardly in his pockets, feeling acutely self-conscious.

'Guilty?'

'What?'

'Feeling guilty?'

'No,' he lied.

'You look like the little boy who cut down the apple tree except you won't own up.'

'Shit. Can I sit down?'

She shrugged. He sat down in the nearest armchair. It was the first time he'd sat alone in any chair in her apartment.

A long silence followed. They had come together in the most unpromising of circumstances and it was perhaps inevitable that it would come to nothing, he was thinking. Yet he had come closer to Janice than to any other woman he had known. They shared a contempt for pettiness and pretension, a sense of humour, an appreciation of the absurdities of life; that was what had held them together. And lust. There had been plenty of that, too. Now here they were, together in a New York apartment that might as well have been a hotel room for all the intimacy it contained.

He looked up and saw she was smiling faintly. Even now they could find amusement in the absurdity of the situation, their juvenile awkwardness with each other. Then she shook her head.

'Oh no,' she said. 'Loving you is just too damn painful, Lynch. You want to put your work ahead of me, we're better

116

breaking it off now. That way I can start getting over you today. Otherwise I have to wait till Jack Halloran calls me one day and tells me I can start grieving because you were killed two months ago in some goddamn slum in Lebanon.'

Lynch hesitated. 'Twenty years,' he said. 'Nearly twenty years. That's how long I've been doing this for a living. It's not work. It's not a job. It's what I *am*. It's the only damn thing I know, the only thing I'm good at. You can't expect me to change overnight. Nobody changes direction that easily.'

'You have a choice.'

'There are lunatics out there terrorising and murdering innocent people,' Lynch answered. 'The crazy thing is that nobody is doing anything to stop them. Nobody. Quite frankly, I don't think it's good enough to sit around with your finger up your bum waiting for them to pull their next stunt. A man says he's going to kill you, I think it's a good idea you believe him and get in first. That's what we're about. That's why I'm in.'

'My,' she said, 'we *are* feeling better.'

Lynch's voice hardened. 'You're not asking me to do something else,' he said. 'You're asking me to be somebody else.' He shrugged his shoulders. 'This is it, I'm afraid. This is as good as it gets.'

'I know,' she said. 'I saw it in your face the moment Jack landed on the boat. You knew what was coming and you were glad. I knew then you were going to take his offer. I guess I'd known for a while.'

'You didn't tell me Jack called you a month ago and asked if I was ready for work.'

She looked away for a moment. 'I told him you were much better. I didn't think he had something for you this goddamn early. I'd hoped we'd have more time together so...'

'So you could work on me a little longer?'

'Yes, goddammit,' she said. 'We haven't exactly had the best start in the world. What chance do I have of competing with Halloran, for Christ's sake? I don't know what it is

117

about that all-boys-together-bullshit but I've been around it enough and I wouldn't even know how to compete.'

Lynch smiled. 'Uh-huh,' he said. 'You've stuck it out this far. Why can't you stick around a little longer?'

'Because I can't,' she said. 'I just can't. You want to go your way, that's making the choice for both of us.'

'You knew I'd go back to work. You told Halloran.'

'I told him I couldn't stop you if you really wanted to. I...' her voice wavered but only for a second. 'I had hoped you wouldn't want to.'

The day outside had grown more overcast. The only sound to scratch the silence was the traffic noise wafting faintly past the window along with a few filthy scraps of paper spiralling upwards on hot air currents from the street below.

'There is something else,' he said. 'I do love you, you know.'

Janice said nothing but he caught a glimpse of something in her eye. It was the first time he'd said it. The phone rang, sounding unnaturally loud. Janice picked it up and listened for a moment. 'Yes, he's here,' she said. She passed him the handset then uncurled herself from the sofa and walked to a window to stare at the Manhattan skyline.

'Mr Prentiss?' It was Mrs Wilson's unmistakeable voice. 'Howard said we might find you there. Mr Halloran would like to know if you can come in to his office this evening — about six o'clock?'

'I'll be there,' Lynch said. He hung up and turned to go. Janice had her back to him. He went to the door.

'I'll send your things to Jack's office,' she said.

He was about to go when one last thought occurred to him. He smiled and turned to look at her. She was still looking out of the window, her back to him.

'Let's see if you give up that easy,' he said.

She spun around.

'Bastard!' Her voice was a disbelieving gasp. But the door had closed and he was gone.

* * *

118

'Goddamn that woman.' Halloran spat the words out. 'Like all spoiled kids — if she can't have it now, it ain't worth having.'

They were in the communications room adjoining Halloran's office. The brilliantly lit, windowless room was all white and about the size of a squash court. It was dustproof, soundproof, air conditioned and sanitised to a germ-free sterility. And it was filled with every state-of-the-art piece of telecommunications equipment modern technology had devised. There were two mainframes, a dozen consoles and monitors with 3-D and glorious technicolour that Lynch had never seen before. The room was swept two or three times daily for bugs. All Halloran's communications channels were on scrambler, the codes changed at random intervals. All communications channels were monitored electronically every twenty-four hours and checked manually several times each day for intercepts. Howard was hovering discreetly in the background in case his boss needed him to get a drink, press a button or shoot somebody.

'You going to be all right about her?'

Lynch nodded. 'Relax,' he said. 'It's only love.'

Halloran shot him a shrewd glance. 'You learn fast,' he said. He turned to business. 'Word from Washington is good. Both candidates confirmed available. I want Reece and Bono on the ground at Fayetteville Airport, North Carolina by tomorrow night. We'll meet them there and drive to Fort Bragg. It's time to lock this thing up. Make sure you take everything you need with you. You won't be coming back for a while.'

'A little tight,' Lynch said.

'Yeah,' Halloran went on as though he hadn't heard. 'We have to assume Reece and Bono will have no parachute experience whatever. They'll have to go through basic training the hard way... and then some.'

From this room Halloran could speak to anyone on earth if they were near a phone, a radio, a satellite receiver, an

119

on-line computer or a fax machine. He could talk to Captain Penny on the *American Endeavour*, no matter where on the high seas it happened to be. The powerful radio, microwave and satellite transmitter-receivers on the roof of the STC building meant he could talk to any vessel or aircraft, civilian, naval or military, belonging to any nation anywhere on the planet. He had direct lines to the Pentagon and the State Department. He could talk to the Kremlin if he wanted to. And he could talk to Sir Malcolm Porter, Control Director, CTC, in Whitehall, London. They were waiting for him to ring now. It would be a little after 10 o'clock at night in London. Sir Malcolm was at an official dinner with the Queen Mother honouring Falklands veterans, but planned to call immediately afterwards.

'We can't rely on Vance and Cooper to carry Reece and Bono when they jump...'

'Excuse me, sir,' a technician in a dust coat interrupted. 'Your call from London.' He gestured to a nearby telephone extension.

Halloran hit the conference button so he and Lynch could both listen in to the British security chief. The scrambler was activated automatically. Lynch recognised the cultured English voice immediately. Cunning old bastard. The last time he had seen Porter had been on the flight deck of the aircraft carrier USS *John F. Kennedy*, sailing with the Fifth Fleet off Libya. Lynch had not been in any condition to carry on a conversation.

'Promising news, Jack,' Sir Malcolm announced, coming directly to the point. 'I think we have a chap who might suit your needs. He's SAS. Extensive experience in the Middle East. Fluent in Arabic, a number of dialects, I believe. At the moment he's in Northern Ireland but I think we can pull him out for a while. How soon will you need him?'

'Can he be here for breakfast?' Lynch interjected.

'God almighty.' There was a pause. 'Is that you, Lieutenant Lynch?'

'Yes sir.'

'Obviously you're much fitter than the last time I saw you.'

'Only suffering from wounded pride now, sir.' Lynch was referring to the subterfuge to which Sir Malcolm had resorted to get him out of England and into Halloran's employ.

'Well, we all have to live with that from time to time, don't we old chap? Tomorrow, eh? Are you serious? CO-SAS won't be too happy about that — it would be different if it was one of our operations. Might have to get the Home Secretary to lean on a few people. Look, twenty-four hours is out of the question as you damn well know. He could be sitting in a foxhole somewhere in south Armagh. I think I can have him with you in a week. That's assuming he's agreeable, of course. Will that do?'

'Agreeable my ass,' Halloran muttered.

'Sorry, old chap, didn't quite catch that.'

'That's fine, Malcolm,' Halloran said.

'All right. Well look, the name of our chap is Gamble. Rather appropriate don't you think? Captain Peter Gamble. Never met him but I've heard he's a good man. I'll get back to you in forty-eight hours and confirm.'

'That'll be fine,' Halloran said.

'Tell him the pay's good,' Lynch added.

'It's an ill wind eh, Lynch,' Porter rejoined.

'As always,' Halloran said, 'I appreciate all you're doing, Malcolm.'

'Don't you worry, Jack,' Porter replied. 'We'll extort an appropriate favour in return soon enough.'

I bet you will, you sly old prick, thought Lynch. It was because of Porter that Lynch would never be able to work in the UK again. He was unable to resist a parting shot. 'Perhaps I can have a holiday in London soon?'

'Yes, we'll have to see about that,' Porter's smug drawl floated back. 'Goodnight Jack... and to you, Lieutenant... and give my regards to your lovely lady friend in New York.'

'She'll be flattered.' Lynch replied. Touché. The bastard

probably had a home video of the more intimate moments of his courtship with Janice.

'So, where does that leave us?' Halloran growled as they strolled back into his office and sat opposite each other on the facing leather couches. Halloran gestured vaguely at Howard and somehow Howard understood they would have coffee. Lynch looked at the time. It had just gone ten. Another day gone. Sixteen days to go before they were supposedly ready to strike and still Lynch felt they hadn't done anything.

'Reece and Bono are standing by for my contact,' he said. 'I might have to charter a plane but I'll have them in Fayetteville by tomorrow night.'

Halloran nodded. 'Tell Howard what you want. He'll fix it.'

'They're two very capable guys,' Lynch added, 'but we can't just assume that they'll be able to breeze through HAHO training. In my view, the less you do of that stuff the better. I'd like to go through it with them and try to hold down the risk of serious injury. If they're going to hurt themselves it might as well be when we're inside Lebanon.'

'Good idea,' Halloran growled. 'When's the last time you jumped out of a plane?'

'About eight years ago — into the North Sea at night. I did three months with the Royal Marines Comacchio Company before going to SBS. Comacchio looks after our North Sea oil rigs in the event of terrorist attack or takeover. Went through a couple of HALO exercises with Comacchio — handy bunch of lads.'

Halloran nodded. 'This ought to be a piece of cake.'

'I could stand some practice.'

'You've already been to Fort Bragg?'

Lynch nodded. Halloran knew damn well he'd spent two weeks at Fort Bragg in 1985 on a joint intelligence sharing programme between British and American Special Forces.

'I'll arrange for you to try out the new 'chutes there next week,' Halloran added. 'Just enough for you, Reece and Bono

122

to familiarise yourselves. Then we'll re-locate to Baja because we're going to have to do at least one rehearsal.'

'Why Baja?'

'Because I've got a place in the mountains in southern Baja,' he said. 'Just a house and a couple of thousand acres of mountainside — but it's secure. I used to spend a lot of time in Baja in the late fifties, marlin fishing. Bought a lot of beachfront real estate when it was a few cents an acre. Course the place is fucked by condos and timeshare shit now and I hardly go anymore but I made a fortune.' He stopped for an instant as though remembering a better, more innocent time. Then it was gone.

'We're going there because the Pacific coastline of Baja is almost identical to the coastline of Lebanon. It even looks the same: ocean approach, coastal mountain range peaking at 3,200 metres — that's almost exactly the same elevation as the Lebanese Mountains which parallel the Lebanese coast. You'll have to exit the aircraft at 8,500 metres above the Mediterranean, about 50 kilometres out from the Lebanese coast, para-glide over the water, across the coastline and over the Lebanon Mountains to drop into El Laboue. It's 32 kilometres from the coast to El Laboue, as the crow flies. That's a 80 kilometre glide from aircraft exit to the landing zone — and you can't drop below 3,500 metres until the last three, four kilometres into El Laboue.'

Lynch sucked in his breath. 'That's a helluva long way to glide,' he said.

'The new 'chutes can do it,' Halloran said confidently.

'They better. And we better damn well hope it's a calm night when we go in. Any kind of a headwind and we have a choice: a dip in the ocean with no chance of a pick-up, Beirut by night, or an unfriendly mountain peak.'

Halloran nodded. 'That's why I'm with you. I don't think we should push our luck any further than one full-scale rehearsal. You, Gamble and the two guys from Delta will be okay. Reece and Bono will just have to wing it the best way they can.' A small smile crossed his face. 'Thank Christ for superior technology. We'll just have to rely on that to get Reece and Bono to the LZ.'

A white-jacketed waiter arrived with coffee for Halloran, tea for Lynch. Halloran motioned to Howard to join them. They drank in silence for a moment and Lynch could see Halloran was kicking something else around in his mind.

'This is the last time I'll say anything about it,' he said finally. 'But I don't want you dwelling on this business with Janice. We have enough problems without our best man worrying about his love life.'

'It's already out of my mind,' Lynch lied.

'Maybe I should talk to her,' Howard said. It was the first time he had addressed Lynch directly that night. He sat in a corner of the same couch where his boss was sitting. Impeccably tailored, legs crossed, cup and saucer in hand, a study in calculated nonchalance. 'Talk some sense into the spoiled little bitch before she causes us any unnecessary problems,' he added.

'Please don't do that,' Lynch said quietly. It was polite but the words fell like drops of acid onto the highly polished surface of the coffee table and smouldered there.

Halloran smiled indulgently. 'No excesses of zeal for the moment, thank you, Howard,' he said. It was the lightest of admonitions. Howard smiled at his boss then looked over his coffee cup at Lynch.

Lynch was sure now that he didn't like Howard. At all.

Panama City, Florida, June 15

Tuckey got the call a little after six am. A buddy from Pensacola Salvage had just won a fat contract. A dredger en route from New Orleans to Mobile had capsized in the Mississippi Sound. The buddy had bought salvage rights but had to act promptly because the sunken vessel presented a hazard to shipping and the job was too big for him alone.

124

If Tuckey could assist in Reef Runner there'd be a fat pay cheque at the end of it for both of them. Besides which the buddy would consider it a big personal favour. Tuckey struggled out of bed to the bathroom, still shaking the fog of sleep from his head. He hadn't recognised the woman's voice. She was the new secretary she explained. That would be about right, Tuckey thought. His buddy was a nice enough guy but had wandering hands and a high turnover in secretaries. The buddy was already on the way and would meet Tuckey in the Sound, 1.4 nautical miles southeast of Cedar Point where the dredger had gone down. Funny, Tuckey thought. That was a well-sheltered waterway and there hadn't been any bad weather lately. Still, things like that happen all the time at sea.

Luisa heard him in the bathroom and padded out in bare feet. She made a face when he told her he'd be away at least two or three days but would call from Mobile as soon as they had re-floated the dredger. She made him blueberry waffles and coffee while he put on his blue jeans and work shirt and got a few things together. She insisted on coming to the marina with him. She could drive the pick-up back home instead of leaving it unattended at the marina for two or three days. It made sense to Tuckey. He went out to the pick-up while she put on a pretty cotton print dress. It was less than a half-hour to the marina and at that time of day there was no traffic. Another beautiful southern morning, Luisa thought, as she snuggled closer to her husband during the short drive.

The marina office wasn't open when they arrived and Luisa promised she'd let them know where he'd gone. She followed him along the dock, past gleaming aisles of yachts, working boats and pleasure craft, to where Reef Runner was moored. They hadn't been down to the boat for a week and Tuckey took several minutes to run his checks and make sure all his dive and salvage gear was where it should be. She waited on deck as he busied himself, her gaze wandering affectionately

125

over the bulky blue and white work boat they had so often used for pleasure trips in the gulf. Cruising, fishing or just pottering along the coast to some secluded beach or bay that no-one could reach except by water, then spending the day lazing, picnicking and making love. Soon there would be three of them and she looked forward to the days they would spend together as a family on their boat. It was a life Luisa had hardly dared dream about until Emmet had left the navy for good and asked her to marry him. There had been some anxious minutes a few days ago when that sinister man had come to their house. He hadn't stayed long, hadn't even finished the beer she brought him. But it was long enough to upset Emmet. Later that night, in bed, he had held her and reassured her that his old life wasn't coming back to reclaim him after all, that he was home for good. She believed him. Until then there had always been a few doubts. She knew he had held an important job in the navy and that some of his work had been secret and dangerous and she fretted silently that one day that world might intrude into their peace and take him away from her again. Now, she knew, Emmet had made a decision. He belonged to her. She had never felt safer or more content. Their baby would be a boy, she knew. Her husband deserved a son. He would be a good father... and there would be more children after that. She wanted a daughter. Luisa liked big families. She had been sixth in a family of nine. They had been poor but her children would be more fortunate. When he was ready they kissed each other and embraced for a long time before she leaped nimbly from the boat back to the dock. He looked at her and shook his head. God, he wished she wouldn't do that. She smiled mischievously back and blew a kiss. Tuckey slipped the mooring, stepped into the cabin and started the engine. Before backing away from the dock he leaned out of the wheelhouse window to give Luisa one last wave. She was waving with one hand and absently stroking her swollen belly with the other when the gas pump nearest to her exploded in a massive sheet of flame.

There were two gas pumps on the dock, each with its own tank, buried in concrete beneath the jetty and each containing 90,000 litres of marine fuel, pumped along a safety line from the marina's central fuel tanks a kilometre away on dry land. It was supposed to be impossible for them to explode, even under the impact of collision. But now they exploded, almost simultaneously, ignited by a pack of high-explosive plastique attached to each pump and triggered by shortwave radio signal. One second Luisa was on the dock, waving to him, the next she was engulfed by a boiling cloud of flame. She didn't even have time to scream. Tuckey watched in horror as the tiny figure of his wife and unborn child flared for a moment then disappeared in the inferno. It was the last image he would have on earth. A split second later the blast wave reached him followed by a searing wall of flame. There was no pain. Only the sensation of overwhelming, all-consuming heat. He felt his flesh ripple, fragment and fall in pieces from his bones, as though it belonged to someone else. Then a wave of molten lava swallowed all remaining consciousness and Emmet Tuckey descended gratefully to his death.

4

DEATH FROM ABOVE

Fort Bragg, North Carolina, June 16

It was almost one o'clock in the morning when two identical
blue Chevvy sedans pulled up to the guardpost at the main
entrance to Fort Bragg in the leafy backwoods of North
Carolina. The corporal of the guard had been told to expect
a senior officer with VIP civilians and when he approached
the first car he wasn't disappointed. He knew a major-general
when he saw one. And he knew enough to go by the book.
As soon as he had saluted the general's rank he asked for
identification. The Pentagon's Chief Liaison Officer to
SOCOM, Major-General Roy Kramer and his driver unsmil-
ingly complied. The corporal looked in the back and saw
two civilians — one, casually dressed, about the same age
as the general, the other a younger man in a cream coloured
suit. The numbers checked with his duty list. He walked to
the second car and again inspected the ID of the military
driver. There were three more civilians in the second car and
that checked too. He had not been given the names of the
civilians and that irked him but his orders were clear. General
Kramer was their passport. He was expected and he had
checked out. The guard could only speculate what it was
all about. He walked back to the first car, saluted the general
again, and signalled the trooper in the guardpost to raise
the boom. The two Chevvies hissed quietly onto the base
and turned in the direction of the Stockade, Delta Force
HQ, while the corporal stepped back inside the guardpost
and picked up the phone.

General Marsh, Commanding Officer, Delta Force, Fort Bragg, was waiting outside the main gate to the Stockade when the two cars arrived. He knew Roy Kramer quite well. Whenever he had a major problem at Fort Bragg, Kramer was the man he had to deal with. Both had gone to West Point though Kramer had preceded Marsh by seven years. Both had attained captain's rank in Vietnam though Kramer had been steered into high administrative duty on his return and Marsh had elected to stay with his original unit, the 82nd Airborne, until his transfer to Special Forces where he had been promoted to General. Despite similar careers they hadn't met until Eugene Marsh had been posted to Fort Bragg two years earlier to become C.O. of a revitalised Special Forces division. Kramer and Halloran got out of the first car.

Kramer walked over to Marsh and saluted. 'Morning, General,' he said. He was followed by Halloran. Marsh returned the salute. They had been on first name terms for a year but the formality was more for the benefit of the civilians they were escorting.

'First names will be fine if that's okay with you, General,' Kramer said.

Marsh nodded. 'Especially considering none of this is happening.'

Kramer turned and introduced Halloran though General Marsh already knew Halloran by reputation. Marsh didn't entirely approve of what seemed to be going on under Delta's nose. There had already been one embarrassing operation too many under the banner of special operations and Marsh had been put in command to make sure nothing like it ever happened again. But Halloran was a man with immense influence. Whatever he was involved in had the approval of the Pentagon, the Joint Chiefs Of Staff and the White House. Marsh had made sure of that much. If it was something that would get Congress hot under the collar Marsh was covered. Higher heads would roll before his. Halloran and the civilians with him had been given the highest security clearance. Marsh knew it had to be something important considering the equipment he had been authorised to show these people and the instruction they were to get in its use. This thing had the stink of dirty tricks all over it, he decided. He also knew enough not to be too nosy. What happened here tonight and in the following few days was classified top secret. Marsh had come too far and was too long in the tooth to jeopardise his remaining years in the army. These visitors would get the full cloak and dagger treatment, as requested. The Joint Chiefs could weather the shitstorm, if it came, he thought. They deserved it. When the duty reports from the guardhouse arrived on his desk the next day they would get a quick trip to the shredder and false reports would be prepared showing there had been no unusual visitors to and from Fort Bragg between the hours of one and six am on June 16. The corporal of the guard would have been surprised to see his own signature flawlessly reproduced on the new reports. Not that he would see them again. Marsh had selected a man for duty that night who was due for transfer to the west coast in ten days. Introductions over, Marsh climbed into his jeep and nodded to the driver. The jeep sped off with the Chevvies close behind.

A few minutes later their little convoy pulled up outside a huge, darkened aircraft hangar. There were no guards, nothing to draw the attention of prying eyes. That was the reason Halloran had insisted on unmarked blue Chevvies to ferry them all from Fayetteville to Fort Bragg, rather than choppers. It was the long way round, but choppers disgorging visitors from the Pentagon and civilians with the dog-eared look of the mercenary about them had the potential to excite comment, even at Fort Bragg. The men emptied gratefully out of the cars and stretched their legs after the two-hour ride from Raleigh. Reece and Bono had been picked up at Hibbing too late to make Halloran's plane at New York. Their chartered jet had been re-routed to Raleigh, and Halloran, Lynch and Howard had waited for them in their cars on a secluded corner of the airport tarmac. This was the first time Reece and Bono had been able to catch up with Lynch since their meeting in the woods. Bono lumbered up to Lynch with a slight limp and a strange humourless smile on his face. He brought the palm of his hand down on Lynch's back with a thud that almost caved in Lynch's spine.

'Really liked the grenade in the shitter,' Bono said breezily. 'Nearly blew my cock off.'

'You're welcome,' Lynch muttered through clenched teeth.

Reece caught up. 'You shoulda been there when he came runnin' backwards out of the can with his eyes shut and his pecker in his hand,' he sniggered. 'Man, there's never a camera around when you need one.'

General Marsh led the way through a side door into the hangar followed by Kramer, Halloran, Howard and the others. Lynch, Reece and Bono lugged bags which suggested they would be staying a few days. Temporarily relieved of the tension of duty, the two Defense Department drivers were able to join their army counterpart to have a smoke and speculate quietly about what the hell was going on. Not one of them came close.

It took the new arrivals a few seconds to adjust to the glare of the harsh fluorescent lighting inside the hangar. When they had blinked away the dazzle they saw an empty steel cavern with a huge, black bird of prey perched in the rafters, with wings outstretched and the body of a man dangling lifelessly from its talons. Then they realised it was a kind of parachute, a voluminous black parachute, fully deployed and suspended from the rafters by a network of wires. The corpse was a store dummy which hung from the parachute's harness. Lynch's eyes were drawn to the apparatus attached to the front of the harness. It was a rectangular black box about the size of a regular lunch box and there were black leads connecting it to the harness straps. He had never seen anything like it before on any of the parachutes he'd used.

Its positioning on the dummy's chest ruled out a reserve 'chute. It could have been a kind of drogue — a mini-chute used to stabilise tumbling skydivers free falling in tandem — but they were usually deployed from leg pockets. Lynch's thoughts were interrupted by the sound of loud, rapidly approaching footsteps. He looked around to see a muscular, balding black man in his late thirties, wearing the uniform of a Master Sergeant of the 82nd Airborne, striding towards them across the oil-streaked floor of the hangar. As he drew closer Lynch saw the name on the man's chest tag was Norton.

'Sir!' The man had a voice like a cannon and the echo rattled the hangar walls. He saluted Kramer and his C.O. and presented himself. Kramer glanced around the odd group of men gathered in the hangar in the middle of the night and deferred gratefully to Marsh, glad his escort role was now concluded. Kramer was fifty-three, a little on the plump side with skin like milk-fed veal and Hollywood grey hair. He was getting a little too old for this sort of thing, he tried to tell himself, but something inside him relished every minute of it too. He felt tired... but his mind was wide awake. Kramer strolled over to a cluster of bleaehers stacked against one wall and sat down, followed by Halloran and Howard. The Major-General knew about the new Samson range of smart parachutes, designed and built by the Purbright Corporation under contract to the Department Of Defense. He knew this model had been eight years in development and costs had been close to $60 million. Production models would cost $40,000 each — virtually all of that tied up in the electronic bag of tricks attached to the harness. He hoped to hell it performed better than the M1 battle tank, which had cost the army a couple of billion dollars and still didn't work properly. But, until now, he hadn't seen the 'zoot 'chute' and he wanted to know how it worked.

Marsh introduced himself and returned the gaze of the men now watching him. Even if he hadn't already known of Halloran he would have recognised the older man's air of authority. Howard, he guessed accurately, was Halloran's flunky. A flunky with a gun under his jacket. He didn't much care for that either. He knew from the way the other three carried themselves that they had seen regular service, but not recently. Marsh let his eyes settle for a moment on Bono. The big man was wearing army surplus baggies, dirty grey sneakers, service issue T-shirt and a blue baseball cap that said 'Destruction Engineer' on the front. Marsh didn't know their names and he wouldn't be told them either. After tonight he would never see any of them again. And that was fine by him too. He knew soldiers who had turned mercenary. He had to concede that they must be good at whatever it was they did or they wouldn't be here. Either that or they were utterly expendable. He wondered if they really knew themselves. Whatever they were up to was dirty and Marsh thought it was probably better that he didn't know. He wanted to retire from the army with some illusions about his country still intact.

Marsh was already familiar with the parachute. Two hundred prototypes had been delivered to Fort Bragg for testing and assessment in field conditions. Because its existence was still supposed to be a secret, a special test unit had been formed to conduct the tests. All the jumps, so far, had been carried out away from regular drop-zones and exercise areas. There was no such thing as regular training hours for Delta. Marsh had made a dozen jumps with the new 'chute himself and considered it to be the most important advance in airborne infantry warfare since the arrival of the C5 Starlifter. He also knew the high-tech parachute was too expensive for conventional deployment. It would be reserved for special operations for some time to come, unless a way could be found to bring costs down, but he was pleased because a new role had been found for the paratrooper in the era of techno-warfare.

'Gentlemen,' General Marsh began, 'what you see before you is the Samson Nighthawk. You only have to look at

133

it to see why it is called the Nighthawk. It is beautiful, it is strong, it is efficient and it scares the shit out of anything else in the sky...' He paused for effect. 'Except maybe a man flying a Tomcat. And he won't even know you're there. It is the most technically advanced parachute in the world. Nothing quite like it has ever existed before. In a world where conventional tactical thinking says the infantryman is obsolete on the battlefield, the Nighthawk changes the whole scenario yet again. When you try it for yourselves you will understand why. You will know what it feels like to manoeuvre through the sky with the grace and flexibility of a bird. And you have the privilege of pioneering a new era, a new dimension in airborne warfare.' Marsh paused to let his words sink in. 'I believe there are two of you who have never jumped before.' He didn't have to say which two.

'Sergeant Norton is the best jump instructor at Fort Bragg. He paid his dues in the Airborne. He is also the most experienced man in operational use of the Nighthawk... in the world. The usual time-span for training recruits to be paratroopers is twenty-four weeks. We have been given six days to turn you into paratroopers and teach you how to use the Nighthawk. This is impossible. That is why Sergeant Norton is here. Sergeant Norton specialises in the impossible. Gentlemen,' he concluded, 'you and I will not see each other again.' Marsh left the words hanging in the air for a brief moment. 'Good luck,' he added, then turned the floor over to Norton and joined Kramer on the bench. Lynch, Reece and Bono began to feel a little exposed out on the wide hangar floor. Norton took his cue and savoured the moment, taking the time to eyeball each man separately. Nobody avoided his gaze.

'In the Airborne,' he began, 'it is a court martial offence to refuse an order to jump.' The sergeant's voice echoed through the hangar. 'You men are so smart you do not have to take orders. I will not order you to jump. I will tell you to jump. If you do not jump I will throw you out of the

134

aircraft.' He waited for a moment. 'However, you and I know that will not be necessary . . . because no white man in America wants to suffer the indignity of being thrown off an airplane by a black man.'

Halloran stirred on the bleachers. He had forgotten how much fun this was.

'The first few days will be easy,' Norton continued. 'In the Airborne only pussies use a 'chute to jump under five thousand feet. As we all know, because of his ghetto background, a black man can jump five thousand feet with a colour TV set under one arm, a video cassette recorder under the other arm and run a hundred yards in under nine point eight five. However, something may have escaped your attention . . . but it has not escaped mine — you do not have the advantage of being black men. Therefore,' he grinned mirthlessly, 'my expectations will not be quite so high.'

Lynch shook his head. This was more like Broadway than the army.

'What's the matter son, something wrong?'

For a moment Lynch thought Norton was speaking to him but it was Reece who had caught the sergeant's attention. The nuggety little Italian was frowning.

Reece mumbled something.

'What's that, son?' Norton said even louder. 'You'll have to speak up because nobody heard you and we all want to hear what you have to say because everybody likes to laugh.'

Reece looked sullen and mumbled again but this time it was audible. 'I don't like heights.'

'Yes, indeed, that is very funny,' Norton said resuming his stroll back and forth in front of the three men, hands clasped behind his back. 'We are all very happy you have shared that with us tonight.'

Bono looked down at Reece disbelievingly. 'Bit late to tell us now, ain't it?'

Norton raised a finger at Bono but looked directly at Reece.

'Don't worry about it son,' he said. 'You will be doing most of your jumping at night. Therefore you will never know how far off the ground you are.'

Reece groaned softly.

Norton beckoned them closer to the parachute. Lynch stole a glance at Halloran. The bastard was beaming, enjoying the show.

'As you will have noted,' Norton continued, 'the canopy of the Nighthawk has an unconventional configuration, rather like a figure eight. This is to accommodate the vents which give the Nighthawk its superior manoeuvrability. The Nighthawk also has a canopy with a diameter of 200 square metres. That is thirty more square metres of canopy area than conventional parachutes. This also gives it superior lifting power. The Nighthawk can safely carry a load of 545 kilos without any impairment to its performance. Which means it can carry a man and four hundred and fifty kilos of ordnance without adversely affecting performance. The canopy is still made of radar-absorbent carbon reinforced nylon because nothing has been proven better.'

'I thought all parachutes were undetectable on radar,' Lynch said.

'Oh good,' Norton said. 'The class genius. It is true that a single parachute, even a cluster of parachutes, is unlikely to show up on a radar screen. However, most military parachutes carry a quantity of radar reflectant metal, either the armaments the soldier will be wearing or larger objects like howitzers, vehicles, ammunition, and even large field guns. A close formation of conventional military parachutes carrying sufficient armament might create an unusual radar signature which, in certain parts of the world, would attract unwelcome attention. There is the added complication that, in a battle zone, those 'chutes have the unfortunate habit of resembling the kind of metal chaff our friends in the air force eject to confuse heat-seaking missiles. A man in a parachute is peculiarly vulnerable to impact by missile. A

136

formation of Nighthawks, however, is designed to be quite invisible to even the most sophisticated modern radar. It works. We know this from our own exercises.'

Norton paused for a moment. 'You will also have noticed that the Nighthawk is black. This is not to make it sexually attractive to strangers although it has been known to have this effect. As the name would suggest the Nighthawk is intended for use at night. Its colour is designed to make it difficult, if not impossible, for the naked eye to detect in the dark. The airborne soldier is most vulnerable when making his landing approach. It is desirable therefore that people on the ground, including sentries who may be looking for unfriendly objects in the sky, do not see the Nighthawk until it is too late.

'Gentlemen, because you are so smart you will have already determined that the Nighthawk is not a parachute for pussies. However, the military understands that during a covert operation jump or in the heat of battle things can go inexplicably wrong. Men get confused. Sometimes they get hurt. Therefore, the Nighthawk has been designed to think for itself. Even if the soldier is 100 per cent incapacitated. As in dead. Here, gentlemen, are the brains of the Nighthawk.'

Sergeant Norton tapped the satchel-sized black box on the dummy's chest.

'You may have heard of NAVSTAR,' he continued. 'NAVSTAR is a network of eighteen satellites that the US has in space orbit. The last one went up to complete the network in 1988 so what we have here is brand new, gentlemen. NAVSTAR transmits a stream of navigational information which enables any missile, airplane, ship or vehicle on land, sea or in the air to determine its position, speed and its relationship to its destination with unprecedented accuracy. Therefore, by using NAVSTAR technology it is possible to navigate any moving object to any target over long distances... with pinpoint accuracy. The Nighthawk's NAVSTAR sensors also take into consideration wind assistance or resistance and will calculate alterations in descent rate, forward air speed and ground speed accordingly.' Norton paused to let the implications sink in.

'NAVSTAR was originally intended to impress the Russians by letting them know that in a nuclear war there would no longer be any such thing as a near miss. Until now an ICBM which landed within a mile of its target was considered accurate. With NAVSTAR we have been able to show the Soviet generals that they are no longer safe in their underground bunkers with half a mile of mountain and reinforced concrete to protect them. We now have the technology to score repeated direct hits, to put one, two or even three nukes right on top of their heads.'

'Gentlemen, what NAVSTAR can do for a missile it can do for a man in a Nighthawk. It dispenses with the need for homing beacons which requires at least one friendly agent on the ground in covert operations. The Nighthawk turns a man into a missile. A human missile. And, because a man is smarter than a missile, he is potentially more dangerous. If you can put an armed man precisely where you want him, and he can think and act for himself once he is there, then that man is far more versatile, far more deadly than any missile.' Norton rapped the black box with his knuckles. The trio crowded around attentively. They could see four dials on top of the receiver. Lynch guessed them to be altometer, two speedometers, one giving air speed, the other giving compensated ground speed and compass.

'This is the Nighthawk's NAVSTAR receiver,' Norton continued. 'The receiving antenna flows through these leads into the harness, through the 'chute lines and into the canopy seams so the black box receives a constant stream of data, giving it long distance directional accuracy and a degree of control previously impossible in parachute technology. The aerodynamics of the Nighthawk itself are so sophisticated that all the man in the harness has to do is exert minimum effort to monitor the instruments on his NAVSTAR receiver and adjust trim via his steering lines to change altitude, speed and direction. The brains of the Nighthawk will do the rest for him. The receiver will keep the Nighthawk on track and carry the man right to the bullseye.

'Gentlemen,' he paused. 'The Nighthawk is idiot proof.' Then he looked pointedly at Reece. 'Almost idiot proof.'

They were the longest six days of Lynch's life. Each time he woke up and looked in the mirror he swore he looked another year older. For the whole six days, Lynch, Reece and Bono rarely saw daylight. From that first night they were billeted in cots inside the hangar at Fort Bragg and their meals were brought in. The hangar was equipped with toilets, shower facilities, an office with a telephone and was well away from the busy core of the base. General Marsh assigned a couple of dog-handlers to discourage the curious. The army mechanics who normally used the hangar were told a couple of choppers were being fitted with some highly sensitive new night sight equipment. To further mislead anyone who saw the trio they were issued with Airborne uniforms and jumpsuits. Marsh knew that rumours and speculation were inevitable. Like all concentrated population centres the fuel of life on an army base was gossip. He merely saw to it that there were enough contradictory rumours about the activities at hangar nine to ensure nobody really knew what was going on.

Lynch, Reece and Bono crawled into their cots around four am that first day, Norton's booming voice still ringing in their ears. They slept till early afternoon and training began in earnest at 1600 hours the same day. That immediately became their new regime. Each working day started at four in the afternoon and didn't finish until sometime after dawn the following day, when Norton said it did. The Airborne veteran first schooled them in the operation and performance of standard military parachutes. They learned about the equipment. They learned about everything that could go wrong,

139

what they could expect and what they could do to fix it and Reece grew paler and paler.

Norton strung them up in harnesses and put them through a few landing rolls. 'We don't usually do this shit no more,' he commented, as he watched Reece and Bono's clumsy efforts. 'But you know what they say, falling is easy — landing is the hard part.'

They had been listening and learning and training for twelve hours straight when Norton told them they would be jumping at dawn. They would be using standard 'chutes for a simple low altitude jump from 600 metres, he said. Just to let them know how it felt. Lynch was all too aware that it would be his first jump in eight years. God alone knew what was going through the minds of the two ex-Marines as they prepared for the first parachute jump of their lives. He already thought he knew about Reece just by looking at his face. But Norton was a smart and tough operator, Lynch saw. He barely gave Reece a free moment to dwell on his natural fear of stepping out of an aircraft into thin air.

It was just getting light when the Bell Cobra took off at 0530 in front of the hangar. There was no wind as they filed aboard. The air was cool and tasted fresh and Lynch noticed there was a heavy dew. Marsh had found them a pilot qualified to fly choppers and aircraft so they could keep the man all week. Like Norton, the pilot had been made aware that what they were doing had the highest security classification and his promotion prospects depended very much on keeping his mouth shut.

The Cobra thrummed up into a clear, starry sky and wheeled northwest, away from Fort Bragg, and its environs and its busy surrounding highways. The pilot flew out over the protected beechwoods where Delta, the Rangers and other Special Forces groups, conducted their reconaissance and surveillance and other secret tactical exercises. It was going to be a beautiful dawn, Lynch thought. He could just make out the others in the dim, amber cabin light. From the expression on Reece's face he wasn't thinking too much about the dawn. Reece had been under the impression he'd have at least another day to steel his nerve for this first jump. Lynch looked across the cabin at Bono. The big man had his eyes closed, as though he were asleep. Norton wasn't wearing a 'chute and only Norton had a radio equipped helmet to communicate with the pilot. They would jump on Norton's signal. It took barely a minute to reach the drop-zone. Norton shook Bono roughly and signalled that they'd arrived. Somewhere below was the drop-zone, a clearing in the beechwoods about the size of a football field, used for most training jumps at Fort Bragg. The chopper circled once. Norton slid open the Cobra's side hatch and the cabin was suddenly swamped by the unmuffled roar of the rotor blades. Norton said something to the pilot and they circled once more. Lynch stuck his head out of the hatch. None of them were wearing goggles for such a simple jump and the blast from the rotor wash stung his face and squeezed tears from his eyes. Norton was smart, he thought. They were on the cusp of a new dawn — just light enough to make out the surrounding countryside and to see the lighter oval shape of the clearing below amidst the greyness of the trees, yet dark enough to stretch the jumper's senses to the limits. Reece white-knuckled one of the cabin struts as the chopper banked and its open door yawned invitingly at him. It didn't seem to occur to him that he was perfectly equipped for falling out of an aircraft. The chopper circled once more as Norton tried to time the dawn light perfectly. He wanted them to know what it felt like. He wanted them to be scared. But he didn't want them to break a leg. It was a fine line. Norton looked at his watch. Reveille would be in twenty-five minutes. It would have to do. He spoke to the pilot again and the chopper slowed to a hovering position.

Most of the LZ was dirt, grass and scrub, Norton had told them, with a few trees and bushes to make things interesting. In the middle of the clearing was a white plastic cross.

All they had to do was jump, count to four, pull the ripcord and try not to drift too far from the cross. If they did land in the trees, he warned, ball up, try not to break anything important and wait until somebody came to cut them down. With each second of descent they would gain better ground definition and be able to use their steering lines more effectively to stay on course. He had used fully deployed parachutes in the hangar to show them which lines to tug to steer the 'chute left and right, forwards and backwards, up and down. They had each climbed into a harness and hung there, like salamis in a butcher shop, memorising which lines did what while Norton paced back and forth in front of them, telling them what to do. 'Don't tug too hard,' he told them. That could fold or collapse the canopy and they could go into an uncontrolled fall from which there was no recovery. 'Tug nice and gentle,' he said. 'Just like you're tuggin' on your little white pecker.'

Now, in the chopper, Norton had insisted each man wear only one parachute. Fewer complications that way, he said. Besides, they weren't using a static line to open their 'chutes automatically as they exited the aircraft so it was an added incentive to get it right the first time. Lynch looked across at Reece again and saw that his face had assumed an alabaster sheen. He wondered how much incentive Reece could stand. Still, Lynch reminded himself, in all the time he had known them both, living, working and fighting with them, he had never known either of them to quit. They were either too dumb or too brave. He wasn't sure which. But that was why they were here.

Norton tapped him on the shoulder, the signal to jump first. Lynch put everything but his training out of his head, gave the thumbs up to Reece and did a perfect forward roll through the hatch. The roar of the chopper evaporated in the rush of air and he felt himself tumbling through the empty darkness. Zero to 150 kilometres per hour in seven seconds. Better than a Porsche. His fist was already on the toggle.

142

He counted out the four seconds and pulled. There was a loud whoosh of unfurling fabric behind his head and he felt himself yanked to a halt in mid-air. Then the dreamy, exhilarating sensation of a gentle, controlled downward drift. And then it came, that almost forgotten thrill. The delicious charge of electricity, the surge of ecstacy that accompanies that unleashed tide of adrenalin bringing with it the certainty that once more you have risked death... and won. He looked up at the red and white canopy over his head and then around at the stars in the dawn sky, the first blush of the sun in the east. All his exhaustion had been flushed away by that raw, primitive rush of triumph, his senses heightened to an almost sexual pitch. Lynch snapped himself back and looked down. The gloom had yielded to a greater definition. He could see clearly the dark tree line around the LZ and about a hundred metres to his left, slightly to the front of him, a small dirty white X. He tugged the steering lines and the 'chute bucked dramatically throwing him around the sky like a shuttlecock. He took his hands away and he stabilised immediately. No rock 'n' roll today, Lynch decided. He would leave that for the show-offs at airshows. He tweaked the lines more gently and the 'chute responded with a slow, graceful swing to the left and he began to rush down towards the cross. Too fast, he decided. He could see trees and bushes rushing towards him. He pulled back and the 'chute slowed but it was too late. The cross flashed beneath him in a sudden blur. He bent his knees, locked them together and readied himself to roll.

For Reece it was the worst minute of his life. As soon as Lynch had disappeared Norton had signalled to him. Reece had hesitated only a second then thrown himself through the open door. He was terrified. The only sound was the thump of blood in his ears as his heart rate tripled. He had tried not to dwell on it. Like they said in the Marines, 'Don't think about it, just do it'. That was how he solved most of these things. You confronted something so dangerous, so

143

blatantly, horrifically dangerous that it made no sense to go any further... but you did. You shut off all the instinctive, primeval signals sending shrill warning messages to the brain... and you went ahead and did it anyway. And up till now that had always worked for him. But now the engine that drove him was stalling.

Reece wasn't a coward. He knew that — he'd tested himself too often. He knew what fear was. This was something else. All night, listening to Norton's theories, going over the equipment, dangling in that stupid harness he had known he was going to have problems. At first it was a niggling sense of unease, the queasy, unnerving suspicion that something just didn't feel right. Then he remembered that time when he was fourteen and he had gone on vacation with his family. He and his mom and dad and younger sister had piled into the family wagon and they had gone west to stay with relatives and see the sights and they had gone to Arizona to see the Grand Canyon. When they got there they had walked out onto one of the look-outs and he had looked over the railing. That was the first time he'd felt the fear. He thought he knew what to expect; a spectacular chasm, a giant hole in the ground. But he wasn't prepared for the abyss that waited for him when he looked over that railing. To him it had felt like he was looking off the edge of the planet. Almost immediately he had felt some invisible power, some evil, irresistible force come rearing up from far below, between the glowing red walls, trying to take hold of him and pull him over the edge, to drag him down to the bottom of the canyon to his death. He hadn't been able to fight it. He turned around and walked away on shaky legs and bought himself a Pepsi while he waited for the others to finish taking pictures of each other. Leaning against the railing with their backs to the void, for Christ's sake. For years afterwards he had had nightmares about falling. As he grew up and more important matters consumed his interest, like getting laid and surviving the Marine Corps, the nightmares were shunted off into some dark and forgotten attic of his mind.

144

Until now. Now he had to face it again. When Reece propelled himself through that open hatch, into the hissing blackness, it was with a kind of numb, dread fatalism: the sure and certain knowledge that whatever happened was beyond his control. He was back at the mercy of all his unresolved childhood fears, the plaything of some evil, unseen force and it alone would decide whether he should be put down gently or hurled disdainfully to the ground.

Reece had his fist clenched so tightly around the toggle of the ripcord he thought his fingerprints would be moulded into its shiny plastic surface. 'One chimpanzee... two chimpanzee... three chimpanzee...' He counted too quickly, pulled the ripcord and nothing happened! A scream formed on his lips but his throat was too dry to give it form. There was a sudden loud snap followed by the terrifying sound of ripping, shredding fabric. Then he was jerked to a dead stop in the sky and held there like an insect seized by its wings. He began to float gently earthward. He was stunned into disbelief for a moment. Then Henry Reece began to believe that this time he might live.

'Okay, you pussies...' Norton's deafening bellow burst in upon Reece's fragile calm. He was lying on the cool, damp ground unhurt, immobile, suffused with relief.

'C'mon, move it...' Norton was calling to them with a loud hailer from the door of the chopper as it settled beside the white plastic cross. 'We got time for one more before breakfast.'

Reece got up awkwardly. Something crackled beneath his feet. He looked down. He was standing on one arm of the plastic cross. He stifled a jittery laugh and then, for a moment, thought that he was going to be sick.

June 19

On the second day they made two jumps from the hovering Cobra. This time from 1,500 metres and by starlight only. Their only guide was the white plastic cross picked out by ground lights. On the third day they jumped from 1,500 metres while the chopper circled at 100 kph in the dark. Norton was trying to push them as far as he could with each successive day without actually breaking their nerve. Lynch and Bono were coping. But he could see Reece was struggling. Every time Reece went up it was like he died anew.

On the fourth day they jumped for the first time using the Nighthawks. They boarded a Hercules C-130 at 0400 hours sharp. The Hercules was a lot of aircraft for three jumpers but this was the plane they would be using for the operation. With its walk-off rear ramp, it was the paratrooper's perfect jumping platform. They gathered in the belly of the Hercules, three of them geared to jump, Norton wearing only his usual olive green jump suit and clipped to a safety line. After the chopper, Lynch felt there was something almost sedate about strolling down a ramp and diving gracefully into 3,000 metres of fresh air at 200 kph. Norton told them it was a simple jump for the Nighthawks but they would all be able to appreciate what the revolutionary new glider 'chute could do. He also wanted them to know how it felt to jump from the Hercules at night and at a reasonable altitude before they went higher and had to use oxygen. Tonight, Norton said, they would jump with a light following wind of two to three knots. Enough for the Nighthawks to carry them to Palm Springs, he said. This meant they would not be directly over the DZ before leaving the aircraft and when they exited the C-130 they would not see anything but pitch blackness for a few moments. The wind and the Nighthawks would carry them over the DZ where they would then be able to see the illuminated white cross and complete their descent as usual.

The roar inside the fuselage from the four throttled down Allison turboprops was deafening. No-one tried to talk. Lynch was fascinated by the luminescent red figures spinning through the dials on top of his Nighthawk NAVSTAR receiver. It was uncanny. Wherever the plane went, whatever its heading, whatever its altitude, the Nighthawk receiver copied it perfectly. Except the receiver wasn't tuned in to the aircraft's instrumentation. It was getting its own data from a string of 18 satellites hanging thousands of miles away in the heavens. Lynch felt a tingle of excitement. He could hardly wait to exit the aircraft and test the performance of the Nighthawk for himself even for what he knew was a mere boy scout jump.

The co-pilot twisted around in his seat and gave the stand-by signal. Norton motioned the men to get ready. They each unclipped their safety hooks and turned to face the exit ramp. The moment the ramp swung open and the howling black mouth of the night appeared Reece knew he wasn't going to jump. The last half dozen jumps had been bad enough. Each one was worse than the one before. Each one had shredded his nerves that little bit more, gnawing at his willpower like a rat until now there was nothing left. He had used all his reserves and then some. Reece hadn't slept at all for the previous twenty-four hours wondering where he would dredge up the last few scraps of courage to face this moment. Now he knew he couldn't. The childhood fear that had lain submerged in the darkest corners of his memory all these years had suddenly reared up again. He stared at the gaping black maw of the night, knowing there was nothing down there for 3,000 metres — more than three kilometres. He froze, unable to move.

Norton had been watching. He saw the fear and homed straight in on it. He signalled Reece to go first. Reece clung to a metal stanchion and shook his head. Lynch and Bono watched in silence. Lynch knew what Norton was trying to do. He was trying to work some kind of miracle on the two ex-Marines. Either they learned to jump or they weren't coming on this operation. And it was too late for any of them to back out now. Unless one of them died in training. Lynch had already decided that whatever happened, he wasn't going to interfere. Reece was on his own.

147

'Get outta this fuckin' plane, son,' Norton yelled, his voice punching a hole in the roar of the engines.

Reece turned his head to the vibrating metal fuselage, a deep sense of shame washing through him, but not enough to wash away the fear. He had gone beyond his limit. There was nothing left.

'Shit,' Norton swore. The co-pilot was watching them, waiting. A sickly green light flickered over Norton's face as the co-pilot switched on the go light, assuming Norton had misunderstood. Norton signalled them to go round once more. The co-pilot turned away and the Hercules revved and banked around one more time. Norton unclipped himself and stumbled across the cabin to stand next to Reece.

'Avgas is a bit too fuckin' expensive to keep flyin' around in circles while you find your nerve, son.'

Reece didn't budge.

'Get out or I'm gonna throw you out.'

Nothing.

Norton grabbed Reece's arm.

Reece whirled on him. 'You're trying to fuckin' kill me,' he screamed, a thread of white spittle trailing from his mouth. His voice had a high, unnatural pitch neither Lynch nor Reece had heard before. It was the sound of terror.

'Yes,' Norton yelled hoarsely back. His face only inches away from Reece, the cords on his muscular neck bulging like ropes. 'Yes, I'm trying to kill you. I'm tryin' to kill you because there is no way you can be a paratrooper in one week. I am tryin' to kill you because if you survive me nobody can fuckin' kill you.'

Norton grabbed Reece by the shoulders from behind and pulled. Reece clung to the aircraft with the terrible strength that only naked terror can find. But Norton wrenched him loose. The Hercules had begun a new approach. The pilot and co-pilot could see the small white snowflake of the illuminated DZ cross ahead and below through the cockpit windows. The co-pilot squirmed around in his seat and looked back down the cabin but couldn't distinguish Norton from the strangely tense huddle in the rear. He grinned to himself. He liked it when somebody's nerve failed. It made him feel better. He pushed the switch for the go light again and the sickly green flash washed through the cabin.

The instant the green light came on, Norton moved. He increased his hold on Reece to an unbreakable grip, swung him brutally away from the fuselage then ran with him down the ramp. Norton couldn't have turned back even if he had wanted to. On the last two steps Norton latched onto Reece's back like a limpet, dug his hands deep under the harness straps, wrapped his legs around Reece's waist and they both plunged into open space together. Lynch and Bono watched in disbelief at the two figures as they tumbled over the lip of the exit ramp and disappeared into the blackness.

They turned to look at each other. Bono wore a mildly puzzled expression on his face.

'That's not normal is it?'

Lynch shrugged, took a series of shuffling steps down the ramp and jumped. Bono hesitated only a moment then followed.

Norton and Reece tumbled through the blackness in a deadly embrace. All either of them could hear was the hiss of the rushing wind. Reece hadn't moved a muscle since they had exited the aircraft. Norton had no idea whether he was conscious or whether he was even alive. It wouldn't be the first time a man's heart had accelerated past bursting point in a moment of acute terror. Norton could feel his own heart pounding in his chest as he struggled to find the ripcord toggle without losing his grip on Reece. There was no point in Norton trying to get Reece to do anything. Reece was wearing a jump helmet and Norton's words would have been whipped away the moment they left his lips. Norton thanked his maker that they were jumping with the Nighthawk. He wouldn't have attempted it with any other 'chute. Even so, he wasn't in the best position to execute an ideal opening.

149

The 'chute was between them, sandwiched between Reece's back and Norton's chest. The moment Norton pulled the ripcord the force of the 'chute opening could knock him off. Either that or he could foul the opening, collapse the canopy and the two of them together would make a major impression on the North Carolina woodlands.

Goddamn, he thought wildly. He might have blown it. He couldn't find the toggle. In the back of his mind the seconds were counting down to danger level. They were already accelerating from a tumble into a lethal spin. His fingers scrabbled desperately over Reece's chest. Suddenly he felt Reece stir. A moment late Reece's fist clamped down on his hand. Norton waited. Then Reece's other hand jammed the ripcord toggle into Norton's fingers. Norton unclamped his legs from Reece's waist for a split second, locked them lower down around the knees and squirmed down so his head and shoulders were just below the top of the 'chute pack. The fingers of both men closed around the ripcord toggle and both yanked at the same time. Norton hung on.

The Nighthawk whooshed past Norton's face. A moment later there was a terrific jerk as their fall was abruptly cut and for a couple of seconds they bounced around the sky like a shuttlecock while the Nighthawk tried to stabilise its awkward load. Norton's legs were thrown loose. His arms felt as though they would be wrenched from their sockets. He gripped harder, even if it meant squeezing the last breath of life from Reece's body. Two hundred square metres of reinforced canopy came into play and the Nighthawk stabilised. They went into a controlled descent and Norton wrapped his legs back around Reece's knees. He struggled to look around but could see nothing. The wind flooded his eyes with tears. Norton had no idea how far they had to go but was certain they would land in trees. A few seconds later he was proved right.

He felt his boots clip the first branches and braced himself. They were drifting downwards and sideways at about thirty knots. They hit the next tree like a wrecking ball. It was hard to tell what did the most damage in the blind, confused scramble of broken branches and crashing foliage that followed. Norton felt the skin and clothing flayed from his back and his legs as the smaller branches raked him from head to toe. Then he hit a big branch and despite his grip on Reece he was knocked away, grabbing, scrabbling blindly at anything to stop him from falling, knowing he might be six feet from the ground ... or sixty. He felt himself falling through space again and for a moment he had no idea which way was up and which way was down. He tried to ball himself up and a second later he hit the ground and every ounce of breath was knocked from his body.

Norton had no idea how long he was out before he heard voices. It might have been minutes, it might have been half an hour. They were looking for him. He tried to yell but his lungs refused to work. Shit, he thought — he had broken his back. Now it was his turn to feel the blaze of panic. He flexed every finger and toe and was flooded with relief when they all responded. Nothing serious. Anything else was kids' stuff. He took his time and tried to pump some air back into his winded lungs. That felt better. He propped himself up on one elbow and looked around. The beams of searching flashlights danced through the trees about six metres away.

'Over here,' Norton yelled and got groggily to his feet. Everything ached but he was going to be all right.

The flashlights swivelled in his direction, slashing the morning dark and blinding him.

'Here's the other one,' he heard a voice say. That meant they had found Reece.

Two men from the DZ crew crashed through the undergrowth towards him.

'You all right?' one of them asked.

'Shit, yeah,' Norton answered. 'Next time I guess I might use a 'chute.'

One of them took his arm and led him gently to the DZ clearing. It was only forty-five metres away, Norton realised. They hadn't missed it by that much. When he got there he found Lynch, Bono and another two men from the ground crew hunkered around Reece who was sitting on the ground.

They looked Norton up and down for a moment, taking in the tattered jumpsuit, and decided he was indestructible. They turned their attention back to Reece who looked fine except that he was incapable of speech.

'Found him hung up like a Christmas stocking in the woods,' Bono said.

Reece looked up at Norton, his eyes still glazed with shock and disbelief.

'See,' Norton said. 'It's easy.'

June 20

The diagnosis at the base hospital was multiple bruises and abrasions — no broken bones for either of them. Reece and Norton had their wounds cleaned and dressed and were released after a couple of hours.

General Marsh hadn't been amused. No-one told him what had happened. It merely confirmed all his worst fears about what happened when good regular soldiers got involved with mercenaries.

Reece said very little on the ride back to the hangar in the jeep with Lynch and Bono. Lynch asked if he was going to be okay. Reece knew what Lynch was really asking. If he wasn't going to be okay he wasn't going on the operation.

He nodded.

'Sure?'

'Sure.' They had pulled up in front of the hangar before Reece spoke again.

'You ever get scared?' he asked Lynch.

Lynch smiled. 'All the time,' he said. 'All the time.' And he meant it. Reece nodded but said nothing more. He stepped inside the hangar and walked to his cot. He was asleep within minutes.

'You ever get scared?' Lynch asked Bono as they followed.

Bono looked at him, puzzled. 'No,' he said.

Norton, Lynch and Bono still had some winding down to do. It was mid-morning and the sun was high when Norton dug a bottle of Canadian Club out of the filing cabinet in the hangar's sparse office. No-one said anything for a few minutes while Norton and Bono sipped the whiskey and Lynch nursed his hundredth coffee of the morning. The office stank of iodine and whiskey. It was Lynch who spoke first.

'Where did you learn a stunt like that?' he asked softly.

'Stunt?' Norton raised his eyebrows. Then he went back to his whiskey. 'Yeah,' he smiled. 'It is a stunt... that's all it is. A dangerous fuckin' stunt. First did it in 1982. Earned a mention in the record books. The first guy in the world to jump without a 'chute, collect the 'chute from a partner in mid-air, put it on and land safely.'

He emptied his glass and poured in another generous splash for himself. 'But,' he said, 'that's the first time I've come down on the same 'chute with an unco-operative partner. I hope it tells your buddy something about the equipment we're giving you people to play with here. Sure it's scary, especially for a guy who's afraid to jump. But he doesn't have to do much. If he can find the guts to get outta the plane the Nighthawk will do the rest.'

'That was a big fuckin' chance you took out there today, pal,' Bono said.

'Not really,' Norton shrugged. 'I coulda opened the 'chute without him. But I figured the guy would come through in a pinch. All he needed was a little encouragement. Besides,' he added, grinning broadly. 'I know something you don't.'

'Yeah?' Bono's ears pricked up. 'What's that?'

Norton's grin grew even bigger. 'No white man in America wants to be found dead in a field with a black man up his ass.'

June 21

They had one last jump to do and it was going to be a killer. Their first High Altitude, High Opening jump. The Hercules would take them to 8,500 metres and they would jump 80 kilometres northwest of the DZ. Despite everything they had been through it was the first real test of the men and the Nighthawks. The Hercules took off an hour before sunrise and climbed steadily to 8,500.

Once again they were grouped in the rear of the C-130. Norton had gone over everything one last time at the briefing before they took off. All the men wore oxygen masks attached to their jump helmets with a small cylinder containing sixty minutes of oxygen clipped to the front of each harness, beside the NAVSTAR receiver. It was at least fifteen minutes more than they would need. This time they wore thermal undersuits beneath their jump suits to protect against the extreme cold they would feel at 8,500 metres. Once again Norton had reminded them to keep their arms crossed in front of them after they had opened the 'chutes. Even with thermal under-suits there was still a risk of frostbite if they held their arms up over their heads before they went below 3-4,500 metres.

'Soon as you're clear of the plane, open the 'chute and let the Nighthawk do the rest for you,' he had said. 'Keep an eye on your instruments but you don't have to fuck around with the steering till you're below 4,500.'

Once the altometer told them they were below 4,500 they would check their compass bearing, adjust trim via the steering lines and glide into the DZ.

'Remember,' Norton had said. 'You don't have to use a lot of muscle on the Nighthawk's lines. It's a sensitive bird. Pull the wrong line too hard and you'll go straight up through the fuckin' ozone hole and then we'll have a helluva time getting you back.'

The co-ordinates for the DZ had already been fed into the NAVSTAR receivers and unless each jumper made a deliberate effort to defy those co-ordinates and steer a different direction, the Nighthawk would home in on the DZ automatically. For a change they would be jumping into a three knot headwind which would reduce their descent-gliding speed from around 40 knots to 37, a ground speed of around 70 kph. That meant it would take them around an hour before they would sight the DZ, another ten to fifteen minutes to home in and land. Norton had deliberately chosen the hour before dawn for the jump so they would glide most of the way in darkness but have improving light as they approached the DZ. He figured they all had enough on their plates already. It was time to engage in a little confidence building.

The Hercules banked into its holding pattern and they could already feel the cold in the unpressurised cabin. Once more the co-pilot gave the thumbs up. This time Norton was geared up to jump with them. The exit ramp opened with a long hydraulic whine and once again they all confronted the hungry mouth of the night. Norton quickly checked each man's oxygen cylinder to ensure they were switched on and demanded the okay signal from each in turn. He watched Reece's eyes carefully through his goggles but this time there was no sign of anything. The kid had guts, Norton decided. Either that or he had given up caring.

The green light flashed and without another sign to any of them Norton led the way down the ramp and jumped. He had done all he could for them. If they didn't all follow him now that was their problem. Bono was next and then Reece. Lynch thought he saw a moment's hesitation as Reece stepped onto the ramp but then he conquered it and jumped.

Lynch followed him with an ungainly shuffle and dived. It was like throwing himself into a black hole. The roar of the Hercules faded almost instantly and then all he could hear was the hiss of the rushing wind and the sound of his own breathing as he sucked deeply on the oxygen. He forced himself to focus on the altometer and saw the numbers flashing down in a dull red blur. Lynch counted off the four seconds, probably a little too eagerly this time, he thought, and pulled his ripcord. The Nighthawk billowed out over his head, spreading its massive, invisible black wings across the sky, holding him securely in its talons. He looked down at the dials on the NAVSTAR receiver and noted thankfully that the altometer had slowed dramatically. It was better not to look at the altometer at all during free fall, Lynch decided. His speed had slowed just as rapidly. From 150kph to 100, then 80. It flickered through 79, 78, 77 and began to hold in a 70-75 range. The ground speed dial with its built-in compensator told him he was making 65-70 along the ground. Next he checked his compass bearing. He was heading due southeast... right on target for Fort Bragg. Despite his thermal suit and hood his hands and face began to feel the first creeping tendrils of cold. He sucked on the oxygen even harder. Lynch looked around and held his breath. He had forgotten how clear the night sky would be at this altitude and how brilliant the stars were. They floated past him like a parade of cosmic jewels; silent, beautiful, awe-inspiring. All he could hear was the gentle buffeting of the wind. Except for that, all was peaceful as he floated dreamily through the night, feeling for all the world like some mythical wild creature of the Milky Way. The next time he looked at the altometer he had gone through 6,000 metres and twenty minutes had passed. The yanks had built something special in the Nighthawk, Lynch knew. Riding silently up there with the stars it was easy to feel like some kind of god, he realised. No wonder Norton had come along for the ride. Daylight jumping would only be an anti-climax after something like this.

For the next ten or twelve minutes a series of updrafts carried him on an undulating path between 5,250 and 5,500 metres. It wasn't unpleasant, but he realised he had to lose some height soon or he would overshoot the DZ. Lynch tweaked the steering lines and the Nighthawk obediently dropped him 45 metres. It felt like going through a trapdoor and he didn't like it. He forced his stomach back out of

156

his throat and tweaked the lines even more gently. In the next few minutes he glided gently down through the 4,500 metre mark. The first pale fingers of dawn were already reaching over the horizon. He checked his oxygen. Twenty minutes left. Lynch switched to air and took a tentative breath. The sudden rush of cold outside air into his mask set his teeth on edge but it tasted sweet after twenty-five minutes of canned air. According to his reckoning he should be seeing the landing cross soon. There was no sign of it. He gave the steering lines a series of tweaks and descended rapidly to 2,500 metres in a series of long, exhilarating hops through the sky. Just like a giant staircase, Lynch thought. Suddenly he saw it, far across to his left and starting to slide behind him. He was right. He had overshot the DZ. Lynch gently tugged the steering lines again and began a long, slow curve into a downward spiral. He checked his watch. An hour had slipped by in what felt like half that time. Five minutes later he was over the white cross. This time he wanted to score a bullseye. He twiddled the Nighthawk's lines until it held him almost stationary in the sky. It was incredible, Lynch thought. He felt as though the Nighthawk could hold him there all night if he manipulated the lines . . . just so. He tugged the forward steering line and the Nighthawk dipped and floated gently to the ground. Lynch landed at the intersection of the cross on both feet, bent his knees a fraction to cushion the minimal impact, trotted a few feet and collapsed the canopy behind him. The Nighthawk obediently folded its wings and went to sleep for the night.

'Like that?'

Norton's ivory smile materialised out of the gloom.

'What a toy!' Lynch grinned. He was unable to disguise his exhilaration. Norton walked up to him, jump helmet hanging from one hand.

'For those who appreciate it,' he said

Lynch looked around. 'Where's Reece?'

'He's cool,' Norton said. 'He'll be okay.'

Lynch sought Reece out and took him aside for a moment.

'You going to be able to go through with this?' Lynch asked.

It took Reece a while to find the answer. 'I don't like it. I'm scared every time I go up there. And there ain't no way in the world I'm ever going to like it the way you guys do. But I don't need no black man to hold my hand either.'

Lynch smiled. Norton's psychology might be crude... but it was effective.

'The way I figure it,' Reece added, 'there's only a couple more to do. I can do that.'

'You sure?'

Reece shrugged. 'If I don't make it, you're going without me, right?'

'Right.'

'You ain't going without me,' Reece said.

Lynch nodded. It had been a good week's work, he decided. On the ride back to the hangar he thought about the weapon that had been put in their hands. What a tool for covert operations the Nighthawk was going to be. His mind roamed over the possibilities. For more than a decade America had been held captive by its own blunt force. Now the joint chiefs had acknowledged the role of Special Forces, opened up the purse strings and the result was the development of a weapon of infinite subtlety whose only application was covert warfare. A weapon with the potential to enhance the effectiveness of Special Forces almost beyond description. The Nighthawk would give the right men the ability to strike anywhere on the globe with surgical precision. No-one would know they were coming. No-one would know they were there. Small units of elite troops, delivered to the right places by airborne stealth, could change the face of politics in the Third World, the battlefield of the twenty-first century. The Nighthawk could deliver a dozen men, two dozen men, to a palace rooftop in Oman, into a besieged embassy in Tehran, a drug baron's villa in Colombia... the heart of a terrorist compound in Beirut. In the dead of night and in complete silence. Death from above. The Americans had always had the power. Now they had the subtlety to exercise it.

The cars arrived at 11 o'clock the following night to pick them up. The jeep carrying General Marsh was in front, this time followed by three Defense Department Chevvies, carrying Kramer, Halloran and Howard in the rear. Lynch, Bono and Reece were waiting, their kit bags packed. Norton was back in his shiny green uniform of a Master Sergeant in the 82nd Airborne, trouser creases so sharp they could slice bacon. Time had dragged since the last jump. There were a lot of awkward silences between men who had been through all they had in six days. But they had to admit, Norton had shown them a thing or two.

The hangar door clanged open and General Marsh strode in followed by Kramer, Halloran and Howard. This time there were two new men with them, wearing jeans and sports shirts but carrying army issue kit bags. Lynch realised that they were Vance and Cooper, the two new men on the team.

The three veterans and the two newcomers eyed each other carefully while Norton completed a quick briefing for Marsh. Vance looked big, hard and fit. By comparison Cooper looked like a weakling. But there was something in his eyes. Lynch remembered. Cooper was a sniper. He'd killed a lot of men in cold blood for his country.

It was time to go. Norton saluted and turned for a final few words to the trio he had just trained to use the Nighthawk.

'You ain't Airborne,' were his opening words, 'and don't leave here tonight thinking you are...'

Lynch saw Vance and Cooper exchange knowing glances. They must have heard about the fun with Reece and no doubt were wondering what they were getting themselves into.

'... but you do know how to get from an airplane to the ground without using a ladder now,' Norton continued. 'That's my business. What happens next, gentlemen, is your business. And I must say, I am mighty pleased not to be going with you.'

With that Norton snapped off a final salute to the officers,

159

turned smartly on his heel and marched away across the echoing hangar floor and out of their lives.

'We'll miss you too...' Bono rasped as the sergeant's footsteps died away.

Halloran drew Lynch aside as the men filed out to the waiting cars.

'Howard will go to the airport with you to make sure everything goes okay,' he said. 'You're going to Mexico on my plane tonight. I have business here to take care of. You'll have a couple of days in Baja to shake down Vance and Cooper. Gamble will be joining you there within forty-eight hours. As soon as you're all together I'll join you.'

'Any news?'

'About what?'

'About the Rose Bowl parade.'

'What?'

Lynch sighed.

Anger flashed across Halloran's eyes for an instant.

'It's been a hard six days, you know?' Lynch said.

'Everything is under control,' Halloran said, his voice harsh.

'How much time do we have?'

'Eight, maybe ten days.'

'Jesus Christ.'

'We got a problem here I should know about.'

Lynch looked away. 'No,' he said. 'Everything is A1.'

'Good.' Halloran gave him one final hard look. 'See you in Baja in three days.' Then he turned and walked away.

It was too late for formal introductions. Lynch, Reece and Bono rode in the back of one car with Howard up front with the driver. Vance and Cooper followed in the next car. They cleared the guardpost at the main gate and drove out onto the All American Freeway, heading for Fayetteville Municipal Airport. By the time they crossed Santa Fe Drive the huge, austere military base had faded from view and they were blending into normal traffic — young people out for the night, families going home late from visiting relatives.

It all seemed so abnormally normal after the week they'd been through. A huge weight began to lift from Lynch's shoulders. He looked at Reece and then Bono. Suddenly, unexpectedly they all found themselves grinning at each other. Reece was the first to laugh followed by Lynch and then Bono.

'Wasn't he some kinda cunt?' Bono gravelled.

Lynch and Reece laughed harder.

The good humour didn't last long. Howard waited for his moment then turned around to look at them.

'There's been some bad news, I'm afraid.'

Janice was the first name into Lynch's mind. But he waited.

Howard dragged the moment out, enjoying it. Nobody spoke.

'I think the boss wants to tell you himself,' Howard said finally and turned back.

Hostility flickered inside the car like sheet lightning.

'Asshole.' It was Bono.

Howard twisted around again. He looked at the three of them coldly. 'What was that?'

'You're an asshole, pal.' Bono said it as if he were explaining a simple matter of fact to an idiot. The driver sniggered.

'Okay,' Howard said, a strange smile on his face. 'Emmet Tuckey is dead.'

The shock of the news overwhelmed any anger they felt at Howard's petty power game.

'When?' Lynch asked.

'Few days ago at Panama City. He and his wife were killed in an explosion aboard his boat.'

It had only been a week since Lynch sat with Tuckey in the backyard of his home. And his pretty wife. Luisa... that was her name. Six months pregnant. Freshly dug foundations for a shadehouse in the back yard.

'Shit,' Bono muttered.

'Any ideas?' Lynch asked.

Howard sighed as if it were all a little too much trouble

161

now he'd enjoyed his moment of power. 'We never let anything like this go uninvestigated,' he said. 'The FBI is taking care of it. Because of Tuckey's... curious service record they'll go over it pretty carefully. But...' he shrugged as if it were hopeless. 'There's always a lot of loose ends in a thing like this. If it was a hit, there's more than one place it could have come from and for a lot of different reasons. And it may not be a hit. It could have been an accident. Accidents happen on boats all the time.'

'An accident?' The contempt was audible in Lynch's voice.

Howard shrugged. 'From what I understand there's not a lot left to go on.'

'What kind of explosion?' Bono asked. He was the explosives expert on the team.

'Gasoline, they think. The boat was moored at the pumps. Looks like Tuckey and his wife were going out for the day. There's no record of any jobs around that time. Somehow the gasoline ignited. Who knows... a cigarette, an engine spark? There's nothing left of either of them, there's nothing left of the boat, there's nothing left of a half dozen boats that were near them at the time and there's not a lot left of the dock.'

'Big bang.' Bono acknowledged. 'But gasoline... there's always failsafes on those pumps just in case some asshole drops a match or a lit cigarette. The flame might blow back into the pump but it gets choked off automatically at the first valve. To ignite the amount of gas it would take to generate an explosion of that magnitude would mean a violent rupture of the main holding tank...' He took a deep breath. 'You're talking about a little outside help here, pal.'

'You can be sure of one thing,' Lynch muttered softly. 'It wasn't any fucking accident.' He looked at Howard. 'What does Halloran say about this?'

'That's why Mister Halloran...' Howard placed the emphasis on the mister... 'that's why Mister Halloran wants you out of the country tonight.'

Lynch brooded. There were two ways of looking at that. He recalled Halloran's words about Tuckey at STC's New York office a week ago. '... if there's a danger, even the suspicion of a threat that he might jeopardise this operation...'

The hairs on the back of Lynch's neck prickled.

Twelve hours later they were in Mexico.

5
HARVEY'S LAST SUPPER

Beirut, June 22

Bill Wallace called him Harvey. He wasn't quite as appealing as the big white bunny in the Jimmy Stewart movie but for three months he had been Wallace's only friend. Harvey was easier than his Latin name: *Cimex Lectularius*. About the size of a matchbox and coffee brown with raised vertical ridges across his hard, glossy back, Harvey was the biggest, fattest bedbug Wallace had ever seen. At least some creatures were growing fat on Lebanon's misery, Wallace had concluded. He had reacted with revulsion when he first found Harvey on his bed in the cellar. The captive American scholar had been lying on the filthy mattress, under a single blanket, trying to postpone that moment when he'd have to sit up and face another day and he had heard a faint rustling in the pillow just behind his right ear. Then he had felt something tickle his cheek, ever so gently and he had recoiled in horror because he knew it had to be something vile. He shook the bedbug violently onto the floor and watched as it skidded across the dirty bare concrete on its back and ricocheted off the far wall with an audible clack. His first instinct had been to kill it but he held back because he had bare feet and the idea repelled him. His captors had taken away his shoes to make it harder for him to escape. Suddenly, Wallace was amused by the irony of his situation. He had been given the power of life and death over another living creature. At that moment he decided to give the bedbug a reprieve. It

164

was a gesture, he decided, to demonstrate the noble resilience of the human spirit, an absurd and modest triumph for a man who had spent four years in the most miserable, de-humanising captivity. The moment Wallace granted Harvey his reprieve he felt a sudden pang of guilt that he might have injured the bedbug as he hurled it across the floor. He walked over and studied it. It was still on its back, spindly black legs waving feebly in the air. The bug was too fat and sluggish to right itself. Obviously the pickings were good for bedbugs in this part of Beirut ... wherever that may be.

Wallace had been moved at least half a dozen times since his capture that night, another lifetime ago. He had long since given up trying to calculate his location. Despite the blindfolds, the pushing and shoving, the long rides in car trunks that accompanied every move, he knew he had once been held captive in the basement of the Iranian Embassy. He had overheard his captors talking and recognised Farsi, the language of Iran. They switched back and forth between Farsi and Arabic because the Hezbollah militiamen did not speak Farsi and the mullahs were impatient. He could hear the contempt in their voices as they berated the militiamen. They were the early, heady days of the Ayatollah's revolution when it looked as though his Shi'ite *Jihad* really would sweep the Middle East. But things had changed since then. Wallace didn't know it but Khomeini was dying. His revolution lay in blood-soaked trenches on the battlefront with Iraq. The Iranian despot had found an enemy as brutal and as savage as himself and had been fought to a standstill. Wallace had been able to glean that much from his guards. Things had changed since then. He had been moved several more times, his captors growing more arrogant and indifferent to his suffering with each passing month. In all his long months of captivity Wallace had never seen nor spoken to another hostage. For all he knew, he was the only Western hostage left in the Lebanon. Time passed with excruciating slowness and there were days when he worried about his sanity as he struggled to occupy his mind with games, riddles and reminiscences. His health had almost collapsed. Usually his captors gave him a bowl of greasy homos or boiled yellow peas called termis with a piece of bread a couple of times each day. He was given nothing to drink but water brought in a plastic soft drink bottle. The water was usually bad and had never been boiled to kill the parasites which contaminated it. In the first months he suffered chronic stomach pains and dysentery, often fouling himself where he lay because he was too weak to move. Sometimes his captors came in to scoff at the weakly American. Sometimes they left him for days to wallow miserably in his own vile mess. Never a sturdy man, Wallace's weight had plummeted till it looked as though he might die of malnutrition and dehydration. Then the guards would drag him roughly to a nearby courtyard, strip him and sluice him down with a few buckets of water. One of the guards would give him an orange, half a cucumber or a piece of cold, cooked eggplant and let him sit in the sunshine for half an hour while they hosed out his cell. Then they would put him back and somehow he would get through the next few days. He had no idea what his weight was now but it had fallen below forty-five kilos at one point, he knew that. His captors must have decided they didn't want him to die just at that time because they brought a doctor to see him and the doctor had given him a vitamin injection and medicine to settle his stomach and his bowels.

Wallace had absolutely no idea if anyone was negotiating his release. His captors never discussed it. But he could determine his value to them through their fluctuating moods. There were days when they treated him almost kindly, gave him an extra meal, a few fresh vegetables, a tin of condensed milk. Every few weeks they would allow him to shave. Wallace found that the most amusing. They always left a guard with him in case he tried to kill himself with a disposable safety razor. When his own clothes had become too dirty and tattered they brought him a new shirt and pants, looted no doubt from some camp or home. Then there were days when the mood changed with terrifying suddenness. Wallace had no way of knowing if it was the shift in international affairs, the downgrading of his hostage status, a new militia commander or just the crazed volatility of the religious zealot. A few of them would come into his cell in the middle of the night to kick and slap him, to rave and scream about American imperialism and yell slogans extolling the Immam and their sacred cause. The following weeks would be hell as the routine jolted back to reflect their hatred of everything American. The food would stop for a day or two and when it resumed it was a single bowl of homos again and a bottle of water a day. He would not be allowed to walk up and down the corridor or have half an hour outside. Instead they would throw a latrine bucket into his cell and then not empty it for days until it overflowed and streamed across the floor, filling the room with its stench. There was no getting away from it. All he ever had was a mattress on the floor and he would spend two or three days and nights huddled in a corner of the mattress trying to stay out of the filth and get a few miserable hours sleep.

Then, something must have happened because the mood had changed again. He was pleasantly surprised because he had come to believe he had no value whatever as a hostage. Even as a spy, which is what his Hezbollah captors believed him to be. There were many times when death would have come as a relief. His intellect prevented him from contemplating suicide but, nevertheless, if death were to come by any other means it would not be entirely unwelcome. Yet, here he was, still alive, still rational. To a point, he conceded, looking at Harvey. Wallace was tougher than even he had realised. It was always the skinny little bastards who seemed to last the longest, he reflected. He was in the same tiny cell where he had spent the past six months. By his calculation it had been six months. He knew there could be a month or two on either side because all he had to go on was memory, observation and the passing seasons. His kidnappers had taken away his watch on the first day of captivity and done their best to keep him disoriented ever since. Whenever he asked for the date they either swore at him or gave him a meaningless answer. 'The anniversary of the holy martyrs' was the one he heard most often.

Then, without warning two weeks ago, his diet had improved markedly. They had begun bringing him three meals daily. Tabouli salads of parsley and tomato, mashed beans with onion called bosara. One day they brought him chicken with rice. It was saturated with oil but Wallace still thought he had never tasted anything quite so delicious in all his life. They let him shave and exercise again for an hour each day and brought him another shirt. They even brought in an old army cot and threw the mattress onto it so that after four years he would no longer have to sleep on the floor.

Wallace waited and wondered. His prison cell was the storeroom of a large house or office building, he suspected. Its dirty brown paint was peeling and the floor was cold concrete. He felt quite sure he was still somewhere in the southwestern suburbs, on the wrong side of the green line. The intermittent sound of automatic weapons fire and the occasional explosion of something heavier, like a tank shell, told him that much. The only light came from a series of small ventilation holes high in one wall at street level that projected a moving pattern on the opposite wall as the day progressed. It was just enough to give the room a permanent dusk during the daytime. The single light socket in the ceiling was empty and dead. They hadn't wanted him cheating them of the pleasure of execution by plugging himself into the light socket. Wallace had learned to pass much of the time sleeping, dozing or thinking in the gloom. He estimated he could pass up to sixteen hours a day like this and speculated that he would never be fit for work again. The Stockholm Syndrome hadn't come into operation with his captors. He saw so little of them there was no time to form even the pretence of a sympathetic relationship. Besides, the guards changed constantly and when they did speak to him they made it clear they considered him to be something less than human. There was only Harvey, he thought, eyeing the fat bedbug at the foot of his bed. He had told Harvey everything he knew. Everything. Harvey had repaid Wallace's confidence by listening with infinite patience. Not once had he spoiled any of Wallace's lectures with a single interruption. And now he was the best-informed bedbug in the world. Wallace was a little worried about Harvey's weight though. He often wondered how Harvey got so fat. He never seemed to touch any of the tempting morsels Wallace laid out for him each night. And Wallace refused to let him back into bed. Every night he prodded Harvey into the corner furthest from the bed with a bare toe. It was undignified, Wallace knew. But friendship only went so far. And every new day when Wallace woke up, Harvey had moved to a new location. But he had never been able to get back up the metal legs of the army cot. What did he live on, Wallace pondered. He knew bedbugs were blood-suckers but he couldn't work out how Harvey managed it. Perhaps when Wallace was asleep, Harvey silently, relentlessly scaled the bed, found the tastiest piece of pallid thigh, inserted his needle-slim proboscis through the skin, quietly drank his fill and then scuttled back down to the floor to sleep for the night. Wallace did wake up with the occasional bite but he was sure they were lice or fleas. What *did* Harvey live off, he wondered.

There were footsteps in the corridor. Wallace got up and looked at the frieze of sunlit dots crawling across the wall. He guessed it was mid to late afternoon. Too early for supper. The tray with two empty bowls from lunchtime were still uncollected on the floor. He heard the bolt slide back and then the door banged open. As usual, it took him a minute to adjust to the sudden infusion of light. A Hezbollah guard in army greens stepped into the room, his AK47 unslung

169

and pointed at Wallace. He was followed by another man, a stranger in a beautiful pale brown suit with well barbered hair. He had a handsome Arab face and looked to be in his mid-30s. The guard ordered Wallace to sit on the side of the bed and jabbed the barrel of the rifle at him. Wallace sat down. Obviously they were afraid the emaciated American professor was going to overpower them both and fight his way out of Beirut.

The man looked around for a moment and wrinkled his nose delicately in distaste at the stench inside the room. Wallace hardly noticed it anymore.

'My name is Ziad,' he introduced himself in English. He had a cultured voice and almost no accent. Probably educated in England, Wallace thought.

'There has been an important development in your situation,' he said.

Wallace tensed. Imminent release. It had to be.

'Yes, professor,' the man said consolingly, 'what is it the Americans say — I have good news and bad news.' He smiled charmingly.

The bastard is playing with me, Wallace thought.

'The good news is that you will be leaving here soon,' he chuckled. 'The bad news is that you won't be going home.' His face assumed a sympathetic look. 'Your government doesn't care about you. They are not the slightest bit interested in what happens to you, Mr Wallace. They have been made many very reasonable offers and they have declined them all. It is a pity, Mr Wallace. Many other hostages have been taken and released in the time you have been a prisoner of war.'

He shrugged. 'Other Western governments have a more pragmatic approach. They appear to value the lives of their citizens more highly than the Americans.' He paused. 'You must be a very unimportant man, Mr Wallace.'

'Yes,' Wallace agreed. 'Mind if I go home now?'

Ziad smiled, stepped forward and gently patted Wallace's

cheek. 'I love your sense of humour,' he said.

Wallace pulled back. 'If I'm not going home, where am I going?' he asked.

Ziad drew a deep breath and looked thoughtful. 'Our friends at Hezbollah have wanted to dispose of you many times, Mr Wallace. I think you can believe that.'

Wallace believed it. But he was thinking. 'Our friends at Hezbollah...' Then this Ziad wasn't with Hezbollah.

He took a punt. 'You're not Lebanese?'

Ziad shook his head. 'Palestinian.'

Wallace was confused. Four years of confinement and a bad diet did nothing to improve a man's reasoning powers. 'What business does the PLO have with Hezbollah?' he tried.

'What makes you think I am with the PLO?' Ziad answered.

'Who are you with...?'

Ziad smiled indulgently. 'There is no need for you to know everything,' he said. 'All you need to know is that arrangements have been made on your behalf and you will be leaving here soon. Even if you are of no interest to your own government, Mr Wallace, you do have a certain... curiosity value. The rest of the world might be interested to know how the American government looks after its people when they get into difficulties.' He paused and adjusted his pristine shirt cuffs.

'Used properly at the right time and in the right place, you and some of your colleagues could yet turn out to be quite influential, Mr Wallace. I merely wanted to ensure that you are still in good health.'

That was it, Wallace realised. He had been swapped in some kind of deal between the militias. Part of a package deal along with a few other poor bastards like himself. Being taken off to God knows where to be used in a propaganda exercise to humiliate his government even more. Ziad was undoubtedly right on one score. Wallace and the other hostages had been forgotten by America and the rest of the world. To drag them back out onto the world stage en masse

171

with the threat of public execution and a new set of demands was one way to make the whole world sit up and take notice. Whoever Ziad represented had decided to up the ante dramatically. Wallace realised that once again he was a pawn in a game over which he had no control, a game with a terrifying new deadline. And that could only mean one thing. If America didn't give in to the new demands Wallace and the others would be slaughtered for the world's media in a stark and bloody escalation of the terrorist agenda. Abject misery flooded through him as the realisation sank home.

'Well, are you...?' Ziad was asking.

'What...?' Wallace hadn't been listening.

'Are you in good health, Mr Wallace?'

Wallace smirked. 'No,' he answered. 'I'd like a new room with a bath, a colour TV, a case of scotch and a months supply of pastrami on rye. That would make me feel a lot better.'

Ziad smiled. 'They tell me you spend a lot of time talking to yourself, Mr Wallace.'

'It's the only way I can get an intelligent conversation,' Wallace shrugged.

'Is the food all right?'

'If you're a monkey.' The words were out before he could stop them. Wallace wasn't a racist. He had studiously avoided anything that might provoke his captors into beating him simply because he could not withstand pain. But suddenly, that was all irrelevant now. Wherever Ziad was going to take him, death would follow soon after. He was certain of that. Emboldened by that realisation, the fear Wallace had lived with for four years left him. All he wanted to do now was lash out in whatever pathetic, insignificant way he could to try to return some of the suffering he had endured for what felt like an eternity.

Ziad smiled but Wallace saw a dangerous new look in his eyes.

'Don't you like our food, Mr Wallace?' The cultured English

172

voice sounded like dripping ice water. Ziad looked around the squalid room. A moment later something caught his eye. He walked to the end of Wallace's bed and bent down. When he straightened up he was holding the fat bedbug in his hand.

Wallace recoiled in horror and disgust as he realised what Ziad intended to do. The guard sniggered. Ziad's empty hand lashed out and grabbed Wallace by the scruff of his thin, bony neck. He jerked the American professor's head back savagely and Wallace gasped in pain.

'Bon appetit, professor,' Ziad said and pushed the insect towards Wallace's mouth. Wallace saw the fat brown body and the spindly black legs wriggling and felt the vomit rise in his throat. Ziad shoved Wallace's head over the side of the bed and waited till he had finished retching. When there was nothing left to bring up Ziad yanked the American upright, pushed him brutally against the wall and shoved the live insect into the limp open mouth. There was a brief choking sound and then Ziad brutally ground Wallace's jaw shut, crushing the insect's body in his mouth. The American somehow found the strength to wrench free and began vomiting and spitting again across the floor.

Ziad stepped back smartly, afraid of getting his shoes or smart suit pants splashed.

'Such weak stomachs, you Americans,' he said, then adjusted his shirt cuffs and motioned to the guard that it was time to leave.

Baja, Mexico, June 23

The Beechcraft 2000 with the STC company logo on its tail landed at San José Del Cabo, near the southernmost tip of the Baja peninsula, a little after five o'clock in the morning. It had been a long night, first the two-hour drive to the airport at Raleigh, North Carolina and then the five-hour flight aboard Halloran's private jet to Mexico. All the way down, Lynch, Reece and Bono smouldered about the news of Tuckey's death. It wasn't a good time to get to know Vance and Cooper. The two Delta Force men sat in the back of the nine-seater jet while the others dismantled the seats to stretch out and catch up on lost sleep as best they could. Howard had introduced Lynch briefly to the pilot at the airport and then left. No-one had seen or heard from the pilot since take-off. Obviously Halloran wanted it that way.

The next they heard from him was when he announced over the intercom that they had begun their descent into Baja. The sun was already half over the eastern horizon, warming the Sea Of Cortez and turning the Baja desert a soft, dusty pink. Once on the ground the tower directed them to a corner of the tarmac, away from the pink ochre terminal, even though the airport was deserted. The sole Mexicana 737 on the ground was still dark and unattended, awaiting the first rush of sunburned Californians going home to Los Angeles after a week of margaritas and mariachi. The plane taxied to a halt near a blue and white 4WD Cherokee Chief with a roof rack parked inside the perimeter fence. Lynch saw four men: two Americans and a Mexican wearing casual clothes, the fourth man was wearing the electric blue uniform of a police officer.

The pilot reappeared briefly, opened the hatch and threw out the stepladder.

'Hi.' The curly, sun bleached hair of a man far too young to be involved in Halloran's business, appeared in the open hatchway. 'Welcome to Mexico.' Lynch recognised him immediately as Dennis, the former USN midshipman who had been their steward at the villa in Malta during their last job. His hair was longer but the engaging grin and sunny manner were the same. It had been about a year since Malta and obviously he had risen in STC's corporate empire. But then, Lynch knew, sudden vacancies weren't uncommon among Halloran's staff.

'That's it?' Lynch asked.

'That's it, we're free to go.'

'What about him?' Lynch nodded at the cop.

'He's cool,' Dennis said. 'The other guy is the airport manager. He's taken care of immigration... and there are no customs for you.'

Cool. Another word for bought, Lynch realised.

They climbed out into a day that was already hot and dry. There was a slight breeze but it felt as though someone was opening and closing an oven door. Lynch was glad to see the car had air conditioning. The Cherokee was crowded once they had all climbed aboard, even with their luggage overhead in the roof rack. Lynch sat up front with Dennis. Reece and Bono sat in the second row with the second man in their welcoming committee, whom Dennis introduced as Brad. Brad was nowhere near as communicative as Dennis. He chewed gum, looked tough and communicated with nods and meaningful looks. He was the only one wearing a jacket, a light green cotton windcheater. Lynch knew why. Beneath the jacket was a holster containing a machine pistol, probably a baby Uzi. Lynch was in a bad mood. He wanted to take Brad's gun away from him and hit him with it. Vance and Cooper sat in the back seats again. They still hadn't said much. But, Lynch noticed that their eyes were working overtime.

Dennis drove the Cherokee across the deserted car park in front of the terminal, out onto Transpeninsular One and turned north. Another shitty day in paradise, Lynch thought as the climbing sun beat a hot metal path across the Sea of Cortez to their right and inflamed the sawtooth mountain ridges of the Sierra de la Laguna to their left.

'Where are we going?' Lynch asked.

'To Mr Halloran's ranch — '

'I know that,' Lynch interrupted. 'Where is it?'

'Place called El Triunfo... about an hour's drive.'

'Is there a phone before we get there?'

Dennis shot him an anxious glance. 'Our orders are not

to stop anywhere, Mr Lynch. We have to take you straight to the house at El Triunfo. There are phones there you can use.'

'Dennis.' Lynch kept his tone even but there was a note in his voice that everyone in the car heard. 'I want to make a phone call before we get to the house. Now either you stop at the next phone box or I stop the car for you.'

'Mr Halloran's ord — ' Brad began. Brad obviously wasn't too smart because when he got into the car he had allowed himself to be sandwiched between Reece and Bono. His words were cut off when Bono grabbed the back of his head and shoved it between his knees. Reece pulled up the windcheater and fished out the Uzi, the gun Halloran issued to all his bodyguards. He checked its safety then passed it to Lynch. Lynch put the gun on the seat between him and Dennis.

'Oh shit,' Dennis said. The car was silent except for the muffled grunts and threats coming from Brad as Bono shoved his head further down towards his ankles.

'Okay,' Dennis said. 'We'll be coming to Miraflores in about twenty minutes. There's a Pemex station just on the other side. They might have a phone. You'll have to slip the guy a few bucks.'

Bono took his hand off Brad's head and the angry guard jerked upright. His face was flushed, his hair awry and his eyes blazed with wounded pride.

Bono gave him one of his best smiles. 'Now,' he said. 'What was it you wanted to do to me the minute you got loose?'

A road sign said 'Camino Sinuoso' and the road obediently twisted and turned up into the mountains of Sierra de la Laguna. On another day it would have been a pleasant drive. The landscape was filled with spectacle and drama. Raw ribbed mountains soared from deep, rubble-strewn arroyos and moulded themselves into fantastic, jagged turrets against the sky. Organ pipe cactus saluted from the roadside as they drove past. Just when it seemed the parched browns would go on forever there would be a sprinkle of vivid yellow from the tiny flowers of the *pitahaya* cactus and then the sudden, unexpected lush purple splash of wild bougainvillea.

No-one in the car spoke until they reached Miraflorés. Christ only knew what was going through Vance and Cooper's minds, Lynch thought. But this wasn't the time for long and involved explanations. They would just have to roll with it, he decided. It would be a reasonable test of their mettle. The road struggled through a cleft in the mountains and abruptly came out on to the small town of Miraflores. Dennis drove slowly through the still sleeping town and just when it looked like they were clearing the outskirts he pulled into a tiny gas station with an ancient pump and a new Pemex sign. Lynch handed the Uzi to Reece and got out. The heat almost took his breath away. Even though it was still early the town seemed to cower beneath the pitiless glare of the sun. Everything looked dead. The only sign of life was from the turkey buzzards wheeling high overhead searching for carrion. They never seemed to feel the sting of the sun. Dangerous country, Lynch thought. He liked it. The garage looked shut and it took him a few minutes to stir the owner but the moment Lynch produced a fifty dollar bill the man's objections melted magically away. *Mortida* — bribery — was still the most persuasive language in Mexico. The air inside the garage was rank and stifling. It wasn't just oil and gas fumes. There was something else, a foul, rancid smell he couldn't quite put his finger on. Then he noticed the steer hides hanging in the back of the garage. The owner ran his own small tannery and sold hides and leather goods to the tourists. The smell came from the fats putrifying on the animal hides as they dried.

Lynch dialled Janice's number and calculated the time difference while he waited for the call to go through. It was almost seven in the morning in Baja. Midday in New York. The phone rang twice and then a familiar voice came on the line. It sounded strangely tinny, even for long distance.

'Hi, this is Janice... I've gone away for a few days but

177

please leave a message after the beep and I'll get back to you as soon as I can... promise.'

Lynch slapped the phone down in disgust.

'Stupid bitch!' He knew it made no sense to be angry with her. She didn't know the danger she was in. That was the hell of it. Even knowing Halloran as well as she thought she did, she couldn't possibly have guessed that her life would be in danger from the very man who had once been her most benevolent protector. Lynch knew he was safe. For the moment at least — the operation was everything, it was sacrosanct. Halloran had already demonstrated that. No matter who had to be sacrificed until it was all over. Even then, Lynch wondered, would he be safe? He forced himself to think about Janice. There was no way of knowing how long that tape had been on. He hadn't spoken to her for more than a week. Tomorrow would be Monday. She had probably taken a long weekend, he rationalised. She would be back tonight or tomorrow morning. He would have to wait. His face told the story as he walked back to the car. They drove on in silence again for forty-five minutes until they came to another small town, Dennis flicking the occasional sideways glance at Lynch. Lynch stared ahead through the windshield, stony faced. Thinking.

From a short distance El Triunfo was a pretty little place squeezed into a tiny valley at the northern tip of the sierras before the Transpeninsular Highway began its winding descent into La Paz, thirty-two kilometres away. Close up it was a few straggling streets of forlorn houses and shops on either side of the two lane blacktop. A few of the houses were derelict. There was a cafe on one side, a cantina on the other, both closed. The men's eyes were drawn to the biggest building in town, a twin-spired church painted a violent lime green with lurid aqua trim.

'God sure is colour blind in Mexico,' Bono muttered.

'Aren't there any fucking people in these towns?' asked Reece.

178

'El Triunfo is almost a ghost town,' Dennis volunteered, trying to sound helpful. 'Used to be a silver mining town with a population of 10,000 but the ore ran out a long time ago. Now there wouldn't be more than 600 people in the whole place. A few gringos are coming in, buying up old houses, turning them into vacation homes. It isn't popular though — too far from the beach. Makes it perfect for us.'

He turned left at the first intersection and drove up the hill past the church. The blacktop ran out a moment later and they found themselves drawing a long dust plume on a dirt track that curled away from town and into the mountains. A few minutes later El Triunfo had disappeared in the dust haze. The road continued to wind deeper into the hills until it reached a small plateau tucked improbably between the bony shoulders of the mountains. The vegetation thickened with a thin coating of dirt to cling to and there were stands of white-barked mimosa and ironwood between prickly islands of cactus. They came to a set of old wrought iron gates forged into Spanish lace and set into an adobe arch. The gates were open and a dilapidated dirt-brown adobe wall reached briefly away on either side, a vain civilising gesture by the architect in such desperate country. On the other side of the gates, a dusty driveway was flanked by a double row of tall, dowdy palms. Lynch thought they had the look of a threadbare honour guard. A moment later they emerged from the avenue of palms onto the circular driveway of what had been a grand home and now had the ambience of a folly. The dirt road circled a low brick wall, which protected the remnants of a cactus garden. One survivor remained, a thick clump of *pitahaya* whose crooked fingers reached ten metres into the air like a giant, arthritic claw. Once past the entrance to the house the driveway diverted briefly to a long, red-tiled open garage then looped around the cactus garden and lunged back toward the palm drive as though eager to escape.

The house was a block-shaped, two-storey Spanish

hacienda of fading pink ochre. A series of narrow arches punctuated the walls of a great front porch, giving shade to a short flight of wide steps which led to an imposing front door built from solid ironwood and stained by time to the colour of ebony. The wings of the porch fanned across the front of the house into a shady high-arched verandah, making the whole house look as though it had been raised up on a platform to separate and distinguish it from the starkness of its surroundings. It should have looked grand, Lynch realised, but it didn't. Its grandeur had faded to a weary, worn-out look. There was a new Ford pick-up and an empty open truck parked near the porch. A glistening new satellite dish and a bristling nest of antennae on the roof emphasised the building's air of obsolescence. Behind the house they could see a fenced pasture rising briefly to the mountains on three sides. The fencing had long since broken down and Lynch guessed the garage had once stabled horses. Now, they all realised, there was only one way in. And one way out.

'Used to be the mine manager's house,' Dennis said as he halted the Cherokee in front of the steps and waited while the trailing cloud of dust swept past them. 'In the old days they shipped the silver from here to the coast and then to San Francisco. Company directors would stay here with the manager's family. Used to be a pretty fine house. Mr Halloran hasn't done much to the outside. Doesn't want to attract attention. Inside it's okay.'

Lynch held his judgement in reserve as he climbed out of the car. The windows of the house hadn't been cleaned, the pink ochre paint was peeling, exposing patches of adobe clay brickwork underneath and there were tiles missing from the front steps. The old girl looked like a dowager with some teeth missing, Lynch thought.

'How secure are we, Dennis?' he asked. It was a loaded question but if Dennis understood Lynch's true meaning it didn't show. Lynch wanted to know how much trouble he might have getting out when he wanted.

'We've got a couple of guys with Uzis out on the perimeter now,' he answered. 'We've only been here five days ourselves. Most of our gear started coming in yesterday. We'll have a command post set up in the garage by morning and we'll have an early detection electronic sensor network laid across the mouth of the valley by tomorrow night.' He shrugged. 'You can see how hard it is to get in and out of here without somebody knowing. There's only one way in and that's through the front gate.'

Lynch had heard that before.

'Anybody who wants to come in the back way has to get over those ridges.' He thumbed over his shoulder to the mountain peaks soaring another twelve hundred metres above their heads. As far as Lynch could see the last hundred metres or so of the crests and shoulders were vertical rock. It wouldn't be an easy climb in and out, he conceded. But it could be done. At night, not during the heat of the day.

'The other guys are armed for general security.' Then he added sheepishly; 'I know you guys can take care of yourselves.'

The others had begun climbing out of the Cherokee and pulling their bags down from the roof rack. Lynch took a bag. He was coming back for more when he noticed something suspicious about Brad. The guard was marking time, hovering a little too close to Bono as the big man lifted the bags down. There was a glint of malevolence in Brad's eye as he watched Bono and Lynch saw the guard was choosing the moment to strike.

Bono yanked a heavy kit bag down, turned and threw it to Brad.

'Here,' he said amiably. The guard reached out reflexively and caught it in both hands with a grunt. Bono's right foot suddenly swung up and caught the guard between the legs with a sickening thud. Brad screamed, dropped the kit bag and fell on top of it, groaning and clutching at his crotch.

Bono stood over him. 'That's just for thinking about it,

181

you sly motherfucker,' he said. 'You ever try something, I'll kick your nuts so hard people gonna think you're wearin' funny earrings!' Then he yanked the kit bag away and Brad's head hit the ground with a thump.

'Jesus...!'

It was Vance. He had seen what happened. It was the first time Lynch had heard him speak except to be introduced. The brawny Delta Force man walked over to Lynch.

'Do you guys carry on like this all the fucking time?' he asked.

Lynch shook his head. 'No,' he said. 'Today was a good day.'

The inside of the house resembled a mansion near the front in wartime Europe. The front door opened directly onto a huge reception room bustling with a purposeful chaos. All the furniture had been shoved against the walls and the floor was taken up by half a dozen of Halloran's employees emptying packing cases of all manner of hardware and gadgetry. They were all men, all with the look of the ex-serviceman about them — almost certainly ex-USN or Marine Corps. The contents of the packing cases were stacked on a slate floor the colour of dried blood. Piles of neatly-folded jump suits and olive green uniforms, belts and webbing, boots still wrapped in greaseproof paper, rapelling ropes and harnesses, ballistic helmets, stacks of ammunition clips, colourful coils of electronic wiring, computer keyboards and screens. Lynch saw one man check a Heckler and Koch MP5A3 sub-machine gun from a rack in a case stamped 'STC Mining Machinery — Export Only'.

From the corner of his eye Lynch noticed Vance nodding. Obviously this was more like it.

'Where do we sleep?' Bono asked.

'I'll show you,' Dennis said. He threaded his way across the floor to a staircase at the opposite end of the room. It was a wide, newly-carpeted stairway and it led up to a

182

balcony which circled the whole room. The balcony walls were lined by empty bookshelves. A corridor on each side led off to half a dozen bedrooms, Dennis said, leading the file of five men up the stairs. When they got to the top Lynch noted that you could see the entire first floor reception and drawing room from any point on the balcony. There were eight bedrooms in all, Dennis explained. Two more were downstairs next to the kitchen and had been turned into a dormitory for Halloran's men. Lynch and his team would have to share the upstairs bedrooms, two men to a room. Halloran and Howard would have the other two bedrooms and the remaining bedroom would be converted into Halloran's temporary communications centre. The computer electronics they had seen downstairs would be hooked up to the radio and satellite antennae on the roof and Halloran would have his empire at fingertip control.

Unfortunately, Dennis apologised, there were only two bathrooms on the top floor. One was for Mr Halloran in the master bedroom and the other was at the end of the corridor, which they would all have to share. But, he added, it was only for a few days. Lynch didn't need to be reminded.

It was after ten before Lynch got to sleep. The wallpaper in his room was badly faded, the curtains ancient and the windows opaque with dirt. His room faced the front of the house and when he cleared a hole in the grime he realised he could see right down the neck of the valley, between the mountain peaks and across the shimmering brown savannah beyond to the Sea of Cortez. In the middle distance he could see the square, lime green steeples of El Triunfo's church. There was an antique wardrobe, a chest of drawers, a couple of photographs of strangers wearing Victorian clothes on the walls and two new fold-away army cots. Lynch decided that Halloran had bought this place and never even stayed here. The house and its two thousand acres of rough mountainside had been bought as a hideaway or a casual investment, depending on which need became most urgent. Lynch wondered how many other such places Halloran had tucked away around the world, patiently awaiting their transitory moment of glory.

At least Lynch would have the room to himself for a couple of days before Gamble arrived. He told the others he would see them at supper, pulled off his clothes and slumped into bed, expecting to go to sleep immediately. But he couldn't. He was exhausted in mind and body but his alarm circuitry wouldn't switch off. Deep inside him there were warning lights flashing. He thought about Janice and Halloran and Howard and the operation. He thought about himself and wondered how safe he would be when the operation was over. He didn't doubt his own ability to survive the operation in Lebanon, whatever its outcome. But he wasn't sure about the fallout afterwards. Whatever the result, he decided, this would be his last job for Halloran.

He woke up a little after seven that night after a restless sleep. He felt physically better for the sleep, but his mind hadn't rested. He had had dreams — ugly, disturbing dreams. He pulled a clean pair of jeans and shirt from his kit bag and went down for supper. As he walked downstairs he saw the big room had been transformed. The packing crates and military hardware had disappeared as though they had never existed. Instead there were a couple of cheap pinewood sofas and six director's chairs grouped around a fake wood coffee table in front of a big empty fireplace he hadn't seen before in the mess. Perhaps it got cold in the mountains of Baja in winter, Lynch mused. Obviously Dennis had wanted to impress his boss by economising on the furniture. Then again, Lynch reminded himself, it was only for a few days. But the tackiness of Dennis's taste was more than made up for by the dining table, a great black slab of newly polished antique timber surrounded by twelve high-backed Spanish chairs. The red velvet upholstery on the chairs may have faded, like everything else in the house, but they at least still had an aura of dignity. Reece, Bono, Vance and Cooper were already at the table, eating. Lynch had smelled cooking the moment he left his room and by the time he reached the table his mouth was awash. It was a basic meal, chipped beef, creamed potatoes, corn and pumpkin, followed by a choice of apple or cherry pie with ice cream. It was navy cooking from a navy cook, but it was filling and there was plenty of it. There was no tea in the newly stocked kitchen and Lynch was obliged to drink coffee with the others.

The five of them sat around one end of the dining room table for a while, drinking in silence. Only Cooper smoked. Hand rolled. The habit of a man used to spending long periods of time on his own. They had got to know each other a little more over dinner but the two newcomers were guarded and it was obvious they had reservations about what they were involved in. Lynch still had to hear the sound of Cooper's voice. But then, as he well knew, half a million dollars could silence a lot of doubts. Lynch watched the slim young Alabaman for a while. His dirty blonde hair was brushed straight back from his forehead revealing thick dark eyebrows which gave him an oddly cadaverous look. He observed everything through sleepy, half-closed eyes and he had the long-term smoker's mannerism of letting the smoke drift out of his mouth in thick, grey-blue ribbons only to be sucked into his nostrils and back into his lungs. Clearly he wasn't overly worried about his long-term health.

Vance was over six feet tall, powerfully built, no flab. He was typical of the kind of men recruited to US Special Forces and quite unlike their British counterparts who tended to be thin, wiry men like Lynch. Lynch recognised the self-assurance of the paratrooper in Vance, the confidence that said he had proved himself a long time ago and had a right to wonder whether these men he was joining were up to his standard, and whether he would be able to rely on them in a tight spot. So far he looked unimpressed. But then, Lynch realised, no-one had gone out of their way to impress him.

185

'This it?' Vance asked suddenly.

'This what?' Lynch said, putting his coffee cup down.

'This the team or is there more to come?'

'One more to come,' Lynch said. 'Guy from England. SAS. Should be here tomorrow.'

'Another Brit?'

'Yeah.'

'How come this is a British led operation?'

Vance said it politely enough but his meaning was clear. Why were two Britons going on a mission to rescue American hostages?

'Experience,' Lynch said. He knew Vance had taken part in the successful storming of a hijacked aircraft, killing four of the hijackers.

'You heard of the Falklands?' Bono asked Vance. Lynch didn't need Bono to fight off a challenge to his authority but he wanted to see how Vance performed. He waited.

'You heard of Grenada?' Vance replied.

'Yeah, I heard of Grenada,' Bono paused. 'Marines took eighty fucking per cent of Grenada because Delta went surfing in their choppers.'

Lynch suppressed a smile. It was brutal but true. The invasion of Grenada by combined US forces in 1983 had been a disaster for Delta Force which lost five helicopters in a bungled attack on the Grenadan army barracks at Fort Frederick. Other SEALs and Ranger units were pinned down by Cuban and Grenadan soldiers and it had been left to the Marine Corps to take the bulk of the island.

'You guys Marine Corps?' Vance asked.

Bono nodded. 'The only casualties we took at Grenada were three Marine pilots dead when we tried to rescue a Special Forces outfit who shit themselves in the governor's mansion when they thought they'd come under fire... and fucking lied to get help. What's your next job... you gonna invade Key West? I understand there's a lot of faggot bartenders down there who might drive you off with harsh language.'

Vance smiled faintly but kept his cool. Cooper still said nothing. He just sat and listened and smoked and watched everything through those oddly reptilian eyes.

'That was a SEALs team that panicked in Grenada,' Vance corrected Bono. 'Not Delta. And if it makes a difference I think they should have been court martialled.'

'Court martialled . . .?' Bono echoed. His voice trailed away in disgust.

Lynch sighed and decided it was time to impose his authority. The last thing he wanted at this point was a challenge to his leadership. He switched his voice into officer mode. 'This is a covert operation using the best talent currently available from our nations' combined forces,' he said. 'Because of the special nature of the group we tolerate a degree of informality that would not be permitted in other circumstances or operations. That is because every man recruited to this team is a specialist and is expected to behave accordingly.' He paused. 'This is not the first time our two nations have co-operated on covert operations of this nature — and because of past successes it is likely that it will not be the last.' He let the unspoken threat hang in the air. He wanted Vance and Cooper to understand clearly that there was a precedent for what they were doing and it was something to live up to.

It was after nine o'clock when Lynch decided to try Janice again. He summoned Dennis and the former mid-shipman blanched when Lynch told him he would be taking a car into town.

'The phones are working here now, Mr Lynch,' Dennis pleaded.

Lynch couldn't tell him he didn't want any record of whom he was calling, or why. It was enough that Dennis would have to report that Lynch had disobeyed Halloran's clear instructions to go directly to the house from the airport and stay there under the protection of the men he had provided. Dennis reluctantly handed over the keys to the Cherokee. No-one tried to stop Lynch as he left the house. It was Sunday night and El Triunfo was dark and deserted. If the cafe and cantina had opened at all during the day, they were shut now. Perhaps Dennis knew that and it was why he hadn't put up a bigger fight, Lynch thought. He checked the gas in the car and decided to drive to La Paz. Lynch knew he was breaking a major security rule. La Paz was the biggest city in southern Baja and had a population of 150,000. If he had an accident or ran foul of the local authorities it would be harder to hush over and he could blow the whole operation. There wouldn't be enough time to mount a new strike if a scandal erupted over the presence of a team of international mercenaries in Baja. The reason they had flown into San José Del Cabo and not La Paz was to avoid attracting the attention of an overly officious policeman or immigration officer.

It took him half an hour to reach La Paz. The city was alive with tourists and residents enjoying the restaurants and clubs and the summer night. Lynch spent a few minutes cruising around looking for the post office. He accidentally spun the wheels of the Cherokee while taking off at one of the dirt and gravel intersections and earned a dirty look from a cop in a cruiser. Lynch sweated and drove slowly down the block waiting for the whoop of a siren but none came. He finally found the post office and pulled into an empty parking space. Lynch gave the operator his credit card number and waited while Janice's phone rang. It was nearly ten at night in Baja. It would be between four and five am in New York.

'Hi, this is Janice... I've gone away for a few days but please leave a message after the beep...'

Lynch swore and almost hung up again but he caught himself and waited for the beep. She could have just been woken up and, still drowsy, was listening to the call on the machine to see if it was worth answering.

'Janice, this is Colin,' he said. 'If you're there and you can hear this I want you to pick up the phone. It's important.

I'll wait five minutes and call back. If you're there please pick up the phone.'

Lynch kept the phone to his ear for five long minutes, pretending to make a call in case anyone else tried to use it. Nobody came near him.

'Hi, this is Janice...' He waited and then tried to inject just the right note of urgency into his voice so she would understand his instructions were not to be ignored. 'I want you to go to my place immediately and wait for a call,' he told her. 'Whatever time you hear this, do it straight away. It's important. Just do it... I love you.'

Lynch sighed and hung up. If nothing else would convince her — that ought to do it. In twenty-four hours he would try her apartment again and then his house in Vermont. It wasn't the best plan in the world but it was all he could do for the moment. Lynch walked back to the car. For the first time in a long time he prayed. He prayed that she was still alive.

Far away in New York, in Janice's darkened apartment, a shadowy figure played back Lynch's message. An elegant, slim-fingered hand opened the machine and delicately removed the message tape. The figure turned towards the door and crossed a sudden shaft of light from outside, revealing a satisfied smile. Howard was still smiling as he let himself out.

6

THE BOYS FROM BAJA

June 24

Lynch kept his mind on work. It was an effort but it was where training and all those long, lonely years of hard experience paid off. He had always possessed an uncanny ability to shut out distraction and focus on the task at hand. Disarming landmines at night in the numbing cold with the wind driving blinding ice particles into his eyes while Argentine snipers tried to blow his head off had been ideal for refining that kind of discipline. Janice thought it his single most annoying characteristic. But it had helped keep him alive. And now it kept him from agonising over her fate.

He had thought of her first when he woke up this morning. Then he remembered — six days! Only six days before he was supposed to have the team ready to drop into Lebanon and pull out the American hostages. He had put together a team of specialists, perhaps, but it was a team which had never been in action as a unit before, a team with no idea how its other members would perform under extreme pressure, a team which hadn't even had a single full-scale rehearsal yet. He decided that it was time to begin the forging process.

'Okay,' Lynch announced over breakfast at the big table. 'The honeymoon is over. We're going mountain climbing. Get your things together.'

He led the men in single file across the dusty paddock behind the house to the lower flanks of the bald, basalt ridges which formed the Sierra de la Laguna. At Lynch's instruction they wore sneakers, green army coveralls and peaked caps, and each man carried a water bottle. Lynch and Vance each wore a rapel harness and had ropes slung across their shoulders.

The sky was clear, the sun hot and they were all starting to sweat by the time they arrived at the lowest mounds of rubble. Lynch spent a few minutes examining the escarpment, looking for the best way up.

'That looks good,' Vance indicated a nearby fissure.

'We'll go this way,' Lynch decided, nodding in a different direction. Vance shrugged and they began navigating a path between huge granite and basalt boulders from old rock falls. They stopped at the chimney Lynch had selected and looked up. The blunt, narrow fissure reached halfway up the mountainside like a crooked finger then faded out into what looked like sheer rock face. To Reece and Bono it looked terrifying.

'It isn't as hard as it looks,' Lynch said for their benefit. 'It's about 120 metres to the top. We'll be able to walk up this chimney for about seventy five metres and then we'll have to make a little effort to get the rest of the way. It should take us no more than two, three hours at the most. When we get to the top we'll rapel back down. That's the fun part.'

'Do we put the ropes on now?' Reece asked.

'What for?' Lynch looked at him.

'In case somebody falls.'

Lynch shook his head. 'We don't need ropes for this. Besides, there's no point in losing two men.'

'So . . . what if I fall?' Reece persisted.

'Try not to,' Lynch answered.

'This the guy who couldn't jump either?' Vance asked.

'Fuck you,' Reece said.

'Cooper, you follow me,' Lynch ordered. 'Then Bono, then Reece. Vance, you pick up the rear. Catch Reece if he falls.'

'Sure . . .' Vance looked at Reece and smiled. 'Trust me.'

191

Lynch started climbing. The first thirty metres were easy. There were plenty of ledges and cracks to give firm, easy holds. Then it got a little harder. The holds became harder to find and further apart. After an hour he estimated he had climbed about sixty metres and stopped to see how the others were doing. Cooper was about six metres behind him and making it look easy. Snipers had good balance, Lynch smiled. Bono was another fifteen metres behind him with Reece and Vance close behind. Lynch was pleasantly surprised. Reece was doing better than he expected. It was Bono who was holding things up. The big man was overweight and he wasn't as fit as everybody else on the team. His nerve was good, Lynch knew, but he was built all wrong for climbing.

Lynch waited for Cooper to catch up, then they both waited for the others.

'How you doing?' Lynch called down to Bono.

'Great,' Bono lied.

Lynch grinned. Bono would rather die than admit a weakness. Somewhere beneath that thick ugly hide and that obscene, violent persona was a whole encyclopedia of neuroses, Lynch suspected. Which was, no doubt, why he had chosen this kind of work too.

'Gets a little tricky now,' Lynch yelled. 'Take your time.'

A few minutes later Lynch reached the end of the chimney and was confronted by a threatening bulge in the rock face. It wasn't an overhang and if it had only been two metres off the ground it wouldn't have presented a problem. But it was sixty metres off the ground and the mind behaved differently at that height. Lynch dug his toes into the last chimney ledge and reached up over the rock belly, fingers wandering, searching for something to hang onto. He found one and then another, not too far apart. Just a couple of faintly raised knobs in the rock, enough for him to hang onto for a few precious seconds while he hauled himself up and then wormed the rest of his body over the bulge. He dug his fingers in and heaved. His hands were sweaty and he had no chalk. Ticklish rivulets of sweat ran down his back under the cotton coveralls and soaked his running shorts. He could feel the sun burning the back of his neck. His fingers held. He squirmed over the lip of the rock and pulled himself onto the narrow ledge beyond with a grunt. Two to three metres at the most. That's all it was — but far enough and hard enough to shrug a man off and kill him at this height. There was enough room for two men to sit atop the rock swell and he rested for a moment with his back against the rock wall. He saw Cooper's hands appear from the underside of the rock, fingers probing for a hold. A moment later Cooper was beside him too. They looked at the rest of the climb together. It really wasn't as bad as it looked from the ground. The rock face ran at a steep incline to the mountain crest so they would be able to clamber the rest of the way fairly easily. Easily but carefully. They were still a long way off the ground. But, Lynch realised, they had just negotiated the hardest feature of the climb.

'I can't do this.' It was Bono's voice from beneath the gentle overhang. 'I'm not a fucking spider. I can't get over this.'

'Whatsamatta pussy?' Reece's voice floated up. He was mimicking Norton. Mocking Bono. 'Want a ladder?'

Lynch shook his head. How soon they forgot.

'Vance, can you help him?' Lynch yelled.

'I can try,' the words came back.

They waited while Vance climbed past Reece to reach Bono. Lynch took the rapelling rope from his shoulder and fastened the clip to his harness.

'You ready?' he shouted down.

'Ready,' came Vance's reply.

Lynch played the end of the rope over the rim and down to Vance then leaned back flat against the rock face and dug the heels of his sneakers hard into the ledge. He had a descendeur on the rope with a dead man's stop but he didn't know how long he could support Vance's weight if the Delta Force man were to fall. Hopefully it would be long enough for Vance to regain control and get a fresh foothold. Cooper took some papers and tobacco from a breast pocket and impassively rolled a cigarette.

'Clip it on,' Lynch shouted to Vance. 'I'll hold you while you help him up.' He wrinkled his nose in distaste as a wisp of smoke from Cooper's cigarette caught him in the throat.

Both sides were working blind, separated by the suddenly insurmountable belly of the rock wall. Lynch felt Vance take the end of the rope, pull in the slack and clip it to his own harness.

'Okay,' Vance yelled. Lynch pulled in the slack as Vance climbed up beside Bono. He pressed his face close to the big man. 'Okay,' he whispered. 'We're going to a lot of trouble here for you... so now you can climb this little hill you bit fat stupid fucking pig.'

'Oh-ho,' Bono grunted. 'The old courage-through-anger ploy. Jam it up your ass, pal. It won't work. We're not talking about nerve here. There's just no way I can hump my ass over this thing. That's it.'

'We're asking you to climb it, not fuck it,' Vance said between clenched teeth.

Bono took a deep breath. He wasn't used to turning back, even when his body refused to do the things he wanted. His legs felt watery, his arms were aching, he was bathed in sweat, he had ripped one leg of his coveralls and his knee was bleeding. He couldn't go up and he couldn't go down. Everybody waited.

'It's not that far,' Lynch yelled down to him. 'The lip is the hardest part. Pull yourself over that and you're home. I'll grab hold of you.'

'I knew we should have been roped up,' Reece mumbled.

'Reece?' Bono called down.

'Yeah?'

'Do me a favour, will you, pal?'

194

'Yeah?'

'Jump.'

Bono squinted up at the insurmountable bulb of rock that confronted him. He took a deep breath and began feeling over the rock with his fingers, just as the first two had done.

'That's the way,' Vance coaxed. 'Make sure you get a good hold and when you're ready — pull like hell. I'll give you a push and there's a man waiting up there to grab you. It couldn't be much easier, for Christ's sake.'

Bono found something, hesitated then heaved himself upward with an almighty grunt ... and fell. His sweaty fingers slipped, scrabbled desperately at the hard rock but couldn't get a hold. He slid downwards on his belly, legs flailing to regain the precious foothold he'd had just a moment ago — but he couldn't find it again. He felt the unforgiving power of gravity pulling at him, eager to claim him for his foolishness, peeling him off the mountainside like a strip of wallpaper. An involuntary yell escaped his lips. Vance grabbed at his belt with one hand and held but it wasn't enough. Bono was too heavy for him. Acting from pure reflex Vance let go with his other hand, grabbed Bono around the waist and they both fell off the mountain together.

The rope leaped in Lynch's hands as the two biggest men in the team fell into space. He ground his heels deeper into the rock and braced himself. A moment later the descendeur bit and the dead man's stop brought the rope to a sudden halt. The combined weight of the two men must have been over 200 kilos. Lynch yelled as the shock hit him and almost plucked him off the mountainside. There was no way he could hold them for more than a second or two. The harness felt like it was trying to tear his body in half. The strain was intolerable. Somehow he held — but only for a fraction and then his feet began to slide. Cooper grabbed onto the rope with both hands, cigarette still jammed between his lips, and hauled back with Lynch. But the two of them together weren't enough to hold it for more than another couple of seconds. They both began to go. Lynch took one hand off the rope and scrabbled desperately for the release clip on his harness. He was going to let Vance and Bono go before he went with them.

The rope slackened. Lynch thought it must have snapped. He gasped at the sudden shock of relief and sagged against the rock face. He had miscalculated badly. The exercise that was to begin bonding the team together had turned into a disaster.

'They're okay...' Reece yelled a moment later. 'They hit the side with a crack but he's got a hold and they're okay.'

Lynch and Cooper had only been able to hold for two or three seconds but it had been enough for Vance to swing them back into the rock chimney and wedge himself and Bono against a good ledge while they caught their breath. Lynch rolled his eyes skyward and breathed deeply. Then he coughed. He looked at Cooper.

'Would you do me a favour?' he asked.

Cooper shrugged.

'Put that cigarette out.'

When they had all caught their breath they transferred Vance's harness to Bono then hauled him over the bump like a side of beef. It was undignified but they all knew it was the only way he would make the top.

An hour later they stood on the jagged crest, a barren spine of basaltic vertebrae just wide enough for them to sit down, drink some water and take in the view. To the east lay the glamorous blue of the Sea of Cortez, to the west a gigantic rumpled carpet of bare, brown mountains. The minor team triumph Lynch was hoping for had been tarnished by the major tragedy they had narrowly avoided. Nothing was working out as it should have been.

'Nice view,' Cooper said. They were the first words Lynch had heard from him and he knew what they meant. A man up here with an M21, an M40A1 or a masterful example of sniper technology like the Heckler and Koch G3SG would control a lot of country.

Lynch looked down at the house and saw a lone figure watching them from the back paddock. He couldn't make out who it was but whoever it was he was interested in them.

'Bit sloppy,' Peter Gamble said drolly as the team straggled back towards the house, tired, dirty and sweaty.

They had taken almost an hour to rapel back down the escarpment. Lynch had not wanted to risk any more serious injury to his team. He and Vance had shown Reece and Bono how to use the rapelling equipment then Cooper had rapelled down first to show how it was done. The two ex-Marines had followed with Lynch and Vance controlling their descent from above. Even so Reece and Bono bumped and slid most of the way, cursing as they went. Vance went next and then Lynch. After the incident with Bono neither of them wanted to push their luck any further today and they had both walked down the mountainside, resisting the temptation to try a few spectacular leaps and bounds.

Gamble introduced himself and he and Lynch shook hands while the others filed past, preferring to get into the shade and a cold drink.

'How long have you been watching?'

'Couple of hours.'

'Did you see the — ?'

'Yes.'

'We weren't trying to impress anybody,' Lynch smiled apologetically.

'You succeeded,' Gamble grinned.

'When did you get in?' Lynch asked.

'Missed you by twenty minutes, otherwise I might have come along. Flew Heathrow to Mexico City last night. Your friend, Mr Halloran, had a charter plane waiting for me there.'

'And how are things at Supply And Stores?' Lynch used the old Special Boat Squadron nickname for the SAS.

Gamble smiled. 'Business as usual. Always plenty of naughty people around needing to be spanked.' They skirted the garage where Halloran's men had set up a security post and walked around to the front of the house. Gamble stopped when they reached the top of the steps in the shade of the great front portico, wanting to have a quiet word with Lynch before they went inside.

'More to the point,' he asked, 'how are things here?'

'Under control,' Lynch said.

Gamble looked back at him. He was a fraction shorter than Lynch with ink-black hair, dark eyes and swarthy, deeply-tanned skin. Like all men in their line of work he wore nondescript clothes, jeans, sneakers and a loose green sport shirt. The accent was Oxbridge but he looked as though he had mixed blood and Lynch realised that was what made it easier for Gamble to blend into the background when he was working in the Middle East. The right robes, a turban and a rifle and Gamble could easily have been *mujahadeen*.

'In all seriousness,' Gamble added, 'what I saw up there this morning wasn't very encouraging.'

'No,' Lynch conceded. 'But try not to worry about it,' he said, breaking off the conversation to go into the house. Not another leadership challenge, he thought as he went upstairs. If Halloran learned how low the morale of his team was he might be tempted to cancel the whole operation anyway. Now that the thought had occurred to him, Lynch concluded, it might not be a bad thing. He kicked it straight out of his mind again. It was defeatist thinking and not like him. It had to be Janice, he decided. Worrying about her was undermining his concentration.

He took a long shower and while he was changing in his room Dennis knocked at the door with some news.

'Mr Halloran will be here tomorrow afternoon,' he said. 'He wants to see you first, about four. There will be a full briefing for everyone at six and then dinner afterwards.'

Conversation was desultory at best around the dinner table that night. Lynch didn't want it that way but the team divided itself automatically with he and Gamble exchanging minor titbits of news and information about common acquaintances

198

and issues. Reece and Bono bickered back and forth like an old married couple who were sick of each other, though that was normal. Vance and Cooper both ate quickly and went their separate ways.

After dinner Lynch took the Cherokee and drove into La Paz again. He called Janice's apartment first and got the same infuriating recorded message. When he phoned his own place in Vermont there was no answer. He got back to the house shortly after eleven and went to bed. Gamble was already in his cot, sleeping soundlessly. Five days, Lynch thought as he went to sleep. Five days.

June 25

'What the fuck have you been playing at down here?'

Halloran was not happy.

Lynch sat in a new director's chair in the master bedroom as Halloran paced the floor. Lynch noticed the room was twice the size of any other bedroom and had a much better equipped bathroom. In fact, Lynch thought, the fittings in Halloran's bathroom looked new. He wouldn't have put it past Halloran to have his own quarters fitted with new facilities while the rest of them made do. A pair of double doors to the adjoining bedroom were open and Lynch could see all the electronic paraphernalia of Halloran's temporary communications post. He could also see Howard hovering among the equipment, pretending to work. Listening. Smirking. Lynch noticed Howard wore beautifully tailored slacks and a designer safari shirt.

'You wilfully disobey my instructions to come right to the house and to stay here...' Halloran was saying. 'Then, when you get here, you take my guys on a hiking trip and you nearly get one of them killed. On top of that you've been sneaking out to La Paz every night and making secret phone calls. This operation is supposed to be one hundred per cent secure now. Who have you been calling?'

199

'Janice.'

Halloran gave an exaggerated sigh. Lynch watched his eyes carefully. There was no sign of anything.

'I wanted to know if she was all right. I still do.'

'Janice is all right.'

'How do you know?'

'I know. Take my word for it. Now, are you going to be able to keep your mind on the job here or what...?'

'My mind is on the job,' Lynch said evenly. He didn't believe for one minute that Halloran was telling the whole truth about Janice.

'What about Tuckey?' he asked.

'What *about* Tuckey?' Halloran sounded exasperated.

'Got any leads?'

Halloran threw his hands up in the air. 'It's far too early to tell. They haven't finished all that forensic shit yet. There's not a lot to go on. Did Howard tell you?'

'Yes.'

Halloran nodded. A fleeting look of contrition crossed his face. 'I'm sorry. Damn shame. He was a fine boy... a real fine boy.'

'His wife was having their kid too,' Lynch said.

'What? Oh... yes... I know. Terrible. Awful. I've already talked to a couple of people at the State Department and the FBI. There's nothing yet. No leads... nothing.'

And probably never will be, Lynch thought.

'Why didn't you call Janice from here?' Halloran demanded suddenly.

Lynch hesitated only a second. 'Because I didn't want you or anybody else to know I was calling,' he said. It was the truth.

Halloran nodded. 'She's fine. I talked to her yesterday and she's all right. You don't have to worry about her.'

'Did she say anything about me?'

This time Halloran hesitated. 'No.'

'Has she been home in the past couple of days?'

'Yes, I think so. She had to collect a few things. She's gone away for a few days till this thing between you and her blows over.'

Lynch knew now he was lying. He nodded slowly. His questions had blunted the thrust of Halloran's own anger.

'What's the news about the hostages?' Lynch asked.

Halloran stopped pacing and sat down on the edge of the bed to face Lynch. He was wearing a creased linen suit with the shirt collar and tie undone and he looked haggard and more tired than Lynch had ever seen him look before.

'The PLO deal for the hostages is going ahead as expected. Our intelligence says they're taking the hostages to Ba'albek from all over southern Beirut, the Beqa'a and southern Lebanon right now. It looks like we'll have to move in five to ten days. You going to be ready?'

Lynch nodded.

Halloran looked unconvinced. 'Don't let me down on this one, Lynch,' he warned. The note in his voice was unmistakeable.

They all gathered again in the big reception room at six, as ordered. Halloran had a slide projector set up on the dining room table pointing at a whitewashed wall. The men sat around the table and listened. The doors were closed and the only other man in the room was Howard. Lynch hadn't seen too many of Halloran's guards or employees in the past few hours at all. Since their boss had arrived on the premises, Lynch realised, every man but the cook would be armed and on alert around the house and throughout its grounds.

Halloran had showered and changed into clean slacks and khaki shirt and appeared reinvigorated, though Lynch noticed the bags under his eyes were a lot darker and more pronounced than usual. The first slide to appear was a map of the eastern Mediterranean showing Turkey, Lebanon, Cyprus and Israel. Only the main population centres were shown.

'We will leave for Turkey five days from now,' he said. 'We will use the company plane to fly to Istanbul. At Istanbul we will stay in low profile quarters and maintain strict security until we get word from intelligence that the mission is "go". When we receive that word we will fly direct to the NATO base at Ankara. Because the mission is deniable and the government is under certain treaty obligations, our time on the base will be kept to an absolute minimum. We will leave my plane and proceed directly to a NATO Hercules where our equipment will be waiting. If there are sufficient night-time hours remaining we will take off immediately. If not we will wait until nightfall to ensure you all get to the DZ and rendezvous under cover of darkness. The destination of the Hercules will be the Turkish occupied sector of Cyprus. Because it will be an unscheduled flight the NATO base commander will inform Nicosia in the usual way. This is not an unusual occurrence. Turkey operates unscheduled military flights between Ankara and Cyprus fairly frequently. The pilot of the Hercules will inform Nicosia of his flight plan when airborne. Anybody doing any eavesdropping will assume it is another unscheduled NATO flight by Turkey. The distance from the NATO base to Cyprus is 600 kilometres — about one hour's flying time in a Hercules C-130H. Once over the Mediterranean the Hercules will deviate from the flight path to within 45 kilometres of the Lebanese coast. NATO will keep us informed of all other aircraft movements in the region at that time. The plane will climb to 8,500 metres and make one pass only. You will exit the aircraft to commence your own approach over the Lebanese coast and into the interior, using the Nighthawks. The moment you have left the aircraft it will resume its stated flight path to Cyprus.'

He thumbed the remote for the projector and the map was replaced with a satellite map of Lebanon with borders, main highways, cities and towns superimposed. The village of El Laboue and the town of Ba'albek, to its south, were highlighted in bold white type.

'Your NAVSTAR receivers will be pre-set exclusively with

the co-ordinates for El Laboue. All you have to do is follow those co-ordinates and you will pass over El Laboue. You will have to navigate the Nighthawks precisely onto the DZ. El Laboue is approximately ten klicks north of Ba'albek on the main highway through the Beqa'a Valley. There is only one highway and one town on those co-ordinates. On the southern extremity of the town there is a series of large citrus groves adjacent to the highway.'

He flicked up an enlargement of a satellite photograph showing a small town with mountains on both sides, a major road running through it and what looked like a cultivated area to the south. There was a white cross on the highway just south of the town.

'That is your DZ,' Halloran said. 'You will land there, stow your 'chutes and effect your rendezvous there. You will be on your own. There will be no-one on the ground to assist you. Your rendezvous, therefore, should be effected with extreme caution. I don't want you guys getting nervous and blowing each other away. The rendezvous point will be on the western perimeter of the highway, precisely one kilometre south of the village of El Laboue, where we have marked the X on this photograph. Even if you land spread out you should be able to negotiate your way through the fields and citrus groves around the town to the RV point. You must make every effort to reach the RV by dawn. If any one of you is unable to do that the operation will proceed without you and you will have to make your way to Israeli lines the best way you can.'

He thumbed the remote again. A tourist snapshot of some Roman pillars against brilliant blue sky flashed up.

'Gentlemen,' he said grandly. 'The temple of Jupiter Heliopolitanus, chief of the Roman gods. These columns and the extensive ruins beyond are all that remain of Jupiter's temple at the southern approach to Ba'albek. The Greeks knew him as Zeus and he was a serious motherfucker. His weapon was the thunderbolt. Rather poetic, don't you think?'

'Yeah,' Bono agreed.

Halloran punched the remote again and another satellite picture of a large town appeared.

'This is Ba'albek,' he said. 'Dates back to 3,000 BC. Seen a lot of action down through the years...'

'Going to see a little more,' Reece muttered.

'The large rectangular structure near the top right corner is what concerns us,' Halloran said.

He punched up an enlargement of what was unmistakeably a fortified military barracks. They could see a solid perimeter wall protecting a cluster of what were probably administration buildings. There were a dozen long white buildings which had to be troop barracks and a couple of other solid looking structures, one of which had to be the magazine, the other probably the motor pool.

'Sheikh Abdullah Barracks, gentlemen. Home to 500 Hezbollah militiamen. Probably more when you get there. This is where the hostages will be. We do not know exactly where yet. We hope to know before we leave Ankara.'

'That's nice.' It was Vance.

'Do we have plans of the barracks?' Lynch asked.

'No,' said Halloran. 'This satellite picture is all we've got.'

'We'll need to spend some time with this,' Lynch added.

'We have still photo enlargements for everybody,' Halloran said. He went on: 'We do know that the perimeter wall is approximately four metres high. It's mostly clay brick and concrete, though there has been some additional reinforcement recently. There are eight sandbagged towers with heavy machine guns and the wall between the towers is topped with razor wire. There are sentries posted throughout the day, including at prayer times which happen four times a day. There's a mosque in town which they use for pep rallies and there are usually half a dozen mullahs at the barracks. Radical bastards, even by Iranian standards. Vehicles come and go all the time, mostly shitheads in Toyota pick-ups with tripod-mounted M60s in the back. There are six truck-mounted anti-aircraft guns around the barracks and at least two SAM emplacements with SA-8s and SA-9s. There is always an armed group at the main gate, sometimes numbering 20 to 30 men, and they usually have a couple of pick-ups with M60s parked there. Seems they just like to hang out trying to impress each other with the size of their dicks. They must feel pretty secure because the gates are usually open. We have to assume the gates will be closed while the handover takes place — but that won't stop you, will it... gentlemen?

'That's the nut you have to crack — that's where you earn your pay. There will be a heavy Shi'ite militia presence in and around the town and around the barracks too — as well as regular Syrian army units. We estimate Hezbollah could have at least a thousand militiamen in the area, as well as 500-plus inside the barracks. We believe there are two or three hundred Iranian Revolutionary Guards still at the barracks too, despite worsening relations between Tehran and Hezbollah. These are Guards who think Tehran has softened its line with the West too much and have opted to throw in their lot with their Shi'ite brethren in Hezbollah.

'Remember...' Halloran raised his voice and punched the words out. 'These people are fanatics. They are not the most disciplined fighters in the world but they are ready to die for their cause. They believe that when they die fighting for Islam they will immediately go to paradise. That makes them brave and it makes them reckless... and it makes them dangerous. So when you hit them — don't fuck around. Don't hold anything back.'

The room was silent.

'Okay,' said Bono.

Halloran smiled. 'On top of that,' he added, 'we can expect between 100-200 PLO fighters at the barracks to provide an escort for the hostages. And... there's more good news. The Syrian army will have checkpoints at El Laboue and Ba'albek. Ba'albek is on the main route from the Beqa'a Valley

205

to Damascus. And Ba'albek is closer to Damascus than it is to Beirut. That means the Syrians will be there in strength. We know they have T-72s deployed at several checkpoints and on the approach to Sheikh Abdullah Barracks.'

There was a low murmur around the table and Halloran held up his hand.

'When you land at the DZ you will be carrying enough ordnance to erase half of Lebanon,' he said. 'In addition to automatic weapons, grenade launchers and high explosive grenades, Mr Bono and Mr Reece will carry additional charges of plastic explosive, to be deployed at Mr Lynch's direction or at their own discretion, to accentuate confusion and diversion.

'Gentlemen,' he said, 'the success of this operation depends absolutely on the efficiency with which you apply the guiding principle of all covert operations: stealth, swiftness, surprise ... and maximum violence in minimum time. It is worth remembering that everything that makes Lebanon so dangerous will also work to our advantage. At this point in its history Lebanon is a true anarchy. The only law is gun law. The country is in a perpetual state of turmoil, violence and confusion. This means a team such as ours can gain a lot of ground under the cover of that confusion. The entire operation should not exceed twenty-four hours. You have an additional twenty-four hour margin. The moment you exit the aircraft the Israeli government will be asked to alert its border forces to the possibility that our people will be coming out within that forty-eight hour period. If you exceed that we will have to assume you have failed. That is likely to be a realistic assumption because the hostages will have been removed and you will all be either dead or disabled. Whatever happens on the ground, when that forty-eight hours is up, you're on your own.'

He paused to let the words sink in.

'Because you will be moving quickly and travelling light you will carry no food rations beyond a few high concentrate

206

glucose pills to keep your energy up. Anything else you need, whether it's food or water, you will take on the ground. Once on the ground five of you will pose as Shi'ite militiamen. For that purpose you will all stop shaving today in order to acquire that authentic shithead look. Mr Bono, Sergeant Vance and Mr Lynch will have to apply some black hair dye before leaving here. Because this operation is government deniable, neither you nor your uniforms will carry any identification. Once you have disposed of your 'chutes, jump suits and helmets you will be wearing only appropriately soiled and creased militia style uniforms. When you have assembled at the RV point you will commandeer transportation on the ground. At least three vehicles. Two will be the absolute minimum.'

'Five?' Cooper drawled. 'You said five militia men. What about the sixth man? Shouldn't I dye my hair? There's no way I can pass for an Arab.'

Halloran nodded. 'Thank you, sergeant. We need you exactly the way you are because you look like an American and because you are going to be our hostage.'

'What?'

'Yes, sergeant. You will pose as an American hostage being taken to the Sheikh Abdullah Barracks by Shi'ite militiamen for the handover. If you are challenged by Syrian checkpoint guards or Hezbollah militiamen, Captain Gamble will try to talk you through. Neither Syrian ground forces nor Hezbollah patrols can know exactly how many hostages have been taken to the barracks, from what direction the other militias are bringing them and over precisely what period of time. Not even the PLO knows all of that, only Hezbollah Command and some of their mullahs. It's a subterfuge that just might work long enough to get you inside the barracks. However, if you are challenged and it looks like things are going bad you will neutralise whatever opposition you encounter. But you must try to minimise actual combat and preserve the element of surprise until you reach Sheikh Abdullah

Barracks. Any major conflagration in the area before you actually arrive at the barracks will only endanger the lives of the hostages.'

'What's likely to happen if the PLO has taken delivery of the hostages but hasn't left the barracks?' Vance asked.

'We don't know,' Halloran smiled. 'We have to assume the worst case. The PLO may not like it but they'll be outnumbered and Hezbollah could simply shoot the hostages. With any luck they'll fight each other — that would only assist us by adding to the confusion, but we can't count on it.'

He continued: 'Mr Lynch will divide and deploy the team according to the situation on the ground at the time. However, you will need a major diversion at the barracks. Something of a catastrophic nature to create maximum confusion while the rest of the team gets to the hostages and pulls them out ...'

'We could blow away half the fort,' Bono volunteered.

'As long as you make sure it's the right half,' Halloran said. 'Once you have the hostages you will commandeer the appropriate vehicles and proceed south, towards Israeli lines.' He thumbed the remote and an enlarged map of southern Lebanon and northern Israel appeared showing all the highways, including a highlighted road directly south from Ba'albek to a town called Metulla on the Israeli border.

'That's a distance of one hundred kilometres. It's rough country but that's to your advantage and the roads are surprisingly well maintained. You could do it in two hours. As you approach the border you will prominently display a white flag. If you are successful you should reach friendly lines within twenty-four hours of exiting the aircraft.' He left the rest unsaid.

Nobody spoke.

'Okay,' Halloran added. 'Here are the nine hostages we expect to be handed over to the PLO.'

The map was replaced by a display of nine passport type photographs. The silence seemed to intensify as they studied the faces. Even though they knew why they had been brought together, this was the moment when it hit them all like a hammer blow — the first time they had studied the faces of the hostages in close up. Halloran clicked the remote and separate blow-ups of each hostage appeared, one at a time. He rolled off the names, jobs, where each man had been snatched ... how long each one had been held hostage.

'...William Randolph Wallace...' Halloran was saying. 'Aged fifty-seven. Political science lecturer at the American University in Beirut. Married with two kids. Helluva wife. She's held her job and her family together through this for nearly five years.'

The picture was an official mugshot, probably from the university. It showed a narrow-faced man with thinning grey hair brushed back from a high forehead. Jacket, shirt, tie knotted loosely under a prominent Adam's apple. His eyes had an almost startled look, as though the photographer's flash had caught him by surprise. It made him look vulnerable.

'Wallace was employed by the NSA for eleven years before he took the university posting in 1972. They kept in touch through our people at the Embassy in Beirut and he did occasional, low level research for them. Nothing major. What he did certainly didn't present a threat to anybody.'

Lynch and the others studied the picture. Wallace didn't look like he could present a threat to a butterfly.

'Somebody got their information screwed up somewhere.' Halloran continued. 'Hezbollah snatched him in September, 1987. Thought he was a spy. They tried to trade him for big bucks but they've since learned he's not that important. He's been allowed no contact with the Red Cross, no messages to or from his family ... nothing.'

'Are we sure he's still alive?' Gamble asked.

'Oh he's still alive,' Halloran confirmed. 'They're all still alive... in a manner of speaking. Christ knows what this has done to their minds.'

The photographs went on: a clerk from the US Embassy

in Beirut, an agricultural advisor, a TV sound man from the NBC, a freelance journalist, a 70-year-old Catholic priest, an airline clerk, a retired businessman, a student from the American University... and Wallace. A parade of faces pathetic in their ordinariness. Through it all ran the narrative thread of Halloran's litany of misery, the details of their unjust imprisonment, the families devastated, the lives and minds irreparably damaged. When it was over there was not a man in the room who could speak. Halloran switched on the lights and looked around the table at their faces. Every one of them was ready to go that minute.

June 26

A hail of bullets smacked into the rock face sending slivers of granite and ricochets howling across the valley. The echo reverberated around the mountain peaks and rolled back down on the knot of men in the dusty paddock behind the big house.

'The M16A2 has an effective range of 800 metres,' Lynch said, lowering the smoking weapon. 'Thirty round magazine, 5.56mm cartridge, auto, semi-auto and three-round burst capability.'

It was about 500 metres up a gentle incline from the back door of the house to the mountain face at the end of the valley. Because there was plenty of open space and they were shielded on three sides by mountains it made a perfect shooting gallery. Lynch decided it was time that the men got in some practice with the weapons they would be using for the assault on the Sheikh Abdullah Barracks. All of them were familiar with the two basic assault weapons he had selected, the American-made M16A2, which was the latest version of the M16, and the Heckler and Koch MP5, the weapon preferred by Special Forces the world over for close work such as hostage rescue. However, not all of them had worked with the refinements he had adopted.

Lynch had set up a couple of folding metal tables and laid out a long strip of blue plastic sheeting on the ground covered with an elaborate pattern of weapons and ammunition. A couple of Halloran's guards had wandered over to watch the show although there was no sign of either Halloran or Howard. Lynch hadn't spoken much to Halloran at all after their tense exchange the previous night. The briefing was followed by dinner and Halloran had made a special effort to make it enjoyable, telling scandalous stories about rich and powerful friends, expounding on his patriotic philosophies, drawing out the three newcomers, seeking their opinions, encouraging them to tell their own stories. He had done a good job, too, Lynch had to concede. He even got Cooper to talk a little about the relative merits of modern sniping rifles. The atmosphere had been more relaxed at the end of the evening than at any time since they'd arrived. Only Lynch had appeared not to enjoy himself.

He bent down to pick up a rifle identical to the M16A2 except that the forestock was fitted with a second, much fatter barrel underneath. He held the weapon in one hand and hefted a yellow bullet about the size of a spray can in the other.

'The improved M203 grenade launcher, gentlemen,' he explained. 'It can deliver a spin stabilised grenade 400 to 450 metres.'

He dropped the grenade into the launcher, raised it and aimed it at the far mountain face.

'From this distance we should just about make the foot of the mountainside,' he said.

Bono yawned. He had seen what the old M203 could do.

Lynch pulled the trigger, the launcher coughed and jumped against his shoulder. A full second later they saw a vivid flash of flame against the foot of the mountain. It was followed by a huge fountain of shattered basalt and dirt and an instant later the shockwave hit them with an almighty crack that almost split their eardrums. They all flinched in surprise and

211

watched incredulous as the dirt and stone boiled into a cloud which grew until it seemed to blot out half the mountainside. They heard the first shower of small debris hitting the ground less than a hundred metres from where they stood. The dust began to clear and instead of a continual line of rubble at the bottom of the mountain there was now a gaping wound. A few seconds before there had been boulders the size of cars jumbled together with smaller, fallen debris. Now there was just a ragged, scorched crater, the big rocks smashed and shrugged aside by the blast.

'Jesus,' Bono blinked.

'Each one the equivalent of fifty sticks of gelignite,' Lynch said. 'Enough to turn a T-72 into a backyard barbecue or demolish a house. Half a dozen of these will make the Sheikh Abdullah Barracks look like Jupiter's temple. Each man will carry six.'

He put the rifle and grenade launcher back on the plastic mat and picked up an MP5.

'You are all familiar with this,' he said. 'The Heckler MP5 uses 9mm Parabellum, fires 800 rounds per minute and has a 30-round magazine. We will use it once we are inside the barracks. Some of you, however, will not be familiar with this.' He rolled a copper clad bullet with a black tip between his fingers.

'This is the Glaser Safety Slug. It is teflon coated, it has high penetrating power and is ideal for hostage rescue operations because once it has hit the target it fragments and does not pose any threat to hostages or other members of the team from ricochets.'

Lynch plucked a body armour vest off the sheet and threw it to Reece.

'Put this on,' he ordered.

Reece caught the vest. 'You sure about this?'

'Trust me.'

Reece put on the vest and Lynch ordered him to stand behind one of the metal tables he had set up nearby. On

212

the table was a one-gallon oil drum filled with water.

'Turn around,' Lynch ordered.

Reece turned and Lynch dropped to one knee six metres from the table, about nine metres from Reece. Reece had barely completed his turn when Lynch fired a single shot, the oil can leaped and Reece staggered forward under the impact of the slug against his right shoulder.

'You coulda fuckin' told me it was coming,' Reece yelled.

'You were never in danger,' Lynch smiled.

There was a neat hole in the side of the oil can where the slug had entered, a jagged metal gash where it had exited, and the right shoulder of the body armour vest was impregnated with deadly shot fragments.

'If the can was a door and Reece was an unprotected terrorist on the other side of that door...' Lynch needed explain no further.

He ordered everybody to stay put, quickly set down the sub-machine gun and picked up a chunky, rugged looking pistol.

'The famous 9mm Browning High-power comes with non-slip grip and red spot sighting,' Lynch smiled. 'We won't have time for red spot sighting, gentlemen. We will have time for this.' He rolled a new bullet between his fingers then inserted it into the clip and slammed the clip into the pistol. Reece had just slipped off the body armour and was flexing and rubbing his shoulder and mumbling about the bruise he would have. Lynch took the vest from him, dropped it over the still emptying can of water and fired.

The vest and the can jumped as though hit by a baseball bat and toppled to the ground. Lynch quickly retrieved them and dumped them back on the table. The oil can had fresh entry and exit holes. So did the vest.

'Shit.' It was Reece. He had forgotten about his shoulder.

'High velocity, armour-piercing rounds, bronze alloy, teflon coated,' Lynch said. 'Not preferred for hostage situations because innocent people can get hurt. Very effective, however, for subduing the gentleman who hides behind a wall or is wearing body armour. We may need it.' Lynch returned the Browning to the plastic sheet and picked up another vest. It was the same dark blue colour as the ruined vest although it was thinner, lighter and festooned with loops, pockets and pouches. 'This is a load-carrying assault vest,' Lynch said. 'We will be carrying a lot of gear when we go into the barracks. There will be no further need for disguise then. Indeed, in the confusion it will be essential that we recognise each other immediately.'

He began stacking the vest with ammunition clips and grenades.

'The vest is made of layered kevlar so it offers some ballistic protection too,' he said. 'But its great advantage is that it makes carrying everything easy.'

When he was finished Lynch had the six grenades secured, two clips and another 300 rounds each for the rifle and the MP5, including sixty rounds of Glasers and two clips of high velocity shells for the Browning in a side holster. The MP5 was clenched in his left fist, the other hand free.

'We'll only need one gun at a time,' he said. 'We'll be carrying 3,000 rounds per man when we make the drop. We take that with us to the barracks in the commandeered vehicles and we'd better have some left to get us to the border afterwards.'

He gestured at a couple of empty belt clips attached to the vest.

'Built-in rappelling harness,' he explained, looking at Bono. 'Just in case we have to do any clever stuff.' He put down the MP5, removed the vest and handed it to Gamble. Gamble left the ammo in the vest and began picking through the groundsheets for his own equipment.

'So far we've talked about all the force and violence we're going to be applying during this operation,' Lynch said, dropping his tone to let them know he'd finished the war toy talk.

214

'It is comforting to know that we're going to have all this firepower and the best assault gear in the world at our disposal but I'd still like to think we can rely on the element of surprise when we get there. With any luck at all the bastards won't be expecting an attack. The odds are very good indeed that they'll assume no-one would be crazy enough to attempt a rescue in the heart of the Beqa'a Valley. If we get there undetected there's a chance we can lie low during the day and attempt a covert penetration after dark. I'd like to give it a try before we just kick in the fucking front door and start shooting everything that moves.'

'Not by strength, by guile,' Gamble said sardonically. The SAS man had quoted the SBS motto.

Lynch smiled. 'Captain Gamble is going to demonstrate the benefits of stealth and skill.'

Gamble set off towards the escarpment they had scaled two days earlier, an enormous length of rope wrapped diagonally across his torso. Lynch watched him go for a moment then turned to Cooper.

'You care to show us what your weapon can do, sergeant?'

Cooper had agreed to demonstrate his gun at Lynch's request but the way he hesitated and looked at everyone through those heavy-lidded eyes seemed to imply that the world was always demanding too much of him. He walked over to the second table and picked up a battered leather rifle case. He unzipped the case, pulled out the rifle and looked at it for a moment as though it were an old friend. Everyone crowded around. Most of them had never seen a Russian sniping rifle before. Lynch had only seen one, captured from a Spetsnaz soldier in Afghanistan. It was strikingly different from any Western equivalent and, with its long barrel and cut-away butt had an old fashioned, cut rate look about it. Lynch knew that despite its appearance, the SVD or Dragunov was reputed to be one of the best balanced and most durable sniping rifles in the world. A semi-automatic based on the AK-47, it fired 7.62mm shells, had an effective range of 1,000 metres, and an unusually large magazine capacity of ten rounds for a sniper rifle. The Dragunov had two other unusual features. Instead of a bipod for added stability it had a shoulder sling. This gave the sniper the considerable advantage of mobility as well as stability. There was no need to set the rifle down on a bipod for accuracy. The sniper could simply drop to one knee, stabilise the rifle on the sling and snap off a series of devastatingly accurate rounds. The second intriguing Soviet innovation was incorporated into the sight, which had a graduated range-finding scale based on the height of the average man. By fitting the target into the sight grid, the sniper got an accurate idea of the range. Simple, but effective.

Cooper couldn't conceal his pride as everyone wanted to inspect the Dragunov. By the time they were all satisfied they had forgotten about Gamble. Lynch looked up towards the escarpment but couldn't find the SAS man. He glanced at his watch. Half an hour had passed; Gamble should have at least started the climb. Then he realised that he was looking too low. His eyes ranged up the mountainside and found Gamble, barely fifty metres from the summit. It had taken him a quarter of the time it had taken the rest of the team two days earlier. The men switched their attention to Gamble. They watched as he vaulted over the last few ramparts of granite and then began walking nimbly along the mountain's ragged spine. He was heading further up towards the summit to where the mountainside was at its steepest ... a terrifying sheet of vertical rock glinting in the morning sun. Cooper took his rifle and strolled quietly away from the others as they focused their attention on Gamble. He tested the balance of the Dragunov in his hand and smiled then raised it to his shoulder. He adjusted the shoulder sling and then squinted through the sight at the small figure nearly 600 metres away on the mountain ridge. He began adjusting the grid to get Gamble's height just right. It wasn't easy because the SAS man kept bobbing and ducking as he negotiated the rocky crags. Cooper took his time.

A few minutes later Gamble reached the summit and stopped to give a cheery wave to the distant group of men.

'Yoo-hoo,' Bono growled.

They watched while the tiny figure secured the rappelling rope and estimated the distance to the ground. Lynch guessed it was more than 250 metres. He hoped Gamble had taken the right length of rope.

Gamble jumped. He leaped away from the summit and began to free fall. A moment later his feet connected with the rock face and then something astonishing happened. Gamble thrust his body forward like a runner leaving the blocks and started to sprint down the sheer face of the mountain.

'Shit,' Reece gasped. 'That can't be done.'

'Fast roping, gentlemen,' Lynch said. 'That's how it's done.' They couldn't hear it or see it but Lynch knew Gamble's rappelling rope, his umbilical to the summit, was unravelling behind him with blinding speed as he ran down the side of the mountain. He had set his three-speed descendeur to give him rapid descent for the first 200 metres, then the brake would come on. He would slow to medium descent and then slow for the last few metres. To Gamble it felt exactly the way it looked from the ground — as though he were sprinting down the side of a mountain to a rocky brown wall waiting for him at the bottom.

Cooper slammed a round into the breech and followed Gamble through the sight. The Briton had caught him by surprise. He didn't like that. It took away the shock value of what he was going to do.

When it seemed Gamble had lost control of his descent and must slam into the ground in another instant he suddenly slowed. The descendeur bit and the nylon rope pulled him back to a fast walk. Two seconds later the descendeur grabbed again, Gamble shortened his stride and appeared to just stroll off the mountain.

Cooper fired. Everyone froze. Gamble seemed to stagger and go into an awkward crouch.

217

Lynch saw it first. The severed rope was falling away from the mountain summit in a series of graceful loops and coils until it fell in a heap around Gamble on the ground. Gamble took his hands away from over his head and began to straighten up.

'Thanks, sergeant,' Lynch said. 'Saves him going back for it later.'

'Hi, this is Janice ... I've gone away for a few days ...'

Lynch hung up. It was a little after nine at night at the La Paz post office. Close to midnight in New York. He decided to try the building's security and quiz whichever doorman was on duty. He knew most of the security men in Janice's building — it was one of the most expensive buildings on Park Avenue and employed one of the best security firms in the city. More importantly — they knew him. Trade always recognises trade and most of the security men who protected Janice's building knew Lynch was at the top of his. He had made a point of cultivating them all. He never knew when he might need them as an early warning for himself. In the beginning he had asked a few pointed questions so they understood he knew the security business, though he was careful not to antagonise any of them by flaunting his superior knowledge. They knew Janice too and liked her. Apart from the fact that she was a beautiful woman who was never offended by their smutty jokes, Janice believed, like Lynch, that it was good insurance to keep the doormen on her side and every Christmas each one of them got an envelope with a card enclosing a couple of hundred dollar bills. It was the kind of gift they appreciated. Lynch had made a point of always stopping to chat for a minute, going in or out. Now, he decided, it was time to put all that groundwork to the test.

'Park Towers security ... can I help you?'

Lynch recognised the voice.

'Martin, this is Colin Lynch, can you hear me okay?'

218

'Mr Lynch? Hey, how y'doing… where you been? Long time no — '

'Yes, Martin,' Lynch interrupted. 'Look, this is important. I've been away on business a couple of weeks and I haven't heard from Miss Street. I need to know she's all right. Have you seen her lately?'

'Yeah, well, I tell ya, Mr Lynch, it's none of my business, y'know but I was kinda wondering about that myself.'

The line started to fade. Lynch swore.

'Sorry, Mr Lynch?'

'What's been going on there, Martin?'

'Well, I don't want to speak out of turn, y'know. I mean, what you and Miss Street do in your private lives is your business, y'know?'

Martin was in his mid-30s, a working class guy working his way up. He was decent, reliable and respectable, but security work was the only way he would ever make it to Park Avenue.

'Martin… this is very important. I am very worried about Miss Street's safety. She could be in danger. I may have to cut short my business trip. Have you seen her these past few days?'

'No, I been working nights. I haven't seen her for two, three days.'

'How was she when you last saw her?'

'Not good.'

'Fuck… Martin?' Lynch almost yelled. 'What do you mean not good?'

'She was with another guy.'

'What kind of guy.'

'Well, that's what I mean by not speaking out of turn, y'know. I mean, maybe it's Miss Street's private business y'know? Maybe I got it all wrong, anyway. Hey, I shouldn't have said anything.'

'Martin… you better tell me what you saw that didn't seem right, because if Miss Street gets hurt out of any of this I'm going to take it very personally and I'm going to come back up there tonight and I am going to be so upset I am going to turn you into a fucking invalid.'

There was a sudden pause.

'Martin?'

'Yeah, okay. All right. I just... well, I saw her leave the building three days ago with this other guy. It was late, real late. One o'clock in the morning, something like that. And she ain't been going out that time of night for a long time, not since you and her... y'know?'

'Yes... what else?'

'Well, even though it was night-time and the guy was dressed real sharp, like he was going somewhere special, she just had ordinary day clothes on.'

'How did she look?'

'Like she got dressed in a hurry. Kind of messy y'know... for her. And she looked tired, like she hadn't slept much.'

'What else?'

Martin took a deep breath. 'Well, she looked upset about something. I thought she looked upset. Like this guy had brought bad news or something. And she looked like she didn't want to go with him. Like, she had to... but she wasn't very happy about it, know what I mean?'

'Do you know where they went?'

'No.'

'Did she have any bags?'

'No. I can tell you something else though. They went away in a company limo. One of those limos STC uses. I know them and I know the drivers. It seemed strange to me because they haven't been calling for her for a long time either.'

'What did the guy look like?'

'Oh, tall, long blonde hair, expensive haircut, sharp clothes, plenty of style, y'know? Some women really go for that type but he seemed kinda... slimy to me, y'know. Tell you something else though... she seemed scared of him. That surprised me. She wasn't her usual self at all. She just said goodnight and then kind of looked at me for a long time like she was trying to tell me something. Then she got in the car...' he rambled to a halt.

'That's all I can tell you Mr Lynch, honest. Maybe it doesn't mean anything, y'know. Maybe it doesn't mean anything at all. Mr Lynch...?'

The handset was swinging uselessly on its steel cord where Lynch had dropped it. He was already in the Cherokee. In the security booth in the lobby of Janice's building in Manhattan Martin heard the angry roar of a powerful car engine all the way from Baja then it faded away and there was nothing. Martin hung up and shook his head. For a good looking couple like that who looked like they had it made, he thought, they had some serious problems. He would find out soon enough. He shrugged and went back to the *New York Post*.

Lynch drove back to the house in less than half an hour. He nearly lost the car over the side of the road at one point and he took another bend wide and nearly collected a truck with a terrified old couple in the front. He forced himself to slow down as he drove up the track, under the adobe arch and between the avenue of sagging palms. Even so, the guards knew immediately that something was very wrong. Lynch pulled up outside the front porch and got out of the car, leaving the door open and the lights on. The two guards at the security post in the garage wandered out to see who it was. They saw Lynch take the steps three at a time and hurl open the ironwood slab door with a crash that shook the house. The two guards looked at each other. One of them pulled out his pocket radio and called Dennis. The other carefully unholstered his Uzi and went after Lynch.

Vance, Bono and Reece were sitting in the big room talking when Lynch hustled past them and ran up the stairs. Bono started to say something then stopped. Lynch reached the landing and broke into a trot along the balcony and down the corridor towards Halloran's room. The door to Howard's room opened and Howard stepped out to see what the loud crash downstairs had been. Lynch saw him with perfect clarity. Howard was wearing a gorgeous silk paisley-patterned dressing gown, the old-fashioned kind that guys like Noel Coward used to wear. Howard saw Lynch striding towards Halloran's room and made one of the biggest mistakes of his life.

'What the fuck do you think you're doing?' he demanded, and stepped in front of Lynch.

Lynch hardly altered his stride. He made a slight sideways turn to compensate for the angle, then his left foot lashed out like a bolt of lightning. The ball of his foot landed squarely under Howard's jaw with a sickening crack and, for a moment, it lifted Howard right off his feet. Howard's head snapped back as though hit with a pick-axe handle and a sudden spurt of blood and teeth sprayed from his mouth. He slammed back hard against the doorjamb and bounced forward. But he was already unconscious and his legs buckled. Howard crumpled soundlessly to the floor like a discarded paisley scarf, a thick stream of blood from his shattered jaw running out of his mouth and onto the carpet. Lynch's adrenalin was surging. He didn't wait to try the door handle to Halloran's room. His foot lashed out again, the handle and lock disintegrated in a blizzard of splinters and broken metal and the door flew open. Halloran's room was empty. The door to Halloran's private bathroom was open and that was empty too. Lynch saw him through the double doors in the temporary communications room from where he could still run his empire, yelling at generals, bullying politicians, ordering and destroying lives. Halloran had heard the noise and was standing up in front of the computer screen where he had been working. The room was in a kind of eerie green twilight, illuminated only by the glow from the three PC screens he had arranged around him in a semi-circle. Lynch strode towards him, even now not entirely sure of what he was going to do and whether he could stop himself.

Halloran watched him with a strange fascination on his broad, green-tinged face. There was no sign of fear or apprehension in his eyes, just the brute knowledge that events had suddenly, dramatically escalated right out of his control. His fate was in the hands of the man rushing towards him with murderous determination and for the first time in ages there was nothing he could do to stop it.

Lynch found his way barred by the arc of desks supporting Halloran's computer terminals. He grabbed the middle terminal in both hands and hurled it across the room like a toy. It shattered against the wall with a tremendous explosion, sending shards of glass flying across the room. Lynch didn't seem to notice. He reached across the desk with both hands, grabbed Halloran by the shirt collar and hauled him off his feet and across the desk top towards him. Halloran was bigger and heavier than Lynch but he was nowhere near as fit or powerful. Lynch's biceps stood out like rocks under his navy blue T-shirt and the cords in his neck bulged like ropes.

'Where is she?' Lynch asked, his voice a hoarse, deadly whisper. 'Tell me now or God help me I'll kill you right here.'

Lynch heard the ripple of automatic weapons being cocked as the first guards ran into the room, then more of the soft, sinister clicks as the other guards arrived. They fanned out quickly and softly behind Halloran to get Lynch in a crossfire without hitting their boss. The muzzles of six Uzis began to close in on Lynch.

He didn't seem to notice. He never took his eyes away from Halloran's face. His hands were bunched around his employer's throat, clothing and soft flesh seized in the vice of his clenched fists. Lynch didn't care how many bullets hit him. It would take him less than a second to rip the rapidly pulsing carotid artery from Halloran's neck. And he could do that with his dying breath if he had to.

'She's safe,' Halloran gritted. It was almost impossible for him to speak under Lynch's grip. One of the guards began edging closer towards Lynch, the muzzle of the Uzi aimed at his head.

'You lied to me, you fucking bastard,' Lynch screamed.

223

There was an undercurrent of pain in the voice. 'Where is she?'

He intensified his grip and there was an ugly, strangled rattle in Halloran's throat. A thin stream of saliva began to ooze from the corner of his mouth and trickle down his chin.

The guard with the Uzi edged closer. He had made up his mind. He was going for a kill.

'One more step, pal, and your head is going right out the fucking window.'

It was Bono. Everyone had forgotten about the team. Bono stood in the open door to the corridor, a Browning High-power in his hand pointed at the guard edging closest to Lynch. Beside him was Reece with a raised MP5.

'Time to choose, fellers,' Bono added. 'What's it gonna be? We gonna start winding this thing back a little or we gonna fuck it all and go for gold?'

'She's okay,' Halloran grunted. 'She's safe. I had her taken somewhere safe, for Christ's sake. What's the matter with you?'

Lynch still looked murderous. He shook Halloran like a dog with a rag and thrust his face closer till they almost touched.

'Where is she?'

'She's in one of our safe houses.' There was a tremor in his voice. Halloran was starting to crack. 'I had her taken to a safe house till this thing is over. I want her safe too, for Christ's sake ... I love her too.'

Lynch let go and Halloran fell onto the desk like a sack of chaff. No-one moved for what seemed like an eternity. Slowly, very slowly Lynch began to straighten up, his fists still clenched in front of him, the knuckles white. The whole room seemed to sigh. The closest guard stepped swiftly towards Lynch, pressed the Uzi sideways across his chest and pushed him up against the nearest wall. Lynch didn't resist. His face looked grey and suddenly seemed drained of all expression. Dennis arrived looking anxious and switched on the light. The room was a mess. Bono and Reece stepped inside, guns lowered.

'Hey,' Bono grabbed the shoulder of the guard holding Lynch against the wall. 'Show a little respect. This guy is worth two hundred of you, shithead.'

The guard seemed unconvinced.

'Let him go.' It was Halloran. Two of the guards had helped him to a chair and Dennis had brought him a glass of water. The mood in the room was still tense but everyone sensed that the real threat had passed. The guard stepped away from Lynch. He still didn't seem to see everything clearly.

'Where's Howard?' Halloran asked.

'Well, Howard is next door,' Reece shrugged, 'but his teeth are in Acapulco.'

'Jesus.' Halloran drank the water and massaged his neck and shoulders. There were still livid white finger marks around his neck and shoulders where Lynch had held him. There would be massive bruises there in the morning. He looked at Dennis.

'Take Brad and get Howard to the hospital in La Paz.' he ordered. Dennis vanished from the room with the guard in tow.

'Come and sit down, Lynch,' the big American said. 'Let's get this thing clear.'

Lynch looked at him.

'Everybody else just fuck off,' Halloran grunted. The tough old bastard was getting his composure back, they realised. 'It's over. It's okay. Just go back to what you were doing. We'll clean this up later. Mr Lynch and I are going to have . . . a little chat.'

Slowly, reluctantly, they filed out of the room. When they had gone Halloran got up and closed the doors. He pulled a swivel chair up beside the desk for Lynch and slumped back in his own chair. Lynch still hadn't moved.

'Come on,' Halloran gestured to the empty chair. 'Sit down.'

Lynch took a long time but finally he stirred, crossed over to the chair and sat down. The two men looked at each other in silence. The murder may have gone from Lynch's face, Halloran realised, but there was still danger there.

'Yeah,' he nodded slowly. 'It's true. I love her. Did she ever tell you about us?'

Lynch didn't move.

'Well,' Halloran said. 'There wasn't a lot to tell, I suppose. And it was a while ago... for her. Nearly ten years. Seems like last week to me. I had just pulled her out of Radcliffe, introduced her to a way of life she'd only glimpsed until then. I had wanted her to do a certain kind of work for me.' He looked at Lynch.

'You know what I'm talking about?'

Lynch nodded.

'She did well too. She was beautiful. And smart. And tough. And everything else. The problem was, I ended up falling for her myself. We had a... fling I guess is what it was. I could still impress and intimidate her then but she soon got past that. As soon as she realised she didn't have to sleep with the boss she wanted out. She was twenty-one years old. She didn't love me. Oh she liked me well enough and she liked the things I could do for her but she didn't love me. Who the hell can blame her? She told me she would still work for me but only as a free agent and on her own terms. And she meant it. And I bought it. Because there's something special about Janice, isn't there? You've seen it. You're in love with her. She's everywoman, every man's dream. A lady and a whore. And all these years it's been a kind of sweet agony because I could have her close but I could never touch her. Instead I had to watch her... service all these other bastards. Worse than that, half of them were friends of mine and she was doing me favours by helping me put together the organisation that I have today. And I'm not talking about the business side of it, Lynch, you *do* understand that? I'm talking about *this* side, the operational

226

side. The side that gets things done. And if getting things done and getting what I wanted meant Janice had to sleep with somebody in the Cabinet or one of the joint chiefs... or the President of the United States then she did it... and she grew stronger and richer doing it.' He chuckled for a moment but it hurt his throat and he had to cough. 'Then, in the end, what happens? She goes and falls for a fucking hit man. A sailor. And all the time, you know, I loved her. Pathetic for an old man isn't it?'

'Where is she?'

Halloran nodded. 'I had Howard pick her up before we came down here. We dropped her off in Washington first and she's been taken to a safe house there for a few days. She'll be moved to another one after a few days and then another one until this operation is over.'

'Why did you lie to me... why did you tell me you didn't know where she was?'

'Because you didn't have to know,' Halloran said. 'You might not like it but you didn't have to know. And besides... you wanted this operation. You walked away from her.'

The fire flared in Lynch's eyes but only for a moment because he knew Halloran was right.

'Are you certain she's in danger?'

'After Tuckey I'd say there's a reasonable bet that we're *all* in danger... wouldn't you?'

Lynch fixed him with a strange look. He believed Halloran this far. He believed that he might still be in love with Janice and he believed that he wanted her safe. But he also believed that Halloran was capable of ordering Tuckey's death to save the operation. Everything he had said tonight had served to confirm that. He had used the woman he supposedly loved as a whore for ten years, to help him build the clandestine operational empire he now controlled.

'Who is she in danger from?' Lynch asked.

Halloran heard the new emphasis in Lynch's voice but appeared not to understand it.

227

'We still don't know,' he shrugged. 'The FBI is looking, the CIA... Christ, Lynch, it's being investigated. But there are half a dozen groups in the US alone, and another dozen around the world who would like to get at us, me, the people in my organisation. It's going to take a while to find out. There's a long process of elimination involved here. But when we do find out...' he leaned forward and touched Lynch's arm. 'We'll hit the fuckers with everything we've got.'

Lynch leaned back and pulled his arm away.

'I hope so,' he said, standing up. 'Because if you're still lying to me and I come back from this operation to find she's been hurt — I'll kill you.' He got up to go.

'And all this,' he added, glancing at the computer hardware and the debris of the shattered terminal on the floor, 'all your power, your plans, your vital operations, your big organisation, everything you've ever built in the last forty years... will all die with you.'

7
DANCE OF THE NIGHTHAWKS

June 27

Spray whipped Lynch's face as he rode the launch out to the *American Endeavour*. Halloran's yacht had arrived the previous night from the Caribbean via the Panama Canal, and was moored in the outer harbour at Cabo San Lucas, the tourist boom town at the southernmost tip of the Baja peninsula. The rest of the team sprawled around the afterdeck of the launch as it butted easily through gentle swells. Another achingly perfect day in Baja, Lynch thought. Clear sky, blue water, enough of a breeze to cheat the sun of its sting and the rejuvenating kiss of sea spray. The events of the previous night had already been replayed several times in his mind. He regretted none of it.

The chopper from the yacht had picked up Halloran at the house earlier that morning. Dennis had arranged for the rest of the team to be at the dockside in Cabo by eleven. The youthful former midshipman had aged overnight, Lynch thought. Obviously the mayhem between Halloran, Lynch and Howard and the sudden, shocking prospect that the whole operation could be ripped asunder before it started had shaken him. He told them on the dockside that he hadn't got back from La Paz till three in the morning. He looked like he hadn't slept at all. Howard would spend a few days at the hospital in La Paz and then fly home to convalesce. The jaw was broken in at least eight places, Dennis said. It would be wired and set in a cast and Howard would have to eat

229

through a straw for three months. When the cast came off he would be fitted with dentures. The doctors said he was lucky. The impact from the blow could have driven bone splinters up through his sinus cavities into his brain. It was a peculiar injury, the doctors said, and they speculated on what kind of blow would cause such damage. Dennis had told them it had been a blow from a golf club in the hands of an inexperienced golf partner. The doctors seemed surprised but Dennis had paid cash in advance for Howard's treatment and they hadn't pressed it. Dennis eyed Lynch warily as he spoke and Lynch wondered if the youngster was really cut out to be Howard's replacement.

The launch bumped past the protective granite knuckles of the Cape which guards the harbour, policing the rowdy Pacific swells, softening and subduing them before they could disturb the serenity of the Sea of Cortez. *American Endeavour* was anchored in the middle of the outer harbour, barely sixty metres from the spectacular sea-worn arch that marks the tip of Cabo San Lucas. Miffed by the appearance of the big private yacht the lesser luxury yachts self-consciously turned their backs while a vulgar flotilla of pongas flirted around the big ship, trying vainly to catch its attention. Tourists aboard the pongas unashamedly tried to guess which movie star, fugitive politician or business tycoon might be on board. They craned their necks even harder to see who was aboard the launch as it pulled up alongside the boarding stairs to the *Endeavour*. The tourists were disappointed by the file of scruffy, unshaven men who decanted themselves from the launch to the ship. They didn't look at all important. They looked like returning crewmen or tradesmen summoned to do some dirty work for the owner. In that sense, at least, the tourists were right.

There was no-one to greet the team when Dennis led them on board. They caught a brief glimpse of Captain Penny in his correct, starched whites watching them from the bridge.

'How's it hangin', Hornblower?' Bono called up to him.

Penny turned away. He had seen them before and didn't approve.

Lynch looked around. It felt like a different ship. He glanced towards the fantail. Seventeen days had passed since he and Janice had lounged out there after making love for the last time. It might as well have been seventeen years, it seemed so distant and unreal to him now. The Puma was still there on the helipad, the same chopper that had brought Halloran and his irresistible offer to them at Andros Island. The world had turned seventeen times since then and a few people had fallen off.

Halloran was waiting for them in his stateroom. He wore a plum coloured Ascot under his shirt to hide the ugly, purple bruises which had appeared around his neck and shoulders since last night. Lynch thought he looked haggard but felt not even a twinge of sympathy. Halloran had another man with him, a tall, bony, dark haired man wearing a flight suit. Lynch recognised the chopper pilot.

'This is Will Lipscombe,' Halloran said, his voice husky, as though he was suffering from a sore throat. 'He's going to take you on a joy ride over the mountains to the Pacific side and show you what you'll be flying over tomorrow night. We'll do one full-scale rehearsal, using the Nighthawks, and that will have to do. I've chartered a good plane from Aeronaves and Captain Lipscombe will be the pilot for the jump. We'll set the NAVSTAR co-ordinates for the highway one kilometre south of El Triunfo. It's as close as we can get to the real thing before you go. However, we will have a few vehicles circled there with their headlights on to show you the DZ. You won't have that at El Laboue.'

'That's a main highway,' Gamble said. 'What are you going to do about traffic?'

'We'll still be on my property, about a hundred metres in from the road,' Halloran said. 'There's a screen of trees between the road and the DZ, just like the orchards at El Laboue. We'll make it look like a little cook-out for a bunch of tourists. They do that at the dude ranches here all the time. We'll have a couple of my men at the roadside to discourage anybody who gets too curious.'

'What about the cops?' Vance asked.

'Won't be too many cops using that road at one o'clock in the morning,' Halloran said. 'They don't exactly work themselves to the bone down here. If somebody does come along we'll slip 'em a little *mordida* and tell 'em to fuck off. If that doesn't work, well, we might have to get a little more heavy-handed.'

'Why can't we make the jump in the daytime?' Reece asked.

'Because we don't want every vacationing American and nosy cop in southern Baja wondering what half a dozen guys are doing floating around the sky in big black parachutes,' Halloran said.

'Apart from that,' Gamble added, his head inclined slightly toward Reece, 'it's a lot rougher to fly over mountains in the daytime. You get a lot of thermals and wild air currents swirling around the mountain peaks and up from the valleys from the heat of the day. It would be a little like riding a wild bull in the middle of the sky. The middle of the night is the coolest, calmest time... much more civilised.'

'Much,' Halloran repeated.

'And on top of that,' Gamble added, turning his head back towards Halloran. 'You have two highly inexperienced jumpers here. Are you sure they should be chancing it tomorrow night?'

'They have to know what the real thing is going to be like,' Halloran said. 'I know it's taking a chance. This entire operation is one big chance. Besides —' he stopped and smiled awkwardly. 'I have a lot of faith in Mr Reece and Mr Bono. More importantly, I have a lot of faith in the equipment. We'll put tracking devices on the 'chutes for this jump and my men aboard the *Endeavour* will be able to track each one of you for a radius of eighty kilometres. We'll know where each of you is the moment you leave the plane. Even

232

if they don't score a bullseye on the DZ, it doesn't matter. We'll have a couple of guys in a pick-up on the road to collect them if they overshoot and land on the highway. The *Endeavour* will up anchor tomorrow morning and cruise up the coast with lights blazing. She'll be hard to miss. If any of you overshoot the DZ by a long shot, you'll see the *Endeavour* from eighty kilometres away and that's your cue to turn around and steer back inland to the DZ. If you really fuck it up, a couple of my boys will have the launch in the water to pick up anyone who lands between the beach and the ship. In the event that any of you should land in an area where there are people, you will explain that you are a member of a hang-gliding club and you will pay for any damages. For precisely that reason you will not be carrying any ordnance on this jump, unlike the jump into Lebanon when each man will be carrying an additional 115-130 kilos of equipment. That means you'll be jumping light this time — so it should be that much easier.'

He looked pointedly at Reece and Bono then at the other four men. 'The Nighthawks and NAVSTAR will get them to the drop zone. They have to know what it means to glide over mountains in the dark and to keep their cool, whatever happens.'

Gamble shrugged. 'It's your party,' he said. The look on his face said he had grave doubts whether Reece and Bono would survive to make the jump over Lebanon. He wasn't the only one. Reece and Bono were right behind him.

The Puma lifted gently off the *Endeavour's* helipad, hovered briefly then climbed and streaked inland over the town of Cabo San Lucas. Lynch, Gamble and Bono were squeezed into the cabin behind Lipscombe. They watched the ribbon of white sand between blue ocean and brown earth slide below them. All along the coastline they could see new condo cities going up, crowding greedily on what had once been open, pristine shoreline. They flew over the miserable huts and shanties of the real Cabo San Lucas, hidden behind the condo compounds, then climbed up over the Sierra de la Laguna. The chopper bucked a few times as they hit updrafts from the mountain range and Lipscombe took it higher. After a few minutes they saw the wide blue swathe of the Pacific beyond the mountains and ten minutes later they crossed the coastline.

'El Pescadero,' the pilot said through helmet speakers and pointed down towards a small town on the coast. 'Good fishing.'

'Next time,' Lynch answered. Lipscombe banked the chopper hard around and they watched the horizon swerve dizzily beneath them. He completed the turn and they headed back across the coastline towards Cabo.

'Hear you gave the old man a bit of a fright?' Lipscombe said.

The question was directed at Lynch but the other two heard it through their helmets. Lynch said nothing. There was a pause.

'Far as I understand it, nobody ever set hands on him like that before . . . nobody has dared,' Lipscombe pressed.

Lynch still said nothing.

'Maybe it should happen more often,' Bono answered for him.

Lynch hadn't thanked Bono for the previous night. They both knew there was no need. It was reassuring to know he had friends in what had increasingly begun to feel like an enemy camp. The chopper bucked suddenly as they hit rough air and Lipscombe broke off the chat to concentrate on flying. They hit a brutal updraft and the chopper reared like a frightened pony until Lipscombe got it back. Lynch caught Bono licking his lips but the big man said nothing. Neither Bono nor Reece liked anything to do with heights, Lynch thought. God help them tomorrow night.

June 28

It was a little after eleven pm when the convoy of three cars crunched through the dark streets of El Triunfo and turned south down the Transpeninsula Highway, heading back to the airport at San José Del Cabo. The sky was clear except for a little haze which softened the stars and blurred the pockmarked albino face of an almost full moon. The weather forecast said conditions were calm throughout the Baja region and there was only a slight westerly breeze of perhaps one knot. Halloran sat up front in the Cherokee with Dennis at the wheel. Vance and Cooper sat behind them with a couple of Halloran's armed security men in the rear. Lynch, Gamble, Reece and Bono followed in two pick-ups driven by Halloran's guards. The men were already wearing jump suits. Their Nighthawks, helmets, face masks, oxygen cylinders and NAVSTAR receivers were securely packed under canvas in the back of the two pick-ups. The airport was quiet and empty except for the airport manager, a security guard at the gate and a couple of nosy cleaners who had been shooed away to the furthest end of the terminal. The convoy drove through open gates onto the tarmac and pulled up beside the only lit aircraft, a five-year-old Fokker Friendship. Lipscombe was already on board and had been there all evening, running maintenance and safety checks. Halloran climbed onto the plane to talk to Lipscombe while the others piled out of the vehicles and began unloading the equipment. Lynch saw Dennis stroll over to the terminal to chat with the watching airport manager and assumed a fat envelope was changing hands. It was a little after midnight by the time they were all geared up and Lynch had checked each man to his own satisfaction. They were beginning to sweat already under the insulated jump suits and the weight of the equipment in the warm night air.

When they were ready to go Halloran climbed out of the Fokker and stood to one side, silently giving every man a reassuring tap on the shoulder as they filed past. Lynch was last. Halloran squeezed his shoulder a moment longer than necessary and held his eyes.

'It's going to be okay,' he said.

'I know,' Lynch answered coolly and climbed through the hatch.

Lipscombe had done a lot of work on the Fokker during the day and had removed half the seats so the men would have room to move. Each of them found a space against the fuselage where he could lean back on his 'chute. Lipscombe spent a couple of minutes securing the Fokker's rear exit hatch so it would remain open for the flight.

'It'll take us about half an hour to reach the jump zone.' he told them. 'When we get there I'll circle at 8,500 and keep circling until you're all out.'

He paused and looked directly at Lynch. 'I'll leave the cockpit door open and give you the thumbs up on each pass so you know when you're clear to jump and you can count your men out. Keep your eyes on me because we won't be able to communicate verbally once we're airborne.'

Lynch nodded.

'Because we'll be flying all the way unpressurised I'd give it about ten minutes then switch your oxygen on,' Lipscombe added. 'And I hope you remembered to put your long johns on because it's going to be cold up there.'

He turned back towards the cockpit and was just about to duck into his seat when he looked back.

'Have fun,' he said.

The men put on their helmets, adjusted their oxygen masks and made themselves comfortable. They heard the twin turbo-props cough into life and the Fokker began to move. Lynch caught a quick glimpse of Halloran and Dennis watching them as the plane taxied towards the runway. A moment later they were airborne. The engines howled deafeningly through the open hatch as the Fokker wheeled, then climbed steeply to clear the mountain peaks. Lynch put on his helmet to shut out the noise and got up on one knee to look through a cabin window. He saw the lights of San Jose Del Cabo slipping further behind them to be replaced by the dense blackness of the barren sierras. He searched for the airport and saw three sets of headlights swinging back towards the highway as Halloran and his men began the drive back to the drop zone at El Triunfo. Lynch sank back on his haunches and waited. Lipscombe shut off all but a handful of cabin lights and the men were left alone with their thoughts in the amber gloaming. Ten minutes later Lynch felt the temperature inside the plane start to plummet and switched on his oxygen. He glanced around the cabin and saw that most of the others had done the same. Reece was daydreaming. Lynch kicked the bottom of his foot and Reece started, then obeyed Lynch's signal to switch on his oxygen. Lynch saw Gamble shake his head. This was one area where he and Halloran were in agreement, Lynch realised. If Reece and Bono couldn't make it now it was their tough luck and they wouldn't be any use on the mission anyway. Lynch wondered momentarily if he was being unjustly harsh then pushed the thought out of his mind. The sweat beneath his thermal-lined jump suit cooled and dried, sending an involuntary chill through his flesh. He got up on one knee again and saw they had just crossed the Pacific coast. The faint lights far below to the south had to be El Pescadero. There were no towns at all where they would be crossing. No towns, no roads, nothing on the coast or in the mountains until they reached El Triunfo.

Lynch checked his NAVSTAR receiver and saw that the Fokker had reached 8,500 metres. He glanced quickly around the cabin, adjusted his goggles, and focused on the cockpit door. The plane began to turn. The men looked through the open hatch but there was little point. All they could see was icy blackness. Unlike the others, neither Reece nor Bono could bring themselves to look up through the cabin windows at the moon and the stars. It only told them they were jumping out of an aeroplane on the edge of space. If anything, Reece had discovered some truth in Norton's cruel joke. He preferred jumping at night precisely because he couldn't see the ground. He couldn't see anything. If he concentrated hard enough he could almost forget he was falling, until he had to monitor that damn receiver and remember to keep tweaking the steering lines to keep himself on course. He had no idea whether he would make the drop zone. He planned to keep a high altitude until he was certain he had cleared the mountain tops then head for the nearest lights and let Halloran sort it all out later. He too had confidence in the Nighthawks and the NAVSTAR navigational system but he had no confidence at all in his ability to guide the 'chute accurately enough for those last precious miles. He had already come perilously close to collapsing the canopy on his second Nighthawk jump at Fort Bragg when he pulled one of the forward lines too hard. It had felt like falling through a trapdoor. He let go of the line immediately and the Nighthawk promptly began to soar away with him in a new direction. The figures on the NAVSTAR receiver were spinning in a unified blur, like the symbols on a fruit machine, so he could make no sense of any of them. And this jump was going to be the hardest yet. Still, he reminded himself, when this one was over there was only one more left — and then he would never jump out of an aeroplane again for the rest of his life. He had promised himself that much.

The Fokker banked around again and Lynch sensed that Lipscombe was making the first live run. He pulled himself up into a crouch and signalled Gamble to move towards the exit. The SAS man got up and shuffled towards the open hatch. Lynch had given them the exit order in advance and he nodded next to Cooper, then Vance, then Reece and then Bono. Lynch would be last to leave the plane. He looked back up towards the cockpit and waited. A moment later Lipscombe's arm jutted out with the thumb raised. Lynch leaned forward and tapped Gamble hard on the shoulder.

Gamble stepped forward, dived smoothly into the blackness and vanished. Cooper counted to three then followed without prompting and three seconds later Vance went after him. Lynch motioned to Reece and Bono and the two men shuffled awkwardly towards the door. He looked back up towards the cockpit and Lipscombe's arm had vanished. He signalled the two men to wait. A moment later the pilot's gloved hand appeared, thumb raised again and Lynch signalled Reece to go. He saw Reece step towards the door, shut both eyes tight behind his goggles and jump. Three seconds later Bono too followed, without prompting.

Lynch readied himself and looked up towards the cockpit but Lipscombe was signalling him to wait while he banked the plane around for a fresh approach. Lynch wasn't concerned. Five men had gone in one run. It suited him to follow ten minutes later. That way they should all be safely on the ground when he reached the DZ ten minutes after the last man. He would use the mild headwind to brake his gliding time further to avoid overtaking even the slowest man. It had gone with a reassuring efficiency, Lynch thought as the Fokker turned into its second run, parallel to Baja's Pacific coast, thirty-two kilometres away. Perhaps they would surprise everybody and make a perfect jump after all. Lynch steadied himself beside the open hatch, eyes on the cockpit door. Lipscombe's gloved hand appeared again with thumb raised and Lynch dived.

For a second he was tempted to keep diving, to slap his arms by his side, turn himself into a human bullet and savour the exhilarating, cleansing rush that came with free fall. But he couldn't risk a HALO with over 3,000 metres of rock between him and the DZ and he yanked the toggle. The liberated Nighthawk burst from its cage on his back and spread its wings. Lynch was hauled to a stop in the infinite blackness and felt himself swing into a perfect, gentle glide. He looked down at the receiver on his chest and watched the numbers scroll by. The compass told him he was drifting

239

southeast. He gave the steering lines a tug and swung back onto his true heading towards the DZ a little less than eighty kilometres away on the other side of the Sierra de la Laguna. Eight kilometres beneath his feet Lynch pictured the deep, groaning swells of the cold black Pacific waiting for him if anything were to go wrong, and a delicious thrill of unaccustomed fear made him shiver. He turned his mind back onto the figures and gently tweaked the steering lines again.

About forty-five minutes later he crossed the coast at 4,500 metres. All he could hear was the muffled murmur of the wind outside his helmet. He checked his oxygen. Each man had gone up with ninety minutes supply. He had thirty minutes left. He had hardly been breathing at all for the last half hour's ride, he realised. Lynch thought he could vaguely make out the ragged silvery line of the surf far below but it faded quickly into the dense, dark cloak of the sierras. He watched the NAVSTAR instruments carefully and marvelled at their precision. 38,000 kilometres over his head a satellite collected data from its seventeen companions around the planet and obediently relayed it in a silent ceaseless stream into the electronics inside the little black box strapped to Lynch's chest. He floated magically between heaven and earth, guided safely between the stars and over the peaks and valleys below by the invisible hand of man's genius. A sudden gust caught the canopy and threw him upwards and sideways. The instruments blurred then stabilised again as Lynch gently coaxed the Nighthawk back on course. It had been an unexpected thermal, he realised, a rising current of warm air released late from some arid, still cooling valley far below. He checked his watch. Just over an hour. Any minute and he would be able to see the lights of La Paz to the north and perhaps San Jose Del Cabo to the south. The instruments told him he was steering a true course. He followed his instincts and brought the Nighthawk down to 3,500 metres. By his reckoning he still had at least 400 metres between him and the mountain tops, probably more. A moment later he saw the glimmer of city lights on the northeastern horizon. That was La Paz. Using it as a fix he gazed around and then found the smaller, dimmer glow of El Triunfo dead ahead on the Transpeninsular Highway. He strained to see through the goggles, and made out a smaller, brighter tiara of jewels just to the south of the town. It could be nothing else but the DZ. Lynch glanced down and saw the last great shadows of the sierra melt away beneath him and began to circle down and around for his landing. Further out to the east on the Sea of Cortez he could see another shining crown, the *American Endeavour*. Lynch smiled despite himself. For the first time in days he began to feel that things might finally be going well for them all.

Bono was lost. He had been lost since he left the plane. He had done everything he was supposed to do and still he was lost. He studied the compass and struggled to keep the Nighthawk on course but like Reece he was afraid of losing height too soon and running into the mountains. His 'chute had arrested him at 8,000 metres and he had held it there for an hour. Consequently he hadn't had a single visual fix. It was only when his oxygen began to run out that he brought the Nighthawk down to 4,500 metres. For half an hour he had been staring desperately through the blackness, hoping for a glimpse of something familiar. All he could see was more blackness. Bono began to feel uncomfortable. It wasn't fear, it was something worse than fear — the sure and certain realisation that if he didn't kill himself he was about to make a spectacular fool of himself again in front of men who did not tolerate fools lightly. He brought the Nighthawk down another 300 metres and gazed around. Still nothing but darkness. He wondered how long the Nighthawk could stay aloft. It felt as though it could keep him airborne forever, if he wanted. Perhaps, he thought, he could just keep circling until daylight. He looked at his watch. Dawn was only about five hours away, he reckoned. Suddenly there was a glimmer of something in the corner of his left eye.

241

He grunted, twisted in the harness and strained to see. Lights. The first ground lights he had seen since leaving the airport what seemed like twelve hours ago. But they weren't where they were supposed to be: they were on the far northern horizon. Bono held his altitude and steered the Nighthawk north by northwest. It wasn't the direction he had been told to follow and the figures on his receiver told him he was going the wrong way but he ignored them and began homing in on the distant lights. Bono didn't give a damn where they were. He wanted his feet on the ground.

It was only ten minutes later that Bono realised he was approaching land. There wasn't a hint of a mountain peak between him and the lights and he brought the Nighthawk down to 1,500 metres. The lights began to multiply and they spread out like a welcoming embrace along the coastline. Beneath him there was only ocean. Then it struck him. No wonder he had only seen blackness beneath him since leaving the plane. He had been gliding over open ocean the whole time. A sickening awareness spread throughout his body as he realised he had somehow missed the mountains entirely. He had drifted scores, perhaps hundreds of kilometres off course. He might have missed the peninsula completely. He looked at the instruments. They still made no sense. He ripped his mask off and swore to ease his anger and frustration. He had no idea what town or city he was approaching, or where he was going to land. All he could be sure of was that he was about to cause profound embarrassment to Lynch and his employer.

The lights grew stronger and more numerous. He began to make out buildings and streetlights. He saw the headlights of cars and the lights of boats on the water. He squirmed around for any sign of the *American Endeavour* but she was nowhere to be seen.

'To hell with it,' Bono muttered to himself. He would land the best way he could and figure it out from there. He yanked on the forward lines and began a swift descent towards the beach. If he could land on the beach, he decided, he could at least hide the 'chute somewhere then stroll into town and find a phone. That was if he could land without hurting himself and if the beach was deserted.

The beach disappeared. Bono blinked and stared again but it had gone. Then he saw why. He had dropped below the horizon and some jagged, unknown headland had reared unexpectedly in front of him, obscuring his view of the town and obstructing his path toward a safe landing. If he couldn't turn or gain further height, Bono realised, he was going to run smack into the face of a cliff. He squirmed around in the harness and saw another string of lights barely two miles away along the shore to his left. He pulled on the steering lines and the Nighthawk swerved sharply to the left and down towards the shore lights. The big man and the Nighthawk began a final relentless swoop towards land.

Bono stared through his goggles as a cluster of buildings materialised rapidly in front of him. He saw a series of long, low white adobe buildings, palm trees and a garden of sand warmed by a forest of orange lights. It looked like a hotel fronting directly onto the ocean with a huge, invitingly empty beach. Then he realised too late that the descending Nighthawk was gathering speed. He yanked on a line and the 'chute reared crazily upwards for a second then continued its headlong rush into the shore. Bono saw breaking surf flash beneath his feet — less than thirty metres between him and the ground and descending rapidly, he figured. The beach rose rapidly from the surf line towards a series of ragged cliffs and buildings which were tucked into the base of the cliffs. He saw people on the footpaths between the buildings, going back and forth between what appeared to be a bar and a nightclub.

Bono pulled desperately on the riser lines again to try and brake his landing but all he managed was another sudden spastic leap into the air, another giant uncontrolled hop up the beach. He looked down. It was too late. People were

243

staring up at him, mouths agape. A thatched roof rushed up to meet him and he bent his knees. His boots clipped the roof and ripped away a shower of palm fronds. He caught a glimpse of startled drinkers looking up at him in disbelief then careened off the roof of the bar towards a courtyard where a huge crowd of people appeared to be waiting for him. Then he saw... they were dancing. Something hard smacked against his right leg and he lost all pretence of control, cannoned off the side of a building and down towards the dancing people. At any moment the canopy would collapse or snag onto the corner of a building and pull him to a bone-breaking stop. Something grabbed at his legs and tried to pull him to the ground. He stared wildly down and saw that his feet had hooked under a table and he was dragging the table across a red tiled floor. Food, dishes and cutlery spewed everywhere. More people screamed and threw themselves out of his path, knocking over more chairs and tables, and spilling more food and dishes across the floor. A stream of foul words poured from Bono's mouth as he flew across the floor, arms flailing for a hand hold, legs trying vainly to kick off the screeching metal table that had hooked onto his feet like a wrought iron anchor. Dancers and waiters scrambled to get out of his way. Still the vengeful Nighthawk wouldn't put him down. He caught a glimpse of a mariachi band, clipped a corner of the bandstand, lost the table and braced himself as the plate glass windows of a restaurant raced towards him.

Suddenly it stopped. Robbed of its support within the sheltered confines of the nightclub courtyard, the Nighthawk lost all power and collapsed with a soft, rustling sigh. Bono had his eyes shut and was tensed for the impact of splintering glass.

Instead the Nighthawk set him down gently in its dying grip. He landed unexpectedly on the balls of his feet, fought to get his balance, stumbled into a series of desperate, staggering steps and came to a breathless halt against the window panes, his gloved hands pressed flat against the glass. Behind the windows Bono could see the stunned faces of late diners still at their tables, unable to move, transfixed by the spectacle of a sky diver landing in their midst.

Then there was nothing but silence. Bono turned slowly and looked around at the scene of appalling devastation. People stared back at him in disbelief. For some reason Bono's eyes were magnetically drawn to the two matching gouges the iron table had ploughed across the dance floor.

'Hey,' he looked around. His throat was sticky and phlegmy and he had to stop to hawk and spit. 'Is this Maui?'

Somebody began to clap.

Lynch landed gently in a pool of light formed by the headlights of the circled cars. They had given him a drop zone the size of a football pitch. He quickly collapsed the canopy and shrugged off the harness. There were four figures walking towards him. He pulled off the helmet and goggles and looked up. He saw Gamble first then Vance followed by Halloran and Dennis. He saw the red tip of a cigarette near one of the pick-ups. Cooper was the only man in the team who smoked.

'No sign of Reece or Bono?' he asked.

Gamble shook his head.

'We've got two cars checking the highway north and south,' Halloran said.

'How long has everybody else been here?'

'Cooper landed twelve minutes ago. He was the last. We tracked all four of you perfectly from the plane. But Reece and Bono...' He took a deep breath. 'We never really had them. They went out of range almost immediately they left the plane.'

'Jesus Christ.' Lynch looked around. 'They could be anywhere. They could be in the ocean.'

'We picked up one signal for a little while about thirty-two kilometres north east from here,' Halloran added. 'Then we lost it.'

Lynch looked at him. 'That's La Paz.'

245

'Yeah.'

'Any idea who it is?'

Halloran shook his head. 'They're only tracking devices. Could be either one of them. We'll keep looking. We'll find out soon enough.'

Henry Reece knew he had made a big mistake. And as he watched the glittering lights of the big city drift prettily beneath his feet he wondered how he was going to put it right. As far as he could see there was nowhere to land. Not unless he wanted to attract a crowd. Yet the city only 150 metres below seemed to go on forever. He had already passed the same sports stadium twice. At least he thought it was the same one. But that would mean he was going around in circles and he didn't see how that was possible. He had to make his mind up soon. He had been losing height steadily for the past half-hour and if he didn't find a landing spot for the Nighthawk, the Nighthawk would find a spot for him. Reece looked at the instruments again but they still didn't tell him anything. He knew what he was supposed to do and had been so proud to navigate successfully across the mountains that he simply hadn't realised he had drifted so far off course. At least he was on the right side of Baja. He knew that much. But he hadn't expected to steer so expertly into the biggest city on the southern half of the peninsula. He was quite sure he had found La Paz and that El Triunfo was about thirty-two kilometres to the southwest from here. But he had already lost so much height on his descent down the eastern slopes of the sierras that it was impossible for him to re-route to El Triunfo. He had spent the past half hour trying to steer a course southwards out of the city but every time he thought he was on course he seemed to drift out towards the open sea and he panicked and pulled too hard on the steering lines. And so the Nighthawk duly took him on another sightseeing tour of La Paz by night.

At least there wasn't much traffic about, Reece thought.

And not too many people. Halloran would be thankful for that. Although he had been spotted by a gang of street kids playing soccer on a vacant lot and they had yelled and waved excitedly to him. He had waved back because it seemed churlish not to and they had grown even more excited and gone and told their friends and families. When he passed near the vacant lot a second time Reece estimated that there had to be at least fifty or sixty kids down there. It was a beautiful still night and he could hear the chorus of their thin young voices drifting faintly up to him. The Nighthawk drifted a little lower again and the kids swarmed, mutated, formed and re-formed into a pack and they began running along the street, following him, shouting and waking people up. This was a big occasion for them, Reece realised. He tugged the riser lines again and gained a little height. He picked up speed and began to lose them again and then he saw the sports stadium coming around for the third time. There was a main highway running beside the stadium and Reece guessed it was the Transpeninsular. If he followed it south it would lead him back towards El Triunfo. He had tried that before but over-compensated on his seaward drift. This time he was careful. The Nighthawk seemed to be responding. He was following the highway. Reece looked down and saw a motorcycle cop parked at an empty inter-section. The cop seemed to be looking up the highway back towards La Paz. Reece twisted his head around and saw why. A mob of what looked like 200 screaming children and adults was pouring out of a side street about three kilometres away, fanning out across the main highway and running towards the intersection. The cop stayed put and watched the oncoming crowd. Reece saw him pick up a radio and speak into it.

The Nighthawk seemed to be gliding painfully slowly now, Reece thought. He meandered lazily southwards, following the highway, a small, helpless figure beneath a huge, elegant black parasol caught in a friendly airstream. He had lost a little more height too, he thought. He had to be under 120 metres now. He looked back and saw that the crowd had almost reached the motorcycle cop. He had covered three or four kilometres at most, he thought. He could see people shouting to the cop, laughing and pointing in his direction. The Nighthawk seemed to stall in the sky. It stood quite still for a moment as though looking for a place to roost. A couple of hundred metres away he could see a Pemex station. The Nighthawk saw it too and descended towards the empty gas station. Coming the opposite way on the highway Reece could see a pair of headlights travelling at speed. He gave an inward shrug. It would be all over for him in minutes, he thought. Almost certainly he had blown the operation. He tried to push the big black bird further up into the sky but she refused to respond. Tired, Reece thought. He could understand that. He was coming in harder than he expected. He lifted his feet but it was too late. His boots crashed through the tall neon Pemex sign in front of the station and sent a great wave of fine glass splinters cascading across the forecourt. There were lights on inside the station too, he saw, even though it was closed. There seemed to be a group of men inside playing cards or something. Their heads jerked up in unison as they heard the Pemex sign explode and they watched in awed disbelief as Reece landed gently between the pumps. He tried to make it graceful but missed his footing, skidded on the broken glass and crashed to an undignified halt on his buttocks. The great black wings of the Nighthawk flared briefly then settled protectively around him. The Pemex operator walked slowly out of the office followed by his two friends, their mouths slack.

Reece grinned at them. 'Hi there,' he said. 'Can I use your phone?'

The oncoming headlights swerved into the Pemex station and a blue pick-up screeched to a halt beside Reece. Two brawny men wearing furious expressions leaped out, heaved

Reece bodily into the pick-up and pushed the 'chute in with him. One of the men jumped in the back with Reece and sat on the 'chute to stop it billowing. He swung around to face the rear and in one hand he carried what looked like a sub-machine gun to discourage anyone who looked like following. The other man jumped back behind the wheel, slammed his door, gunned the engine and the pick-up screamed out of the Pemex station, threw a wild U-turn onto the highway and roared off southwards into the night.

The three Mexicans watched them go in silence and then looked around at the suddenly empty service station. All that was left was a shattered Pemex sign and a forecourt coated with glass gravel. A moment later the motorcycle cop pulled into the station and yelled at the stunned Pemex man. A couple of miles down the road they could see a crowd of kids hurrying to catch up, laughing and shouting as though on their way to a fiesta. Somewhere behind them they could hear the distant wail of a police siren. The Pemex manager haltingly explained what they had seen and the cop listened in silence. They left the bit about the gun till last. The cop's eyes widened. It wasn't just some sporting stunt gone wrong after all, he thought. A paratrooper at night... men with machine guns. He picked up the radio to La Paz police headquarters again and upgraded his earlier call to a major emergency. They should also alert the army garrison in La Paz, he said. He might have stumbled on a terrorist attack, a major drug run... or the start of a coup. A moment later a police cruiser crunched across the broken glass and pulled up beside the motorcycle cop. The two cops in the cruiser conferred briefly with their colleague and then made up their minds. They checked their guns, the motorcycle cop climbed back on his bike and then followed the cruiser out of the Pemex station and headed south after the blue pick-up.

'Sir... it's Bono, sir.' Dennis was calling to Halloran from the cab of the Cherokee, still at the drop zone. They had assembled the cars and switched off the lights.

Halloran, Lynch and the others hurried across.

'They just relayed a call from the house. Bono says he landed at a hotel in Cabo called Club Solmar. Did a little bit of damage to the bar and the nightclub. He says they're cool and they're buying him drinks. But he says to come soon... and bring a lot of money.'

Halloran shook his head, slumped down on the bumper of the car and put his head in his hands.

'Oh...' Dennis added tentatively. 'He said don't worry because he's not hurt.'

'Jesus...' Vance hissed.

Lynch turned away and wiped his mouth with the back of his hand, trying not to smile.

'Somebody's coming,' Cooper said.

They all looked up as the blue pick-up swung off the road and bumped to a halt beside them with Reece in the back. The driver switched off his headlights and leaned out of the cab.

'We better move or we're going to have company real soon,' he said.

Halloran stood up. 'Time we weren't here,' he said.

Twelve hours later they were out of Mexico.

8

ONLY THE LONELY

Istanbul, June 30

'Fleet's in,' Bono grunted.

They looked through the portholes of Halloran's Beechcraft 2000 as it circled low around the Golden Horn and back out to the Sea of Marmara for the final descent to Attaturk Airport. Bono was right. The blue-grey waters of the Horn and the approaches from the Bosphorous, the narrow strait which links the Sea of Marmara to the Black Sea, were filled with warships. Lynch counted twenty-three before the plane banked around and the city slid from view.

'Tomorrow is Navy Day,' Halloran explained. 'People forget Turkey has a big military budget, blue water navy, second biggest army in NATO.'

'Navy day,' Bono whooped and gave Reece a hard shove.

'Better padlock your underwear, Henry, or them Turkey sailors are gonna take one look at your sweet little ass and be into you like a rat up a drainpipe.'

Reece looked insulted.

'You talk a big game for somebody who's next to fucking useless,' Vance said to Bono.

It was finally out in the open. The tensions in the team had been building ever since they arrived in Mexico. Until now they had simmered along, just beneath the surface. Finally, Vance had had enough. The haste in which they had been forced to get out of Baja had angered him. Not because he couldn't cope with hasty departures. He was used to that. It was the sloppy, undignified manner in which they

251

had been forced to leave, one step ahead of the local authorities whose tolerance had finally been exhausted, leaving Dennis behind to try and smooth things over and spread enough *mordida* around to satisfy everyone. The La Paz police department had costs approaching $50,000, according to the police chief and the chief magistrate. The nightclub and hotel estimated damage at close to $10,000. There had been half an hour to get their gear back at the house while Lipscombe, the pilot, left the Fokker at the airport, collected the chopper and shuttled them back to the *American Endeavour* where they would be out of harm's way. Mid-morning the next day, the Beechcraft arrived and they all transferred from the chopper to Halloran's private jet along with Halloran and two of his men. Apart from a couple of refuelling stops at San Juan, Puerto Rico and Santa Cruz in the Canary Islands, they had been confined to the nine-seater jet for almost eighteen hours. Everyone was tired and edgy. The way Vance saw it Bono and Reece were a pair of lethal incompetents who threatened the safety of the team and the viability of the operation, a couple of blunt instruments who were out of their depth in an operation that involved a high degree of finesse. Vance couldn't bottle up his hostility towards Reece and Bono any longer and the contempt showed on his face.

Bono looked stunned by Vance's outburst. Nobody ever talked to him like that and walked. He made a point of it. His face darkened and he leaned towards Vance. The man from Delta Force tensed but he didn't back off.

'That's enough,' Halloran snapped. The sound of steel was back in the old man's voice, Lynch noticed. He was tired of playing Mr Nice Guy too.

'Any more of this, from anybody...' He looked pointedly at Reece and Bono and they too saw that the old pals act was over. 'Any more fuck ups by any man,' Halloran continued, 'and he's out of the operation... in fucking pieces.'

Lynch looked back through the porthole at the smudgy brown haze that cloaked Istanbul in the late afternoon sun.

The city stretched from horizon to horizon, the slender needles of its minarets reaching up from the uniform brown suburbs to pierce its permanently smoggy stratus. To the north were the vineyards of Soviet Georgia and then the steppes of central Russia. To the west lay Turkey's ancient enemy, Greece, and the corrupt socialist republic of Bulgaria. To the south and east lay the former conquered territories of the Ottoman Empire, now known as Iran, Iraq, Syria and Lebanon, still seething with bloodshed and hatred more than sixty years after Ottoman rule had ended. Istanbul was the great bulwark between East and West, rival to ancient Rome, catharsis of empire, capital of intrigue when London was a riverside village. No city in the world had seen more grand designs, more great armies, more wars... or more blood.

On the ground the plane taxied towards a hangar with the Turkish Airlines emblem on the doors. Halloran and the pilot climbed out first. A tall, balding man in suit pants, white shirt and tie walked over to meet them. He was accompanied by two other men, both Turks, one wearing an expensive suit, the other in dark blue uniform. The balding man introduced them to Halloran and the four of them engaged in deep discussion for several minutes. Lynch heard the first man's accent. American. State Department, he guessed. The two Turks would be government officials, probably one of them was from Turkish military intelligence, the other from customs or immigration. Almost certainly they were there only as observers. Lynch knew that Turkey had a long and consistent record for co-operating with the US.

Finally Halloran nodded, then walked back to the plane and stuck his head through the door.

'Get your things and follow me,' he said. 'We've got a couple of cars waiting.'

The pilot had already unloaded most of their bags. Everything else, Lynch knew, would be waiting for them at the NATO base at Ankara. Lynch watched amusedly as, despite the heat, Halloran's two guards put their jackets back on

253

to conceal the Uzis they carried. They picked up their bags and followed Halloran, the State Department man and the two Turks into the hangar. It was only when they were out of the glare of the late afternoon sun that they saw the two jeep-loads of armed soldiers parked in the shadow of the hangar. Lynch spotted a couple of other men in plain clothes. Turkey was still ruled by the military; it made for much smoother military-civilian co-operation on occasions such as this, he reflected. They walked the length of the hangar and out into the sunshine again through a small door in the rear. There was a short walk to a double gate in a perimeter fence watched by two more soldiers and half a dozen plain clothes men. The two groups eyed each other appraisingly. In accordance with Halloran's instructions none of the men but Cooper had shaved for several days now. They were beginning to acquire that authentic Islamic militia look. In their creased grab bag uniforms they must have looked like the most inefficient and unimpressive cutthroats the Turkish security men had ever seen, nothing like the usual Special Forces groups who occasionally flew in, Lynch thought.

There were three black Mercedes limos waiting just outside the gate. Lynch noticed the man in the blue uniform turn back once they had walked through the gate. At least his part of it was over. Halloran stepped into the first car with the balding State Department man and one of his guards. Lynch automatically chose the second. This time Vance threw his bags in too and made a point of climbing into the backseat alongside Lynch. Cooper got in the front seat beside the Turkish driver and they closed the doors, leaving Bono, Reece, Gamble and Halloran's other guard to squeeze into the last Merc.

Lynch got a glimpse of himself in the rear vision mirror for a moment. With the four-day growth of beard and recently dyed hair he hardly recognised himself. He sank back into the cool leather upholstery, closed his eyes and breathed deeply. He had endured almost three weeks of intense, calculated insanity. There were four days, perhaps a week to go. It had been a cramped eighteen hours on the flight from Mexico, with all nine seats in Halloran's jet occupied. He hadn't slept much at all in the past forty-eight hours. Once again he was looking forward to bed. Any bed.

'Let's dump those two clowns and get two fresh guys,' Vance said suddenly.

Lynch blinked and looked at him.

'Can't be done,' he said.

'We could have two new guys from Fort Bragg here by tomorrow night,' Vance persisted. 'Better trained, better suited for this operation... better men.' He jerked his thumb back towards the following car. 'Those two guys are fuck-ups,' he said. 'Even your limey pal agrees with that.'

'How do you feel about this, sergeant?' Lynch asked Cooper.

Cooper shrugged. 'They ain't what you'd call a class act,' he said.

'No,' Lynch had to agree. 'They're not.' He pulled himself up in the seat. If the driver understood English there was little sign of it. They had left the airport and were driving east on the expressway into Istanbul. The traffic looked hideous. Lynch had never been to Istanbul before. Under other circumstances he might have found it interesting.

'First off it's not that easy to pull men out of regular units at twenty-four hours notice,' Lynch said, taking a deep breath. 'Even Special Forces. This is a highly secret, government deniable operation. If anything, the presence of Reece, Bono and myself for that matter — enhance that deniability. A lot of work went into the selection process before you two were approached. We had to be reasonably sure you'd jump for the money. There's no going back to regular units after a job like this for you guys. Your government doesn't work that way. Not like the SAS. You take on a job like this and it's a one-way ticket out of the army. So, even if we wanted to, we probably couldn't find two men to replace

Reece and Bono in the time available to us now to execute this job. Secondly, I agree that they're a little rough around the edges...'

Vance opened his mouth to speak but Lynch held up his hand. 'I've read your record, Sergeant Vance. I know your background. You're a very capable man and that's why you're here. You and Cooper. And while they may not look it, so are Reece and Bono. They are both combat experienced. They are experts with explosives. They're tough. They don't crack under pressure... and they can be counted on to do what I tell them. Even though they fucked up that last jump there's still a better than even chance they can get to where I want them. They don't have to score a bullseye. If they can just get into the region of the drop zone we can find them. And I want them to try because we are going to need them on the ground — because when it comes to the job we have to do those guys could make the difference. And just remember something, they don't find jumping out of planes easy, like we do. They're scared to death every time they go up there... and I mean really scared. But they've been doing jumps it takes recruits three months to work towards. That makes those two the only guys on the team who have been pushed to their limits every day for the past two weeks — and they're still here. And they're still cracking jokes. That makes them the bravest men on the team so far, sergeant. Because the rest of us still have to see what happens when you hit your limits.'

Vance looked as though he were about to argue but thought better of it and sat back in his seat. They travelled the rest of the way in stony silence.

The three Mercedes passed the teeming Topkapi bus station and followed the massive city wall for a couple of kilometres — the walls of old Constantinople and Byzantium before that, Lynch realised — then swung onto a wide main thoroughfare running parallel to the Golden Horn. The driver cut expertly through the swirling melee of the roundabout leading onto Attaturk Bridge and even Lynch, jaded as he was, found himself marvelling at the spectacle of the twin city skylines. After a few minutes they passed the US Consulate and a few minutes later the British Consulate. Consulate country meant friendly country, Lynch thought; Halloran wanted his government contacts close. The cars drove on and then turned into a narrower street. A glimpsed sign in English told Lynch they were on Straselviler Caddesi. Caddesi seemed to be Turkish for street. A moment later they turned into a much narrower, quieter street and pulled up outside an old, nondescript building with the euphemistic title of Plaza Hotel. It looked small, quiet, and unimportant, ideal for people who wanted to get lost in a vast metropolis such as Istanbul.

Halloran and the State Department man went in first with one of the guards. A moment later the guard appeared and signalled to Lynch and the rest to follow. They bypassed the main desk in the small, empty lobby and took the elevator to the fifth floor, the top floor of the hotel. There were a dozen rooms and Lynch realised Halloran had booked the whole floor. There were only two exits, a fire door to a staircase and the elevator. Lynch sauntered down the gloomy, wood-panelled hallway and chose a small room with a spectacular view of the Bosphorous. The furniture was old, bordering on the antique, but the bed was soft and the room was clean. There was a bath and he had it to himself. Luxury, he decided. He opened the window, then closed it again when the roar of the city flooded into his room. The hotel had a stuffy, smoky smell, he thought, created by a century of Sobranie cigarettes and illicit affairs. The Plaza seemed just the hotel for a clandestine romance. He would just have to live with the smell.

He looked outside and saw Halloran's two men had each taken up positions, one on a chair beside the fire exit, the other next to the elevator.

'To stop people coming up,' Halloran said as he noticed

Lynch checking. He waved Lynch across and introduced him to the blonde man.

'Jimmy Slater, US Consulate,' Halloran said. 'He's going to keep an eye on things while you're here. A couple of Jimmy's guys will be in the street around the clock. My guys will be relieved in a couple of hours but they'll stay in the rooms up here with you. We can keep things pretty tight on the outside and if there's a hint of trouble we'll pull you out and go direct to NATO, Ankara.'

Lynch nodded. Halloran drew him aside and lowered his voice out of Slater's earshot. 'It's not the outside I'm worried about anymore,' he said. 'The biggest threat to this operation is from the inside. I don't know what is going on with this team, Lynch, but I hope to hell you know what you're doing... and if you've got a strategy for pulling them all into line it's about fucking time we saw it.'

'They're big boys,' Lynch said. 'They'll do the job.' It had become his stock answer where Halloran was concerned. Halloran looked sceptical.

'Where are you staying?' Lynch asked.

Halloran hesitated briefly. 'I've got a suite at the Pera Palas. I come here two or three times a year and it's where I'm expected to stay. It's not far from here, if you have to contact me urgently don't use the phone. Get one of my people to call the Consulate. Their lines are protected. They'll send somebody around and I'll come personally... but only if it's urgent, understand?'

Lynch thought it a little strange but said nothing. He had long since given up expecting Halloran to be completely forthright with him. A few more days and it wouldn't matter anyway. He would have discharged his final obligation to the powerful American and their association would be at an end.

Halloran raised his voice and called the men out of their rooms. They straggled back down the hotel corridor and gathered around Halloran near the elevator.

'I want you all to stay here until I tell you to move,' Halloran said. 'My men understand that they cannot force you to stay. They are here for your protection only, I want you to remember that. But I also want you to know that if any man breaks security now — the operation is off and you're all finished. If just one man fucks up you're all out in the cold. No pay, no nothing. I'll cut you loose right here in fucking Istanbul and you better not try to come back to the States in my lifetime. So, from now on you sleep here, you eat your meals here, you shit here, you don't move from here. I don't want you drinking booze from now on, I don't want you getting any broads sent up to your room. Anything else, we'll have delivered to the floor. Books, papers, magazines, VCRs, whatever you want. But I will tolerate no more fucking around. Any man breaks these instructions and you're history, all of you.'

'We can't go take in a few of the sights?' Bono asked.

'You stick your big ugly head out the window and I'll know about it,' Halloran answered. 'We are counting down to the launch of this operation. I want you all here and ready to go when I say so. That could be tomorrow, it could be a week from now...' He paused. 'But it will be soon. So take this opportunity to get plenty of rest because you're going to need it.' He looked pointedly at Lynch then turned, nodded to Slater and they both got into the elevator and disappeared from view.

Bono looked at Lynch. 'Takes this kinda seriously, doesn't he?'

'Go to bed,' Lynch said. Then he walked back to his room, pulled off his grubby army greens, fell into bed and went straight to sleep.

Baghdad, July 1

The chairman of the Palestine Liberation Organisation was chatting with an earnest and pretty young journalist from

Paris Match in the drawing room of his Baghdad compound when the call came through. A dark-suited aide picked up the phone, spoke briefly then walked over to the chairman and whispered confidentially into his ear. Yasser Arafat excused himself in heavily accented French, pulled himself out of a thickly cushioned couch and crossed the room. He perched on a marble-topped row of cupboards, which divided the big airy room, picked up the phone and said simply: 'Arafat'.

The French journalist understood English and pricked up her ears to eavesdrop.

'Are you comfortable?' Arafat seemed solicitous, as though speaking to a friend.

'Good,' he said. 'Within twenty-four hours. Please stay where you are. We'll send a car.' There was another pause. 'Yes,' he said. 'I think I can give you the information you need.' He hung up and smiled to his aide. 'The Americans are so impatient,' he smiled. 'It does them good to wait a little while.'

The journalist sighed. It couldn't be anyone or anything too important.

Halloran hung up the phone in his hotel's Diplomatic Suite and walked over to the window. From the top floor of the Oberoi Hotel in Baghdad it was possible to pick out one particularly large oasis of tall palms and to glimpse the high stucco walls of the PLO compound only a dozen blocks away. It had been three months since Halloran had last stood in this exact same spot, awaiting the summons from the PLO to say that the chairman was able to see him at last. A four day wait and then it had been two o'clock in the morning when they finally sent a car. Halloran wasn't used to being treated like that, not even by the President of the United States. But Arafat treated him that way and Halloran had to take it, because Arafat had what he needed. Halloran stared at the PLO walls for a long time and remembered his own words '... it was a confident man who thought he could outsmart Yasser Arafat.'

Halloran had flown from Istanbul to Baghdad in his private plane overnight. There had been only himself, the pilot and one guard. When the call came that Arafat was free to see him he would have to leave even them behind and go alone and unprotected into the heart of the PLO. The timing of this meeting with Arafat had been excruciating. He couldn't see the PLO chairman at his Tunis headquarters because Tunisia was crawling with American diplomats and the international media ever since the PLO's rapprochement with the US. But Arafat never broadcast his movements in advance to anyone. The survival instincts of the PLO leader were legendary. There had been the time in Beirut, seven years earlier, when Arafat had gone to a meeting of all the squabbling Palestinian factions. It had taken months to set up the meeting. It was vital to the progress of their cause and it was unlikely it would be repeated in a hurry. Arafat had arrived in the bunker in southern Beirut, unannounced as usual, and walked around for a few minutes, checking the place out. He had waited impatiently for a few of the first speakers to finish then stood up abruptly and advised everyone they should get out immediately. His instincts were respected, even by his enemies, and everyone had obeyed. Half an hour later Israeli jets bombed the entire block where the bunker was hidden and turned it into rubble. Since then, no-one challenged Arafat's instincts. He flitted around the Middle East like a shadow, turning up one day in Tunis, the next in Baghdad, another day in Damascus, then Cairo, Algiers, the Yemen. Sometimes he disappeared for days at a time. Halloran had seen intelligence documents showing a dozen known PLO bases, ranging from elegant compounds like the quarters in Baghdad, to a palace in Tunis, a country estate in the Tunisian mountains, a fortified retreat in the Madagascan countryside outside Antananarivo. Arafat's survival depended on his unpredictability. The most he would ever indicate to anyone was that he would most probably be in a certain city at a certain time. But precisely where and precisely when was always left to that two am phone call.

And since the assassination of his lieutenant, Abu Jihad, by an Israeli hit squad, Arafat had grown even more circumspect. If the Israelis could be sure of Arafat's whereabouts for just a few hours, Halloran knew, they would move heaven and earth to exterminate their country's greatest enemy. There was little Halloran could do but wait... until Arafat was satisfied it was safe to see him.

'Let's go play some blackjack, John,' he called to his guard. Despite his bloodshot eyes and his body's aching need for rest, Halloran couldn't sleep. It was all coming to the boil. Three months of frantic planning and activity. It had been one of the most complex operations he had ever attempted and half a dozen times it had almost been thwarted. After the debacle in Baja Halloran had to get the team out before the White House heard about it and killed the operation. If Arafat could give him the information he needed he could launch the operation in the next forty-eight hours and until then he could simply pretend to be out of contact. Like Arafat, he smiled. In the meantime, the Oberoi had a casino in the basement and Halloran had always found blackjack a therapeutic way to pass time, even though financially, it mattered little to him whether he won or lost.

It was Thursday night and the huge lobby of the big hotel was filled with wedding parties. The racket was deafening. All Iraqi couples seemed to get married on Thursdays and Fridays and it seemed like they all wanted to hold the reception and honeymoon in the Baghdad Oberoi in a room overlooking the Tigris on the same night. The lobby and gardens were filled with the grating cacophony of gaudily jewelled women making the high pitched warbling sounds that Iraqi women make at weddings and funerals. Halloran looked around. There were a lot of flushed and excited male faces and pale, apprehensive female faces in the crowd. Halloran remembered that Iraqi women had to be virgins when they married. Their lives depended on it.

'How many, John?'

'I stopped counting at fifty, sir.'

'Jesus H. Christ almighty,' Halloran shook his head. 'That's a lot of pussy gonna get mauled tonight. I hope they're all the hell away from my room.'

Halloran left his whereabouts with the Indian concierge and headed down the wide, pink marble staircase to the basement. If anything, it was noisier. Arabs loved to gamble and the casino was jammed. The bodyguard changed US$2,000 into chips and Halloran finally found a seat at a blackjack table. He looked around. They were the only Americans amidst a sea of robed Arabs and expensively suited European, Indian and Asian businessmen. Wheelers, dealers and arms traders from all over the world were flocking to Baghdad these days to syphon off a few of President Sadam Hussein's oil dollars as he rebuilt his economy in the wake of the war with Iran and prepared for the next round, which everyone knew was inevitable. Italians, French, Germans from East and West, Arabs from all the Gulf States, Japanese, Taiwanese, Koreans, Singaporean Chinese. All trying to sell a shipload of Toyotas here, a petro-chemical plant there, a new hotel somewhere else... and perhaps a consignment of the latest surface-to-surface missiles along the way. It amused Halloran to know that, despite this room full of secrets, he held the greatest secret of all. And no-one could possibly know who he was. Halloran had not had a photograph taken of him for twenty-three years. Just one look at him was enough to know he was an American. But *who* exactly — freelance oil man? CIA station chief? Renegade arms dealer with a shipload of TOW anti-tank missiles? The Middle East swarmed with wealthy, anonymous, dangerous-looking men and no-one pried too much. It was bad for business. One or two strangers in the room would have an idea who Halloran was, even if they did not know exactly what he was doing here. Hussein had been informed of his visit both times via the State Department and indicated he had no objections. The Iraqi president knew the American was seeing Arafat but was led to believe it was all part of the new US-PLO dialogue. At least he seemed to believe it. No-one could ever be sure of anything in the Middle East. And Halloran knew Hussein would have a couple of his men here too, somewhere among the players, keeping an eye on the American. He laid the chips on the green baize and pushed a $50 chip out first. The Indian croupier glanced at the money. Halloran was the cheapest player at the table. Just because he was rich didn't mean he liked to throw his money away. His senses prickled into alertness and he felt better than he'd felt all day. Jack Halloran wanted to play blackjack.

The call came a few minutes after five the next morning, as usual, when he least wanted it. Halloran looked at the bedside clock and groaned. He had only fallen asleep about ninety minutes earlier. He picked up the phone. It was the concierge.

'A gentleman is here to collect you, sir.'

This was it; it was the way the PLO had called for him the last time.

'I'll be right down,' he said. Halloran splashed some water on his face, gargled some mouthwash and pulled on a pair of dark pants and a light blue sports shirt. The door opened and he saw his guard silhouetted in the light from the sitting room.

'Time for me to see the chairman, John,' he said. 'Just wait for me here, like I said. There's nothing more you can do.'

The guard nodded and disappeared back into the room. He could catch up on his own sleep now. Halloran pulled on his black leather loafers and let himself out into the deserted hallway. It felt strange to walk unaccompanied to the elevators, push the button for himself and then ride down to the lobby alone. Strange but not unpleasant. Playing this waiting game in Baghdad had been a surreal interlude. Here he was, one of the most powerful private individuals in the world, waiting to unleash his own private army on a country ripped asunder by war... and he had been playing blackjack like a man on vacation, and winning. That had been the best part. Halloran never got tired of winning. It wasn't the amount that was important. There were many more higher rollers in the room than him but few who got more pleasure from the game. Halloran had left the table at three in the morning, after five hours play, with US$11,000 in his pocket, enough to cover Bono's gatecrashing at that club in Baja, he chuckled. He stepped out of the elevator and into a blissfully quiet and deserted lobby.

A black-suited, tough looking man with a moustache and bad skin was waiting alone near the front doors. There were two clerks at the front desk as Halloran walked past, his rubber soles squeaking on the polished marble floor, and neither of them looked up.

'Mr Halloran?'

'Yes.'

'The chairman will see you now.'

Exactly like the last time. In the dead of night, while the rest of the world slept, Arafat worked on. It was another part of the Arafat legend; the chairman never slept... and no-one knew where he would turn up next. The PLO man led the way to a waiting Mercedes. Halloran knew it. Tinted, bulletproof glass and heavily armoured black bodywork. A car like this was supposed to survive a direct hit from anything but an artillery shell. He had half a dozen just like it in various garages around the world. The man opened the door for Halloran and then climbed in the front beside the driver. The door had barely shut when the driver screeched away and turned left through the gates, accelerating quickly down the road between huge, stately date palms towards the PLO compound. It was still dark but Halloran saw sand flurries dancing in the yellow cones of the street lights as the fingers of a desert dust storm furtively probed the city.

Halloran checked his watch. Two minutes later the driver

pulled smoothly up to the first checkpoint at the entrance to Arafat's compound. A gate blocked by a black and white striped boom barrier and a wooden guardpost to one side. The gate was manned by three armed Iraqi soldiers and the top of the wall was crested with coils of barbed wire. Halloran glimpsed another sentry strolling near a distant corner, one of half a dozen soldiers who ceaselessly patrolled the outside of the compound, which was about the size of half a city block. The corporal of the guard bent down to check the occupants of the car, then signalled his comrade to raise the gate and waved them through. There was a short drive between well-tended gardens and then a maze of darkened buildings until the car made a left turn and came to a second inner compound. As usual, there were guards everywhere — PLO men. The Iraqis kept the perimeter secure, but the PLO was responsible for the chairman's security inside the walls of the compound. Two armed men wearing the olive drab uniforms and black berets of the PLO showing the blue and yellow olive sprig insignia, guarded the second gate. They waved the Mercedes through into Arafat's inner sanctum and the driver pulled up in front of a short flight of steps leading to a solid front door. There were at least six heavily armed men at the dimly lit front door to Arafat's house. Two were wearing PLO uniforms and had AK-47s slung across their shoulders. The other four were wearing dark suits and carried sub-machine guns which Halloran recognised as Czechoslovakian-made Skorpions, accurate up to 200 metres with a rate of fire of 840 rounds per minute. A powerful weapon, Halloran knew. The moment the car appeared they snapped to attention.

The PLO aide jumped out of the front seat and opened the car door for Halloran. Another aide welcomed Halloran by name while another opened the door to Arafat's residence and escorted him inside. They stepped into a small vestibule and one of the guards turned to Halloran with an apologetic smile.

'Please, Mr Halloran?'

Halloran knew the drill. He raised his arms and submitted to a quick, expert search for only the second time in his life.

'Thank you, sir.' The guard spoke English well. Halloran noted the intelligent face, the assured manner, the courtesy in the voice and the expensive grey suit. All Arafat's aides were creamed from the best in the PLO. Many were drawn from PLO camps as children, sent to the PLO's secret training camps for the Palestinian Young Tigers in Tunisia and Algeria, schooled, trained, indoctrinated to the cause then sent abroad to the best universities in Europe and North America. The Sorbonne, Heidelberg, Oxford, Cambridge, Harvard, Yale and UCLA had all unknowingly scholared PLO students at one time or another. When they returned to Arafat these young men and women were more dedicated than ever. They owed everything to the PLO and they would willingly die for the chairman. Many were sent out to PLO missions and offices in more than seventy countries around the world, pursuing diplomatic careers, running major PLO businesses, farms and properties, collecting taxes, administering finances, promoting the cause of Palestinian statehood. Some joined Arafat's personal staff.

Another aide opened the door to a large, empty waiting room and Halloran stepped through. He was ushered quickly through the waiting room to another, much bigger room divided into a sitting room and conference area. The room was well lit and empty except for another couple of aides and a young, moustached man in uniform without his beret. Halloran watched as the young man snapped off a salute that would do credit to a marine, clicked his heels, turned and walked briskly from the room with a sheaf of documents under one arm. Whatever the Western world thought of Yasser Arafat — that he was a terrorist, a fanatic, a murderer, a high-tech brigand with medieval hates in search of a country — here it was all different. This was another world. A world where the superpowers were temporary aberrations to be negotiated, treated and manipulated into neutrality and impotence. The Soviets were clumsy, unsophisticated godless vulgarians with an obsolete ideology, the Americans were naive and volatile children with guns, dangerous only in their passions and unpredictability. In his world, Yasser Arafat was a hero and a fighter. Throughout the Arab and Islamic worlds, and to hundreds of millions of people on a quarter of the earth's surface, Arafat was accepted as a head of state and treated deferentially. When he visited any Arab country he was given head-of-state status. He was on familiar terms with kings, princes and potentates, comfortable in their palaces, at ease in the highest circles of power. Within the PLO he was regarded as the president-in-exile of the Palestinian state, head of government, chief of all the armed forces and the only plausible saviour of his people. Here, Jack Halloran was reminded, he was in the presence of a national leader and everyone was expected to behave accordingly, including him.

Arafat smiled as only Arafat can. The chairman of the PLO came into the room, saw Halloran and walked towards him with hand outstretched, his greying, whiskery jowls folding into a broad, engaging grin that was almost impossible to resist. But behind the smile Arafat's glistening dark eyes told Halloran nothing. The chairman was a little shorter than Halloran recalled. Perhaps it was because this time he had left off his trademark black and white check keffiyeh. Without his head covering Arafat was revealed to be quite bald, except for a dark horseshoe of hair around his ears. The chairman wore drab olive green battledress with the only dash of colour a black and white cravat. They shook hands and Halloran noticed the handshake was firmer this time, if a little too moist.

'Good to see you again, Mr Halloran,' Arafat said. 'Please come into my office.'

The PLO chairman still had difficulty pronouncing Halloran's name but the American had to concede that Arafat's English was a helluva lot better than Halloran's Arabic. Arafat led Halloran into a small, plainly furnished office with a desk and three chairs. The wall behind the desk was filled with books and there was one floor-to-ceiling window looking out onto a tiny, private courtyard. It was still dark outside although the light from Arafat's office revealed tiny drifting sand dunes across the courtyard tiles.

'Can I offer you something to drink, Mr Halloran? Tea, coffee, a fruit juice perhaps?' Arafat asked.

Halloran declined politely and Arafat nodded to his aides to wait outside, then closed the door, walked quickly behind his desk and gestured to Halloran to take a chair. Arafat always seemed to be moving, Halloran recalled. Even when sitting down he was the kind of man who appeared to need to do two or more things at the same time. Sometimes it was damned offensive when he picked up a document and appeared to be reading it while you talked. Then, he would ask two or three pertinent questions which went right to the heart of the matter and prove that he had heard and considered everything. Then, to add insult to injury, he would sign the piece of paper and hand it to one of his aides to show he had finished that too. Arafat was wearing a new gold and steel Rolex on his left wrist, Halloran noticed, and had a battery of pens in a sleeve pocket on his left shoulder. The chairman looked tired and older than his years. He pulled a leather wallet from a breast pocket and put on a pair of glasses. Halloran had forgotten that Arafat was short-sighted and suffered from eye strain.

'How can I help you, Mr Halloran?'

'You know damn well,' Halloran answered gruffly. He had played his part but now they were alone he was too tired and edgy to put up with any more unnecessary protocols or subtle intimidations. Halloran waited and watched the chairman. Arafat had to be one of the success stories of the twentieth century. He had gone from renegade and terrorist in the 1960s to the head of his own corporate state in twenty-five years, an achievement which ranked with the greatest tactical and corporate accomplishments of the post-war era, Halloran conceded. Along with his own. How different history might have been if this Palestinian refugee, former engineer and bridge-builder had been allowed to migrate to the United States from Lebanon in 1955 as he had requested. He might have wound up working for Halloran. Instead he had been refused and gone on to build his own billion-dollar empire with global tentacles — and Halloran was working for him.

Arafat smiled. This time it was more restrained.

'You realise the value of what I am giving you, Mr Halloran?'

'Both myself and my government are well aware of your influence and the constructive part you have played in these arrangements,' Halloran answered, slipping into diplomatic parlance. 'And we are appropriately appreciative.'

'And... when is the world likely to see the fruits of this appreciation?' Arafat queried. 'The Palestinian people have waited a long time for the Americans to accept the legitimacy of their claim. They are impatient for further progress, for a greater demonstration of commitment from the Americans.'

'We're doing all we can for the moment,' Halloran bristled. 'If everything works out all right — and I stress that's a mighty big if — you won't exactly be disadvantaged.'

Arafat plucked a pen from his sleeve pocket and tapped it against his lips. 'I am putting a great deal of faith in you, Mr Halloran.'

Halloran smiled. He enjoyed being personally threatened by the chairman of the PLO.

'Both our peoples stand to gain if there is a satisfactory outcome to this series of events,' he said. 'You, Mr Chairman, will gain more personally and more immediately than anyone.'

Arafat nodded thoughtfully. 'Perhaps,' he said. 'Assuming your arrangements are sound.'

Halloran took a deep breath. 'Where are our people now?' he asked.

'They are at the Sheikh Abdullah Barracks,' Arafat said. 'You already know that.'

'All of them?'

Arafat hesitated and looked uncomfortable for the first time in their meeting.

'My information is that the last of the hostages will be taken there two days from now,' he said. The smile came back. 'You understand how it is, Mr Halloran, the Shi'ites are not well disciplined. There have been many ... difficulties.'

That was an understatement, Halloran thought.

'Some of our people have been held captive in Lebanon for five years, Mr Chairman. That's a long time too.'

Arafat looked out the window into the courtyard. 'My information is that Hezbollah will have the last of the American hostages at Sheikh Abdullah Barracks within thirty-six hours. We expect ... our people to take charge of them forty-eight hours from then.'

'The last of the hostages will be there by midnight tomorrow?'

'Yes.'

'And your people will pick them up some time between midnight tomorrow and midnight on July 4.'

'We believe so ...'

'You *believe* so?'

Arafat shrugged. 'It is impossible to be more specific. There are many factors — you know that. If you want the transfer to take place at all — then I tell you it must be after midnight tomorrow. It is close to the date you wanted, yes? Your Independence Day?' He raised his hands in a gesture of resignation. 'That is a miracle in itself. You must decide what you will do. I have done all I can for you now.'

It took an effort, but Halloran held his tongue.

'Tell me,' Arafat asked. 'Is Mr Colin Lynch one of your people?'

271

Halloran tried not to look shocked.

'That's confidential,' he said. But his voice gave him away.

'Of course,' Arafat smiled.

There was a long silence. There wouldn't be another opportunity like this. Halloran had to ask. 'Where have you heard Colin Lynch's name?'

'We are aware of him ... and many others like him,' Arafat said casually. He fixed Halloran with a long, knowing look. 'The reason I ask is that the British have more experience at this kind of thing.'

Sly bastard, Halloran thought. 'Okay,' he said, steering the conversation back where he wanted it. 'If you've kept your word, we'll effect the ... transfer ... within that time frame. I just damn well hope your information is good.'

Arafat looked pained. 'Mr Halloran,' he said. 'The information I have just given you was good as of two hours ago. That is the problem with intelligence. It ages very rapidly. The rest is up to you ... and Allah.'

Halloran took a deep breath and switched back to protocol. 'Okay. Thank you, Mr Chairman. You will know within four days whether our ... arrangements have concluded satisfactorily. For any of us.' Halloran got up to go. 'Now, if you will excuse me, I have a plane to catch.'

Arafat nodded and got up to walk his visitor to the door. 'Tell me, Mr Halloran,' the PLO chief said, keeping his voice innocently conversational, 'with all your absences and other interests ... will STC be issuing a share dividend this year?'

Halloran spun around, the shock on his face undisguised. 'You haven't ...'

Arafat smiled. 'The PLO is always interested in improving its portfolio, Mr Halloran. Your company has performed very well for the past four years. I think you may have exposed yourself on some of your rolling stock loans but your property investments are very sound.'

'How much?'

Arafat grinned. He was enjoying himself. 'Oh, just a token

of our support, considering our other... joint interests. A couple of million. Perhaps as events unfold we will be able to consolidate our association and make it more profitable for both parties.'

'Jesus Christ...'

'A much overrated Western deity,' Arafat said. 'Trust in Allah. It's better for business.'

The uniformed guards snapped to attention as Arafat appeared while the aides bustled around Halloran, opening doors, escorting him to the waiting car.

Arafat stepped outside for a moment, sniffed the approaching dawn then raised his hand in farewell to the American.

'Safe flight, Mr Halloran,' he said, then disappeared back into his fortress. And there hadn't been a trace of irony in his voice, Halloran noted.

The eastern horizon was rimmed with the crimson of a rising sun as Halloran rode back to the hotel in the back of the PLO car. His mind raced through a series of calculations. He assumed Arafat had been talking US dollars. Two million. STC shares were around $9.50 when he last checked. Arafat would have used agents via the Arab Bank or a Swiss holding company so the shares would be hard to trace back to the PLO. Even if he could there was no guarantee that Arafat would sell them back — except at a hefty profit. He swore softly to himself again. How in hell was he going to explain the PLO at the next shareholders' meeting?

Istanbul

'Vance and Cooper have gone.'

The words hit Lynch like a slap in the face. He had been dozing contentedly after a long, healing sleep when Bono threw open the door without knocking and marched in. Lynch sat up and swung his legs over the side of the bed.

'What do you mean... gone?' He was still groggy. He

rubbed his face roughly with his hands, trying to clear his head. The curtains were drawn, the room was dark and he had no idea of the time. He looked at his watch. It was a quarter to eight. He pulled the curtains and looked at the neon signs winking through the dusk on the buildings opposite. He blinked in disbelief. It was a quarter to eight at night. He had slept the clock around and then some. No wonder he felt groggy.

'Gone...' Bono persisted. 'As in... not fucking here.'

Lynch stumbled around his room for a moment, fumbled in his kit bag for a pair of jeans and started pulling them on.

'What room... are you sure...?'

'We're sure they ain't on this floor.'

'Who's we?'

'Me, Reece, Gamble... the boss's guys.'

'Shit.' Lynch hurried into the bathroom, filled the sink full of cold water and shoved his head in. The fog inside his head dispersed in a moment. He pulled his streaming face out of the water, mopped himself dry with a towel then hunted out a clean shirt and a pair of sneakers.

'Has anybody told Halloran?'

'Not yet,' Bono said. 'I told the guard to wait while we got you. I told them I'd break their fucking legs.'

'Good.' Lynch strode out of the room and down the long, gloomy corridor to where the others were gathered in a tense group beside the elevators.

'Did either of you see them go?' Lynch asked the guards.

They shook their heads. 'They didn't leave while we were here,' one of them said. 'We've been on duty since midday.'

'Which room were they in?'

The guards led Lynch to the two rooms nearest the fire exit. He checked Vance's room first and looked out the window. The answer was next to Cooper's adjoining window, an iron fire escape ladder which ran straight up the wall beside his window to the roof. From there they could have got into the fire stairs and walked down to the lobby and out into the street.

'Mighty fucking unprofessional, if you ask me,' Bono gloated.

'I don't think they've busted out of the operation,' Lynch said tersely. 'Their clothes are still here... everything.' He picked Vance's wallet up off the dresser. 'My guess is they've seen how everybody else fucks around in this Mickey Mouse outfit and they've gone out for a couple of beers.'

'Yep, mighty unpro —'

'Shut up,' Lynch snapped. 'We'll have to assume they're going to do what every other tourist and off-duty serviceman would do with a few hours to kill in Istanbul. They've gone to the red light district.'

He turned to the guards.

'Has either of you radioed the Consulate or told Halloran about this?'

The guards looked at each other then shook their heads. They knew what was coming.

'Have you been told the nature of this operation?'

The two men nodded cautiously.

'Give me till midnight to find them,' Lynch asked. 'If I haven't brought them back by then... blow the whistle.'

'Mr Halloran told us...'

'I know what Mr Halloran's orders were,' Lynch interrupted. 'But if we're going to save this operation we've got to get those two assholes back safely. That's if they weren't seen by any of Slater's men from the street.'

The guards looked at each other.

'Okay,' the bigger of the two said. 'We go off at midnight. If you're not back by then we radio in.'

'Good enough,' said Lynch. 'Now give me your gun.'

The guards tensed and backed away but Lynch moved too quickly and pulled the baby Uzi out of the big man's holster.

'That's...' he started to protest.

'A precaution,' Lynch said evenly. 'Give me a spare clip.' The man hesitated then rolled his eyes in defeat and passed Lynch a clip.

'They told me you were the good guys,' the guard said. 'Just do it fast because my ass is in the wringer now.'

Lynch hoisted his shirt, jammed the Uzi into the waistband of his jeans and let the shirt fall back. 'Bono, you come with me,' he ordered and headed for the fire door.

'Hey, Lynch?' It was Gamble.

Lynch had no time to argue.

'You have your talents, Peter,' he said. 'Bono's talent is street fighting.' Then he was gone with Bono hurrying after him.

They trotted down the five floors to the fire exit, slipped quietly into a back alley and hurried down to the main street. They saw no-one before joining the crowds on Straselviler Caddesi but Lynch knew that didn't mean they hadn't been seen. They were going to need a lot of luck, he realised. More luck than they'd had on this operation so far. The second taxi they flagged stopped for them. They climbed into the back and Lynch pulled out a ten dollar bill, folded it and wagged it at the driver.

The driver spoke little English but understood the language of the American dollar. Bono made a drinking gesture with his fist then formed a circle with the thumb and forefinger of one hand and began poking it vigorously with the index finger of the other. In case the driver still didn't understand he gave an exaggerated wolf whistle and made a hideous, lascivious face that was intended to convey lust.

The driver nodded his head furiously.

'Don't try so hard, he'll think you want to marry him,' Lynch hissed.

'Istiklal Caddesi,' the driver said and the taxi sped off through the traffic.

Both men recognised the street even though neither of them had seen it before in their lives. It was exactly like a hundred other red light streets they had seen around the world. Noise, neon, sleaze, cheap food, crowds of tourists, servicemen, hard looking pimps, pushers and dealers, junkies, drunks and the dissipated faces of women who had been working the street too long.

'Hi, honey, I'm home,' Bono yelled as he climbed out of the cab. Lynch threw the driver the ten and ten more. The driver looked ecstatic and indicated he would wait if they wanted him to. Lynch shook his head and he and Bono pushed their way into the crowds seething along both sides of the street. Everywhere he looked there were white uniforms. Sailors. Then he remembered. This was the Turk's Navy Day — the red light district would be even busier than usual. Lynch looked at his watch. Nearly 8.30. Something told him it was impossible.

'You work that side of the street,' he told Bono. 'I'll work this side. If you find them first, bring them out here. I don't care how you do it.'

Bono grinned then turned and threaded his way between the crawling cars to the opposite side of Istanbul's sleaze strip.

'Hey … American … how much for your girlfrien'?'

Vance stared at the half empty bottle of Efes Pilsen and knew it was about to get them both into a lot of trouble. It was his second beer in half an hour. The only beers he'd had in almost a month. He had decided back at the hotel that if he was going to put his life on the line with a bunch of goddamn amateurs he was damn well going to have a contemplative beer or two first. Cooper had needed only a little persuading. The little quiet man from Alabama wasn't hungering so much for a drink. He wanted a woman. And he'd been of the same mind as Vance. This could be his last chance for a little carnal pleasure before he went on a job that might just be his last.

They had deliberately avoided the bigger, flashier places

at street level with the storefront windows. Too conspicuous. Instead they had looked for something smaller and quieter and had checked out this club which had only a doorway and a neon sign of a Turk's head with a winking red fez. A flight of filthy stairs led down to a basement club with a bar, a few tables, half-moon booths along two walls and vintage pop music. It took the two men a few minutes to adjust to the foggy gloom and the smoke even caught in Cooper's throat. The Turks enjoyed their tobacco. But it wasn't too crowded and more importantly for Cooper, there were women there. A middle-aged woman in a blue sequinned dress showed them to a table. Vance didn't like it and insisted on a booth. The woman had indicated the booths were reserved until Vance slipped her five bucks. He noticed she had a lot of gold in her mouth and she had an antique beehive hairstyle that looked as though it hadn't been combed out since Elvis was a boy. When she left he caught a gust of body odour unsuccessfully masked by cheap perfume. She brought them a couple of beers and they settled down for a quiet hour. Vance figured on putting away a six pack before heading back to the hotel and Cooper said he might slip out with one of the women for a few minutes, if it was that sort of place. Their eyes had adjusted to the gloom and it looked like that sort of place. There were a lot of sailors, a lot of men in cheap black leather jackets, turtleneck sweaters and three-day-old beards. The only man in the room who was clean shaven was Cooper. With his blonde hair it made him look even younger. He was the only man who didn't seem to notice. There were about a dozen women, most of them too old and too overweight, even for his basic needs, Cooper decided. When they ordered their second beer the hostess indicated they might like a little company. A couple of women had already started in their direction. Vance knew all they were expected to do was be suckered into buying a few overpriced drinks and he was prepared to play along for the sake of international harmony. Cooper decided oth-

saw that the sailors weren't alone. There were a few leather jackets trying to get in some licks too. Vance and Cooper hit the floor kicking and punching for their lives but it did no good. Vance felt a tremendous crack to the back of his head and almost blacked out. The heel of someone's boot jammed into his kidneys and he winced. Then the blows seemed to blur into one agonising, merciless tattoo. Cooper had rolled himself into a tight ball with his knees protecting his genitals and his arms over his head, but it only incensed the crowd even more and they kicked at him savagely, looking for an opening, trying to scar and maim. Vance never dreamed he could endure so much pain and remain conscious. He found himself on all fours and scrambled desperately, trying to butt his way through the mob and claw his way to the door but there was another brutal blow to the side of his head from somebody's boot and he felt blood pouring across his face as he went down again. He began to hope for unconsciousness but it wouldn't come. The Turks wouldn't stop punching and kicking and the terrifying realisation came to him that he was going to die here and now on the floor of this filthy Turkish dive. There was a sudden, ear-splitting scream and Vance thought somebody must have taken a knife to Cooper. Vance knew he was next and somehow found the strength to roll over on his back and kick up at the sea of furious, hate-filled faces above him. One of the faces suddenly disappeared as though plucked away by a giant hand, then another. Vance heard a huge crash and a sudden roar, then the beating stopped and the mob pulled back. Vance looked up through a curtain of blood to see the face of someone he recognised.

'Relax guys,' Bono said. 'The Marines are here.'

Somebody hit Bono from behind. A sailor had launched himself onto the big man's back, trying to knock him to the ground. Bono stumbled momentarily, reached behind him, seized the man's head and shirt in his huge hands and pulled him viciously off his back. The man slid forward over Bono's head and shoulders and Bono changed his grip and heaved him across the room. The seaman landed heavily on his back about ten feet away and the floor trembled. The man rolled and tried to scuttle back onto his feet but Bono took two steps and kicked him brutally between the legs. The sailor's feet lifted off the ground then he crumpled back to the floor and lay in a ball, gagging and moaning.

'Now don't get up,' Bono grunted.

He turned and pulled Vance to his feet. Vance gasped as pain lanced through every fibre of his body but forced himself to stand upright. The crowd fell back and stood in a sullen menacing circle around the two men.

'Get up Cooper,' Bono growled. 'If you can walk we're walking outta here now.'

The huddled figure slowly uncurled and Cooper got unsteadily to his feet. Vance wiped away the blood still pouring from a cut in his scalp and looked around. He and Cooper were battered and shaky and their clothes were in bloody rags but they could see four Turks lying amidst the shattered furniture who were worse, and more bloody faces in the crowd. Bono began moving slowly towards the exit with Vance and Cooper behind him. It was only six metres to the door and then the stairs to the street, but even with Bono, Vance wasn't sure they would make it. They moved a few feet but the crowd muttered and their ranks hardened. They weren't falling back anymore. Somebody aimed a bottle at Bono's head and he instinctively ducked and raised his arm to protect his face. The bottle hit his elbow and shattered in a shower of glass.

The sailor who had started the brawl lunged forward out of the crowd. His face was pulpy and bloody but his injury had only enraged him more and he wasn't about to let the Americans leave till he'd satisfied his brutal pride. Somebody had given him a weapon. It looked like a length of thick black rubber but it was filled with cement. He swung savagely at Bono and the big man stepped back. It was all the crowd

282

had been waiting for and they surged forward. Vance thought he caught a glimpse of a knife and his blood chilled.

'Shit,' Bono grumbled at Vance and Cooper. 'What did you say to these guys?' He ducked away from the murderous, flailing blackjack and caught the sailor by the wrist. There was no time for finesse. Bono yanked the arm high into the air, turned and broke it across his shoulder. The elbow joint made a sound like a pistol shot as it cracked and the man screamed in agony and dropped to his knees. A shattered table leg connected with the side of Bono's head and he staggered. Somebody grabbed him around the waist and tried to drag him down. Vance fought with every scrap of his remaining strength but still reeled backwards under the on-slaught of half a dozen men. He lost sight of Bono and Cooper. If he went down this time, he knew, he was finished. He fought desperately to stay on his feet.

A series of muffled explosions filled the room. There was the sound of breaking glass, screams and then silence. Every-thing stopped. More explosions echoed through the basement room for several seconds, showering the stunned crowd with splintered wood and chips of shattered masonry.

'Now!'

It was Lynch's voice. He was crouched at the bottom of the stairs with the Uzi. The three Americans struggled out of the cowering mob towards the door. Vance and Cooper stumbled up the stairs first. Bono turned to look around and saw a rash of bullet holes around the walls of the wrecked basement club. Then he turned, stepped back into the room and sank his boot into the ribs of one of the Turks crouched nearby. The man yelled in pain and rolled away.

'That's what I like about you,' Lynch said as they backed carefully up the stairs, the Uzi pointed downwards. 'Deep down you're rather a spiteful man, aren't you?'

Bono took it as a compliment.

'Took your sweet fucking time, man,' he said.

Lynch stopped at the exit to the street, tucked the Uzi

back under his shirt and grimaced as the hot barrel touched his belly. 'Wouldn't have found you at all if it wasn't for Slater's men.'

Bono looked outside. Jimmy Slater was standing on the footpath with three men in suits, one of them a Turk. The State Department man looked agitated and was signalling them to join Vance and Cooper in a waiting Mercedes. A crowd was just starting to gather. The Turk held up an official badge and began moving the people along. Lynch and Bono hurried out to the car and climbed in. Slater jumped in the front beside Lynch and the driver and the Mercedes took off.

There was a long pause until the lights of Istiklal Caddesi receded behind them. Vance and Cooper dabbed at an array of cuts and bruises and probed for broken bones. There didn't seem to be any.

'Welcome to Istanbul,' Slater said dryly.

'Nice town you got here,' Bono said.

'Does Halloran know?' Lynch asked.

'Not yet,' Slater answered.

'Why not?'

Slater hesitated. 'Because he's not here, that's why.'

'Where is he?'

'Had to go out of town on business for a few hours. He'll be back... tonight, tomorrow maybe.'

'You going to tell him?'

Slater gave a short humourless laugh.

'Somebody's going to have to tell him.'

'Can you fix it with the local authorities?'

Slater pursed his lips. 'They have gang fights in that part of town all the time,' he said. 'Lot of drugs in Istanbul. The Turks will help us out. They don't have a lot of choice because they're in deep enough already. But they won't like it. You've been naughty boys.'

'Then why did you let me handle it?' Lynch asked.

'They're your guys,' Slater shrugged. 'Better somebody they know.'

'You guys were watching us?' Bono interrupted. 'And you wouldn't help till the shit hit the fan?'

'Hey,' Slater said, his voice betraying his suppressed anger. 'You guys are supposed to be able to take care of yourselves. My people were asked to keep an eye on you but not to intervene unless they had no choice. You came close, let me tell you. We knew where your two pals had gone and we knew you were looking for them. We were in radio contact all the time and, I have to say, I thought things would sort themselves out when you found them. When the three of you didn't come out of that dive we figured something must have gone wrong. That's when I told my people to identify themselves to Mr Lynch here and I came down to see if he could pull you out fast and quiet.' He paused and looked at Lynch. 'It wasn't as quiet as I would have liked.'

An uneasy silence settled in the car.

'Yeah, we're fine, thanks,' Vance said after a while.

They all ignored him. Lynch began to recognise the streets. They would be back at the hotel in a few minutes. He checked his watch. It was a little after ten.

'What are you going to tell Halloran?' Lynch asked finally.

Slater hesitated. 'The way I see it you all got out in one piece. But I don't want you in my town anymore. You've been here two days and you've overstayed your welcome. You can tell him what you want. I'm going to tell him things have changed and I want you all out of here in twenty-four hours.'

'Thanks,' Lynch said. And meant it. Maybe the State Department wasn't full of assholes after all.

The car dropped Slater off at the front of the hotel then drove around to the back alley where he opened the fire exit door for the rest of them. Vance and Cooper climbed out of the car like men crippled by arthritis.

'Hey!' Vance called after Bono.

Bono looked back.

'Thanks,' Vance said.

Bono grunted. 'Special fuckin' Forces my ass,' he said and disappeared up the stairs.

Lynch waited till his men were inside then shook hands with Slater.

Slater hesitated then smiled unexpectedly.

'I know what you're doing,' he said. 'Just get those poor bastards out of Lebanon . . . okay?'

Lynch nodded. 'Okay.'

Lynch trudged up the five flights of stairs smiling ironically to himself in the dark. He finally had a team that could depend on each other. Perhaps it hadn't been such a bad night after all.

9

THE GUNS OF EDEN

Beirut, July 2

Bill Wallace was awakened by the barrel of an AK47 jabbed roughly into his bony back.

'Get up, American,' the Hezbollah guard ordered. 'It's time.'

The guard ripped the blanket off the bed, took Wallace by the arm and pulled him upright. The American professor hadn't heard the door open. Electric light flooded the room and hurt his eyes. He had no idea how long he had been asleep, he had taken to sleeping even more than usual, hoping that one time he might drift into blissful unconsciousness and never wake up again, however much he yearned to see his family — his wife who was growing old without him, his daughters who had grown up without him.

'Hurry... hurry... stupid old man.' The guard grabbed the professor's shirt and trousers from the end of the bed and flung them at him. All these months of nothing, Wallace thought, and now they were in a hurry.

'American.' That was all they had ever called him. As though his real name, his real identity, his uniqueness as a human being were unimportant. But they *were* unimportant, Wallace realised, to a class of fanatics who had generated a pathological hatred of all things American. He doubted that they had ever thought of him as a human being, let alone a gentle, learned man who had never wished or done them any harm. They had only ever treated him as a sub-human. How ironic, he thought, that these medieval zealots should demand, at the point of a gun, that the whole world recognise their sacred cause, their ancient principles and their basic rights as a people — while denying them so casually to others. Now he hated them with every atom of his being.

He pulled on his clothes and the worn shoes with no laces and shuffled clumsily into the corridor in front of the guard. There were several other militiamen in the corridor, all armed. Wallace looked for a window and saw that it was still dark outside. Maybe this was it, he thought. His last moments on earth. Maybe that creature, Ziad, had been lying. Maybe he had been wrong. Things changed all the time. Maybe he suddenly was worthless to them all. He felt nothing. It seemed like a lot of soldiers to execute an old man: one quick bullet in the back of the head from a small calibre pistol would have done it. The guard slung his rifle, pulled Wallace's hands behind him and handcuffed them together. Another militiaman pulled a dirty pillow case over Wallace's head and they began half pushing, half pulling him down the corridor. They came to a flight of stairs and Wallace stumbled. The guards cursed him and pulled him up. He lost a shoe. They dragged him along another corridor. There were a few sharp, jostling turns and he began to feel dizzy. A final short flight of steps and he felt a sudden coolness and realised he was outside.

He heard car engines running and men shouting. He strained to hear but there were so many voices jumbling into one another. They were talking about him and about which guards would ride in which vehicle. He wasn't going to be executed after all, he realised. They were going to too much trouble. He felt two pairs of hands lift him up by the shoulders and by the feet and then they slung him into the back of a truck like a sack of chaff. His head cracked against a sharp metal corner and he cried out involuntarily in pain. Somebody barked a rebuke to the guards and Wallace was amused. They didn't want him too badly damaged before he got wherever it was they were taking him. He had landed on his side and he tried to wriggle up into a sitting position

but someone grabbed him and shoved him down into a corner
with his hooded face pressed against the side of the truck.
The metal rattled with the engine vibrations and he shifted
his head a little to get more comfortable. Someone kicked
his feet and he pulled them up tight. He felt several men
climb into the truck and settle down around him. There were
more shouts and then the engine revved and the truck lurched
forward and began bumping over a rough road. Somewhere
in the distance he heard the rattle of automatic weapons
again. He hadn't heard that in a while. Just as he had thought,
he was still in Beirut. But where were they taking him next?
Events were moving towards an unknown climax for him
at last, Professor Wallace realised. Just how long did he have
left to live now, he wondered?

Ankara, July 3

The NATO Hercules trundled down the runway, lifted into
the hazy night skies over central Anatolia and began climbing
steadily. The American pilot levelled off at 6,500 metres, set
his cruising speed at 500 kph and confirmed his bearing for
Cyprus. The Turkish co-pilot checked the bearings, then
radioed their flight plan to Nicosia. If anyone was eavesdropping this was just another Turkish military flight to their
garrison in the Turkish sector of the island. The men riding
in the belly of the Hercules sat in silence, conserving oxygen
and energy, alone with their thoughts. Jack Halloran rode
in the navigator's seat, wearing a flight suit and helmet. His
eyes behind the oxygen mask betrayed nothing of the thoughts
that seethed through his mind. He had arrived back in Istanbul
thirty-six hours before to find two of his men sporting some
ugly cuts and bruises and his State Department contact pres-
suring him to get his team onto the NATO base at Ankara
without delay. No-one would tell him what had happened.
Vance and Cooper claimed they had given each other the
bruises. Halloran didn't buy it. Lynch would only tell him

that their minor morale problem had now been solved. He was more willing to believe that because of the obvious change in the attitude of the men towards each other. Even Halloran's own guards couldn't or wouldn't shed any more light on what had happened. In the end he had no choice but to let it go. As exhausted as he had been he had gone back to the airport, turned his plane around and they had all flown to Ankara, leaving a much relieved Jimmy Slater behind. That had been yesterday afternoon. The NATO base commander had not been pleased to see them. There had been a flurry of calls between the base, Ankara and Washington, and Halloran had to give some big assurances to the State Department that the mission was still on track and should not be cancelled. They had been billeted overnight in government VIP quarters. At least it had given Vance and Cooper time to have their injuries treated at the base infirmary. Vance had had five stitches put into the gash in his scalp and both men had been told to rest for a few days. They had promised to try. After a night's rest Lynch and his men had spent all day in the hangar with the Hercules, checking and rechecking their equipment. Halloran confirmed that take-off would be at 2200 hours.

Halloran had tried to say something to the men before they geared up but it hadn't worked. Everything had been said. Everything had been done that could be done in the insanely short space of time he had been given to mount the operation. He had pledged to the State Department that he could do it, but as the weeks had passed he had begun to have his doubts too. For the first time in his life Jack Halloran believed he might be attempting an operation that could not succeed. The men sensed it too yet still he pushed them, and still they went. Halloran knew they were no longer doing it for him. Every man on the team had his own reasons. There was a gulf between Halloran and this team that had never existed on previous operations. He might have put it all together, he realised, but he was no longer one of them.

They trusted Lynch more than they trusted him: he was one of them, Halloran never could be. And the gulf between himself and Lynch yawned perilously wide; Lynch simply did not trust Halloran and he did not believe in him anymore. He would see the job through, but afterwards, things could never go back to the way they were — not that it mattered, as far as Halloran was concerned. He was a pragmatist. Lynch might be a good man, but even good men could become more trouble than they were worth. And the surly, unpredictable Lynch might solve all Halloran's problems for him yet, the American knew. Men had died for him before and left uncollected pay cheques. It was ultimately their decision. Halloran had achieved what he had set out to do. These men would do the job, or they wouldn't come back. Lynch included. Whichever way it went down, Halloran couldn't lose. He and Arafat had made sure of that.

After half an hour they crossed the Turkish Mediterranean coast and entered international air space. Halloran heard the pilot's voice through his helmet speaker. He had started climbing, he said, and was flying a new course for the launch zone. The pilot thumbed a switch on the dashboard and a red light began flashing in the hold. Lynch looked up as the red glare began washing over them. Another twenty minutes to jump time. The men switched their oxygen onto full as the Hercules began to climb. The air inside the plane grew even colder. Lynch felt the temperature change through the thermal suit and the layer of creased military greens he wore beneath his jump suit. He ran a quick equipment check again. The compass on his NAVSTAR receiver registered the new heading and the altometer told him how quickly they were climbing. The air speed and ground speed needles were off the dials. They weren't calibrated to register aircraft speeds and the needles would only flicker back to give useful readings when the Nighthawk had been fully deployed and was travelling at below 100 knots. Lynch could feel the 'chute pack between his back and the fuselage. The M16A1 was strapped to his torso beneath the NAVSTAR receiver and the only other unfamiliar piece of equipment was the black polycarbonate gear capsule strapped to his waist and thighs. It meant that when he sat back against the aircraft the capsule sat snug against his belly and rested on his lap like a sinister black egg filled with 115 kilos of high explosive. His MP5 and Browning High-power were inside the capsule along with his load carrying vest, grenades, ammunition, glucose pills... and 45 kilos of extra plastique for Bono and Reece. Every man carried an identical load, as Halloran had promised. It was enough to blow away half of Lebanon.

In the cockpit Halloran heard the pilot's voice again.

'Weather's clear in most of the Eastern Med, according to the Turkish airbase tower on Cyprus,' the pilot said. 'Prevailing easterly winds of two to three knots from the Syrian and Lebanese coast... some summer storm activity believed over the Lebanese mountains, strength hard to gauge. I can't press them on it. Want to tell your guys?'

'No,' Halloran said. 'They'll find out soon enough.'

The pilot glanced around at him then shook his head and went back to the controls. A few minutes later they arrived at the launch zone. Lynch saw the green light come on first and then the rear exit ramp of the Hercules yawned slowly open with a high pitched hydraulic whine. Lynch got to his feet and signalled to the others to line up behind him. Gamble was next, then Vance, Cooper, Bono and Reece. If Reece froze this time, they all knew they were leaving him behind. The gaping mouth of the night roared at them like a mythic beast and Lynch waddled awkwardly down the ramp and toppled into its bottomless black throat.

He pulled the ripcord and the Nighthawk rushed from its pack with a comforting whooshing sound and spread its great wings. Lynch felt himself hauled into the protective care of the great bird and then it began its eastward glide towards the coast of Lebanon, thirty-two kilometres away. Lynch looked around but could see only blackness. There must have been some haze, he realised, or even some cloud because he couldn't see a single star in the sky. He concentrated on his instruments and registered his altitude at 8,040 metres and descending gradually. His bearing was slightly off and he tweaked the steering lines to adjust his course. Next he checked his oxygen and saw that he still had fifty-five minutes left. For the next half hour Lynch sailed through the freezing void unable to see anything but the reassuring twinkle of his NAVSTAR instruments. He was down to around 6,400 metres but still gliding blind and decided he could afford to lose a little more altitude. He took the Nighthawk down to 5,500 metres and held it. A moment later he saw a few wisps of cloud whip past and then the lights of a huge coastal metropolis slid into view far away to the south. Beirut, Lynch realised. He was on course. Then he saw and heard something that worried him. At first he thought it must be the distant flicker and grumble of shell fire but then he realised it wasn't. It was thunder and lightning rippling malevolently through the mountains ahead. Lynch knew very little about para-chuting through storms except that he'd heard of a Luftwaffe pilot who supposedly drowned in mid-air during the war when he parachuted from his crippled plane into a huge rain-bearing cloud. Lynch tugged the Nighthawk to get some height and the glider 'chute responded, giving him almost 200 metres. That was one of the few benefits of a three knot headwind, Lynch thought, checking his air speed against his ground speed. He stared ahead through his goggles, breathing a little faster now. There it was again. A silvery ripple of light through a mountain valley, illuminating the rugged slopes. A couple of seconds later he heard the grumble of thunder again, a little louder this time. Lynch pulled on the lines and gained another sixty metres. All he could do was the same as the pilot of any light aircraft would do — try to fly over it. God help Reece and Bono, he thought. Wherever they were.

Henry Reece felt the fear again. He had held it under control for so long but now he could see himself drifting inexorably into the terrifying embrace of a waiting thunder-storm it surged uncontrollably through his body once more. Reece had tried but he knew he couldn't navigate his way through or around the storm. It was no longer a matter of skill, it was a matter of nerve. He had spent hour after hour studying the instruments and going over compass bearings with Bono until he was sure he had it right. After that it was all an effort of will. He had summoned enough of it to jump from that plane one last time and when the Nighthawk opened above him again it seemed like a vindication of all his struggle. He was going to make it. Despite the blackness of the night he had strained to monitor the instruments and done everything he had been told. He too had been rewarded by the lights of Beirut, far to the south. He wasn't to know that Lynch was gliding about 600 metres below him and about 300 metres to his right. All he had eyes for was the flashing teeth of the storm as he flew closer and closer into its arms. Reece checked his altitude. He was shaving 6,700 metres. Another lightning flash and then another rumble of thunder. Reece sobbed. He was going to take her down. He tugged on the lines and the Nighthawk began a rapid, spiralling descent. Reece looked at his altometer. Going down through 5,500 metres. The highest peaks were supposed to be around 3,800 metres. He could see the lights of a few small villages below. He would try and steer for a place between the lights, maybe land on one of the lower slopes and hide out for a few days until the mission was over and then try to make his way south to Israeli lines. And what then, he wondered? How would he face Bono, Lynch and the others? He couldn't. Reece knew that he was finished. His nerve was gone for good. A sudden updraft caught him and the Nighthawk bucked wildly in the sky and Reece heard himself scream. He pulled on the lines but he couldn't stop it. There was another vivid flash of lightning and a second later a deafening crash of thunder. The storm had reached out and claimed him. Reece felt himself thrown around the sky like a ping pong ball. He sucked on the oxygen and began to choke. His oxygen was running out, he'd flown too high and consumed too much. Reece felt panic sweep in on the heels of fear. His insides seemed to freeze. He fought the fear and he fought to control his 'chute but the Nighthawk wouldn't respond. He ripped the mask off his face and gulped clean air. He checked his altometer. He could hardly focus on the numbers because of the buffeting from the storm. 4,500 metres and falling. Just a few seconds longer. He began to babble a prayer. An invisible hand swatted him across the sky, the harness tore at his shoulders, one of the thigh straps to the gear capsule tore loose. He felt himself thrown through the sky in a great sickening arc and another giant hand tried to wrench him from the Nighthawk's talons.

Reece felt the Nighthawk let him go. The canopy collapsed and the great black bird of prey dropped him from it claws. As he fell Henry Reece believed the gods were finally punishing him for his fear. It was the last sane thought he had before he died.

Lynch pulled away his oxygen mask and breathed deeply. The air was the sweetest he had ever tasted in his life. He checked the gauge. The needle was below empty. Lynch laughed. His arms and shoulders ached from the nightmare passage through the storm. It had taken everything he knew to ride the boiling air currents over the Lebanese Mountains, wondering all the time whether a man in a parachute was an efficient conductor of lightning. Twelve minutes he estimated, before he was through the worst of it, the longest twelve minutes in his life. The last few had felt like a joyride by comparison. He had brought the Nighthawk down to 4,000 metres and was staring through the darkness for any sign of the lights of El Laboue. He saw nothing and began looking for a bigger town. If he found Ba'albek first he would be able to find the drop zone at El Laboue. Lynch decided to take a chance and brought the Nighthawk down to 3,000.

This was below the highest peaks of the range, he knew, but instinct also told him he was over the mountains' spine. A moment later he saw the dim yellow lights of a large town. He squinted through the goggles and found a smaller cluster of lights a few kilometres to the north. He checked his coordinates on the NAVSTAR receiver. He had found El Laboue. Lynch tugged the steering lines and the Nighthawk swooped gracefully around to the north and carried him silently down towards the small Lebanese town. He checked the altometer at 1,200 metres. He was almost directly above El Laboue now and he scoured the empty streets for any sign of a threat. There seemed to be a small town square with a few brighter lights. He descended another 300 metres and curved smoothly down towards the south, carefully calculating his approach to the drop zone amidst the orchards. A large villa glided beneath his feet and Lynch saw a couple of cars out front. They would do for transport to Ba'albek, he decided. Everything was peaceful as it should have been. The countryside south of El Laboue was in uniform darkness. There were no headlights on the road. Bedtime in the Beqa'a, Lynch thought. It must have been one of the last peaceful places in all of Lebanon, precisely because no-one dared challenge the rule of the Shi'ite terrorist militias in their own domain. Lynch made up his mind, took the Nighthawk below 300 metres for landing and bent his knees in anticipation.

A heavy machine gun opened fire. Searchlights blinked on. An electrical current of pure horror coursed through Lynch's body. More searchlights. He saw red tracers lancing through the night sky, crisscrossing searchlight beams. The lights sliced across tree tops and lit up the foothills of the ante-Lebanese range. Lynch was so close he could see oranges on the trees. He was in the right place. Then he saw the tanks. He heard men shouting, tank engines roaring, headlights switched on and the tanks began moving, searchlights sweeping the sky for raiders. God almighty, Lynch thought, someone had tipped off the Syrians. And the Nighthawk had obediently carried him straight into the ambush. Lynch yanked on the steering lines and the Nighthawk veered wildly away from the hell that had erupted beneath his feet. He was losing height rapidly. It was too late to climb, to try and gain some height and land a few kilometres down the road. He fought and coaxed as much height out of the 'chúte as he could, knowing that every precious metre could save his skin. Then he saw tree tops rushing up to meet him. He steered for a patch of darkness between the trees and braced himself. Just before he landed Lynch snatched a desperate look back towards the firing and saw a Nighthawk helplessly impaled on a searchlight beam, red tracers streaming up towards it.

Cooper hauled on the steering lines and the Nighthawk danced like a moth caught in a spotlight, but he couldn't escape. The blonde young Alabaman watched with a peculiar self-detachment as the tracers licked towards him like the deadly tongue of some lethal giant insect. Between every one of those red dashes were three rounds of 12.7mm, he knew. Cooper pulled savagely at the lines again and the Nighthawk shook him, irritatedly, like a puppet. He could hear the rattle of small arms fire between the heavy metallic chatter of the large calibre machine guns. He struggled to unclip his rifle and return fire. There was one clip in the magazine. Cooper knew it was futile but he wasn't about to float across the sky like a clay pigeon, waiting to be shot either. He finally pulled the M16A1 loose, swung it down and squirted off a long, blistering round at the ground below. It wasn't the same as his own rifle but it made him feel better. Cooper would have been happy to find a perch in those mountains somewhere and take on these bastards with his Dragunov. Then he would make them work, he thought. With his hands off the lines the Nighthawk lowered him into the hornet's nest. A sudden shock of pain swept through his body as a hail of machine gun bullets sliced across both legs. A moment later a stream of red tracer poured into the gear pod strapped to his front.

Lynch was almost a kilometre away when the forty-five

kilos of plastique, six high explosive grenades and all the ammunition in Cooper's gear capsule went off. The flash illuminated the sky and Lynch caught a glimpse of an entire Syrian tank squadron grouped in the orchard south of El Laboue. He knew then that it wasn't an ambush. They had just been unlucky. The Syrians had pulled in for the night and a sentry had spotted something in the sky. No doubt the moment the Syrians switched on their searchlights and caught sight of a Nighthawk they believed the area was under assault by Israeli paratroopers. If they had known what was in those gear capsules they would never have risked firing. Lynch rolled behind a couple of trees, flattened himself against the ground and waited. The sound of the explosion reached him an instant later and it sounded like the crack of doom. Then another and another. He lost count of the number of explosions as they melded into one shattering crescendo. His eardrums groaned under the jump helmet and then he felt a sudden wall of heat roll over him as the blastwave tried to melt him into the ground. A great storm of debris lashed him from head to toe as torn metal and splintered trees flew through the orchard like javelins. And then it stopped and there was an unnatural silence. Lynch struggled to his feet. He hadn't time for minor pain or grogginess now. He tore off his jump helmet and looked around. If the Syrians had planned it they couldn't have arranged for the explosion to have a more devastating effect. Lynch realised he had survived something fantastic in the history of warfare. A tank squadron, nine Soviet built T-72s, had just annihilated itself. By detonating a concentrated pack of 115 kilos of high explosives a hundred feet in the air they had created an explosion as devastating as a small, airborne nuclear blast. A direct hit by a missile couldn't have done more. The blastwave had created a circle of destruction half a kilometre across and everything directly underneath had been flattened, as if by a giant hammer. Nine main battle tanks had been turned into molten scrap metal and every trooper in the squadron

298

cremated. Several trees were still burning and Lynch could see the trunks of the trees that had sheltered him studded with shrapnel and lethal wooden shards.

God only knew who it had been in the Nighthawk, thought Lynch. Whoever it was had bought the rest of them some time. He unclipped the M16A1 and the gear capsule then tore off the parachute harness and thermal lined jump suit. There wasn't much point in hiding the 'chute and capsules anymore, he realised. Word would get to Ba'albek within an hour and militiamen would be sent to investigate. They had to get to the Sheikh Abdullah Barracks before the word of parachutists got back. So much for lying low and attempting a covert entry, Lynch thought. He unscrewed the cap to the gear capsule and hauled out his armament. He clipped the Browning to his belt, pulled the already loaded vest over his green army shirt and slung the MP5 across his back. The plastique was packed in ammunition pouches and he slung them over one shoulder. Lynch picked up the M16A1 in his free hand and began circling through the trees and away from the devastated drop zone. He didn't worry about being spotted by unfriendlies. The explosion would give him at least five minutes before anyone was brave enough to venture close enough to make sense of what had happened. He was wrong. He was almost at the road when a figure stepped out between a clump of orange trees with a weapon raised.

Lynch dropped to a sitting position, swung up the rifle and prepared to fire.

'The Ayatollah sucks.'

Lynch got back to his feet as Gamble walked towards him.

'What the fuck was that?' Gamble asked.

'One of our boys.'

'Do you know who?'

'No . . . not yet.'

'Shit,' Gamble turned. He was carrying the same load as

299

Lynch. 'Let's get a car and get the Christ away from here.'

The two men reached the road. South towards Ba'albek was still dark. North to El Laboue they could see lights moving. Headlights.

'We'll move in closer and take the first car,' Lynch said. The two men slipped back into the shallow ditch at the roadside and began a slow trot towards the town. It was only as they got closer to the blast site that they realised the full extent of the destruction. They found the bodies first. Men and pieces of men in grotesque positions, dangling from scorched and shattered tree limbs. They came on a tank that was still burning, the hatch blown off and the flames licking up from its own exploded magazine. The next few tanks were just hulks. There was a jeep on its side and more mangled bodies. As they passed near the epicentre of the blast, both men stopped for a moment to gaze at the horrific scene. For a radius of perhaps 200 metres there was nothing: just metal hulks glowing dim red, the stumps of burning trees… and scorched, naked earth.

Firing. Both men listened but it stopped. It had been an automatic weapon, but the firing had been too brief to tell what type. They hurried across the blast zone and made some cover among the trees still standing on the other side. They were about 800 metres from the edge of El Laboue. The 115 kilos of armament each man carried was starting to take its toll. A pair of headlights bounced suddenly into view and they heard the sound of a racing car engine. Gamble dropped his plastique into the ditch and scurried across the road. Lynch hurried forward a few metres then stepped out into view, rifle pointed threateningly at the oncoming car, poised to jump if he had to. Gamble stepped out a dozen paces behind him on the other side of the road so the driver would know he might get past the first man but he wouldn't pass the second. The sound of screeching tyres filled the air as the car slid to a stop a few metres in front of Lynch. The two men hurried forward, Gamble opening his mouth to speak in Arabic.

Bono stuck his head out of the car. 'Man, have I been busy,' he said.

Gamble and Lynch flung their belts of plastique into the back of the blue Datsun sedan.

'It's only a piece of Japanese shit,' Bono apologised, 'but it's got wheels and a motor.'

Lynch took off his vest and heaved it gratefully into the back seat too.

'Had to nail a couple of guys to get it,' Bono was saying. 'Came down the other side of town and walked in. What was the bang? Broke every fucking window in that place, I can tell ya.'

'One of our guys,' Lynch said.

'Reece?' Bono's voice went up a beat.

'No way of knowing.'

'You mean this is it?' Bono looked around at the three of them.

'Maybe,' Lynch shrugged. 'We'll drive up and down a few times, see if there's anybody else out there. Stick your big ugly head out the window. If Reece is out there he'll see you.'

They piled into the car with Lynch at the wheel and Gamble in the back. Lynch turned the Datsun around and accelerated back up the road to El Laboue. Another pair of headlights swung into view. Lynch pulled the car across the road and waited. He could see people silhouetted against the streetlights further up the road, waiting, afraid to venture from the protection of their homes to see what had caused the almighty blast. The car stopped cautiously about twenty metres away. It was an ancient black Citroen with four men inside. They looked like they'd been blown out of bed by the blast, Lynch thought.

'Tell them to go back into town and stay there,' Lynch ordered Gamble. 'Put a burst over their heads to show we mean it.'

Gamble leaned out of the car and yelled at the men in Arabic. They looked back at him then at each other but the car didn't move. One of them leaned out and shouted something but Gamble produced the rifle and fired two rapid bursts over the roof of the Citroen. The car reversed away, did a rapid U-turn and fishtailed back into El Laboue. Lynch turned the Datsun around and they drove back down the road, headlights on, scouring both sides of the road for Reece, Vance or Cooper. They found nobody. Lynch repeated it two more times and still they saw no-one.

'Okay,' he said. 'That's it. We go without them.'

'No,' Bono yelled. 'I'm not leaving Reece.'

Lynch glanced at Bono but kept on driving. 'You know the rules, Sam,' he said. It was the only time Bono could recall Lynch using his first name.

'You know the rules... and so does he.'

'Leave me here,' Bono said. 'I'll wait for him.'

Lynch slammed the car to a stop in the middle of the road and faced Bono, his voice dangerously low.

'He's probably dead. If he's not he could be anywhere. I'll leave you here if you want. All it means is that we lose another man. Think about it.'

Bono's face darkened with inchoate fury. 'You're as bad as that cunt Halloran.'

Lynch grabbed Bono's shirt and pulled his face close.

'Look at me,' he gritted. 'We can't waste any more men. We can't waste any more time. We've come this far... we do the job. Or it's all been a waste... all of it. Reece too. We do the job because that's all there fucking is now.'

Bono took Lynch's wrists in his hands and prised them loose. The two men stared at each other for a long time.

'Okay,' Bono said at last. 'Let's go.'

The words almost choked him. But he knew Lynch was right. Staying longer to search for Reece or the other two men was pointless.

Bono hung his head and shook it disbelievingly. 'You dumb fuck, Reece,' he mumbled. He looked back at Lynch through glazed eyes. 'The little bastard could be in fucking Cairo now.'

Lynch nodded. 'Yeah,' he said. Then he started the engine, stamped on the gas pedal and the car sped down the road toward Ba'albek.

'Wait . . . there's somebody.'

Gamble was right. They had gone only a couple of kilometres when they saw a figure crouching by the side of the road. Lynch slowed down. Whoever it was had a cannon pointed at them. The mouth of the M203 grenade launcher.

'Hey, Special fucking Forces,' Bono muttered. He didn't try to hide his disappointment. 'Now we're gonna be all right.'

'I was beginning to think I was it,' said Vance. He threw his gear in a heap on the back floor and climbed in beside Gamble.

'Is this everybody? Is there another car?'

'This is everybody,' Lynch said. He accelerated away and the four of them rode in silence for several minutes.

'What the hell was that explosion?' Vance asked. 'I saw all kinds of shit going down when I came in. I got the fuck away. Next thing I knew there was a bang nearly blew me outta the sky.'

'Reece or Cooper,' Lynch said evenly. 'Maybe both. We'll probably never know.

'We've lost two key men,' Lynch said. 'One of our demolitions men and our sniper. We've probably lost the element of surprise too. That means we go in fast and hard.'

'I've got Cooper's gun.' Vance said.

They looked at him.

'He wanted me to carry his gun. Said it was safer with me if we had to do some heavy carrying.'

Lynch nodded. They had pulled off onto a dirt road halfway between El Laboue and Ba'albek to get their breath and decide on a new plan. They were hidden from the main road by a protective screen of tall, leafy plants. The same crop stretched for field after field as far as they had been able to see from the road in the pale starlight. When they got out onto the dirt track they saw the plants were taller than Bono and the air was filled with a strange, sweet smell.

'What is this shit, anyway?' Bono said. He grabbed one of the thick stemmed plants and pulled it through his hand. A thick gooey resin stuck to his fingers.

'Grass,' Gamble said.

'What kind of...?'

'Dope... hemp... marijuana.'

The four men stared slowly all around them.

'Lebanese Gold,' Gamble said. 'It's the biggest cash crop in Lebanon... the Beqa'a Valley is thick with it.'

'Jesus H. Murphy Christ...' Bono breathed.

'Yeah,' Gamble said. 'That's where they get a lot of their money. Pushing this stuff on the streets of Europe and the United States then using the cash to buy arms to take Americans hostage. Nice arrangement, isn't it?' He pulled one of the plants through his fingers and sniffed.

'By the look of this I'd say it was ready for market. They must be having distribution problems. Must really be hurting for cash by now. That's why they're selling the hostages. Can't wait. They need the dough.'

'Okay,' Lynch looked at Vance. 'Can you use the Dragunov?'

Vance nodded.

'Good... once we get to Ba'albek we'll check the place out, ditch the car and split up.' He looked at his watch. 'I want you to get into a position to start picking off the guards at the gate by three. That's two hours, forty-two minutes from now. Set your watches.'

Bono set his watch then looked around. 'Know what day it is guys?'

'Shit,' Vance said.

'That's right,' Bono answered. 'Sweet, ain't it?'

'Bono,' Lynch interrupted. 'I want you to play hell with the place. I want you to lay time staggered charges all over that fucking town. Time the first one to go off at 3.10, after

304

Sergeant Vance has started bothering them a little, ten minute intervals after that for an hour to keep 'em reeling. Captain Gamble and I will go into the barracks over the back wall. We'll grab the hostages, take one of the militia wagons and ram our way out through the front gates. Bono, it would be a big help if you could lay some charges around the barracks. When you see us coming you tag on behind and we go like hell for the border.' He paused. 'Don't ask me if it'll work. If anybody has a better idea, let's hear it.'

The men stood in silence.

'I want to lay a little diversion now,' Bono said. Lynch stared at him. 'Okay,' he decided. 'Do it.'

Half an hour later they pulled back onto the main road and drove south again towards Ba'albek. They had only gone a couple of kilometres when the horizon behind them lit up with a brilliant yellow and crimson flash. Lynch pulled the Datsun over and they looked around. A long, crooked finger of flame was reaching deep into the heart of the vast marijuana fields.

'What the hell did you use,' Vance asked. 'Napalm?'

Bono shrugged. 'A little plastique can go a long way.'

'That stuff is ready to burn too,' Gamble said. 'Going to be a lot of smoke in the valley tonight.'

Lynch started the car again. They had already done a lot of damage, he thought. And they had yet to reach the Hezbollah stronghold.

A few minutes later they drove over the brow of a hill and were almost run down by a Toyota truck coming the opposite way. Lynch veered off to the side of the road and saw a second pick-up flash by. The first Toyota screamed to a stop and began reversing. There were two militiamen with a heavy machine gun mounted on the back, a Soviet 12.7mm anti-aircraft machine gun. The same weapon the Soviets and Syrians had on the T-72s.

'Hezbollah,' Gamble hissed. 'Don't any of you utter a fucking word.'

305

Lynch glanced quickly around the car. The weapons were on the floor. Lynch slid the Browning from its holster and held it by the side of the seat. He thought they looked scruffy enough to pass for militiamen. But would the men from Hezbollah? Bono ripped a length of material from his shirt, turned it into a bandana and wrapped it around his forehead like a sweatband. They waited. Two seconds later the pick-up screeched past them and jolted to a stop less than four metres away. The gunner in the back swivelled the heavy machine gun down at the Datsun. Two militiamen jumped out carrying Kalashnikovs and strode towards the Datsun yelling. Gamble was already out of the car, empty hands gesturing and yelling back. He jabbed a finger animatedly back down the road towards the burning marijuana crops and yelled even harder. Lynch looked back and saw the second pick-up had stopped in the middle of the road. He also saw that it had half a dozen armed militiamen on board.

One of the militiamen walked around the car, stooping down to peer in the windows, rifle poised. Vance and Bono followed him closely. If anything started he would be the first to go. Lynch eased the door handle of the Datsun down with one hand and slipped the safety off the Browning with the other, poised to throw himself out of the car. Gamble waved his hands more and Lynch sensed things weren't quite working out. Gamble was pointing towards the town. The Hezbollah group leader shook his head vigorously, raised his voice and began shouting at Gamble. Then he looked back towards the northern horizon where the flames in the marijuana crop were already getting higher and he made up his mind. He yelled and gestured threateningly at Gamble and the car then turned back to the Toyota.

'Allahu Akhbar,' Gamble yelled and punched his fist at the sky.

'Allahu Akhbar,' the men in the Toyota answered his salute. The militiamen jumped back into their vehicle and it revved away. Gamble turned, leaned both arms on the car roof and sighed. Lynch slipped the safety back on the Browning.

'Told them we were from El Laboue,' Gamble said. 'Somebody had set the fields on fire and we were on our way to report it. He asked what the explosion was. They were on their way to check it out. I told them it must have been the petrol used to start the fire. I don't think he really bought it. Not surprisingly he didn't know what we were supposed to be doing at El Laboue and he certainly didn't want us going into Ba'albek. Told us to wait here till they got back.'

'Sure,' Lynch said, 'Get ba — '

Bono kicked his door open, dropped to one knee and aimed his grenade launcher at the departing Toyota. The launcher kicked and a second later the Toyota bucked into the air and disintegrated in a ball of crimson fire, sending a flaming comet of wreckage spewing down the road and into the waiting pick-up. Men leaped from the truck in flames and Bono squeezed off a series of bursts. One of the militiamen screamed and fell.

'Jesus...' Lynch yelled. He jumped out and the others followed. They grabbed their weapons and dashed down the road, firing as they went, making sure there were no survivors. When the last militiaman dropped Lynch turned and ran back to the Datsun where Bono was feeding a fresh clip into his gun.

'What was that...?'

'Fuck 'em,' Bono cut him off. 'Why let 'em go?' His voice was harsh and his face set like stone. He was no longer willing to argue with anybody after losing his buddy.

The four of them squeezed back into the Datsun. They could see the lights of Ba'albek only five or six kilometres away beyond the next rise.

Lynch slowed the Datsun to a crawl for the last couple of kilometres then pulled off into the shadows at the side of the road. The four of them climbed out and hurried up the brow of the hill in single file. The marijuana fields stretched

307

to the mountain foothills on both sides of the road and almost to the outskirts of town, giving the four men perfect cover. When they reached the crest of the hill they crouched down and looked out over the town of Ba'albek. The first sight to greet their eyes was the Sheikh Abdullah Barracks less than two kilometres away atop a small hill, overlooking the town. They were unmistakeable even without the Syrian T-72 and cluster of armed trucks gathered at the front gates. The barrel of the tank was pointed straight down the road to where Lynch and his men now hid. The barracks were set entirely on their own with clear, shallow slopes on all four sides. The nearest buildings of the town were perhaps eighty metres from the southern perimeter wall of the barracks. The men counted six machine gun posts but knew there were probably two more hidden from view. Floodlights on all four walls lit up the area all around the barracks so that even an ant would cast a shadow. Lynch realised that no-one would be able to approach the fortress without being seen.

'We're going to need some mighty diversions, Bono,' Lynch muttered.

Bono mumbled something. Laying waste to the Shi'ite stronghold of Ba'albek was only a technicality now as far as he was concerned.

They could see armed men moving around the vehicles at the front gate to the barracks and other shadowy figures on the walls. No other vehicles came and went. There was no sign of activity inside the barracks. Either the PLO hadn't arrived yet or they had already left — there was no sign of the kind of convoy that would be needed to move and protect nine American hostages. But Halloran had been right about security. There was one road up to the barracks gate and the fork from the main road was guarded by another Syrian checkpoint: another T-72, a sandbagged machine gun nest, a couple of army trucks and an open fire around which soldiers boiled tea. Such obvious security, Lynch figured, indicated that somebody important was inside.

308

The town looked quiet except for the occasional patrolling militia truck with its rear-mounted AA machine gun. Shops, houses and public buildings were shuttered and dark. The tall, slender needle of the minaret of Ba'albek's modern, high-domed mosque presided over the town like an ominous sentinel, its smooth circular walls mottled a leprous grey by the night shadows. The streets were empty as far as they could see. At the other side of town was Wavell Camp, the former British army base which was now a Palestinian camp. It was possible the exchange had been made and the hostages had already been moved there. Lynch didn't think so. Once the PLO had the hostages they would get them as far away from the Beqa'a as possible and into their own territory.

They would soon find out.

'Found a spot?' Lynch whispered at Vance.

Vance nodded. 'I'll get up to that minaret first. Soon as I've picked off a couple, I'll move.'

'See that gun post on the roof of the building against the rear wall?' Lynch pointed out a sandbagged strongpoint on the roof of the administration block. There appeared to be three men behind the bags.

Vance stared. 'Yeah.'

'That's the highest point inside the barracks. The men up there can see everything that comes over the wall or moves around inside. You have to take them out.'

Vance took a deep breath. 'One way or the other... they're gone.'

'Okay,' Lynch said, 'we'll split up here. Gamble and I will wait for the first bang from Bono then cover that empty ground at the rear of the barracks as fast as we can and go over the walls. After that,' he shrugged, 'give us half an hour and if the shooting stops and we're still not out... go home.'

No-one spoke.

'Good luck,' Lynch said. He and Gamble hurried back to the car, grabbed their vests and weapons then melted into the dark, rustling fields and began working their way around to the rear of the barracks. Vance put on his own vest, shouldered the Dragunov with the M16A1 and the MP5 and followed them into the fields. They had left Bono with his own weapons — and 160 kilos of plastique. He went to work.

'Sshh!'

The Syrian checkpoint guard at the fork between the town and the barracks heard it first and signalled to his comrades to be quiet. They listened but could hear nothing. The guard walked away from the fire and up the road a little then cocked his head. There ... that was what he'd heard. Music. He could hear music drifting tinnily down the road between the darkened marijuana fields. He waved the others over and a couple of the soldiers idly wandered up the road beside him and listened. They walked back and woke up the lieutenant in charge of the checkpoint who had been asleep in the back of a truck and told him what they'd heard. He frowned and ordered the three of them to take a jeep and see what it was. The three Syrians jumped into the jeep and drove up the road and over the brow of the small hill. When they crested the hill they saw a small blue Datsun parked at a crazy angle at the side of the road about two hundred metres away with its lights on and the door open. The driver switched off the engine and listened. The music was louder and definitely coming from the car. They listened. It was an American pop song. They couldn't understand the words. The car radio was tuned to the US Forces waveband and turned up as loud as it would go. The driver ordered his two comrades out, re-started the engine and they walked cautiously down the road, one on each side of the jeep, rifles raised.

As they drew closer they saw the Datsun was empty. It looked like the car had run off the road and the driver had staggered off somewhere. Stupid Lebanese bastards, the Syrian soldier in the jeep thought. Stupid country. There were no road rules, no licenses, they couldn't drive for shit. The jeep and the two soldiers stopped about seven or eight metres from the Datsun and looked around. Still no sign of the driver. One of the soldiers shouldered his rifle, walked to the car, reached inside and switched off the radio. The music was too loud and starting to annoy him. Melissa Manchester was telling the three Syrians that whatever it was, it would wait till the morning.

None of them felt a thing. The blast disintegrated the Datsun, the jeep, the three Syrians and left a crater two metres deep in the middle of the road. Nobody would be using the road north out of Ba'albek for a day or two. The Syrian checkpoint guards heard the explosion and saw the bright tulip of flame from behind the hill and began yelling. The Syrian soldiers and Hezbollah militiamen at the front of the barracks turned and looked. There was another explosion and then another. Huge gouts of earth, flame and roadwork leaped high into the air. They seemed to be marching along the side of the road towards the town.

'Bombs,' somebody screamed. They were under attack from high altitude, laser guided bombs from Israeli warplanes. That was why they hadn't heard any aircraft engines. The Israelis were trying to bomb the barracks using smart bombs. A soldier leaped onto the tank at the checkpoint, switched on the searchlight and began scanning the sky. Soldiers at the second T-72 did the same. The Hezbollah militiamen piled into their trucks, fanned out down the road and began pouring machine gun fire into the black night sky. The men on the barracks walls hoisted their own weapons skywards and joined the deafening roar of gunfire. A lacework of red tracers filled the sky with deadly, beautiful, useless patterns.

'Jesus . . .' Vance swore. He checked his watch. Just a little after 2.30. That crazy bastard Bono had started without them. He broke cover from the wall that guarded the square in front of the mosque and clattered across the mosaic tiles towards the door near the base of the minaret. He was about

311

to kick the door open, but stopped and tried the handle. It opened. Vance looked inside. There was a wide, arched corridor where the faithful could leave their shoes and beyond those arches he could see a circular, polished marble floor and a pulpit. Dim, yellow electric lights were set atop alternate pilasters around the domed chamber, revealing a mosaic frieze which girdled the room, and when Vance looked up he saw the great curved roof was painted a brilliant blue — the colour of the imagined skies of paradise, no doubt. Vance waited. He heard nothing. The mullah was either still in his living quarters or at the barracks. The mosque must have been presumed the safest place in Ba'albek. Vance crossed a mosaic floor to the raised pulpit. A large portrait of Aya-tollah Khomeini hung from the front of the pulpit. Behind the pulpit was an open arch and through the arch he could see stone steps spiralling up inside the minaret. He started running up the steps, panting and sweating under the weight of the lethal load he carried on his shoulders.

Lynch and Gamble were caught in a side street when they heard the first explosion. They still had a couple of hundred metres to go until they reached the last houses before the barracks. They had almost been trapped once by patrolling militiamen and been forced to break the lock on the door of a small machine shop and hide inside till the truck had passed. Security must have been good, Lynch thought. There was no need for burglar alarms in Ba'albek, perhaps no point either. Now he and Gamble looked at each other, threw caution to the wind and began running. They ran past the lamp posts and walls plastered with pictures of Khomeini and all the other fanatics of the Islamic world revolution. The faces of hate. Lynch had no idea how the citizens of Ba'albek would react to explosions and gunfire. Perhaps, like sensible citizens anywhere, they would hide under their beds and wait until the murderers outside had finished their bloody work. Two minutes later they reached the end of the street and were confronted by the bare slopes of the rocky hill climbing sharply towards the barracks wall another eighty metres away. Both men were panting under the burden of their equipment. Without a word Lynch unclipped the rappelling rope on his vest and attached the vicious metal hooks of the grapple. The two men scanned the walls of the barracks. There was a machine gun post on each corner but the gunners had their weapons aimed at the sky and were firing apparently endless rounds of ammunition into the empty sky. They ditched the M16A1s under a nearby pile of rubble and stripped down to the weapons they needed for close-in work. Lynch took a deep breath, nodded at Gamble and the two men broke from cover and began sprinting up the brilliantly lit slope of the hill towards the distant wall.

Vance reached the top of the minaret, threw down his gear and slumped into a gasping heap. It had been a punishing couple of hours, even for a strong man. He knew he had no time to catch his breath and peered over the parapet of the tower where mullahs usually stood to call the faithful to prayer. Vance knew that this mosque had been used to dispense a special kind of propaganda these past years. He pulled the Dragunov up, slammed in a 10-round magazine and smiled to himself. Tonight the mullahs' tower of hate would be used to dispense America's answer. He got onto one knee, rested the rifle on the lip of the parapet and squinted through the sight. It had been fitted with an infra-red night sight enhancer but he hardly needed it, thanks to the lighting provided by the militiamen in the barracks. He swivelled the gun sideways seeking out his first target. There were so many. He looked for officers, leaders... kills which would create the most chaos. The echo from the last explosion had faded several minutes ago and some of the machine guns had stopped firing, the militiamen having satisfied their immediate surge of machismo and realised they were simply wasting ammunition.

Vance picked his first target. Hezbollah militiamen displayed no rank so it was impossible to know who had the authority until someone gave an order. A man on the ground in front of the gates was hurrying back and forth between trucks screaming and shouting at his men to stop firing. Vance adjusted the sights, willed away the trembling of exhaustion from his hands and gently squeezed the trigger.

The man on the ground had stopped to yell orders to the machine gunner in the back of a red pick-up. The gunner took his hand off the trigger and looked down at his commander. He started to argue then stopped as the commander staggered briefly then dropped to his knees and toppled backwards into the dirt, eyes staring emptily toward the equally empty sky. The bullet had hit the Hezbollah commander between the collar bone and the shoulder bone, angled down through his body, pulped his heart and exited between the third and fourth ribs. The gunner stared. His commander looked unmarked ... then he saw the spreading dark stain on the dirt underneath and began jabbering and waving to his comrades.

The second-in-command at the gate hurried forward to see why the machine gunner was yelling and took Vance's second bullet just above the left eye. Vance swore and adjusted the sights a fraction. He heard the roar of a truck engine below and thought he'd been spotted but it was a Hezbollah truck rushing back through town towards the barracks. Vance watched it speed down the street towards the checkpoint at the fork then tried a snap shot at the driver. He wasn't sure if he'd done it so he followed the truck and fired a second into the cabin. The truck began to waggle crazily throwing the two men on the back onto the road. He may have got the driver but someone else in the cab was trying to steer the truck. Whoever it was failed. The dead man must have had his foot jammed on the gas. The truck swung wildly towards the checkpoint then lost all control and slammed into the T-72. The truck disintegrated on impact, the gas tank ruptured and a burning wave of petrol washed over the tank, pouring torrents of flame into every open hatch and crevice. A soldier scrambled out of the tank and then another, both covered in flames. Vance let them go. They were no longer a threat. He turned his attention back to the barracks. All but a couple of the trucks had stopped firing — but now they had a new enemy. Panic and confusion. They were being attacked but they didn't know from which direction and by whom. Vance swung his sight along the top of the barracks wall. It was time to give Lynch and Gamble a hand. He found the sandbagged machine gun post on the roof of the administration block and adjusted his sights. Three men. One with a spotlight pointed uselessly towards the heavens, the other two looking towards the burning tank at the checkpoint. Vance zeroed in, fired and the man on the spotlight vanished. The spotlight danced crazily then swung down and went out. The other two men spun around to see what had happened to their comrade and Vance caught one in the back of the head. He snapped off a shot at the third man and thought he'd winged him in the back or shoulder before the man ducked from view but he couldn't be sure. Vance checked his magazine. Six shots gone. Five hits. Four shells left. Cooper would be proud of him so far. A sudden hail of bullets swept the tower. Someone had finally spotted his muzzle flash. Vance chanced a glance back over the parapet and saw the T-72 rotating its turret to bring its gun to bear on him.

'Shit,' he swore, grabbed his gear and began scrambling down the stairs. A moment later a shell screamed overhead. He crouched down and waited. Nothing... then the sound of a distant explosion. The shell had overshot its mark and exploded harmlessly in the distant hills. He got back to his feet, hurtled the rest of the way down the endless, spiralling stone steps and had almost reached the bottom when a thunderous explosion rocked the building and the inside of the minaret suddenly filled with dust and falling debris. Vance hurled himself down the last few steps and through the open arch onto the floor of the mosque. He rolled onto his back and a second later saw a giant slab of falling masonry crash onto the bottom step, splintering the stone and jamming the stairwell. He scrambled back to his feet and ran headlong into a huge man with a rifle.

'Things starting to warm up nicely, wouldn't you say?' Bono rumbled.

The grapple bit and Lynch hauled himself up the wall of the barracks towards the roof of the administration block. It was about a dozen metres, and took him less than fifteen seconds, carrying all his gear. He reached the top, swung over the lip of the wall onto the roof and crouched in the shadows. There were no shots, no yelling. No-one had seen him. Lynch crept silently towards the sandbagged machine gun post. Gamble appeared behind him a moment later, moving like a black ghost. Somebody shouted, the strangled, desperate shout of a man in pain. Lynch realised that one of the militiamen on the roof had only been wounded and was calling out for help. He pulled a knife from his vest. All Special Forces men carried knives, most of them customised to certain preferences. Lynch preferred a short-bladed diving knife with a serrated edge cast from a single sheet of steel. He slid over the edge of the sandbags without making a sound, wrapped one hand across the wounded man's mouth and expertly cut his throat with the other. He snaked back over the sandbags and nodded to Gamble. They shuffled quietly to the edge of the building and looked down.

Lights were flashing on inside buildings and barracks huts everywhere. Men were pouring out of buildings, some with weapons, some unarmed and half dressed, still bleary from sleep. They milled around on the square below, shouting and yelling. It was pandemonium. Lynch smiled — they had no idea who was hitting them nor from where. The tank at the gate fired and all the men inside the barracks froze for a moment. The tank fired again and an instant later they saw the bulbous tip of the minaret, a few hundred metres

316

away in town, disappear in a puff of smoke. The men below
began running towards the front gates and the guards on
the walls turned their attention towards the town to try and
determine the threat. Lynch and Gamble saw their moment.
Gamble pulled the rappelling rope up onto the roof, secured
it to the parapet on the inside and ran it through the descendeur
on his harness. Lynch picked up the M16A1 to give him
covering fire, Gamble nodded and then jumped over the edge.

The administration building had four storeys, each with
a window. Gamble trotted down the wall as though he were
jogging along a garden path, the descendeur braking him
at just the right speed, freeing both hands to hold the MP5.
The men inside the building didn't know what hit them.
Gamble flashed by each window, assessing the situation inside
at a glance. If there were no hostages the room got a burst
of concentrated 9mm fire. Gamble had done the exercise
a thousand times in the killing house at SAS headquarters
in Hereford. Now it was for real. A man in army greens
with a rifle in both hands was leaning from the top floor
window trying to see what was going on. Gamble kicked
him hard in the face and the man flew back. There were
only two other men in a room full of tables and maps, both
Middle Eastern and wearing olive green. The room got a
burst. The next window showed a room with a man dressed
in a mullah's robes and a portrait of the Ayatollah Khomeini
and other Islamic leaders. The mullah stared at Gamble open
mouthed. It was no time for mercy and Gamble knew the
mullahs showed none. He fired and the mullah catapulted
back into the room, hit the wall and crumpled, leaving a
series of bloody streaks smeared across the faces on the wall.
The next window opened onto a room full of militiamen
scrambling to arm themselves. Gamble gave it a prolonged
burst then dropped to the ground and swapped clips. The
ground floor window opened onto a corridor running parallel
to the outside wall. Men were pouring from rooms on either
side. Gamble swung and fired a series of short bursts one

way and then the next. He saw half a dozen men scream and fall. The others panicked and began scrambling back to the cover of their rooms. Gamble allowed himself a grim little smile. The militiamen weren't used to this kind of combat. Their idea of fighting was to take turns hosing down distant buildings with machine gun fire until they got lucky and hit somebody. They hadn't seen room-to-room combat before. They were about to get a brutal lesson. Gamble unclipped himself, readied the gun and climbed through the open window into the now deserted corridor.

It had taken Gamble nine seconds to clean out the administration tower. Lynch watched the SAS man disappear into the building then he turned and ran to the steps leading down from the roof to the barracks wall and a doorway into the building. He saw men running towards him along the parapet. The poor bastards didn't know who he was, Lynch realised. With his wild hair, militia clothes and week old beard he looked just like one of them. He fired a long burst and watched them drop. Lynch kicked open the door to the administration tower and began working his way down to meet Gamble. They wanted one hostage of their own. That was all. The first room contained only three bodies. Lynch heard more firing from below. He picked his way cautiously down to the next level.

'Peter?' he yelled.

'Here,' Gamble's voice came back.

'Which floor?'

'I'm on the second. We've got a couple bottled up.'

'I'm on the next one up... I'm coming down.'

'Okay.'

Lynch heard running feet. A door burst open behind him and he spun to see two mullahs with AK47s leading a horde of charging militiamen. He emptied his magazine into the two mullahs and then the men behind and watched the doorway clog with bodies. The clip emptied and he backed down the stairs.

'You all right?' Gamble's voice called up.

'So far.'

Lynch backed onto the next floor, edged around the stairs and saw Gamble pressed against the wall beside a heavy wooden door. They heard a ripple of distant explosions followed by a renewed crescendo of firing and yelling from the far end of the barracks. More of Bono's work, Lynch hoped.

'We've got a couple in here,' Gamble said. 'I gave the room a good squirt but I know I didn't get all of them.'

'Okay,' Lynch said. 'Ask them where the hostages are.'

Gamble rattled off some words in Arabic and they waited. No-one answered. Gamble tried again.

This time there was an angry, muffled reply.

'They say the hostages aren't here.'

'Ask where they are.'

Gamble yelled out the words. There was a pause then the same thick, anguished voice.

'They want to know who we are.'

Lynch grinned. 'Tell them we're American. Tell them we've come for our people.'

They heard a low bout of muttering and then silence.

'To hell with this,' Lynch said. 'I'm not giving the bastards time to think.' He lifted the MP5, took one step back and fired a series of bursts at knee height, waist height and chest height through the wooden door. The door shuddered, splintered and flew apart under the onslaught. They heard screams from inside as the bullets peppered the room but no answering fire. Lynch stepped in followed by Gamble and glanced around. The room looked like a slaughterhouse. It must have been a militia guard post for the mullahs. Lynch estimated a dozen bodies. None of them stirred. They moved through the room, pulling at the bodies, the carpeted floor squelching beneath their feet with spilled blood. Lynch heard a moan and looked around to see Gamble hauling a bloodied militiaman up by the shoulder.

'This bastard's shamming,' Gamble said. 'There's not a mark on him.'

He wiped the blood from the man's face and the guard stared back with a mixture of shock and terror.

'Ask what happened to the hostages.' Lynch said. 'Make him understand . . . we're running out of time.'

Gamble held the man by the shoulder, pulled out a sinister bone-handled dagger and turned it slowly and maliciously before the man's eyes so that the thin, double-edged blade glimmered in the electric light. Then he lowered it and held it to the man's crotch. The man began to tremble as Gamble rattled off a stream of Arabic. When he had finished Gamble didn't take his eyes off the man's face but jerked his knife arm suddenly and slid the knife into the man's groin just a fraction, enough to let the needle point pierce the skin nearest the scrotum. The man screamed and the words tumbled out of him. Gamble shoved him down onto the floor on his back and placed a foot across his throat. The SAS man still kept the knife in his hand, its wicked point dulled by a speck of blood. He stared at Lynch, his face set and grim.

'News isn't good, I'm afraid . . . if he's telling the truth.'

'What did he say?'

'Says the hostages were taken by road to Beirut six hours ago.'

The words hit Lynch like a blow to the chest. He shook his head and looked around the corpse-filled room. After all they had been through . . . only to be too late. 'Is he telling the truth?'

'I told him I'd kill him and cut his balls off,' Gamble said. 'He won't have much fun in paradise with no balls. I believe him. He believes he's going to die.'

'Where in Beirut?'

Gamble spoke to the man and twirled the knife in his hand then lifted his foot and the man jabbered frantically in reply.

'He said the PLO were taking them out of the country. He thinks they were leaving from the airport... it makes sense.'

'Yeah,' Lynch nodded. 'It makes sense... time we were out of here.'

'Israel?'

'No...' Lynch said. He made up his mind. 'Let's see if we can catch them at the airport.'

Gamble looked at him. 'You don't give up easily, do you?'

Lynch shrugged. 'I hate going home empty-handed.'

'What about him?' Gamble nodded at the man on the floor.

'Leave him,' Lynch said. 'I like cowards. He'll tell them what happened. Be good for them.'

The two men backed out of the room and began working their way quickly and carefully back to the roof.

'Better than sex, ain't it?'

Vance looked at Bono and shook his head.

They were trapped in the mosque. As soon as the Hezbollah militiamen had spotted the muzzle flashes from Vance's rifle they had alerted the gunner of the T-72 and then swarmed down into the town after the second shell had sheared off the top of the minaret. Vance and Bono had tried to make a run for it but as soon as they had appeared on the street they were spotted by the machine gunner in an oncoming truck and he had beat an evil tattoo of bullets down the road towards them. They had seen several hundred armed militiamen swarming down from the barracks towards them and had been driven back into the mosque by a storm of bullets. Once inside both men has unleashed an answering fusilade of their own. A couple of grenades from the M203 had persuaded the men from Hezbollah to vacate the street, leaving half a dozen dead and another incinerated truck behind them. Vance had alternated between Cooper's Dragunov and the brute force of the M16A1 to keep the square in front of the mosque clear. Since then they had driven off two frontal assaults. Each time the men from Hezbollah had resorted to Beirut streetfighting tactics. One man would appear suddenly, empty his magazine into the front of the mosque, then vanish, to be replaced immediately by another fighter who would empty his magazine. This was intended to keep the enemy pinned down under a constant and deadly torrent of bullets while the militiamen advanced. Except they had never been confronted by a real marksman before, a marksman with the nerve to hold his position while he made the shot he wanted. The first time Hezbollah tried it they advanced several paces into the square. Then Vance got one of the gunmen in the chest. The one who took his place didn't even get off a shot before Vance hit him in the head. Then a third, then a fourth.

'They're dumb, ain't they?' Vance mumbled absently as he dropped number five. 'Brave. But... dumb.'

A total of eight men lay dead or wounded on the street side of the mosque square before they abandoned that attack. The next assault came a few minutes later and involved a full frontal assault of what seemed like a hundred or more screaming, firing men. Vance and Bono had stood beside two open windows and fired everything they had. When the magazines from the M16A1 were empty they fired two more grenades point blank into the charging ranks. The grenades tore devastating holes in the massed militiamen and broke the assault. The two Americans then picked up their MP5s and emptied the magazines at the dazed survivors and stragglers reeling drunkenly around the square. When the smoke cleared and they saw the full extent of the carnage they had caused, they were staggered. The square was littered with the bodies of perhaps fifty or sixty men. Many more wounded had been dragged off by their comrades.

The Hezbollah commander swore they had been attacked by a company of Israeli commandos and called on the Syrian T-72 from the next barracks. Vance heard the clanking of the caterpillar tracks first and looked up at Bono with dread in his eyes.

'Relax,' Bono assured him. 'What do you think I was doing out there?'

The militia had taken up positions in the shops and houses across the street opposite the square and were keeping a steady hail of fire trained on the mosque. Bono sat with his back against a wall, his head tilted back, eyes closed, apparently dozing. Vance waited. The grinding of the tank treads was getting closer. Bono waited a few more minutes then his eyes snapped open.

'I'd say that's just about right,' he said. He pulled a small radio transmitter from his pocket and thumbed the button. A tiny red light flicked on, confirming the signal had been sent and an instant later the entire facade of the street across the square disappeared with a whoomph of sound and a rolling cloud of smoke and flame. The stained glass windows of the mosque shattered into technicolour confetti and spattered the inside of the building. The two men flinched as the outside wall resounded to a bombardment of flying debris. When the echo of the blast had faded away the men could no longer hear the sound of tank tracks.

Vance looked around the mosque. It was starting to look a little worse for wear. 'Thought they took better care of their holy places,' he said.

'Savages,' Bono huffed. 'Just savages.'

Soon the two men heard the sounds of fresh militiamen arriving and taking up new positions around the mosque and shortly afterwards the rattle and cough of automatic weapons started up again. Bono chanced a quick glance over a ragged window sill then ducked back down.

'Starting to look a little like Beirut out there,' he said.

Vance looked at him.

'Any ideas how we get out of here?'

'Sure,' Bono replied with maddening calm.

'Care to tell me on the grounds that I might be interested?'

'We walk out,' Bono said.

'Oh... how?'

Bono pulled an ammunition belt from around his waist

and counted the pouches. 'Still got nearly seventy kilos of plastique,' he said. 'That's gonna get us outta here.'

Vance checked his watch. It had just gone 3.30. It felt like they had been fighting a war all night. Then he realised that they had. 'If we're going to link up with those other two guys we ought to be out of here now,' he said.

'Yeah,' Bono grunted and got up. He bent low and scurried across the room. He spent a couple of minutes laying charges along the back wall of the mosque then came back and laid charges along the front wall.

'Okay,' he said. 'We bury ourselves till the back wall goes. It's the smaller charge and it'll blow a big hole in the wall. It'll be big enough to move anybody outside out of the way. When that goes we have fifteen seconds to get as far away from here as we can before the front wall goes. Because when this goes . . . the whole fucking building goes.'

'What about the street out back?' Vance said. 'They'll have both ends blocked.'

'Probably,' Bono agreed. 'But I came in that way. It's a row of houses. We don't start running up the street. We go across the street. The blast I set up at the back will push half that wall right through the houses opposite. Anybody who's in the way is gonna be shit. We hit that hole, go right through the first fucking house, out the back and then we do some serious running.'

Vance stared. 'Subtle,' he said, 'but effective.'

'I think we should move,' Bono said. 'I timed that back wall for 3.35.'

Vance looked at his watch. The second hand said less than fifty seconds to go. He grabbed his gear and followed Bono across the floor to a nook behind the solid marble slab that supported the pulpit. Both men crouched down and covered their ears. The blastwave seemed to pass right through Vance's body. He glanced down and was almost surprised to find himself intact.

'Fucking move,' Bono was yelling. They grabbed their guns

and the last of their gear and sprinted through the billowing dust cloud that masked the ragged hole in the back wall of the mosque. They stumbled over the rubble in the smoke and dust which filled the street. The debris pointed the way across the street and carved an ugly gash in the row of old brick and plaster houses opposite. Vance saw a few uniformed bodies under the rubble and there was a brief rattle of small arms fire from one end of the street. A single front door hung crookedly and Bono kicked it flat. They scrambled over a pile of masonry blocking the long hallway, slid down the other side and ran for the door at the other end. Bono didn't even break his stride. He raised his arms with a rifle in each hand and battered his way through the wooden door. The door flew open and they were through. A narrow alley with a stream of foul water straggling down the dirty trough in the middle. People in the houses were screaming. Dogs barked and whimpered.

'This way,' Bono yelled and ran down the alley towards a lit highway at the bottom. They were heading back towards the barracks. A moment later the sky was split yet again by the glare of a tremendous explosion and then a terrifying thunderclap as Bono's last charges went up. The militiamen approaching in a wary skirmish line across the square watched in horror as the front of the mosque seemed to dissolve towards them in a tidal wave of flying, crushing stone. The great dome bulged upward and outward, then cracked asunder, unable to contain the mighty forces unleashed from within. A tongue of flame leaped for the sky and bricks and rubble flew like cannon shells. Vance and Bono sprinted down the alley, ducking and trying to ignore the debris that rained down around them. They only slowed when they reached the end of the alley. Bono couldn't run any further. His breath was coming in painful, burning gasps. He turned to look in satisfaction as a great, flame-tinged mushroom cloud boiled up into the sky where the great dome of the mosque had been.

'Happy Fourth of July, you cocksuckers!' Bono roared at the top of his tortured lungs. Vance looked at him with something approaching awe. The man from Delta had never encountered anyone quite like Bono. They both paused for a few precious seconds to catch their breath. Vance edged to the corner of the alley and was peering down the street. The fork to the barracks was about 150 metres down the road to their left. The road through town led to the right and the junction for the street to the mosque was just half a block away. The junction was blocked by a couple of cars and four militia pick-ups with mounted machine guns. Vance estimated that maybe twenty to thirty men were clustered in front of the vehicles, yelling, jabbing the air with their automatic weapons in fury and despair as they watched the expanding column of smoke that now marked the graveyard of their mosque and of so many of their comrades.

Vance hurried back towards Bono and told him what he'd seen.

'Here's what we'll do . . .'

Bono cut him off with a shake of his big ugly head.

'No,' he said. 'Here's what we do.'

Before Vance had time to argue Bono slipped a fresh clip into the M16A1, dropped a grenade into the launcher, stepped out into the well lit street and strolled towards the yelling crowd of militia only forty to fifty metres away. They were too intent on the spectacle of the burning mosque down the street to notice Bono until he was twenty or so metres away.

'Okay,' Bono's voice boomed out like a cannon. 'Who wants to go to paradise?'

The militiamen turned and stared at the huge stranger in the middle of the street with stunned disbelief. Bono fired the grenade launcher point blank and the two Americans watched as it hit one man, exploded in a sheet of flame and a dozen others seemed to shrivel in the blast. The force of the blast lifted Bono off his feet, blew him three metres down the road and dumped him heavily on his back. Vance stepped out and emptied a magazine at the gunners in the back of the trucks. One of the trucks was on fire. He loaded a fresh clip and trotted down the road towards Bono, firing from the hip at the wounded and the dazed survivors as they staggered about in the light of the flames.

He bent down and rolled Bono over. The big man grunted and opened his eyes.

'Shit,' he said. 'That's some fuckin' gun.'

'You're some fuckin' nut.' Vance answered. He helped the big man to his feet and they shambled towards the nearest truck.

'Can you drive?' Vance asked.

'Yeah.'

Vance leaped up into the back of the pick-up and checked their machine gun. 'Let's go see if our boys are ready.'

'Can you believe this prick?' Gamble said in disbelief. 'He's leaning against the door to stop us getting out.'

Lynch grinned 'Let's give him a second arsehole.' He pulled out a clip of Glaser slugs and slipped them into the MP5.

They had arrived at the top floor, only to find their exit to the roof barred by a number of militia and one powerful and determined individual pinning the door shut. They heard shouts from below followed by clattering footsteps on the stairs. Lynch and Gamble were being squeezed. Gamble watched the stairs while Lynch stepped back and fired a short, three-round burst through the door. A trio of fist sized holes appeared at waist height in the heavy woodwork and there was a grunt followed by a thud on the other side. A moment later a stream of bullets smashed into the door from the opposite side and it began to splinter inward. Lynch leaned back, unholstered the Browning and emptied all fourteen armour piercing rounds through the door. There was a chorus of screams and the firing stopped. Lynch stepped forward, kicked what was left of the door and it collapsed outwards. He ducked into a crouch with the MP5 raised but all he could see was a line of crumpled bodies along the parapet. But he wasn't ready to step outside yet. He fitted a fresh clip into the Browning, aimed it towards the roof and fired a random pattern. A shower of plaster and brickwork cascaded down like snow and he heard more screams and shouts.

'Let's go, Peter,' he yelled and leaped outside, turning and angling the MP5 carefully as he went, spraying the air with a deadly scythe of bullets. He saw the last of the militiamen waiting to ambush them from the roof stagger and fall. Gamble turned to follow Lynch and a stream of bullets poured up the stairs from below. He dropped to one knee in the open door and waited. Another hail of bullets swept the landing and Gamble flinched as stone chips and debris flew around him. Their informant from downstairs appeared first. Apparently he had decided to vindicate himself in the eyes of his comrades... or they were pushing him up the stairs first. The man stumbled onto the landing, AK47 at his hip firing wildly, and screamed with a mixture of fear and bravado. Gamble put three rounds into his chest. The man dropped the Kalashnikov with a clatter, bounced off the stair wall and fell backwards. Gamble fired another series of bursts into the stairwell then ran after Lynch. The two men scurried across the roof to put the sandbagged machine gun post between them and any threat from inside the barracks. They crouched low against the wall and looked around. The sky over Ba'albek was orange with flames and instead of the great mosque that had been there when they went into the barracks, now there was only a shattered, burning shell. They could see rubble in the streets and the tank at the checkpoint was still burning. Everywhere they looked there was only bodies and ruin.

'Good God,' Lynch muttered, 'Bono, what have you done?' The two of them glanced quickly around for the first threatening shapes they knew had to come at any moment. Gamble grabbed the rappelling rope still dangling from the front of the tower. They would have to go back over the wall and hijack a car in town, Lynch knew. Then he groaned. A red Toyota militia truck was bumping across the shallow slopes of the fortress towards them. Then he realised the gunner was pointing the machine guns to the rear — towards the town.

'I think this might be our boys,' Lynch murmured.

A squadron of hornets buzzed past Lynch's ear and he threw himself down below the wall. Another burst peppered the wall below. Gamble and Lynch hunched back to back and sprayed everything they could see. The bullets stopped for a second.

'Are you coming or not?' Bono's voice yelled up.

Neither man needed a second invitation. Gamble set the grapple into the parapet wall, hurled the rope over the edge and went over with it. Lynch followed the next instant. They hit the ground almost simultaneously. Gamble leaped up into the back with Vance, threw himself into a corner and readied the MP5.

'Lot of angry shites down there,' Bono grunted. He mashed the gears. 'No hostages huh? Guess we blew it. Where next, the border?'

'No,' Lynch said. 'Hit the street down there. That's where we ditched our gear.' Then he pointed to the main road through Ba'albek. 'We take that road.'

Bono revved the engine and the truck bucked and bumped down the hill. 'Where's that go?' he asked.

'Beirut.'

Bono stared at him. 'Beirut?'

'That's where the hostages are,' Lynch said. 'We were six hours too late. We're going to Beirut airport.'

'Jesus,' Bono spat. The truck slowed to a halt at the bottom of the hill and Gamble jumped out and collected the rifles and ammunition. He threw one to Lynch, jumped onto the back of the truck again and loaded his grenade launcher. Bono spun the wheels, the truck leaped onto the paved street and roared up between the silent houses where the people of Ba'albek cowered in mortal terror. They swung wildly out onto the main highway and Bono followed Lynch's jabbing finger south and west to a town called Zahle.

A Hezbollah truck screamed out of a side street and fell in behind, the gunner already firing. Windows shattered and brickwork splintered as the bullets went wide and raked the buildings along the main street of Ba'albek. Vance lowered his gun and fired. The windshield of the pursuing truck disappeared in a snowy cloud of exploding glass, the vehicle went out of control and began to roll, hurling the two men on the back out onto the road. The truck rolled sideways down the road after them like a child's toy and then crashed to a halt against a shuttered shopfront. They had barely cleared the town when Gamble fired the grenade launcher at the last corner house on the road southwest out of Ba'albek. The house seemed to shiver for a moment then its whole facade leaped, disintegrated and spilled across the road. No-one else dared to follow.

The truck roared up the road out of Ba'albek and a few minutes later they passed the six pillars of Jupiter's temple. The hillside road behind them was still dark and empty and Bono pulled the truck over at the last corner and they all stared back in silence. The mosque was still burning and a pall of grey smoke hung over the ancient town like a funeral pyre. From here they could see the full extent of the devastation they had brought to Ba'albek and the Beqa'a Valley. Everywhere they looked there seemed to be fire, death and destruction. The marijuana fields still burned in the distance; the whole area around the mosque was a charred and shattered ruin. Upturned vehicles burned in half a dozen places and there seemed to be bodies in every street. The mournful whine of the first ambulances floated up to them.

'You know what this place is supposed to be, don't you?' Lynch said quietly.

'What?' Bono waited.

Lynch looked at him. 'If you believe the bible scholars,

330

this is the site of the Garden of Eden. This is where God gave Man his beginning.' He paused. 'Look what we've done to Eden.'

Bono revved the engine and the truck lurched forward, over the crest of the hill and Ba'albek slid from view.

'Well,' Bono muttered, 'maybe they'll get it right next time.'

10
BACK TO BEIRUT

Beirut, July 4

They sowed a lot of alarm and confusion through southern
Lebanon in the ninety minutes that it took Bono to drive
as fast as he dared through the mountains from Ba'albek
to Beirut. They counted five Syrian army checkpoints along
the route and at one point had to pick their way cautiously
through the town of Zahle. At each checkpoint Gamble
behaved like a madman, waving his arms and screaming that
Israeli paratroopers had attacked the town of Ba'albek and
a convoy of the first casualties would be arriving within the
hour. It worked. The Syrians were already getting confused
radio messages about heavy fighting in and around Ba'albek.
As army officers hurried to their radios to seek confirmation
and fresh orders, messengers were despatched to every hospital
and infirmary between Ba'albek and Beirut to prepare for
a massive influx of casualties. The men in the red militia
truck were waved through to continue their dash and to spread
further panic. Lights in houses, hospitals, army barracks
switched on in their wake. Messages flashed to Druze, Amal
and Christian Maronite militias that something dreadful had
happened at Ba'albek. As word rippled across the country
all eyes turned to the east as everyone sought more information
to learn the truth about what might have taken place there.
When new reports arrived that it had been an American
assault and not Israeli they only added to the confusion.
Syrian commanders mobilised their armoured divisions and
the road behind the racing red Toyota sealed in a grip of

steel. To the south, Israeli army intelligence units confirmed a major alert and mobilisation of Syrian forces throughout eastern Lebanon. Israel's border forces were ordered to full alert. The first satellite pictures of major fires and explosions in and around Ba'albek began to hum into their receivers in Washington and Moscow.   Telephones began to ring and chirp in the homes and offices of generals and national security officers around Tel Aviv, Damascus, Amman, Baghdad, Cairo, Washington, London and Moscow.

It was still an hour before dawn when Lynch, Bono, Vance and Gamble reached the outskirts of East Beirut on the Damascus Road and the whole world knew Lebanon was in the throes of a new crisis. Lynch and Bono were still in the cabin. Vance manned the Soviet AA machine gun with Gamble standing at his side, trying to maintain the pretence that they were militiamen on an urgent mission and not to be challenged lightly. Their first trouble came at a checkpoint in the suburb of Hazmiye when they had to cross the Green Line to get onto the airport road. There were two T-72s and a couple of dozen Syrian soldiers guarding the crossing.

Gamble leaned forward-and yelled to Lynch through the open window.

'I don't know if I can fool these guys,' he shouted. 'They know all the militia groups. If they ask too many questions we're gone.'

'Bullshit as much as you can,' Lynch shouted back. 'We'll slow right down, get as close as we can and then crash the barrier.'

Bono slowed the truck dramatically as the first soldiers stepped towards them, flagging them down with the barrels of their AK-47s.

'Keep it to a crawl, don't scare 'em,' Lynch ordered.

Bono stopped the truck half a dozen metres from the nearest tank. The tanks were arranged in a dog leg so vehicles had to wind between them to get through the barrier boom. One had its gun pointed into West Beirut, the other to the battered ruins of high-rise apartment blocks immediately to the south, on the other side of the Green Line. Lynch also noticed sandbagged AA gun emplacements on both sides. A Syrian officer stepped out, smoking a cigarette and snapped something at Lynch.

Lynch pretended he couldn't hear above the engine noise and leaned out as Bono began edging the Toyota a little further forward. The officer had half a dozen soldiers around him and others ambled out around the truck. They were all armed. A couple of soldiers in Lebanese army uniforms stood idly by in the background, watching. Gamble said something in Arabic and the officer glanced up, said something sharply back at Gamble then returned his attention to Lynch. Obviously the officer had decided that Lynch was the man he wanted to talk to and he wasn't going to be deterred. Lynch unholstered the Browning and leaned further out of the window, opening his mouth as if about to say something. Gamble shouted something again, a note of desperation creeping into his voice. The officer reached towards Lynch, his hand beckoning, voice harsher, demanding. He wanted papers, Lynch realised. Papers... or money. Lynch gave the officer his friendliest grin, leaned over a little further, and then his arm flashed out, wrapped around the officer's neck and slammed him up against the door. Lynch's other hand appeared out the window with the Browning held to the officer's head. Bono stamped on the gas pedal and the truck lurched forward, smashing two Syrian soldiers to the ground and sending the others reeling. The others hesitated just a couple of seconds, afraid of what would happen to their officer. It was all Bono needed. He swung the Toyota brutally around one tank, smashed through the barrier, caught the edge of the second tank and lost a fender... then they were clear. The Syrian officer screamed in panic as his legs were almost crushed between the truck and the tank treads and then the truck slewed across the wide boulevard into West Beirut, dragging his feet in a wide arc across the scarred tarmac.

The first shots erupted from the checkpoint. Vance swivelled the gun toward the rear and opened fire. Gamble followed suit. Bono accelerated away down the nearest street and the officer screamed as his feet were scraped along the ground. Lynch dropped him and snapped off half a dozen shots from the Browning towards the checkpoint as the officer bounced and rolled across the ground. The truck hurtled down the dark, deserted street between tall, disfigured buildings and the first tank fired after them. The shell screamed past them with a terrifying roar and a fountain of dirt erupted from the road about two kilometres in front of them. A second shot boomed and gouged another gaping wound from a scarred high-rise a hundred metres in front of them, cloaking them with dust from the settling debris as they roared past. Bono swerved into a side street to get out of the line of fire and drove across two city blocks before cutting back towards the airport. The tanks fell silent behind them and they were clear.

Bono looked at Lynch. 'What next, boss?'

'When we hit the airport perimeter, kill the lights, stay away from the terminal and we'll go through the nearest gate or fence. When we get onto the tarmac, cruise as quietly as you can. Ignore the commercial planes. We'll be looking for something on its own, probably with a lot of protection. Can't be too many like that going out this time of day.'

'Yeah,' Bono grumbled. 'If they're still here.'

Lynch shrugged. 'We made good time. They had to come the same route we did, pass the same checkpoints. You have to remember — this isn't a regular airport anymore. You have to keep a lot of people happy, grease a lot of palms to get a plane out of Beirut...' His words trailed away. They knew it was a long shot.

Suddenly, they were clear of the high-rises. They came to a major junction with a large, dilapidated building and a battered sign which said Akka Hospital.

'That's it,' Lynch yelled. 'Airport Road.'

Bono slewed the truck around the corner onto the airport

road while Vance and Gamble hung on the back. About three kilometres ahead they could see the lights of the terminal and the gleaming hulls of jumbos from airlines that were still willing to fly into the world's most notorious anarchy-state. Bono slowed the truck, switched off the lights and pulled over to the side of the road, following a perimeter fence which guarded one major runway. Through the wire-mesh they could see the glistening, starlit waters of the Mediterranean stretching peacefully to the western horizon. They prowled slowly along the fence for a couple of hundred metres, unable to find any opening. The terminal was drawing closer.

'Just go through it,' Lynch ordered.

'Keep your heads down, guys,' Bono shouted to the men up top.

He swung the truck back onto the road, shifted into four-wheel drive in low and rumbled towards the fence. The truck moved a couple of feet but then began to stall in the grip of the steel net as the chain links held. He eased the gas pedal down a fraction more, the engine rumbled louder and the truck moved forward another foot. They had nothing to cut the wire links with and Lynch wasn't willing to use anything noisier than the truck just yet. The truck butted forward again and they heard the first links snap, then the ungodly screech of jagged metal scraping against metal as the truck pushed gradually through the widening wire rip. Suddenly they were free and the truck jolted forward, up the grassy verge inside the airport and onto the tarmac. Bono swung the vehicle around, shifted into second to try and keep the engine noise down and they trundled slowly along the runway towards the first hangars.

'Keep well clear of the buildings,' Lynch said. 'Even if they see something moving out here, I don't want them to get too nosy, too fast.'

Bono swung the truck around and they began driving in a slow, wide arc around the terminal, eyes straining through the gloom towards the lights of the different hangars and terminal buildings. They could see the silhouettes of people moving less than 500 metres away. Many of them were men with guns on their shoulders. Various aircraft slid by, large and small, most of them dark and unattended. They passed a Lebanese 747 with its lights on. People were preparing it for a flight later that day. They rumbled slowly around another wing of the terminal and Lynch saw the first pale hint of dawn in the east. It had been a long night, he thought. And it still wasn't over.

'There . . .' Gamble's voice hissed in his ear. Lynch followed the outstretched finger pointing past his window. 'The Caravelle,' Gamble added. 'There are two Red Crescent trucks beside it, a bit of activity.' The Red Crescent was the Arab world's version of the Red Cross.

'Okay,' Lynch said, climbing out. 'Peter, come with me.' He turned to Vance and Bono. 'When you hear shooting you come like a bat out of hell,' he said. 'That plane is our ticket out of here.' He signalled Gamble to go in from the other side and the two of them scurried off into the darkness, forming a two-man pincer, heading towards the small passenger plane a few hundred metres away.

Lynch padded softly across the open tarmac bent low to the ground. As he drew closer he moved to keep the two trucks between him and the men standing closest to the plane. The Caravelle was a French plane, but the livery was red and white and the insignia on the tail was the Islamic star and crescent, Algeria or Tunisia, Lynch guessed, both PLO havens. Adrenalin surged welcomingly through his body. He came within fifty metres and stopped. A man climbed into one of the trucks, started it, swung away from the plane and drove back into the terminal. The headlight beams flashed centimetres over Lynch's head. He could see a handful of men in suits near the front steps. They were shaking hands with men in uniform. They turned and filed aboard the plane. The engine of the second truck started and the uniformed men turned to go. The turbines on the Caravelle's rear mounted engines began to whine. They were leaving. And there was no sign of any hostages. Half a dozen men with rifles began to edge backwards away from the aircraft. There was only one open hatch near the front of the aircraft and a flight of perhaps a dozen steps. Lynch started running. If he was wrong there was about to be an international incident that would blow up in everyone's faces. If he was right . . .

He pushed all doubt from his mind and sprinted towards the open hatch of the aircraft. One of the dark-suited men stood in the doorway of the plane for a moment, then disappeared. A crewman replaced him and leaned out to close the door. A couple of ground crew workers pulled the chocks from under the wheels then walked towards the mobile staircase. Lynch's feet pounded the tarmac. The ground crew workers began rolling the steps back. Somebody shouted. Lynch jumped. One foot hit the middle step hard and he leaped again, clearing the steps in two strides. He flew across the widening gap between the edge of the steps and the aircraft and hurtled through the open hatch feet first, hitting the crewman square in the chest and slamming him against the opposite wall. Gunfire erupted outside, the mutter of Gamble's MP5 and the hard flat bark of answering Kalashnikovs. Lynch scrambled to his feet and raised the gun at six shocked Middle Eastern men in suits who were gathered in the front seats of the aircraft. At the rear of the aircraft Lynch saw another group of heads. A man with a sub-machine gun leaped to his feet behind them and Lynch fired a short burst. The man staggered and fell backwards. Another man, sitting with the group at the front was trying to get clear of his seat and bring his gun to bear. Lynch fired a second burst and the man fell backwards into his seat, his sub-machine gun clattering to the floor, blood from his shattered head and shoulders spattered against the cabin walls and across the pristine white seat covers. All hell seemed to have broken loose outside but a deathly silence descended on the men inside the aircraft.

A stooped thin man from the group at the rear got shakily to his feet and looked at Lynch. The man saw a dirt-smeared soldier with unruly black hair, darkly unshaven face and the baggy olive uniform of the Lebanese militia under a blue vest garlanded with weaponry.

'Is this good news... or bad news?' Bill Wallace asked.

But he spoke in Arabic. Just for a moment, Colin Lynch thought he had made a ghastly mistake.

A rash of bullets peppered the aircraft and everyone ducked. Lynch spun on his heel and fired a wide burst through the door at the encroaching fighters. Gamble shoved the steps back against the plane with a grunt then scrambled up and rolled inside. Lynch fired another burst, then heard the sudden loud chatter of a heavy calibre machine gun. The men on the ground scattered as the red Toyota slewed to a halt beside the aircraft while Vance swung the AA gun back and forth and hosed down the tarmac. Bono miscalculated and smashed into the steps. There was a nerve-shredding rending of metal as the steps dragged against the fuselage, toppled sideways then fell to the tarmac with a crash. Bono pulled the truck up snug with the aircraft, jumped out, vaulted up onto the hood, then used the cab roof as a staircase into the plane.

Lynch looked at Gamble. 'Tell the skipper to get this thing in the air,' he yelled.

The door to the cockpit was shut. Gamble kicked it open and stepped inside. It was empty. Through the open cockpit window he saw the pilot and co-pilot scrambling across the tarmac. One of them appeared to have injured his leg in the jump.

'Oh shit,' Bono looked back at Lynch. Gamble threw down his rifle, slid into the pilot's seat and gave the throttle a gentle pull. The rear mounted engines roared in response. Gamble eased the throttle back, shut off the brakes, settled himself and gripped the wheel.

'You know how to fly this?'

Gamble glanced over his shoulder at Bono and grinned at the big man's amazement.

'Part of the job,' Gamble said. 'Besides... the bigger they are, the easier they are.' He edged the throttle back again and the Caravelle lurched and began to taxi forward. 'Better tell Mr Vance to get on board,' he shouted over his shoulder. Bono stepped back into the cabin and yelled through the open hatch to Vance. The Delta man looked up and saw the door of the plane had moved a couple of metres. He gave the machine gun one last burst and leaped up onto the cabin roof of the truck and hurled himself at the door. Lynch and Bono reached out towards him, grabbed him by both arms and hauled him roughly into the aircraft. The Delta man wore a huge grin of triumph on his face as he realised they had achieved the impossible, then a storm of bullets raked the aircraft and lashed across his back. Lynch and Bono struggled back into the cabin with him but they knew he'd been hit badly by the way his body suddenly went limp. They rolled him over as Gamble taxied the Caravelle towards the runway. There was nothing they could do. There were five ugly wounds across his body. His eyes were already glazing even though the smile remained faintly on his lips. A dark red stain began to spread in the lighter red of the carpet. Vance struggled to focus on Bono and mumbled something about the fourth of July. Then he died.

'What did he say?' Lynch asked.

Bono shook his head. 'It doesn't matter,' he said. But he remembered his words from that alleyway a few short hours ago when the mosque had gone up and he had yelled 'Happy Fourth of July' to the devastated Hezbollah stronghold of Ba'albek, and Vance had looked at him with undisguised admiration.

'This is an outrage...'

One of the men in the first seats had stood up and was standing in the aisle, fists clutching the chairs on either side, his face grey with fury. Gamble had found the runway, the

Caravelle was gathering speed, the ground rushing past the open door faster and faster.

'This is a crime against — '

'Against what?' Lynch asked. 'International law?' He stepped towards the man, pushed him aside, reached beneath the corpse of the gunman in the row behind and stood up with the dropped sub-machine gun. A Skorpion. The preferred weapon of the PLO.

'Since when has the PLO respected international law?'

Ziad looked wildly back and forth. Everything was disintegrating around him. Eighteen months of painstaking planning had been destroyed in minutes. The men at the rear of the aircraft watched with expressions of grim amusement.

'What's the matter, asshole?' Bono stepped forward. 'Dish it out but can't take it?'

'Do you know what you've done?' The words came out staccato... desperate... filled with dread.

'Yeah,' Bono nodded, a terrible smile spreading across his face, a dangerous glint shining in his eyes. 'We've hijacked the PLO... and you can't fucking take it... can you?' His voice rose to a shout, spittle flew from his lips.

Ziad pulled a handkerchief from the breast pocket of his beautiful black suit and wiped Bono's spit from his face. The Caravelle suddenly lurched upwards and they were off the ground, climbing steeply. Ziad stumbled backwards but regained his footing. He saw the lights of Beirut slipping away beneath them. The cockpit door flapped.

'Where to?' Gamble's voice called out.

Lynch turned and walked up towards the cockpit.

'Tel Aviv,' he said. 'Radio Tel Aviv, identify us and request permission to land at Lod International Airport with nine rescued American hostages... all safe.'

'No!' Ziad screamed. His eyes were bright with terror. He clawed his way up the aisle past Bono towards Lynch. 'I demand that you let us off here in Beirut. You cannot take us to Israel... you cannot...'

Bono stepped after him.

'You want to get off in Beirut?'

Before anyone could move, Bono seized Ziad by the neck and waist, heaved him into the air and lunged towards the open hatch. Ziad screamed but Bono would not be stopped. He hurled the screaming, kicking man through the open door and into the rushing black darkness. Ziad's dying scream was whipped from his lips and the only sound inside the plane was the drone of jet engines. Lynch struggled to the open hatch, reached outside and slid the door shut with a slam. Silence fell again inside the aircraft. They looked around. Four PLO men cowered in the first seats watching Bono with horror. The first of the hostages began making their way up the aisle towards their rescuers.

'Is it true?' Bill Wallace asked in English, his voice starting to break. 'Are we going home?'

'Lynch?' It was Gamble. 'You'd better come in here.'

Lynch stepped into the cockpit and took the co-pilot's seat, leaving Bono to cover the terrified PLO men. 'The radio was already on this band,' Gamble said. He motioned Lynch to put on the co-pilot's headset. Lynch secured the headset and listened. A voice was speaking in Arabic and Lynch shook his head. Gamble answered in Arabic then English. 'I repeat... this flight has been rescheduled to Tel Aviv. If you wish to communicate further... do so in English.' The man on the other end hesitated, said something else and then there was silence.

'It's the PLO, Baghdad,' Gamble said. 'They seem a little confused. He's gone to get his boss.'

A moment later a new voice came on the radio, a thicker, deeper voice but one instantly recognisable.

'Christ Almighty,' Gamble said. 'It's Arafat.'

As if to confirm Gamble's guess, the voice picked up strength. 'This is the Chairman of the Palestine Liberation Organisation,' it said. 'Who has taken the property of the Palestinian people?'

'Air America,' Lynch answered.

There was a brief pause.

'Is that you, Mr Lynch?' Arafat asked.

Lynch couldn't keep the shock off his face. He and Gamble stared wordlessly at each other.

'What can I do for you, Mr Chairman?' Lynch answered after a moment, careful to keep his voice even. 'Keep it brief. We have an appointment in Tel Aviv quite soon.'

'So it appears, Mr Lynch... so it appears.' Arafat paused. 'You know... you weren't expected to get this far.'

Lynch felt an icy chill in his gut.

'Then this is a surprise for everyone,' he said, his voice calmer than he felt.

'Including your Mr Halloran, I suppose.'

'What do you know of Halloran?' Lynch asked. The PLO chief seemed to know much more than any of them.

'Mr Halloran and I have... an understanding,' Arafat added. 'It wasn't intended to go quite this far.'

All Lynch's fears seemed to coalesce into one numbing realisation. 'You and Halloran made a deal, didn't you? We were never intended to get the hostages out of Lebanon, were we? That would save both your ugly faces.'

There was another long gap filled only with static and Gamble thought for a moment they'd lost him.

'Let us say, it would have been more convenient for us if you had not left Lebanon... in quite this manner. You and your men have done very well, Mr Lynch. You are to be congratulated. Give my regards to your Mr Halloran when you see him.' There was a pause and then what sounded like a chuckle. 'I do hope you will return the aircraft when you have finished with it, Mr Lynch. It is the property of the Palestinian people... and if you and your men should ever decide to work elsewhere, perhaps you would let me know?'

The radio went dead.

'The cheeky bastard.' Gamble looked at Lynch. 'What the hell was that all about?'

Lynch sat in silence for a long time. When he spoke again his voice was murderous.

'We were never supposed to get out of there,' he said. 'Halloran never thought we could do it. He cooked up a deal with Arafat. We were supposed to die in the attempt, and so were the hostages. As far as Halloran is concerned, that's an acceptable solution to an embarrassing predicament for America.'

'Except...' Gamble started.

'Except,' Lynch interrupted and finished it for him. 'Arafat decided to double-cross Halloran and move the hostages before we arrived. That way we got dead and Arafat got to keep the hostages.' He paused 'I think Halloran met his match with Yasser Arafat.'

'But now we've pulled it off,' Gamble added, 'Halloran's still the big winner.'

Lynch slowly shook his head. 'Only until I can get to him.'

'You won't have long to wait,' Gamble answered.

Lynch looked at him.

'Halloran's waiting at Lod Airport. Win, lose or draw... He was there to get the news.'

'How long till we're on the ground?' Lynch asked.

'About ten minutes.'

Lynch took the headset off, stepped out of the cockpit and slapped his last clip into the MP5. Then he waited.

The hostages cheered when the Caravalle kissed the runway at Lod with a pout of blue smoke. Lynch and Bono waited silently by the door as Gamble followed the control tower's instructions and taxied around to where a cluster of Israeli army vehicles waited. Dawn was just breaking over Israel. It was going to be a beautiful day. Lynch saw that there were a lot of Israeli military police in the area. A lot of soldiers. And a lot of guns. He also saw Halloran's Beechcraft parked near the entrance to one military hangar. Gamble eased the Caravelle to a full stop, put on the brakes and shut down the engines. As he got up he could see people hurrying towards them across the tarmac. He slid open the hatch and breathed the fresh morning air. A chorus of voices rushed up to overwhelm him. American voices, strongly accented Israeli voices speaking in English. A man in a grey suit yelled that he was from the State Department. The ground crew pushed through with the exit steps. Six Israeli commandos were first up, followed by a gaggle of men in civilian clothes. The Israelis took the stunned PLO men out and led them away to waiting military police cars. A stream of ambulances drove out onto the tarmac. There was a sudden silence as the American officials led the hostages out, blinking into the sunlight. Bill Wallace was first. He looked around and hungrily breathed the air of freedom. For the first time in five years the frail American professor allowed himself to cry. Anxious, eager doctors and nurses began helping the hostages into the ambulances. The babble of noise rose again.

Lynch had covered Vance with a blanket and the Americans came to take his body away. More Israeli soldiers arrived to take the bodies of the dead PLO men. Lynch followed them down the gangway, the MP5 dangling by his side, Gamble and Bono behind him. A man rushed up and introduced himself. He said he was from the State Department. Lynch shoved him aside and strode towards the parked Beechcraft with lethal intent. Halloran hadn't been in the crowd on the tarmac. He wouldn't be. Lynch could see someone moving towards the door inside the Beechcraft. Halloran's smiling face appeared. Lynch kept walking. He could hear voices behind him, yelling. The State Department man was yelling to the commander of the Israeli ground troops. Lynch walked up to the Beechcraft and stopped. All he could see was Halloran's face. Halloran opened his mouth to speak. Lynch raised the sub-machine gun. Israeli soldiers swarmed around them. There was the ripple of safety catches being released. Gamble and Bono turned to guard Lynch's back and raised their guns towards the Israelis. Nothing on God's earth was going to stop Lynch from killing Halloran now.

'Lynch...!' The voice seemed to come from another time and place. He couldn't make sense of it. He began to squeeze the trigger. Halloran held his breath.

'Lynch... for God's sake, it's me... Janice.'

Halloran was pushed roughly to one side and Janice's face appeared in the door of the Beechcraft. Lynch stared. She struggled down the stepladder and ran the few short steps towards him then stopped. He could see her, smell her...

'It *is* me,' she said again, her voice pleading, insisting. 'Jack took care of me all the time. I flew to Cyprus two days ago. He picked me up last night and we came straight here... to wait for you.'

A huge wave of fatigue seemed to swamp Lynch. The anger drained from his body and with it his remaining strength. He slowly lowered the gun and looked at her. All around them the tension eased palpably. Bono and Gamble gradually lowered their guns. Lynch stared at Janice for a long time and then back at Halloran who had climbed down to the tarmac and was waiting watchfully. Lynch switched his gaze back to Janice. She looked tired, he thought... Tired and drawn and beautiful. She was wearing jeans and a thin blue sweater. They looked as if they had been slept in. She moved suddenly towards him, slipped her arms around his waist and held him. He lifted his free hand and touched her hair. It felt impossibly, ridiculously soft.

'I thought the bastard had taken you away from me,' he said at last. They sounded like the first tender words he had said in his entire life.

'You talked to Arafat?' Halloran asked.

The three of them were on board the Beechcraft. The door was still open. Bono and Gamble were lounging outside in brilliant sunshine talking to a couple of Israeli officers and men from the State Department.

Lynch nodded. Exhaustion threatened to swamp him with

each passing second. He sat in a seat next to Janice, head back, eyes half closed. She watched him, one hand clasped in his. He lowered his head and looked back at Halloran.

'Told me you and he were old pals... cooked yourselves up a nice little deal between the two of you, didn't you?'

'You don't know it all,' Halloran said.

Lynch laughed tiredly. 'I bet I don't,' he said.

'Sure I made a deal with Arafat,' Halloran added. 'I'd make a deal with Lucifer himself if I thought me or my country stood to gain something.'

'Even if that included throwing everybody else into the meat grinder on the way to glory?' Lynch said.

'Yes,' Halloran said.

Lynch smiled again. At least Halloran was an honest evil bastard.

'The men you took the hostages away from weren't Arafat's men,' Halloran said.

Lynch and Janice stared at him.

'Yeah, they were PLO but they were part of a splinter group inside the PLO that was trying to embarrass Arafat,' Halloran continued. 'That bastard Ziad had been planning to hijack Arafat's deal, take the hostages someplace else, start the whole damn business over again, discredit Arafat and make his own play for leadership of the PLO. Arafat got wind of it and so he offered a deal to me. He came to me... I didn't go to him. That bastard's intelligence is good, believe me. He said he'd tell us when and where the hostages would be if we could go and pull them out and at least give him some of the credit. He wants brownie points with Washington for his own grand designs. He was willing to let us have all the glory up front as long as he got some of the credit behind the scenes. He'll get it too.'

Halloran leaned forward earnestly in his chair. 'I didn't send you guys in there to die, Lynch,' he said. 'Nobody expected those bastards to move the hostages as soon as they did. That's when it started to go bad. What you guys did was... unbelievable. You did it, Lynch... You got our people out of Lebanon. You did everything we asked and more.'

'What will happen to the hostages now?' Janice asked.

'They'll get immediate care in the Israeli military hospital right here,' Halloran said. 'They'll get some decent food, some rest, new clothes... and they'll be flown back to the States tonight. There'll be an announcement from the White House tonight that the remaining American hostages in Lebanon have been released as a gesture of goodwill toward the American people. Arafat will get a mention, something along the lines of a major friendly influence in negotiations.'

Lynch rubbed the sweat and grime from his face.

'So you and Arafat both win, eh?' he smiled mirthlessly. 'We help Arafat by taking out the renegades inside the PLO... and you get the hostages back. And all on the Fourth of July. You win. Congratulations. What about Tuckey, you fucking bastard? What about him? Who killed Emmet Tuckey... and his wife... and his unborn kid?'

Halloran leaned back under the vehemence of Lynch's words.

'We think we know who killed him,' Halloran said softly.

'Oh?' Lynch waited.

'It was a contract hit,' Halloran said, 'We believe it was somebody working inside the States on behalf of Red Jihad. They want everybody who's an important part of my organisation, everybody who's ever done them any harm. That's you, me, Janice, Bono... anyone who's left. They want us all dead, Lynch — and they have the means to do it.'

'Jesus Christ almighty,' Lynch sighed.

'It's true, honey,' Janice said.

Lynch looked at her and smiled reassuringly. 'I could take you away from all of this,' he murmured.

'When do we leave?' she answered.

'Today,' Halloran interrupted. He got up and climbed out of the plane to give Lynch and Janice some time alone. When

348

he reached the tarmac he paused for a moment and looked back.

'We have to nail those bastards before they nail us,' he said. Then he slid the door shut and his words hung in the air inside the plane.

All Pan books are available at your local bookshop or newsagent, or can be ordered direct from the publisher. Indicate the number of copies required and fill in the form below.

Send to: **CS Department, Pan Books Ltd., P.O. Box 40,
Basingstoke, Hants.   RG21 2YT.**

or phone: 0256 469551 (Ansaphone), quoting title, author
and Credit Card number.

Please enclose a remittance* to the value of the cover price plus: 60p for the first book plus 30p per copy for each additional book ordered to a maximum charge of £2.40 to cover postage and packing.

*Payment may be made in sterling by UK personal cheque, postal order, sterling draft or international money order, made payable to Pan Books Ltd.

Alternatively by Barclaycard/Access:

Card No.

Signature:

Applicable only in the UK and Republic of Ireland.

While every effort is made to keep prices low, it is sometimes necessary to increase prices at short notice. Pan Books reserve the right to show on covers and charge new retail prices which may differ from those advertised in the text or elsewhere.

NAME AND ADDRESS IN BLOCK LETTERS PLEASE:

....

Name ——————————————————————————————

Address ——————————————————————————————

——————————————————————————————

——————————————————————————————

——————————————————————————————

3/87